AS THEY LAY SLEEPING

BOOKS BY WENDY DRANFIELD

DETECTIVE MADISON HARPER SERIES

Shadow Falls

Cry for Help

Little Girl Taken

Gone to Her Grave

Catch Her Death

Her Lonely Bones

Grave Mountain

The Crying Girls

The Birthday Party

The Night She Vanished

Please Don't Find Me

AS THEY LAY SLEEPING

WENDY DRANFIELD

bookouture

Published by Bookouture in 2025

An imprint of Storyfire Ltd.
Carmelite House
50 Victoria Embankment
London EC4Y 0DZ

www.bookouture.com

The authorised representative in the EEA is Hachette Ireland
8 Castlecourt Centre
Dublin 15 D15 XTP3
Ireland
(email: info@hbgi.ie)

Copyright © Wendy Dranfield, 2025

Wendy Dranfield has asserted her right to be identified as the author of this work.

All rights reserved. No part of this publication may be reproduced, stored in any retrieval system, or transmitted, in any form or by any means, electronic, mechanical, photocopying, recording or otherwise, without the prior written permission of the publishers.

ISBN: 978-1-80550-196-1
eBook ISBN: 978-1-80550-195-4

This book is a work of fiction. Names, characters, businesses, organizations, places and events other than those clearly in the public domain, are either the product of the author's imagination or are used fictitiously. Any resemblance to actual persons, living or dead, events or locales is entirely coincidental.

For my husband

PROLOGUE

Nighttime closes in as the girl stares with growing horror at the dead body before her. Her legs won't move. A surge of adrenaline makes her hands slick with sweat. Her skin is ice cold, making her shiver deep from within. She can't believe this is happening. Things like this don't happen in real life. Not outside of books and movies. And not to people like her.

"Are you going to just stand there or are you going to help me?" barks her partner in crime. "You're in this as much as I am."

The girl tries to swallow but her throat is too dry, so she almost chokes instead. When she can finally bring herself to speak, she doesn't know what to say. "What... I mean, what should I—"

"Grab the tarpaulin from the backyard. The black one. We need to wrap him up good."

Frozen in place, she can't bring herself to move.

"*Now*, for Pete's sake!"

The venom directed at her spurs her legs into action. She races through the warm kitchen, into the bracing backyard. She can barely see more than a foot ahead of her as it's dark and misty. Heavy cloud obscures the moon and the stars. She blindly feels around in the mist at her feet, cringing at the thought of touching mud or creepy-crawlies. When she finally locates the tarpaulin, she pulls it off the ground and holds it out ahead of her, trying to stop any bugs that might be stuck to the material from scurrying up her arms. She can't bear the thought of it. Bugs give her nightmares. It's all the legs they have and how fast they move, usually unnoticed until you feel their light touch as they advance toward your face. Her friend from school once told her a horrifying fact. Apparently, scientists once discovered that every human being eats at least ten spiders a week while they sleep. They crawl into open mouths and nostrils, their victims unaware. Some even set up home in warm, moist ear canals. After hearing that, the girl had slept with a cotton pillowcase partially over her head for three months straight.

She cringes as she hurries back into the warmth of the house, her arms aching from the weight of the damp sheet. The brightness inside highlights how many different lifeforms have set up home in the tarpaulin during its years of neglect outside. Her stomach churns knowing her left hand almost touched the fattest worm she's ever seen.

"Here." She drops it next to the body at her feet, careful not to let it touch the lifeless form. She couldn't bear to watch the disgusting bugs crawl all over the gray skin and find their way into the eyes, the nostrils and—God forbid—the mouth.

"Help me get him on it."

She does what she's told, reluctantly kneeling on the floor after flicking an escaping beetle out of the way. She cautiously takes one end of the sheet, holding it in place as the dead man is rolled onto it. Once in position, he's looking up at her, so she stares into his glassy eyes, trying to imagine what's happening inside his body right now. He'll never see through those eyes again. Never speak another word from that mouth. Never get to feel the touch of anything on his hands.

His puzzled expression tells her he was taken by surprise, just as she was when she heard the commotion that stopped as fast as it started. She wishes she'd never left the safety of her bedroom to see what was going on down here. She wishes she were asleep. That she could wake up tomorrow and find this was all a terrible nightmare. A sob almost escapes her throat. She presses a hand to her mouth to stop it.

"We need more layers in order to stop the smell escaping. Go fetch the shower curtain. And all the plastic bags you can find in the house. If we wrap him up good, no one will smell him. I need tape too."

The girl stands on shaky legs. She doesn't want to be here. "Where will you put him?"

"Never you mind. Get what I asked for. Then never speak of this again, you hear me? Not even to me. I'll deny it. If you go to the police, I'll blame you." A heavy sigh. "It's best we get on with our lives and forget this ever happened."

The girl lowers her eyes as dread squeezes her lungs. She never intends to speak of this to anyone. But how on earth is she supposed to forget it ever happened?

CHAPTER ONE

Lost Creek, Colorado

Madison Harper closes her eyes as she waits nervously in the midday sunshine. Today, she isn't the infamous detective who spent six years in prison for a murder she didn't commit. She isn't the victim of an assault that led to the birth of her only child, now twenty years old and thriving at college. And she isn't the sister of a woman who tried to ruin her life.

Today, Madison is a bride. And she's waiting for the signal that tells her she can begin her walk down the lawned aisle toward her fiancé, Nate Monroe.

At thirty-nine years old, she's a slightly older bride and has forgone the chance to wear a stunning white gown for something more suited to a cocktail party or a black-tie event. She's chosen a strapless coral dress that accentuates her figure. Usually dressed in black jeans and smart shirts, which in her law enforcement role are quickly ruined with blood, saliva and insults, today offers the chance to dress up, wear more makeup than usual and do more than just comb her shoulder-length blonde hair into submission.

She takes a deep breath to steady her nerves. Being summer, she and Nate opted for an outdoor venue. The intimate location—the Lume Mountain Lodge—is nestled in the stunning mountains that surround Lost Creek in southwestern Colorado. The sun sits high above the peaks, unobscured in the clear blue sky. Sunlight glistens off the clear-water creek that runs alongside the property. Being here on a day like today means she can easily forget the work that awaits her when she returns to the police station in two days' time. Things have been relatively quiet in Lost Creek recently. The police department hasn't had any homicides to investigate for months, which should be a good thing given how much has happened in the last few years, but Madison doesn't trust it. She knows from experience that it won't last. Not in this town.

As she watches the specially invited guests take their seats, she gets a glimpse of Nate standing under an arched trellis covered in white roses, his back to her. Her heart swells with love. Having met shortly after the worst time in both their lives, their relationship hasn't been plain sailing. They irritated each other at first, especially as Madison was recently released from prison, highly defensive and flat broke. She was desperate for money and a reason to get up in the morning. Nate gave her a reason. Working as a private investigator, he let her join him on a missing child investigation in northern California. They managed to find that missing child before he then helped her find her own son and get back on her feet. In return, she helped him overcome his harrowing time on death row and eventual exoneration. But trying to return to life outside prison was harder than either of them could have imagined, and their individual recoveries got in the way of their relationship more than once.

She shakes the memories away. It doesn't matter what they overcame to get here. They're here now. That's all that matters.

"Are you ready?" asks Owen, her only child.

She turns to face him. Suited and smart, and now taller than her, he looks like an adult. She doesn't understand how it happened. It seems like just yesterday that she gave birth. Missing almost seven years of his young life while she was incarcerated cost them dearly, but with Nate's help, they've managed to rebuild their relationship to the point where Owen wanted to be the person to walk her down the aisle. Despite having her son with her, it's difficult not to miss her parents today. She wishes they were still alive to see something good finally happen to her. Without them, her only other family besides Owen and Nate is her older sister, Angie McCoy, but Angie's not invited here today, for reasons Madison refuses to think about on her wedding day.

She nods at her son. "You look so smart." Tears brim her eyes as she tries to hold them back.

"You don't look so bad yourself." Owen glances at the officiant, who nods to confirm that everyone is seated and he's ready to begin.

A violinist dressed in a beautiful gold sequined gown that sparkles in the sunlight begins playing her instrument. Madison's stomach flutters with nerves as Owen offers her his arm.

It's finally happening.

Together they step forward and begin the slow walk across the lawn as the sun warms Madison's face. Not daring to look at Nate again in case it sets her off, she makes eye contact with several guests as she passes. Some of her team from the Lost Creek Police Department are here along with her friends and their children. Everyone looks so happy for her, even Sergeant Adams, who has sworn off marriage since his recent divorce was finalized. They're probably as relieved as she is that this day has finally come because they know what she and Nate have been through to get here.

The front row has been left empty as a reminder of the absent loved ones they've lost along the way. Not just their parents, but the friends and co-workers they so dearly miss. And despite weddings and funerals being notorious for bringing families together, Nate's two siblings weren't invited simply because they wouldn't have come. Standing behind Nate is Vince Rader, owner of the popular local diner and Nate's best friend. When Madison makes eye contact with him, she notices him wipe away a tear. It makes her choke up. She has to look away.

When she reaches Nate and Lloyd Maxwell, the officiant hired by the venue, she turns to Owen, who hugs her, saying in her ear, "I'm so happy for you."

Madison's powerless against her tears now. She shoos her son away to try to regain her composure, but when she looks at Nate, her feelings spill out of her. He looks devilishly handsome in his navy suit. The summer sunshine highlights his sandy hair and tanned skin. He takes her hands in his and leans in to kiss her cheek. Before pulling away, he whispers, "It's about time, right?"

She laughs, grateful to feel something other than overwhelmed. Normally so composed, she doesn't know why she's turned into a blubbering wreck in front of all these people.

Lloyd discreetly passes her a tissue, which she gratefully accepts.

"Do you like Brody's bowtie?" asks Nate.

Madison looks down at the German shepherd–husky mix by his side. The former police dog, who they met during their very first case together, is panting with excitement, his tail bashing the ground in happiness at being with all his favorite people, as well as the delicious aroma coming from the buffet that's currently being prepared behind them. Madison strokes his soft fur. "I love it."

"I managed to convince Owen not to bring Bandit."

She snorts. Bandit is their cat. He definitely wouldn't have behaved himself. In fact, he'd probably be stealing the salmon canapés or vomiting up a hairball at her feet.

Lloyd clears his throat. In his sixties, with white hair and mustache, he has kind eyes and a ready smile that puts Madison at ease. "Are we ready to begin?" he asks.

Nate keeps hold of her hands as they both nod.

"Excellent," says Lloyd. "I like to get this first part out of the way before we go any further, for obvious reasons." He turns his attention to the guests. "Thank you all for joining us on this beautiful day to witness the union of your friends Madison Harper and Nate Monroe. If anyone present knows of any reason why this couple should not marry today..." He pauses before adding, "Keep it to yourself as they don't want to hear it."

The crowd laughs. Madison smiles as she looks Nate in the eye. He mouths, "I love you."

She lowers her eyes to avoid more tears escaping. She expected to be more composed than this but figures she should cut herself a break. It's not like she's at work. She can cry all she likes today.

"Okay," says the officiant. "Let's begin." He shifts position and takes a deep breath, but before he can speak, a loud crack echoes through the air, seemingly reverberating off the trees and mountains around them.

Madison barely notices, her eyes again focused on Nate. She frowns when it dawns on her that someone is hunting nearby. Too close for comfort. When the guests start gasping, she doesn't understand what's happening at first. It takes her a few seconds to realize that their officiant has dropped to the ground beside them.

A scream rings out, followed by others. Some of the guests are running away.

Nate covers her with his arm and pulls her away from Lloyd, who's lying face-down on the ground, the back of his head oozing blood.

It slowly registers that the crack she heard was someone firing a shot at them. She automatically reaches for her service weapon, but of course it's not there. She's unarmed.

Brody takes off before anyone can grab him, running straight toward danger.

Someone shouts, "Everybody down!" She thinks it's her detective partner, Steve Tanner.

Nate pulls her away, but she turns, desperate to find her son. She spots Owen hurrying toward them. "Run for cover as fast as you can!" she shouts.

Owen keeps up with them as they race toward the safety of the lodge. There's no time for thinking. All Madison can do is flee.

CHAPTER TWO

Having called for backup, Madison is painfully aware that the shooter could target the wedding guests while huddled together in the supposed safety of the lodge. Waiting for the rest of her team to show up, she rushes around the building checking the doors and windows to see if she can get her guests out of here safely.

"What are you doing?" asks Nate as he follows her, unwilling to let her out of his sight.

"Checking the exits," she says as she shakes a set of external double doors to ensure they're locked before pulling the heavy drapes closed. "We don't know how many shooters are out there and whether they're on their way here to get inside, which means we're sitting ducks while we wait. They could have explosive devices for all we know." She checks the large window at the front of the lodge, which overlooks the parking lot. The venue was closed to the public for the wedding, so she has fifty-six people inside, including the catering staff, the lodge employees and the guests.

"It could've been an accident," says Nate. "A hunter in the mountains who misfired."

Madison stops and looks him dead in the eye. "On *our* wedding day? Come on, Nate. You know we're cursed."

He takes her hand. "Don't say that. We're past all of that."

She suddenly notices he has blood spray on the side of his face. She looks down at her dress. It's also red in places. She feels defeated. Today was supposed to be different.

Deborah Purdue, the venue's manager, suddenly appears looking frantic. Her dark hair, slicked back in a severe ponytail, is unraveling, making her look disheveled. Chad Peters, the bar manager, is beside her, his eyes wide and his hands visibly trembling. He looks like he might cry.

"Is anyone going to go and help Lloyd?" asks Deborah. "He needs medical assistance!" She and some of the other employees were indoors when the shot was fired. They don't know it's too late for him. That he's already dead.

Madison takes a step toward them both. "I'm so sorry," she says gently. "Lloyd sustained a fatal head wound. He died instantly."

The woman's hands fly to her mouth. "Oh dear God."

"I told you," says Chad to his boss. He sniffs back tears. "His poor wife will be devastated."

"We can't just leave him out there," Nate whispers into Madison's ear as Deborah stumbles away from them to break the news to the rest of her employees. Chad hovers for a second, not knowing what to do. Eventually he follows her out.

Madison knows she can't help someone who's already dead, so she has to focus on helping the people in this building instead. "We're locked down until backup arrives. We'll retrieve Lloyd when we can."

Nate nods, his expression strained. They should be married by now. Instead, they're facing a life-or-death situation. Plus their dog is missing. It's been twenty minutes since Brody took off. Who knows what the shooter will do if he catches up to him?

"How are you holding up?" she asks, gently taking his hand.

"I'm fine, just worried about you," he says. "You really think someone was trying to shoot one of us, don't you?"

She doesn't know, but it's possible. She can't consider the shooter's motives yet, or their intended target. That can wait until everyone is safely out of here. "I don't know. But do me a favor, help keep the guests calm." She can hear sobbing coming from the next room. Steve and Sergeant Adams are questioning people, trying to find out if anyone saw the shooter.

"Sure," says Nate. "Just..." He pauses before glancing at the window. "Stay out of view, in case whoever shot Lloyd is waiting for another opportunity. Okay?"

"I will. That's why I'm closing the drapes."

He leans in to kiss her forehead. "It had to happen today, didn't it?"

She smiles briefly. "It doesn't matter about the wedding as long as you and Owen are safe." She frowns, realizing she hasn't seen her son in a few minutes. "Where is he?"

"Looking for Brody."

Her stomach flips. "You're kidding? He left the lodge?"

"No, he's upstairs, checking the view from the windows. I've told him to be discreet and that he can't set foot outside until you say so."

She exhales with relief as Nate exits the room.

Madison hears the sirens before she sees them. She risks a glance outside by holding one drape open. Several cruisers speed into the parking lot one after the other, lights blazing, which is not something she expected to see on her wedding day. Chief Carmen Mendes beats Officer Luis Sanchez to the lodge. Madison goes to the entrance and unlocks the door, hurrying them inside. They're followed by Officer Shelley Vickers.

"Still just a single casualty?" asks the chief as Madison leads them away from the doors.

"Yes. Lloyd Maxwell, our officiant. He's still out there, but dead. He suffered a gunshot wound to the head. It sounded like there was only one shot fired."

The chief glances out at the picturesque landscape, interrupted only by the crumpled body in the middle of the lawn. "Any sightings of the perpetrator?" she asks.

"None as far as I can tell, but Steve and Adams are questioning the guests and employees. The shot echoed off the mountains, so it's difficult to know which direction it was fired from, but Brody ran east, toward Grave Mountain."

Mendes nods. "The rest of the team is out looking for the shooter." She retrieves her phone and walks away to make a call. Madison hears her request a helicopter and pilot from the police department at nearby Prospect Springs. They've recently come to an agreement that the two departments will share resources in emergencies. The LCPD doesn't have the funds for its own helicopter.

Madison turns to Officer Sanchez, one of their youngest officers at twenty-eight, although he's been with the department for years and is both dedicated and experienced. "Could you help question the employees and guests in the next room?" she asks. "Someone might have spotted something before shots were fired. I heard only one, but my mind was all over the place."

"Sure," says Sanchez before leaving.

Officer Vickers stays behind, looking concerned for Madison. "Are you okay?"

For the first time, Madison falters. "The poor guy was standing right next to Nate. A few inches over and *Nate* could've—" Her throat seizes as she realizes how close she was to losing him.

Shelley hugs her. "Nate's fine. You both are."

When Madison pulls away, she takes a deep breath to compose herself just as Steve joins them. "You okay?" he says, looking worried.

"Yeah." Madison inhales deeply. "My sister better not be behind this."

"Angie wouldn't dare," he says. "Would she?"

Since her sister's release from jail seventeen months ago, things have been quiet. She and Angie came to a mutual understanding that they'll be cordial if they bump into each other in public, but that's as far as their relationship can go. Angie tried to destroy her once before. She won't let it happen again. "Anything's possible with her. And what better day for revenge than my wedding day, right?"

Steve folds his arms over his chest as he considers it.

As Shelley leaves them alone, Madison sighs heavily. "Keep an eye out for Brody. He went after the shooter."

"Yeah, I saw. He ran like a bat out of hell. Nate must be frantic."

She nods. "Brody knows how to take care of himself. I'm sure he'll be fine." Still, he's around seven years old now and a little slower than he used to be. She just has to hope he can dodge a bullet.

"You and Nate should leave," Steve says. "It's meant to be your day off. We've got this."

Madison scoffs. "Yeah, well, it's also supposed to be my wedding day."

He smiles sympathetically, but before he can say anything, Chief Mendes reappears. She's followed by Nate and Owen. "The Prospect Springs PD have promised to launch their helicopter within the next fifteen minutes," says Mendes. "If the shooter's hiding in the mountains, they're best placed to locate him or her. We'll get a drone up too. But with only one shot fired, there doesn't appear to be an immediate risk to life. There's a good chance it was a hunting accident."

Madison raises an eyebrow to suggest that's highly unlikely.

"I appreciate why you'd feel that way," says Mendes, "but let's wait for the facts before we speculate." She rests her hands on her hips as her eyes drift to the blood spatter across Madison's dress. "I think you should go home." Madison starts to protest, but Mendes holds up her hand to stop her. "I insist. You need to get cleaned up. Keep the dress intact for Alex to inspect in case it helps with forensics." She sighs. "Knowing you as well as I do, I'm assuming you'll want to return to work first thing tomorrow instead of using your vacation days as planned. Maybe by then we'll know the shooter's identity, and if it *was* deliberate, you can look into their background and search their property."

Nate steps closer to Madison. "She's right. The guys can focus on getting our guests out of here. Let's go."

"What about Brody?" she asks, reluctant to leave.

Nate glances anxiously out the window.

"Don't worry about Brody," says Steve. "We'll find him."

Madison has no choice. Part of her is relieved she can get Owen and Nate out of here, but she also worries that this is just the beginning of something terrible.

CHAPTER THREE

The next day, Madison struggles to stay awake. She slept fitfully, dreaming of loud gunshots whenever she slipped into short bursts of sleep. Nate slept even worse if his tossing and turning was any indication. He must have been worrying about Brody. And Bandit, their cat, roamed the house all night, wondering why his sleeping companion wasn't home yet. All in all, Madison thinks they probably shouldn't have bothered going to bed.

As she enters the kitchen after showering and dressing, she finds Nate standing at the breakfast bar checking his phone for the hundredth time. "No news?" she asks, knowing he's desperate to see Brody.

He shakes his head and pours her a cup of coffee. "I should've gone to help search for him."

"You weren't allowed, remember?" she says softly. "Besides, you were watching out for me and Owen. And my entire department is looking for Brody and the shooter." Chief Mendes didn't want Nate putting himself in danger just to find their dog, but she underestimated what the dog means to him.

To both of them. The chief has never owned a pet. She doesn't know what that bond is like, and how you can't rest until you know your furry family member is safe. "He'll turn up," she says. "There can't be many people in this town who don't know who Brody is, since he's on the TV news as much as we are. Someone will call dispatch once he's spotted."

Nate nods but he doesn't look convinced. He sips his coffee before pulling Madison in for a hug. "How are you doing this morning? Rough night, huh?"

She links her arms around his waist and takes a deep breath. "Yeah. I thought I'd be Mrs. Nate Monroe by now." Although in reality, she's decided to keep her own last name to become Mrs. Madison Harper. Mainly because she and Owen are the last in her family to carry the name, but also because she's too lazy to change her last name on all her accounts, and there's the strong possibility that people will mistake *Madison* Monroe for *Marilyn* Monroe, and she could really do without the confusion. Nate's suggested they double-barrel their last names, but the thought makes her cringe, although she doesn't know why.

He kisses her forehead. "We could go to the courthouse the minute they open this morning and seal the deal? We already experienced our fancy wedding yesterday. Well, some of it."

She can't say she isn't tempted.

"Not until Brody's home, though," he says. "He's got to be there since he's been with us as long as we've known each other."

The thought makes her stomach flip. If Brody doesn't come home, the house will feel so empty. Especially when Owen returns to college in the fall for his final year. She pulls away and looks up at Nate. "Maybe."

She switches on the small TV in the kitchen and watches the news. Several reporters, including her friend Kate Flynn, are stationed outside the Lume Mountain Lodge, covering yesterday's shooting. Being one of their guests, Kate had a front-row seat to the action. Madison's received several updates from her team since she left yesterday. She knows the venue is closed for the foreseeable, and Sergeant Adams has notified Lloyd Maxwell's wife of his death. Lloyd's body has been moved to the morgue pending an examination by the medical examiner. She also knows the shooter is still at large, so finding them is her priority this morning. But not before she finishes her coffee and eats some toast, or she'll be no good to anyone.

Nate checks his phone again. "You know what? I'm going to cancel my morning therapy session," he says. "I need to look for Brody instead."

She hears footsteps descending the stairs behind them.

"I'll help," says Owen, scooping Bandit up in his arms as he enters the kitchen dressed in gray sweatpants and a blue T-shirt. His blond hair sticks up on the side he favored in bed last night.

The cat, *his* cat, rubs his face all over Owen's stubbly jaw and allows Owen to kiss him in front of the ears. They miss each other when Owen's away at college. He's just finished his second year of undergraduate law at Arizona State University. He originally planned to go to law school once he graduated but had a change of heart. Now he plans to join the police academy so he can eventually become a cop and work at the LCPD with Madison. The thought terrifies her. She'd much rather he fought criminals in court than on the streets, but Nate constantly reminds her that she has to let him make his own decisions. Something that's much easier said than done.

A loud bark outside makes them all look at the front door in unison. For a second, no one moves, until Bandit jumps out of Owen's arms and races toward the door, meowing loudly to be let out.

Madison watches Nate, who's one step behind the cat. He pulls the front door wide open, but she can't see past him as

Owen is there now too. She hears another bark as she steps forward and looks over Owen's shoulder.

Brody's home.

She shields her eyes from the bright morning sunlight and looks up and down the street to see who brought him back, but when she doesn't see anyone, she realizes he got here all by himself. He's so excited to see them that he does zoomies around the front yard. When he finally stops, he lets Nate and Owen hug him while excitedly licking their faces. The cat stays indoors but wiggles his bum like when he's excited to be fed.

Nate eventually guides the dog inside when the neighbors start appearing at their windows, wondering what the commotion is so early in the morning. Madison notices the bowtie Nate dressed him in for the wedding is missing, but it doesn't matter. Bandit sniffs him all over as Brody drops onto his bed in the corner of the kitchen diner. Now he's inside, he seems exhausted. His tail's still bashing the floor excitedly but it's obvious he's had a long trek to get here. He licks Bandit's head as the cat tries to curl up next to him.

Nate prepares a bowl of kibble, which makes Brody get up. He wolfs the food down while Nate checks him over.

"Is he injured?" asks Madison.

"No. He doesn't even have sore paws, thankfully. Although his nails are dirty and split in places from the stony mountain trails." Nate stands. "His lack of injuries suggests he didn't catch up to the perp, or maybe the perp spared him. I don't know. Imagine if he'd been shot. I don't know what I would've done..." He abruptly turns away. "I need to find the nail clippers."

Owen smiles as he heads back to his bedroom with a bowl of cereal. "All's well that ends well."

"Owen?" says Nate before he disappears in his room all day. "If I find the nail clippers, would you cut his nails for me? You're the only one he'll let near them."

Madison hides a smile. She knows the only reason Brody lets Owen do it is because Owen feeds him a small piece of salami between each cut. Nate doesn't allow the dog too much human food anymore as it's bad for him, so they've never told him.

Owen's eyes briefly meet hers and they share a knowing smile. "Sure. No problem." He heads upstairs with his breakfast.

"At least you can still see your therapist," says Madison when he's gone.

Nate stops pulling open drawers and exhales. "I know, right? I need to after the last twenty-four hours," he jokes. The relief is evident on his face.

Madison's phone suddenly rings. She retrieves it from the counter. "Hello?"

"Hey, it's Dina." Dina Blake is one of their dispatchers. She mostly covers the graveyard shift. "Sorry to bother you before you get to work, but you're needed at a crime scene."

Madison sighs at the bad timing. She doesn't want any distractions from yesterday's case until they've caught the shooter, but that's not how this job works. "No problem. What's happened?"

"Two females have been found deceased at their home," says Dina. "Possible homicides."

Madison's stomach flips with dread. "Text me the address. I'll head there now." She scoops up her keys.

"Will do. And Madison?"

She stops. "Yeah?"

"One of the deceased is a young girl. Approximately five or six years old."

A chill goes through her. "Understood. On my way." She looks at Nate after pocketing her phone. "I need to head to a crime scene. Remind Owen to be careful if he leaves the house today. You too, okay?" She's worried that yesterday's shooter could strike again today if one of them was his intended target.

Nate walks her to the front door. "Sure. Call me later. Let's see if we can squeeze in a wedding at some point in the next day or two."

She kisses him, trying to ignore the feeling that each time she says goodbye to him will be the last.

CHAPTER FOUR

Madison is apprehensive as she exits her vehicle and stands in the warm sunshine, snapping on a pair of latex gloves on the sidewalk. The deceased females have been discovered at a small one-story home in an ordinary street. The front yard is unkempt, with a sun-scorched lawn and some overgrown weeds. An old Ford Taurus sits in the driveway, giving no clues as to whether its owner is one of the deceased. The sun bounces off the windows as she looks for signs of life, but other than young Officer Lisa Kent cordoning off the area with yellow tape, no movement can be seen inside the property.

Madison turns when she hears a car engine. Her partner, Steve, has arrived with Alex Parker, their forensic technician. They exit Steve's vehicle and join her on the sidewalk.

"Morning," says Alex as he approaches her.

"Hey." She looks over his shoulder for his chihuahua, Mrs. Pebbles, who usually rides with him everywhere he goes. "Where's your shadow?"

"I left her at the station with the dispatchers," says the thirty-six-year-old Brit. "She's a little grumpy this morning."

She scoffs. "No change there then." Although the tiny dog likes everyone else, she inexplicably has something against Madison. Chief Mendes is relaxed about Mrs. Pebbles and Brody spending time at the police station as long as they're well-behaved. The chihuahua even has her own crate in Alex's cramped office. He's filled it with pink fluffy bedding and a whole range of toys. All she's missing is a crown.

"Ready?" says Steve grimly, as he rolls up his shirtsleeves and pulls on some gloves.

Madison's never really ready to enter a crime scene, but it has to be done. She steps forward as Officer Kent lifts the tape for them to duck under and fills them in on what happened. "The victim's boyfriend says he found his girlfriend and daughter deceased earlier this morning," she says. "This is the home he shared with them. Shelley's inside. She'll be able to tell you more."

Madison nods. "Thanks." At the door, she, Steve and Alex slip on some protective shoe covers before entering. Madison sniffs the air. The home smells of the early stages of decomp, leading her to believe the victims weren't killed this morning. Whatever happened here likely occurred earlier than that, which instantly makes her wonder why the boyfriend only recently reported their deaths.

Shelley is waiting for them in the living room. "Hey," she says, standing in front of a worn couch. She absently bats away a couple of large black flies that probably appeared within minutes of the victims' deaths. More will come if they don't move the bodies soon. The room is furnished with worn couches and tired furniture, perhaps thrifted or handed down. Children's toys are scattered around, mostly dolls and books. The space is small and cluttered, but clean, and there are no signs of a disturbance other than the body on the floor at Shelley's feet. "This is one of two victims," she says.

A slim white woman appearing to be of average height is lying on her stomach with her arms outstretched and her left leg bent at the knee. A laundry basket has been dropped nearby, suggesting she was putting away clean clothes when taken by surprise. The victim's blonde hair covers her face, which is turned to the side. Madison can see no obvious wounds on the body, or blood coming from it, and she doesn't spot a murder weapon discarded nearby. She crouches beside the body and lifts the woman's hair with her gloved hand. It disturbs several flies, which she bats away with disgust. They're a hazard of the job but one she could really do without, as they make her skin crawl. She can't see much of the woman's face without moving her, which she doesn't want to do until Alex has photographed the scene, but the one eye she can see stares vacantly into the distance. Ugly purple marks on her neck stand out against the otherwise pale flesh. "Her neck is badly bruised."

A flash goes off behind her as Alex photographs the room before any of them accidentally disturb something.

Standing, Madison asks, "Where's the little girl?"

"This way." Shelley leads her and Steve to a small bedroom at the rear of the property. It's filled with stuffed animals and children's books, and the walls are covered with the girl's drawings. But Madison's eyes are drawn to the blanket on the floor next to the small bed, obviously covering a tiny body. She wonders who placed that over the child. Perhaps her father after he discovered her.

"Ryan—the dad—says he didn't touch a thing in here," says Shelley, reading her mind. "He couldn't bring himself to look under the blanket."

Which means the killer covered her. Bracing herself, Madison squats down and lifts the blanket. A little girl dressed in yellow pajamas lies on her stomach, her face hidden by her fine blonde hair. A stuffed animal has been placed beside her face as though the pair of them have been tucked in for the night. A single fly buzzes overhead, waiting to make its move. The blanket thankfully kept it off until now. Madison brushes it away, then frowns as she realizes a pillow has been placed under the girl's head.

Steve's as confused by it as she is. "Was she sleeping on the floor when she was killed?" he says, thinking aloud.

"I don't think so," says Madison. "Her arms are outstretched and within touching distance of the bed." She lowers the blanket before moving to the floor by the bed. Fingernail tracks are clearly visible in the carpet. She pulls out her phone and aims the flashlight under the bed. The scratch marks originate from there. Leaning back on her heels, she looks up at Steve. "She was pulled out from under the bed, probably by her ankles. She must've heard what was happening to her mom and tried to hide."

"Damn." Steve sighs heavily.

Madison takes a deep breath. This is horrific. She goes back to the little girl and lifts the blanket again. Her eyes are closed, thankfully. She gently moves the girl's hair away from her neck. A line of bruised skin is clearly visible. Madison drops the blanket and stands, angry at the thought of this child being terrified before she was killed. "Where's the boyfriend?"

"He's in the kitchen." Shelley turns to leave the room, then stops, adding, "He's been inconsolable since I arrived, although he's a little calmer now."

Madison refrains from comment. He wouldn't be the first good actor she's come across at a crime scene. Still, she needs to keep an open mind. Things sometimes aren't as they seem, no matter how many times they are. But experience has her gut screaming domestic violence at her. She's seen it time and again.

They follow Shelley and silently pass Alex in the narrow hallway as he prepares to photograph the little girl's body.

The boyfriend is seated at the kitchen table with his head in his hands, elbows resting on his knees. He doesn't even look up when they enter. His messy light brown hair covers his forehead. Wearing blue jeans and a gray T-shirt with sneakers, he looks to be in his early thirties. Madison can't see any obvious bruises or scratches on his exposed arms or hands, but with both females dying face-down, it's unlikely they had a chance to defend themselves.

She considers whether to take him to the station for questioning but decides he'll probably speak more freely here in his home. Sometimes the early conversations—when the victim's loved ones are still blindsided, or *acting* blindsided—can provide the most valuable information, especially if they're more comfortable in their surroundings.

"Sir?" she says. He looks up. His expression is pained. His eyes are red-rimmed. "I'm Detective Madison Harper and this is my partner, Detective Steve Tanner. I'm so sorry for your loss. And I'm sorry that we need to question you while you're clearly in shock, but I'm sure you can appreciate why time is of the essence in a case like this."

He nods before wiping his eyes with his trembling hands. "Sure."

Madison sits opposite him at the table and pulls out her pocket notebook, while Steve takes a seat to his left. "Can I get your name?" she asks, pen poised to record everything he says.

"Ryan Simmonds."

"And the females?"

"Denise and Lucy Ridgeway. Denise was my girlfriend. Lucy was our—" His throat constricts, stopping him for a second. It's difficult to fake that. He gulps back tears. "She was our daughter."

Steve frowns. "Denise Ridgeway?" He gives Madison a look.

She suddenly recognizes the name. With a discreet nod to

let him know they'll discuss it later, she gives Ryan a second before gently asking, "How old were they?"

"Twenty-nine and five."

The landline rings, an unfamiliar sound these days, and grating on the ears. Nobody moves to answer it. Madison wonders whether Ryan has told Denise's family yet. "What time did you discover them like this?"

He glances at the clock on the wall above the sink. "About two hours ago, around five thirty."

She wonders why he wasn't here overnight. Perhaps he's a shift worker. "Tell me what happened," she presses.

He swallows, and at first she thinks he isn't going to be able to continue. Somehow, he finds the strength. "I live here with them, but I stayed at a friend's house last night. I came home this morning to get changed for work." He pauses. "Oh shit, I need to call my boss."

"That can wait for now," says Steve. "What do you do?"

"I work at the auto repair shop on Nelson Lane. I'm a mechanic." He lowers his eyes before continuing. "I entered the house using my key and that's when I saw Denise." He covers his mouth for a second, before adding, "I didn't understand what I was seeing at first. I thought she was on the floor because she was playing with Lucy."

"You said you used your key, so the front door was locked?"

He nods. "The back door too. I checked."

Which means the killer either had a key or Denise answered the door to them. "Did you try to revive her?" she asks.

"No," he says shakily. "It was obvious she was beyond that. I touched her back when I crouched next to her, but she felt weird." His throat clenches. "I've never felt someone like that before. It was horrendous."

Madison nods sympathetically. Nothing prepares you for

the feel of a dead body and no one can appreciate how it will cause nightmares for months to come, if not longer. "I'm sorry you had to experience that."

"I immediately called for Lucy," he continues, "but she never came, so I ran into her room and found her—" He breaks into a sob, unable to finish his sentence.

Madison shares a look with Steve. It's difficult to know whether Ryan is lying, but his raw emotion feels genuine. It takes some time, and several tissues, for him to compose himself. She feels bad for having to push him, but she needs to know the timeline of events. Gently, she asks, "What time did you last see them alive?"

He clears his throat. "Yesterday afternoon."

"Can you think of anyone who would want to hurt Denise?" asks Steve. "Had she had an altercation with anyone recently? Fallen out with a friend or neighbor?"

Ryan leans back in his chair and takes a deep breath. "No, she didn't do drama. She kept to herself."

"Could she have owed someone money?" asks Steve.

Ryan hesitates for a second while he appears to decide whether to be honest. Eventually, he says, "I guess you might as well know she battled with substance abuse. But she was clean for the last two or three months. That's why we got back together. I thought she was doing well. And besides, nothing has been taken from the house. We haven't been robbed." The landline rings again. "I should probably get that." He stands. "I left an incoherent voicemail for Denise's mom, so it could be her." His face suddenly crumples. "How the hell do I tell her that her daughter and granddaughter are dead?"

Madison's heart aches for him. If he's responsible for this, he's a really good liar. "We can tell her face-to-face if you'd prefer."

Steve gets up. "It's probably best we do, given how upset you are."

Ryan slumps back into his seat, the palms of his hands covering his eyes. He nods before breaking into more sobs. He genuinely appears to be a broken man.

Madison has a horrible feeling he might not make it through his grief.

CHAPTER FIVE

Nate Monroe glances at his watch. He has five minutes left of his therapy session, but all he can think about is going home to check on Brody, even though the exhausted dog will probably want to sleep all day after the exciting twenty-four hours he's had. Once he knows Brody's okay, he can call the courthouse and see what hoops he and Madison need to jump through for a quick wedding. He doesn't care where they get married as long as they do it soon. He doesn't want Madison thinking that the death of their wedding officiant yesterday was a bad omen that means they're not meant to be together. She can be easily spooked. They both can. It comes with being so badly burned in the past.

"So, all in all, you're glad you started coming to see me?" asks Tom Lowery, Nate's therapist. "Because I think it's fair to say you were incredibly reticent to begin with." In his mid-fifties, with a fatherly vibe, Tom has been instrumental in helping him to navigate his anxious thoughts and provide some clarity. Nate's aware he's probably drawn to father figures like Tom and his close friend Vince Rader because he lost his father while he was locked up. He misses the levelheaded advice he could rely on his dad for.

"Oh sure," he says. "I was a mess before I came here. Stuck in a cycle of shame and self-loathing." His face burns thinking about all the terrible coping mechanisms he's used over the years to overcome everything that he's been through. As a teen and young adult he would turn to his faith to get him through hard times, but that felt impossible once he'd been framed for murder by a so-called priest. After that, he turned to drugs and avoidance, but that didn't work out so well for him, and he has Madison and Owen to think of now, so for the last seventeen months he's been working through his issues with Tom, and it's fair to say they've had a lot of issues to cover. Mainly due to Nate's long incarceration. Therapy has helped him see clearly for the first time in his life.

He knows now that he's spent years blaming all the wrong people for what happened to him. His situation wasn't the fault of the state that incarcerated him, or the prison that held him, or the correctional officers who enforced the rules during his imprisonment. Nate finally accepts that what happened to him was the fault of one man only, and that man died of old age while awaiting trial for murder. So he's had to come to terms with the fact that he'll never get justice for what happened, but equally, the man's death means his ordeal is finally over.

It's taken a lot of time and hard work to reach this point. Working with Tom has helped, but so did giving a long-awaited interview about his experience, something he'd always shied away from as he didn't want to relive any of his ordeal. It was Vince who convinced him to appear on his popular amateur podcast, *Crime and Dine*. The only interview Nate's ever given since his release from prison, it got a lot of publicity, but that's all beginning to die down now, and interest in him is finally waning.

Now, he's accepted that he needs to let go of all his

misplaced resentment and anger if he wants to move forward with his life, which he so badly does. He has no intention of ever revisiting the past and is now solely focused on his future with Madison.

"Well, you've certainly put in the work," says Tom. "That's not to say you weren't a little reluctant to truly open up at first." He smiles warmly, remembering how difficult it was to engage Nate during those early sessions. "But I can see the difference in you, so I imagine Madison can too."

"Well, we've already discussed going to the courthouse to get married in the next day or two."

"Excellent." Tom stands, indicating the session is over. "You know, your history is so unique that I worried I was out of my depth in accepting you as a client." He smiles. "But as it turns out, I've learned more about human resilience from you than from anyone else. You should focus on that when the negative thoughts creep up."

"Thanks." Nate follows him to the door. "I guess I'll see you next week." He shakes the therapist's hand before leaving the office, which always brings a sense of relief that the session is over and he can go back to living in the present. As he crosses the near-empty waiting room, he hears a gasp and notices a middle-aged woman staring at him. Dressed in blue pants and a white shirt, she has long brown hair that shows gray roots.

Tom hovers in the doorway. "I'll be with you in just a minute," he says to the woman.

She ignores him and clutches her purse to her chest as she stands. "You're Nate Monroe."

For a brief second, dread runs through him as he worries she's a reporter waiting to tell the world he's in therapy. He cautiously stops. "Right. Do I know you?"

"My name's Pamela Smith." She approaches him without smiling. "Are you still a private investigator?"

He's suddenly glad the waiting room is empty of other patients. "I am."

"Oh good." She seems relieved. "I've thought about approaching you for a while now, so I'm glad I've bumped into you. It must be fate. I know you have an excellent success rate with your past cases, so I wanted to discuss hiring you to find my missing, er... well, a friend of mine who vanished thirty years ago. I wanted to ask whether you would look into her disappearance, but it depends how much you charge. Can we go somewhere to talk?"

Nate's surprised by her directness and wonders whether she came here just to corner him. "Aren't you here to see Tom?"

She glances at the therapist. "Yes. Sorry, I meant afterward. My missing friend is actually the reason I'm in therapy."

Tom smiles reassuringly.

Nate can sense from her desperate expression that she's waited a long time for answers that have never come. And he can't pretend he isn't intrigued. He has a special interest in cold cases. "How about coffee at Ruby's Diner?" He glances at his watch. He has a few errands to run before he's free. "Say twelve thirty?"

She nods, clearly grateful. "I'll be there."

CHAPTER SIX

When Madison reaches the home of Denise Ridgeway's parents, Steve is already there. He gets out of his car as she exits her own vehicle and approaches him. In his mid-forties, Steve is classically tall, dark and handsome, but single, having been through a lot over the last few years, most notably finding himself the victim of domestic violence. Madison worries his experience has put him off any more relationships, but she hopes not. She knows he's happy living alone right now, but he's a caring person as well as a great cop and she wishes she knew someone she could set him up with. For now, when he isn't working, he's either at the gym or doing nerdy stuff at home like playing weird tabletop wargames. In her opinion, he needs a partner to bring him out of his shell.

"You remember Denise Ridgeway's name, right?" says Steve excitedly. "I didn't recognize her at the house since she was lying face-down, but I spoke to her four months ago. I've never met her boyfriend before, though."

Madison nods. "I recall her name from the Dominic Larson case. I've been racking my brain about it all the way here." Dominic is a young father who hasn't been seen since February.

Neither has his two-year-old son, Charlie. Steve led the investigation into their disappearance so he's more clued in than she is on the details, but she knows the pair seemingly vanished from their home without a trace. Nothing has been found to suggest foul play, so the working theory as of right now is that Dominic voluntarily walked away from his life, taking his young son with him. "Denise was Charlie's mother, right?" she asks.

Steve nods. "She told me she had a brief affair with Dominic while she was with Ryan Simmonds, resulting in Charlie being born, but she hadn't even told her parents that she'd had another child because she didn't want Ryan to find out she'd cheated on him. She thought he might dump her for good, and possibly take their daughter away from her. She confirmed she let Dominic raise Charlie because she'd struggled with substance abuse and thought he'd be better off with his dad."

When the press found out that Dominic and Charlie were missing, and that Denise had given Dominic full custody of their child from the moment he was born, they painted her as a bad mother who chose drugs over her baby. "Does Ryan know all this?" asks Madison. "Because he never mentioned she had more children." She figures he must have known Denise was pregnant. You can only hide that for so long.

"It's complicated." Steve sighs. "I'll fill you in on the details later. But the fact her lover and their child vanished four months ago and now she and her other child have been murdered has to be significant."

He's right. And if the two cases *are* linked, it may help them find a lead. But for now, they need to notify Denise's parents of her and Lucy's deaths. "Let's focus on getting this over with." Madison nods to the front door. "Ready?" she asks.

"Not really," he says, running a hand through his hair.

She knows how he feels. It's only midmorning but the sun is getting stronger. The family in the ranch-style property before them should be looking forward to a peaceful summer's day. Instead, their lives are about to be shattered.

She follows Steve along the path that leads to the porch and then climbs the steps. When he knocks on the front door, her stomach flutters lightly with nerves. She wishes she weren't bringing such terrible news. A glance from Steve tells her he's thinking the same thing. They may be trained for this, but it's still the worst part of the job.

The door opens, revealing a tall, overweight man in his late fifties. His graying hair and unshaved jaw show signs of him once being a redhead. He raises his eyebrows questioningly. "Help you?" he asks.

"Morning, sir," says Steve. "Sorry to arrive unannounced, but we're detectives from the Lost Creek PD and we need to have a word. Mind if we come in for a minute?"

The guy goes pale. He seems to freeze, which is understandable, since finding a couple of detectives on your doorstep is everyone's worst nightmare. Eventually, he steps aside. "Is everything alright?"

They enter the spotless living room. The sun streams through the front window, highlighting how clean the oak furniture is, with not a speck of dust in sight. Several vases of fresh flowers are dotted about, and the walls are covered with decorative plaques declaring the importance of family, as well as plenty of family photographs, including several of Denise and Lucy together, smiling and laughing at backyard barbecues.

Madison spots a woman with dyed black hair seated on the couch, magazine in hand. She looks just a few years younger than the man who let them in. When she hears them entering, she stands and removes her reading glasses. "What's going on?"

"Sorry to bother you, ma'am," says Steve. "Would you confirm your names before I continue?"

The male speaks for both of them. "I'm Colt Ridgeway and this is my wife, Bernie. Bernadette."

Steve makes a note while Madison steps forward. "You might want to take a seat. I'm afraid we have some bad news."

The couple don't move. "Just tell us," says Bernie, a hand pressed to her chest, her eyes filled with fear.

Madison takes a deep breath. "We were called to your daughter's home this morning. Denise Ridgeway?"

Bernie gasps and looks at her husband. "Is this why Ryan called us earlier? He left a message but didn't really say anything and quickly hung up. I assumed he butt-dialed us but now I'm wondering whether something's happened. Are the girls okay?"

"I'm so sorry to have to tell you this," Madison replies, "but your daughter and granddaughter were found dead in their home earlier this morning." She would like to break the news using gentler words, like *lifeless*, or *unresponsive*, but they're trained to use words that offer no ambiguity, so that the message is delivered clear and direct and there's no room for false hope.

Bernie screams while dropping forward onto her knees. "No! You're lying! That's not true!" Her animalistic howls make Madison's blood run cold. The woman looks at her husband with desperation, for some reassurance that they're wrong, but he can't help her. The blood has drained from his face as shock overtakes him. All he can do is silently crouch next to her with a soothing hand on her back. Madison goes to her other side and kneels down.

"I'm so sorry." She feels tears prickle her eyes at the woman's traumatized expression but remains composed.

Bernie unexpectedly heaves, causing vomit to cover her knees and some of the carpet. Madison rubs her back with one hand while Colt holds her hair back.

Steve disappears, presumably to find something to clean it up.

A sharp voice comes to them from somewhere else in the house. "What's going on out there?"

Madison looks up at Colt questioningly. "That's Ida," he says. "Bernie's mom. She's practically bedbound. We'll break it to her once you've gone." It's clear from his strained expression that he's in shock.

Bernie wipes her mouth with some tissue that Steve passes her. "Oh my God. This cannot be happening." She's gone pale and looks like she could vomit again.

"It's okay," says Colt, helping her wipe the vomit from her thighs. When he's done, he stands, looking bereft. His wide eyes meet Madison's. "What happened to them?"

Bernie doesn't want to be helped up, so Madison stands. "We need to wait for the medical examiner's report, but unfortunately, initial signs indicate they could have been murdered. I'm sorry. If you know anything that could help us figure out who might have wanted to hurt them, we'll—"

Bernie's head snaps up. She wipes her wet face with her hands. "Where's Ryan? Is he dead too?"

"No," says Steve. "He found Denise and Lucy, and alerted the police right away."

She looks at Colt. "It must've been him. Otherwise he'd be dead too, right?"

"Shh." Colt rubs her hand. "Let's not make accusations until we know what happened."

Madison's heart sinks as she thinks back to Ryan's demeanor earlier. He was devastated. But could it have been an act, to cover up what *he'd* done? The thought of a father dragging his own daughter out of hiding to kill her in order to avoid there being any witnesses to his despicable actions makes her shudder.

CHAPTER SEVEN

"I take it you mean Ryan Simmonds," says Madison. "Why do you think he could've been involved?"

Bernie's rocking back and forth on her knees, trying to contain the tremors caused by the shock that runs through her. Her lower lip trembles as she speaks. "Because we recently found out Denise had an affair with Dominic Larson a few years back," she says. "I think that's why Dominic and little Charlie vanished." Her hand flies to her mouth to contain another sob. "I think Ryan killed them because he was angry at Dominic, and now he's killed our girls too."

Madison shares a look with Steve. There's no doubt it's a possible motive for Dominic and Charlie's disappearance.

Colt helps his wife back onto the couch.

"Did you know Dominic and Charlie?" asks Madison.

"No," he says. "We never met our grandson. We didn't even know he existed until he went missing and it all came out in the papers. This is the only photo we have of him." He goes to a sideboard covered in family photographs and picks up a framed black-and-white newspaper clipping from February. It shows two-year-old Charlie on his bike in a backyard. The blond-haired youngster grins up at whoever's taking the photo, displaying gaps in his teeth. Madison's heart aches for Colt and Bernie. The fact they've framed this photo is gut-wrenchingly sad.

"Why do you think Denise kept it from you?" asks Steve.

"Shame, probably," says Colt. "She must've been embarrassed that she'd had an affair. And she probably knew Ryan would disown her if he ever found out, which means she'd be homeless and he could take Lucy from her, leaving her with no children at all."

"How did Ryan not see she was pregnant with Charlie if they were living together at the time?" asks Madison.

Colt shrugs. "She tends to disappear when she's..." He hesitates, before adding, "Using. Sometimes she's gone for months on end, so we assumed she was back at it. We had no clue she was hiding a pregnancy."

"How did Ryan react when all this came out?" she asks, knowing they're going to have to ask him themselves at some point.

"We have no idea. We don't see that much of him, and Denise wouldn't talk about it. She wanted it all to go away. She kept a lot from us, probably because of her addiction. I assume Ryan told you all about that?"

She nods.

With a disappointed shake of his head, Colt says, "Of course he did. He probably wants to paint her in a bad light." He sighs heavily. "We found out from the press that she wasn't involved in Charlie's life at all. She let Dominic raise him."

Madison suddenly wonders whether Denise couldn't live with the shame of her affair and secret child being revealed. Her and Lucy's deaths could have been an attempted murder-suicide. Maybe she worried about disappointing her parents after everything she'd already put them through with her substance abuse, preferring instead to die, taking her daughter with her. If so, she may have been interrupted by Ryan after harming Lucy. He could have killed *her* in a fit of despair after finding his daughter dead.

Colt looks at her with tears in his eyes. "Did the girls suffer?"

She swallows, unsure how to respond. Does anyone *not* suffer while being murdered? "We don't know yet." She redirects the conversation. "Besides Ryan, is there anyone else you think we should take a close look at? Or any reason Denise would be a target for someone?"

Still visibly stunned, they both shake their heads. "Denise wouldn't hurt a fly," weeps Bernie. "And Lucy was only *five years old*. She was the best thing that ever happened to us. I can't believe we'll never see her again." She screws her eyes shut and clutches the small silver cross dangling from her neck. "Oh dear God."

Torn between wanting to give them privacy and wanting to catch their daughter's killer, Madison has to keep probing. "Were Charlie and Lucy Denise's only children?"

Both Colt and Bernie nod solemnly, but they must be wondering whether Denise hid anything else from them. It doesn't matter how close you are to your children and how much you try to protect them, they will always keep certain things from you for various reasons: shame, guilt, not wanting to disappoint. She's seen it time and again in this role, and it always leaves her wondering what Owen's keeping from her.

The couple in front of her look broken. They've lost both their grandchildren as well as their daughter. Madison can't even imagine how unbearable the coming days will be. "Does Denise have any siblings?" she asks.

Colt nods. "We have another daughter. Denise's older sister. She lives in Denver." He looks at Bernie. "We're going to have to break it to her."

Bernie shakes her head at the thought of it. It's a terrible predicament to be in. Sharing bad news can sometimes be even worse than receiving it.

"Where did Denise work?" asks Madison.

"She wasn't working right now," says Colt. "She was getting her life together. But she previously worked at a grocery store downtown."

Steve clears his throat. "Ryan mentioned Denise used drugs in the past but thought she'd been clean the last few months. Could drugs be a motive for her death? Did she owe anyone money or have bad blood with a local dealer?"

Bernie wipes her eyes and nose with a tissue. "He's just trying to deflect blame from himself. He probably thinks that if you know she was an addict you won't investigate thoroughly, or you'll look for someone who doesn't exist."

Colt soothes her by rubbing her back. He looks at Madison. "Can we stop with the questions now, Detective? We need to process this." He looks like he might vomit too.

"Will somebody tell me what the heck is happening out there!" yells Ida from deep within the house.

"I'll be there in a minute!" Colt yells back, sounding irritated. Living with his mother-in-law might be getting to him, or maybe it's grief. Bernie is rocking back and forth on the couch now, staring into space. She's visibly trembling all over. It's gut-wrenching to watch.

"Of course," says Madison. "We'll be in touch. And if you need any help, there *is* support available to you over the coming weeks and months. I'll make sure we send you details, okay?"

Colt nods. "Appreciate it." He may be staying strong to answer their questions, but his ashen skin and trembling hands suggest he's on the verge of breaking down too.

"If you think of anything that might help the investigation," says Steve, "call us." He hands him his card.

"Now that you mention it," says Colt, "one of our outbuildings was broken into last night. The chain had been cut but nothing seems to have been taken."

"What do you keep out there?" asks Madison.

"Nothing, just junk and tools."

"Did they attempt to get into the house too?"

"Not as far as I could tell," he says. "We don't have security cameras, but you can bet your ass I'm going to get some now."

Madison notes it down, but as the intruder didn't try to enter the house and attack anyone, it may not be relevant to Denise and Lucy's murders.

Colt walks them to the front door. When they're out of Bernie's earshot he asks, "When can we see the girls?"

Madison turns. "Depending on how the investigation goes, Denise and Lucy will be released to a funeral home of your choice in a week or so."

He opens the door and silently watches them leave.

Outside, Madison exhales as she and Steve approach their vehicles. This is the part she feels guilty about. She gets to walk out of the house and go back to her life. The Ridgeways don't have that option. They're stuck in hell with no escape.

"They never even met their grandson," says Steve with a sigh as they stop next to her car. "We need to find out when Ryan learned about Denise's affair and other child. If it was after the press revealed it, his anger with her could've been building up for the last four months."

"And if he found out *before* Dominic and Charlie vanished," she says, "he could be responsible for their disappearance." She thinks of how broken Ryan seemed earlier. Can someone really fake that level of grief? "It's the perfect motive," she says. "He could've killed Dominic and Denise because of their affair. But I don't understand why he'd kill the kids. They're innocent in all this. Sure, Charlie wasn't his, but Lucy was."

"He wouldn't be the first person to destroy their entire family out of jealousy or rage, right?"

She nods. It's true. There's no denying that some people consider murder a better solution than simply splitting up with the person they no longer love. Probably because it's the cheaper option, financially at least. "Do you think Ryan faked his reaction earlier then?"

"I don't know," says Steve, leaning on her car. "The Ridgeways are understandably shocked and angry, so it stands to reason they'd want to blame the boyfriend. But no man is ever good enough for someone's daughter, right? They might just be lashing out. And we need to remember that we have zero evidence that Charlie and his dad have come to any harm. Up until now it felt more likely that Dominic wanted to disappear. Maybe so Ryan would never find out about his affair with Denise, or perhaps Ryan scared him off."

She considers it. "Well, either way, Ryan Simmonds is our best person of interest right now." She thinks about how, in the space of just twenty-four hours, she has two new homicide investigations: Lloyd Maxwell's and Denise and Lucy Ridgeway's. She knew things had been too quiet around here recently.

CHAPTER EIGHT

The morning is almost over by the time Madison receives word that the medical examiner is ready to discuss his findings in both the Lloyd Maxwell case and the Ridgeway murders. The atmosphere in the brick building that houses the medical examiner's office has changed since Dr. Conrad Stevens took over the role and a new assistant was hired to replace one who passed away. It took some time for the team to settle and find a new normal, which Conrad has done his best to facilitate. A kind and wise fifty-five-year-old, he brings a lightness to the role. His professionalism and courteous nature make it a pleasure to work with him, whereas Madison struggled to find common ground with his predecessor.

Skylar, one of Conrad's assistants, greets Madison and Steve in the lobby. She has one child, a thirteen-month-old daughter. "How's Meadow?" asks Madison as she follows her along the corridor and pulls a sweater over her head. It may be warm and sunny outside, but she always comes prepared for the cooler temperatures in the morgue.

Skylar smiles over her shoulder. "She's an angel. I hate

leaving her to come to work, but at the same time I like a little bit of me time too, you know?"

Steve chuckles. "Hanging out with dead bodies is your me time?"

"At least I get to talk to adults here," she says with a grin, holding the door open for them. "And very few of them answer back."

Inside, the morgue is cool and has a chemical aroma. Conrad is hovering over a man's naked body and looks up as soon as he sees them. "Detectives! Welcome to my crib." He grins.

Madison snorts. "Don't tell me you used to watch MTV back in the day?"

"No, not me. But Jerry has been enlightening me about what used to pass for entertainment when he was a teenager in the early noughties."

Madison notices Jerry Clark as he approaches. He grins at her. "Detective Harper." Jerry is half hippie, half surfer dude, with messy shoulder-length hair and a carefree attitude to life. He seems to be a jack-of-all-trades, as every time she sees him, he's working somewhere new.

"Jerry," she says with a nod. "Keeping out of trouble, I hope?"

"Always." He winks at her.

She laughs it off before looking at Conrad. "How's Nora?" Conrad's daughter works at the crime lab up north. She and Alex Parker have a flirtatious relationship, which isn't surprising since they're both forensics geeks. Alex has been trying to encourage her to move to Lost Creek to be nearer her father, and to him, of course. They'd make a good couple, especially as Alex has been unlucky in love up until now. Madison doesn't know how Mrs. Pebbles would feel about another woman in Alex's life, though. The chihuahua seems a little possessive.

"She's great," says Conrad. "She's finally agreed to follow her old dad down to Lost Creek."

Madison smiles. "Really?"

"Yes. I'm trying to convince the lovely Chief Mendes to hire her as a lab technician." As Conrad's in a relationship with the chief, and Nora has helped them with many cases in the past, that shouldn't be too difficult.

Steve frowns. "Don't we need a lab in order to hire a lab technician?"

"Plans are afoot, apparently," says Conrad, with a glance at Madison. "Thanks to Nate's generous donations to the department."

She nods. "And not soon enough. Having evidence processed in-house should speed up our investigations."

Steve approaches the naked body, who Madison recognizes as her wedding officiant, Lloyd Maxwell. She's hit with a stab of guilt as she looks down at him. She's still unsure whether the bullet that tore into his skull was actually meant for her or Nate. "I'm guessing you don't have any revelations about Lloyd's murder?" she says. As it occurred in front of so many witnesses, there shouldn't be any surprises.

"No," says Conrad. "He has one penetrating wound to the back of the head, but I understand the bullet hasn't been located. It seems to have exited here," he points to an area at the side of the bloody skull, "and could be wedged in the lawn somewhere, or perhaps it ricocheted off something. Toxicology results will take a week or so, but I'm not expecting them to reveal anything out of the ordinary. The gunshot wound was the cause of death. Whether the manner of death was accident or homicide, I'll let you determine."

"Sanchez and Shelley are currently searching for a shell casing around the area we think the shot was fired from," says Madison. "What type of firearm could have hit our victim from that distance?"

"I'd say a hunting rifle with a good range. If you can locate the shell or bullet, then from the caliber I can narrow down the possible firearms it came from."

Steve nods. "Whatever they used, they only needed one shot to hit their target, which suggests they're experienced with firearms—perhaps a hunter, or former military personnel."

"That's assuming they *did* hit their target," says Madison. Until they have more evidence, anything is possible, which is what makes the early days of an investigation so difficult. It also means she can't relax, as she doesn't know who the bullet was meant for.

Conrad looks over their heads to speak to one of his assistants. "Jerry, would you fetch the Ridgeways for me?"

"Sure, Doc." Jerry and Skylar quickly get to work arranging Denise and Lucy's bodies on separate mortuary tables before wheeling them over to Conrad.

Madison leaves Lloyd's table and approaches Denise's body first. The young woman's skin and lips have a grayish-blue tinge. Her blonde hair spills out behind her head. Her eyes are closed. The bruising around her neck seems more pronounced now due to the contrast between that and the paleness of her lifeless skin. Madison forces herself to look at Lucy's body. The little girl's eyes are also closed, never to see her friends, her mother or her grandparents ever again.

Conrad solemnly watches Madison. "Awful, isn't it?" he says. "I imagine notifying the loved ones is the worst part of your job. For me, it's working on children and babies." They share a moment of thoughtful silence, before Conrad adds, "What we need to remember is why we do this. We're getting answers for their loved ones, and helping these poor victims to rest in peace."

His words bring a lump to her throat. As a rookie officer, she was always told by the former police chief that showing emotion at a crime scene or while attending morgue visits was a sign that an officer shouldn't be on the force, but now that she's more experienced, Madison thinks he was wrong. The minute she stops being touched by these victims' stories is the minute she should hand in her badge, because it would mean she no longer cares about getting justice for them. "Alex thinks they were strangled with the cord from a lamp found at the house. He's sent it to the crime lab. What do you think?"

"Yes, he showed me at the crime scene," says Conrad. "I agree it would match with the ligature marks around Lucy's neck, but not Denise's."

She raises her eyebrows. "It doesn't?"

"No." He leans in and points to Lucy's neck first. "You can see how the bruising differs. If you look at her mother's neck, we have clear finger marks. But they're not present on Lucy. Her injuries are in a horizontal line."

"So you think Denise was manually strangled?" says Steve.

"I do."

Madison takes a deep breath. "I guess that might mean the killer couldn't bring themselves to strangle Lucy with their bare hands, but is that because she was a child, or because she was a child they knew?"

Steve folds his arms over his chest. "You're thinking of her father, Ryan?"

"Right."

"If I may," says Conrad. "I've worked on several cases where a parent has manually strangled their own child, so keep an open mind about that."

Steve shakes his head. "I hate humans."

Madison sympathizes. It's hard not to feel that way in this job.

"We're certainly a flawed species," says Conrad. "But don't let that blind you to our strengths too."

She likes that even though he sees the worst of humanity every day, it hasn't made Conrad cynical. "Could they have been killed by different people?" she asks. "Perhaps there were two intruders."

He nods. "It's certainly possible. Or it could be as you said: someone who couldn't bring themselves to manually strangle a child. That wouldn't necessarily mean they were related to her."

Madison thinks that if two people were present at the scene, there would be more evidence left behind. And Lucy was able to crawl under her bed to hide, suggesting she heard what the intruder was doing to her mom. If there was a second intruder, she probably wouldn't have had time to do that. "Does either victim have any defense wounds?" she asks. "Because it looked to us like they were attacked from behind."

"I didn't find any on either body, which suggests they were very quickly overpowered," Conrad confirms. "But although Denise might have not seen the attack coming, I believe the killer faced her as he strangled her. The damage to her hyoid suggests thumbs were placed on the bone, which is impossible without facing the victim."

Steve shakes his head. "So she saw her attacker and had to look him in the eye while he killed her. Do you think she knew he'd kill Lucy too?"

"Depends," says Madison. "If she knew him, she probably knew why he was killing her and whether that put Lucy at risk too." Denise's final thoughts don't bear thinking about. She must have been terrified for her daughter's safety.

Conrad inhales. "In contrast, Lucy was dragged out from under her bed. Her fingernails contain carpet fibers. I believe she was killed with the cord wrapped around her neck while face-down."

Madison shivers at the image. "That poor child." She thinks of Ryan. He had no obvious wounds on him, which she initially thought was a good sign, but now she knows it's irrelevant, because Denise didn't have time to react and Lucy didn't stand a chance against an adult. "Okay, let's discuss time of death," she says. "Do you know when they might have died? Because the boyfriend says he found them at five thirty this morning."

Conrad nods. "Judging by a number of factors, such as body temperature and visible skin changes on both victims, I estimate they were killed early yesterday evening or late afternoon. Probably no earlier than midafternoon."

Madison turns to Steve. "We need to check Ryan's alibi. He said he wasn't home last night. Now that we have an estimated time of death, we can probe his whereabouts during the afternoon too."

"Agreed," he says. "If his alibi's solid, we'll need to consider other possibilities, like a random intruder, or someone who followed Denise home. Sexual assault could've been a motive."

"Neither victim was sexually assaulted," says Conrad. "But that doesn't mean much. The killer could've been interrupted by Lucy before being able to assault Denise."

Madison's skeptical about a random intruder or a stalker but knows they have to consider every avenue in order to rule it out. "Maybe Denise had a secret life. If she managed to cheat on Ryan before, she could've been doing it again." She doesn't want to victim-blame, but they have to consider it if it helps lead them to the attacker. She looks at Conrad. "Do you know if she was pregnant?"

"We did a test. Forgive me, I forgot to ask for the result." He looks over at his assistants. "Skylar? What was the result of Denise Ridgeway's pregnancy test?"

"Negative, Doctor."

Madison is relieved. At least there are no more victims in this terrible crime. "Denise's parents want to know when they can see her and Lucy."

Their eyes lower to little Lucy's neck. This is no way for them to remember their granddaughter. "Don't worry," says Conrad. "A good funeral home will cover that." He pulls his latex gloves off and throws them into the medical waste. "I'll write up my report, then if Alex doesn't need anything from the bodies, we can release them to the family."

"Thanks for prioritizing these for us this morning, Conrad. I appreciate it." Madison pulls off her plastic apron and waits for Steve before leaving, aware of just how much work they have ahead of them.

CHAPTER NINE

Once they're back at the station, Madison pours herself and Steve some coffee in the small kitchen and spots a homemade fruitcake in a plastic container with a note telling people to help themselves. As it's past lunchtime, and she's not one to turn down free food, she cuts a slice and wolfs it down. Steve declines because he's healthier than her. They carry their drinks through the open-plan office. As Madison passes the dispatchers' cubicle, she waves to their longest-serving dispatcher, Stella Myers, who's on a call. Several officers are busy coming and going, and she and Steve find Chief Mendes talking to Sergeant Adams at his desk, which is opposite her own.

"Hi, guys," says Mendes. She watches Madison and Steve take their seats. Steve's desk is directly behind Madison's.

Adams leans to the left to get a view of Madison from behind his computer screen. "Jeez, you look how I feel."

She rolls her eyes. You can always trust Adams to be straight with you. "It was a rough night. And this morning hasn't been much better." She takes a deep breath before filling them in on the Ridgeway crime scene. When she describes Lucy's death and how it looked like the child had been dragged out from under her bed, Adams flinches. He has twin eleven-year-old girls who he'd do anything for. When she's done, she adds, "We've notified the victims' family in person."

"I'm not gonna lie," says Steve, "it was tough to watch their reactions."

Chief Mendes peers at him with interest, probably wondering how much emotional strain her officers can take and whether they need to check in with Tom Lowery, who is not just Nate's therapist but someone the department uses when a member of the team needs help coping with the stresses of the job.

Madison gets goosebumps as she recalls Bernie's horrified screams. "They named Ryan Simmonds—Denise's boyfriend and Lucy's father—as a person of interest, and with good reason. Turns out Denise had another child from an affair, a boy, but she wasn't raising him, his father was. He's Charlie Larson, the little boy who's currently missing along with his dad, Dominic."

Mendes and Adams look surprised as Madison explains what she and Steve have learned during their eventful morning. When she's done, Mendes says, "So Ryan Simmonds could be behind the disappearance of the Larsons *and* the Ridgeway murders." She sips her own coffee as she thinks it through. "Was it Ryan who notified us of Denise and Lucy's murders?"

"Yeah, he says he found them," says Madison. "He was beside himself. It would be pretty damn shocking if he was involved in their murders."

Adams isn't convinced. "I've gotta say, Harper, it sounds like an open-and-shut case to me."

"Let's not jump to conclusions," says Mendes. She's always the voice of reason, but she's not the person who attends the crime scenes and interviews the victim's nearest and dearest. It's probably easier for her to remain unbiased.

Madison turns her head at the excited pitter-patter of small paws on the floor, getting nearer. Within seconds, Mrs. Pebbles appears, closely followed by a stressed-looking Alex Parker. He always worries when the chihuahua escapes from her crate in case the chief banishes her from the station.

"Sorry, everyone," he says. "She's having one of those days where she won't listen to a thing I say." He scoops the dog up in his arms. "You'll be the death of me, young lady."

The chief strokes the dog's tiny head. "What was Conrad's assessment of this morning's victims?"

Madison takes a deep breath. "Well, both have bruising around their necks. Conrad thinks Denise was manually strangled but the killer used a ligature on Lucy."

Alex speaks up. "I found a lamp discarded on its side in the family bathroom. It seemed out of place, like it was dropped in a hurry. The cord could've been used as a ligature, so I've sent it to Nora at the crime lab. I'm returning to the scene shortly to see what else I can find."

Mendes nods. "Madison, check the boyfriend's background. He seems a good place to start."

"Will do."

The chief picks up her mug from Adams's desk, but before she can head to her office, Madison asks, "Any update on the wedding shooter?"

The chief stops and looks at Adams. "Sergeant?"

Adams leans back in his seat and takes a deep breath. "The helicopter search spotted two people fleeing from under a canopy of trees on one of the nearby trails, but when they got closer, they realized it was a young couple who were half naked and desperately trying to get dressed." He grins. "They must've gone up there for a little al fresco action, if you catch my drift." When the chief doesn't laugh, he quickly continues. "Officers on the ground didn't find anyone in the vicinity, but they're canvassing the neighborhood to see if they can find any witnesses or camera footage of someone fleeing the scene."

Madison's disappointed. While the shooter remains at large, it's impossible to know who their intended target was.

Mendes turns to Steve. "I want you to focus on that case. You, Madison, can focus on this morning's homicide."

"Can't I do both?" she says.

"No," Mendes says firmly. "We have two detectives for a reason. Split the workload. It could mean faster resolutions for both cases."

Against her better judgment, Madison nods. She looks at Adams. "Get Steve a list of everyone who was present at the wedding yesterday. I know who I invited as guests, so I'll add them, but we need the names of all the lodge employees too."

Adams moves some paper around on his messy desk. "Sure. I have witness statements to work through. We can use them to put a list together."

"The press is expecting an update on that case today," says Mendes. "You can tell them about the double homicide too. Let's get the public's help on both cases." She leaves, disappearing into her office.

Madison turns to her computer, already feeling overwhelmed.

Steve and Alex take a seat beside her. Alex keeps hold of Mrs. Pebbles as he asks, "Did Brody make it home after his valiant attempt to find our shooter?"

"He sure did," says Madison. "All by himself too, with not a scratch on him."

Alex smiles. "That's because he's a seasoned police officer."

Madison laughs, but she thinks about how Brody has slowed down in recent months, almost imperceptibly, but noticeable to her. Like the rest of them, he's aging. They don't know how old he really is because he came with little history, but Nate said the vet thinks he's currently around seven or eight and could live to between nine and fifteen years, depending on his history and health. Being a former police dog may shorten his life expectancy, given everything he's been through physically. So it's a guessing game, which means Madison's sensitive to any changes in him. She doesn't even want to think about him as a senior dog, with a graying muzzle and no longer able to accompany Nate on investigations.

She opens her purse, retrieving the dress she was wearing yesterday, now bagged. She hands it to Alex. "Here. It has Lloyd Maxwell's blood on it. I don't know if it will be helpful considering we all witnessed what happened, but I don't plan on ever wearing it again, so it can remain in evidence if you don't need it."

"Thanks." Alex puts it on the desk. He strokes his dog's pink belly. "The direction Brody raced off in after the shot was fired is the correct trajectory of the bullet given the location of Lloyd Maxwell's head wound."

"Good to know," says Steve. "I take it you didn't catch anything on your drone?"

"Afraid not," says Alex. "The tree canopy was too dense, which is why I couldn't find Brody either. I wasn't sure where to focus the drone's attention as things were a little chaotic. But Sanchez and Shelley are currently on scene. I've told them to concentrate on the direction Brody ran in and look for the shell casing from the single shot. If the shooter left that behind, he could've left evidence of himself too, like tire marks, hairs, maybe shoe prints. If the officers find anything, I'll meet them out there and see what I can get."

The thought gives Madison some hope.

Adams leans over his computer screen to talk to them. "I did a background check on the wedding officiant," he says.

Madison notices some gray roots at his temple. It seems he's finally giving the black hair dye a break and accepting he's now over forty. "And?"

"Lloyd Maxwell has no criminal background or complaints made against him. He worked as an engineer most of his life until he semiretired five years ago and began officiating weddings. When I notified his wife yesterday, she was at a complete loss as to why anyone would want him dead."

"That's not unusual," she says. "Many people live secret lives that don't get exposed until after their death." She looks at Steve. "We should visit her. See who knew Lloyd was going to be at that location at that time."

Steve raises an eyebrow and smiles. "*We?* What about what Mendes just said about splitting the workload? Or don't you trust me to do it myself?"

"Of course I trust you. I just find it hard to let go, that's all. But, fine, go alone if you must."

He looks at his watch and stands. "Actually, I need to head out. I have a doctor's appointment. You go see her and catch me up after, okay?"

"Sure."

When he's gone, Adams says, "We shouldn't rule out the possibility that the shooting was random. Perhaps some punk wanted to see what killing was like and made an on-the-spot decision to pick someone as target practice."

"Or it could've been a genuine accident," says Alex.

Madison would like to keep an open mind until they have evidence, but it's difficult because it happened on *her* wedding day. Mrs. Pebbles starts growling, making her realize she's absently stroking the dog's face. She quickly pulls her hand away.

"Be nice, please," Alex whispers to the dog. Her tiny tail starts batting his arm as she lovingly looks up at him and licks his jaw.

Madison shakes her head. "Your dog is weird."

As if to agree, Mrs. Pebbles emits another low growl.

CHAPTER TEN

Positioned in the warm glow of the summer sunshine, Ruby's Diner always looks enticing as it's frequently busy and guaranteed to be welcoming whether you're local or not. When Nate enters, he finds he's arrived before Pamela Smith, the woman who approached him in the therapist's office.

Vince Rader, owner of the diner, gives Nate a wide smile, his hands full as he takes a pile of dirty dishes to the kitchen. Nate chooses a booth by the large window that overlooks the parking lot so he can keep a lookout for his new client. The waitresses are busy clearing away dirty dishes from brunch while seating people for lunch. A strong aroma of bacon and coffee makes Nate's stomach rumble. The TV over the counter is switched to the local news as always, where the weather guy is telling anyone who'll listen that they're set for wall-to-wall sunshine for the next few days.

Nate's always apprehensive when taking on a new case, especially a missing person case like that of Pamela's friend, but it's not the length of time that's passed that bothers him, even though after thirty years there's only so much that can be done. Leads will be cold, witnesses will have moved on or perhaps even passed away, and the footprint the missing person left behind will have faded away like footsteps in sand. No, what bothers him most about missing person cases is how to delicately manage the expectations of the loved ones. Because once they hire an investigator, their expectations always increase, and understandably so. They think a new pair of eyes will reveal new leads, but often, the police investigation exhausted all leads and that's why the case went cold in the first place.

A white Toyota pulls into the diner's parking lot, and the driver parks next to Nate's vehicle. Pamela Smith gets out and walks toward the building at the same time as Vince approaches Nate's booth. A widower, Vince lives above the diner with his son and grandson. "Madison came in earlier," he says. "I gather Brody found his way home eventually. Is he okay?" As Brody's self-proclaimed uncle, he has a soft spot for the shepsky.

"He's fine, thankfully," says Nate. "He'll probably sleep all day while dreaming about his pursuit."

Vince scoffs. "Shame he didn't catch the asshole who ruined your wedding."

Pamela enters, hovering behind Vince with a nervous smile.

Nate motions to the seat opposite him. "Please, join me."

Vince turns and smiles at her. "Hey, Pam. I didn't realize you two knew each other." He turns the clean cups over on their table, pouring black coffee into Nate's. "What can I get you guys?"

"This is fine for me," says Nate, gesturing to the coffee. "Pamela?"

"Call me Pam. Only my mother called me Pamela and I always hated it." She looks at Vince. "I'll have a green tea, thanks." She places her purse beside her.

"Be right back." Vince disappears behind the counter.

When he's gone, she says, "I'm sorry for accosting you at Tom's office earlier. I was surprised to bump into you, and I guess I took my chance before I could change my mind." She anxiously rubs her hands together, adding, "It's just that I've seen you and your fiancée in the news many times, what with all your success at solving cold cases, so I've often thought about hiring you to find my friend. But for someone to be missing for thirty years... well, it's a long time." She drifts off, her eyes glazing over as she looks out the window. The sunlight highlights her wrinkles and the dark circles under her eyes. She's a petite, delicate-looking woman with slim wrists and no meat on her bones. Nate thinks she's in her early fifties.

"Why don't you tell me what happened," he says, "and I'll see if I can help."

Vince returns with Pam's tea, which he sets down in front of her. "Just holler if you need anything else."

"Thanks," says Nate, catching Vince's eye. He suspects his friend will be curious about what he and Pam are discussing. He won't be able to help himself, despite no longer hosting his *Crime and Dine* podcast.

Pam adds a sweetener to her tea, then cups it in her hands as she fixes her eyes on him. "Sharon was my closest friend. She vanished in May 1992, when we were both twenty-three years old." She tilts her head and gives it a shake of disbelief. "It's hard to believe she's been missing longer than she was alive." Her eyes turn watery. "You see, I have to assume she's dead after all this time, but part of me tries to cling to the hope that she's not. That she's out there somewhere living her best life."

"I'm sorry," says Nate, sensing her sadness. "I'm guessing you have a lot of unanswered questions that the police investigation into her disappearance couldn't answer."

She nods. "I'm sure Detective Harper tried his best—"

Nate frowns. "Wait, you mean Madison's father investigated?" Bill Harper worked at the LCPD until moving to Alaska to join the FBI. He left his two daughters and wife behind for the sake of his career. He recently returned to apologize to Madison, but by then the damage was already done, and in the end his chosen career killed him.

"That's right," she says. "That's also why I've never approached *her* about the case. I don't want her to think I'm accusing her father of doing a bad job, but the truth is, things were different back then. You see," she peers over her shoulder to see if anyone's listening, "Sharon was my *girlfriend*. Even now that's hard to say aloud because there's so much hate for same-sex relationships. But in the early nineties it was even worse. To his credit, Bill Harper didn't get hung up on it, but his co-workers did. His chief and partner especially. Even the way it was reported in the press was judgmental."

Nate doesn't doubt it. He hopes the police department didn't do a bad job on purpose, but it's a possibility.

"I felt like no one cared that Sharon was missing. Not really." She lowers her eyes, getting lost in her memories, until she opens her purse and pulls out an old color photograph with an orange tint to it. "This is us about six months before she vanished."

Nate takes it from her and looks at the two women. One is clearly a younger version of Pam. She's leaning against a dusty pickup truck and shielding her eyes from the sun as she peers toward the photographer. The other is a stunning tall blonde with tanned skin and a bright smile. "She looks like she was enjoying life," he says.

"Wasn't she beautiful? Peering into her eyes was like looking into the ocean." She sighs as she takes the photo back from him, then sips her tea before turning serious. "I don't know how much you charge, and I wish I could say it doesn't matter as long as you find out what happened to Sharon, but it does. As a single woman who lives alone and works in customer service, I don't have much. But I want you to find her, Mr. Monroe. No, I *need* you to find her." The intensity of her delivery suggests Sharon's disappearance has haunted this woman. "She was eight months pregnant when she was taken from me."

A sudden sinking feeling washes over him. "She was *pregnant?*"

The middle-aged woman in front of him suddenly breaks down as if it happened yesterday. It's upsetting to see her get emotional. Other diners start glancing over, wondering whether it's Nate who's caused her upset. He passes her some napkins. "I'm sorry. I can see how much you miss her." He considers whether he can do anything for this woman after so much time has passed. He'd like to at least try. "I'll help you."

She wipes her eyes with the napkins before meeting his gaze. "What if I can't afford to pay much?"

He waves a dismissive hand. "Don't worry about it. It's on the house. But you need to be prepared for the emotional upset this will cause. Looking into Sharon's disappearance will open up old wounds, and it might all be for nothing." At least he knows she has a therapist. It means she'll be supported through this process, no matter what he uncovers.

She seems surprised. "You'd look into it for *free?*"

"Sure." He smiles. He doesn't need the money since he was awarded compensation for his wrongful imprisonment. Money isn't a motivating factor for him being a PI. *Truth* is. And helping people like Pam to finally find some peace. "I can't make any promises about finding Sharon, but I'll try my best to uncover more answers than you currently have about her disappearance." Whether she'll like what he finds is a different matter.

Pam covers her mouth with a napkin as she holds back tears. "Thank you."

Nate pulls out his phone. "Is it okay if I record this conversation? Because I need you to tell me everything you know."

She nods, relief evident in her expression. "Of course. I just want her found."

CHAPTER ELEVEN

SEPTEMBER 1990

Sharon Smith never expected to live with a man, but it was the only route out of a family that despises her. As she lies in bed, staring at the ceiling, her mind makes her relive every mistake she's ever made. It's a regular occurrence, and one she wishes she had some power over. Nighttime is the worst. She'll wake with a sudden jerk, then lie awake for hours as her anxiety increases by the minute, making her want to flee her current situation, never to return.

"Take a shower. You smell." Her boyfriend throws back the sheets and slips on underwear and jeans, followed by a T-shirt he's worn for three days straight without putting it in the laundry to be washed.

"Sorry." She sits up, adjusts her nightgown and heads into the bathroom to wash his smell off her. The bathroom is tiny, like the rest of the single-wide trailer. But that doesn't bother her. It's who she has to share it with that's the problem. She doesn't know how accepting one date because she was sick of the guy pestering her has resulted in living with him for almost a whole year now. Except she does, if she's honest with herself.

The truth is, it's more affordable to live with someone than to live alone. Especially when you have no family support.

Warm water from the shower—never hot enough to really enjoy—trickles down her hair and face. Sharon strokes her stomach, hoping they just made a baby. It's the only thought that gives her any relief from depression these days. She even has a bunch of thrifted baby clothes waiting for the moment when she finally has her own.

They both want a child, but for different reasons. Justin wants to see her barefoot and shackled to the kitchen sink with a baby hanging from each nipple. That way, she'll be bound to him and their awful relationship forever while he gets to do whatever he wants in the outside world, one that seems closed off to her as she spends all her time alone indoors thanks to being jobless and broke.

She, on the other hand, wants a baby in order to shower it with the love she never received from her own parents. She knows she can do a better job of parenthood than they did because it's impossible to do any worse. She'll raise the child differently to how she grew up; no shouting, cruelty or stifling the child's personality. He or she will be allowed to blossom into their true selves.

Justin's voice rises over the water as condensation clings to the bathroom's walls. "I'm going for drinks after work later. Don't wait up." The bathroom door slams closed behind him.

The detachment in his voice scares her. It makes her think he doesn't care about her, just about getting her pregnant. He holds all the cards in this relationship. What he says goes. A shudder goes through her. What if she has his baby and he ruins her experience? What if he doesn't let her and the baby have a close bond? He could turn the child against her. Form a pact, especially if it's a boy. He could take him hunting at weekends, excluding her from spending quality time with her son. He might not let her raise the baby how she wants to.

She tries to shake the unsettling thoughts away, but as she squeezes shampoo into the palm of her shaky hand, an even worse thought occurs to her. What if he *only* wants the baby and not her too? She knows he doesn't really love her. He just likes to own her. If she has a child with him, she'll never be able to leave. He's turning into the kind of person who won't let her. She's spent her life listening to the news, and she's watched too many crime documentaries about women in a similar position to hers. Women like her don't matter to men like Justin. They're simply a means to an end. Women exist first and foremost to satisfy his sexual cravings, and secondly to pretend to his parents and co-workers that he's a family man, when in reality he's anything but.

The shampoo washes through her fingers, never to touch her hair. It suddenly dawns on her. She can't have a child with this monster. How could she have been so stupid? Finally coming to her senses and acknowledging what she's been feeling for months now, she realizes she should never have stopped taking her birth control. Dread swells in her chest as she worries it might be too late. She could be pregnant already.

The thought forces her out of the shower. Dripping water all over the floor, she rushes to her nightstand and pulls the drawer wide open. She can't find her birth control pills! Her wet fingers quickly rummage through everything in desperation. They aren't there. Has Justin destroyed them? Did he not trust her to stop taking them a week ago, when they had the awkward discussion about finally trying for a baby?

She almost cries with relief when she hears the rustle of the foil in her fingers. She pulls out the packet and quickly squeezes a pill into her hand before slipping it in her mouth and swallowing. Her heart hammers in her chest as she wills it to work immediately.

She sits on the bed, trying to calm down. Justin's mess catches her eye. He throws his dirty laundry in a pile in the corner under a wooden chair. Her eyes focus on what's hanging over the side of it. A holster containing a gun.

A shudder runs through her. She looks at the packet of pills in her hand. Perhaps it would be wise to swallow a second one. Just in case.

CHAPTER TWELVE
PRESENT DAY

"Thanks for coming," says the older woman as Madison enters the home. "I appreciate it."

"You're welcome," says Madison. She takes a seat on the couch near to Vera, Lloyd Maxwell's wife. Her sister Susan showed her in. The house is cluttered with antique-looking knick-knacks collected over a lifetime. Everything has accumulated dust, but it just adds to the character. The couch is lumpy but covered in a thick velvet fabric. The arms are worn, and the mahogany coffee table is marked with water stains from countless cups of coffee drunk over the years. The decor is miles away from the clean aesthetic so popular with influencers on social media, and Madison couldn't feel more at home.

"Vera?" says Susan, leaning down to her sister's face. "This is Detective Harper. She's come to talk to you about Lloyd's murder at the wedding yesterday."

Madison's puzzled by the way Susan speaks to her older sister, until she realizes she might be her caregiver.

Vera Maxwell's fine white hair, speckled with some defiant brown streaks, is tied back in a neat bun. She's dressed in a chic silk shirt and beige pants, with gold jewelry adorning her neck and wrists. She looks at Madison with red-rimmed eyes and a strange distant expression. "Hello."

"Hi," says Madison, wishing Adams prepared her for this. Then again, knowing Adams, he probably didn't notice there was anything wrong with the woman when he delivered the death notification yesterday. For a cop, he's not the most perceptive person sometimes. "I'm so sorry for your loss," she says. "I didn't know Lloyd for very long, but when my fiancé and I met him to discuss our wedding, he was so warm and friendly that he put to rest my wedding jitters right away. We knew instantly that he was the right person for the job."

Vera's eyebrows shoot up. "It was you he was marrying when it happened?"

Madison nods, overwhelmed with guilt again. What if she *was* the shooter's intended target? That would mean Vera lost her husband because of her.

"I already told you that, Vera," says Susan a little too loudly. "Remember?" She turns to Madison and whispers not too quietly, "We're waiting for the diagnosis to be confirmed, but we're pretty sure it's dementia given she's about to turn seventy and can't remember to wear underwear anymore."

Madison almost cringes. It feels wrong to talk about someone like that, but family members so often do in this situation—not to be unkind, simply because they're trying their best to make visitors understand why their loved one might not react as expected. "Well, I don't want to add to anyone's stress right now," she says diplomatically, "but I wanted to learn a little more about Lloyd. To see if I can figure out who might have done this to him."

"I'll make coffee." Susan abruptly disappears, blinking back tears. Madison suspects the younger sister is trying to keep busy to avoid facing reality. Perhaps she's overwhelmed with her caring responsibilities, as well as the thought of arranging a funeral. Lloyd was part of her family for a long time, so it's understandable that she's upset by his death.

Turning to Vera, Madison smiles. "How long were you and Lloyd married?"

Vera gets off the couch and selects a photo album from a bookcase. When she returns, she immediately starts showing photos of their wedding. The couple must have been in their early twenties when they wed, as they both look radiant with youth. Vera's simple white gown is beautiful. Lloyd beams at her, looking like he's won a prize. "Forty-nine years. Next year will be fifty." Vera's smile fades. "Or it *would've* been." She dabs her eyes with a tissue. "I'm not as far gone as my sister would have you believe, Detective. And if I wanted to wear underwear, I would."

Madison snorts with relief. "Good to know. I'm sure she's just worried about you."

"Well, she should worry about herself." Vera closes the photo album. "As I told the other officer who came to see me, I can't think of a single person who would want to harm my husband, but that doesn't mean he didn't upset someone. He had a mouth on him when he was angry. Mainly in the car."

"You mean he would get agitated behind the wheel?" Madison doesn't know many people who don't get irritated by other drivers these days.

"Right. He would flip people off if they drove dangerously. Not everyone lets you get away with that. Not these days. My first thought after Sergeant... er..." She struggles for his name.

"Adams."

"Right. After Sergeant Adams told me what happened, I assumed that Lloyd had finally offended the wrong person. I warned him so many times that it would backfire on him one day."

Madison pulls out her notebook and writes it down. She can't imagine the mild-mannered sixty-five-year-old who was about to marry her and Nate getting riled up about anything, but she knows better than most that everyone has their triggers. "Did he tell you about any incidents that I should look into?"

Vera thinks about it. "I can't remember. Maybe. When you're married as long as we were, you tend to stop listening when your other half complains of the same thing over and over." She smiles sadly. "And now, with hindsight, I'll miss those conversations." A tear runs down her wrinkled cheek. Her eyes appear to change as she gets lost in her thoughts.

Susan pops her head around the door. "Cream and sugar, Detective?"

"Just cream, thanks."

When she's gone, Vera grabs Madison's wrist and looks her in the eye. "Who was that woman?"

Madison's heart sinks as she realizes Susan is right about her sister's health.

"Where's Lloyd? Tell him to get rid of her."

Madison pats her hand. "That's Susan, your sister. She's making coffee."

Vera appears to ignore her as she looks down at the photo album. She opens it to the first page. "Lloyd was so handsome back then. Who knew we'd be lucky enough to grow old together? We've bought funeral plots so we can sleep together forever once we pass."

Madison smiles reassuringly, while wondering whether it's a blessing that Vera can so easily forget about her husband's murder. Probably not, as she'll have to relive it more than once. "Do you know if Lloyd knew anyone called Denise Ridgeway?" She figures it's worth asking, although she doesn't believe the cases are linked.

"I don't know anyone of that name, so I doubt he did."

"What name?" asks Susan, returning with the drinks. She tells her sister not to try hers yet as it'll be too hot, and to use both hands when picking up the cup. She sits opposite Madison.

"Denise Ridgeway or Ryan Simmonds."

Susan shakes her head. "I've never heard Lloyd or Vera mention those names." She leans forward to pick up her own coffee. "How much longer until you have someone in custody?"

"Unfortunately, that's impossible to know," says Madison. She sips her drink. "Vera thinks Lloyd may have offended someone while driving, but can you think of anyone else who might have wanted to hurt your brother-in-law?"

After taking a deep breath, Susan shakes her head. "He would get riled up easily, but he'd forgive and forget just as fast. He would never take anything too far."

"So if he did get into an altercation while behind the wheel, would he get out of the car to confront someone?"

"Oh no," says Susan. "Not at all. He was all talk. He'd probably laugh at anyone who threatened him, in a bid to de-escalate the situation."

Madison nods. "I see." Vera isn't paying them any attention now, seemingly lost in her own thoughts. "Do you know who would've had prior knowledge that Lloyd was due to work at the lodge yesterday?"

"Well, both of us, obviously," says Susan. "And probably anyone else he'd spoken to in the days leading up to it. He loved talking about his job."

That doesn't help her narrow down potential suspects. "And he got on well with his co-workers and the rest of the family?"

"Absolutely. You don't become a wedding officiant if you're a mean, negative person, Detective. Everyone loved Lloyd." Her eyes tear up. "That's why I don't believe it was personal to him."

"You don't?"

"No. I think it must've been a terrible accident."

Madison isn't so sure. "If it was an accident, I'd like to think the person who shot him would stick around and own up to it."

"Well," says Susan, "as that didn't happen, and we can't think of anyone who had a reason to hurt him, I guess you should assume that Lloyd wasn't the intended target."

Madison's stomach flutters with dread, because her gut tells her that Susan could be right. And if Lloyd wasn't the intended target, it becomes more likely that she or Nate was.

CHAPTER THIRTEEN

Madison is meeting Steve at Ruby's Diner so they can grab a late lunch while she updates him on what Lloyd Maxwell's wife and sister-in-law told her. When she enters the bustling diner, she spots Nate seated with an older woman in a booth by the window. The way he's leaning in, listening intently, suggests his companion has asked for his help. They appear to have been here some time, as empty plates sit discarded on their table.

Madison catches his eye. Nate's face lights up as he smiles at her. She points to Steve so he knows why she's here and that he doesn't have to stop his conversation. He nods in understanding, and she approaches her partner, who's gone ahead and ordered her the chicken and bacon salad she requested. "Hey." Sitting opposite him at the small round table, she says, "Thanks for this. I'm starving." She hungrily eyes his fries while chewing a mouthful of lettuce. "How did your doctor's appointment go?"

He brushes it off. "Fine. Just a regular checkup."

He's acting flippant, but Madison suspects it wasn't a medical checkup. She thinks he's seeing a therapist to try to process what happened between him and his ex-girlfriend. She hopes he is, because at the time he was inconsolable knowing he'd fallen prey to someone like her. What he needs help to understand is that domestic violence can and does happen to anyone, no matter who you are and what you do for a living.

Chewing on a French fry, he changes the subject. "We don't think the two cases are linked, right? Lloyd Maxwell and the two Ridgeway females."

She looks around to make sure no one's listening, but they're seated in a quiet part of the diner. "No. The MOs are completely different. I can't see a link other than that they occurred on the same day. Lloyd's sister-in-law doesn't think he knew Denise. Lloyd's wife, Vera, is awaiting a dementia diagnosis, so she wasn't much help, unfortunately. But when I asked about who might've wanted Lloyd dead, she did mention he would sometimes get pissed off behind the wheel and flip off bad drivers."

Steve snorts. "I don't blame him."

"I know, right? But maybe there's something there. If he flipped off the wrong person, they could've followed him." She sprinkles pepper on her salad and wonders if she can get away with stealing some of his fries.

"But if they wanted to kill him over it," he says, thinking aloud, "doing it out in the open seems a strange way of going about it. It wasn't very subtle, and was actually pretty risky. They could've discreetly broken into his home and done it there instead."

"True." She considers it. "I guess shooting him from afar was odd."

"Exactly, which suggests it probably wasn't personal to Lloyd or to you, if you're still thinking you or Nate was the intended target. It genuinely could've been random or accidental."

Madison's gut tells her it was no accident, but maybe she's wrong. They finish their lunch in silence as they consider the possibilities. When she's done with her food, she says, "Adams has put together the full list of everyone present at the lodge. If I were you—"

He cuts her off. "You'd start with figuring out who makes a better target than Lloyd Maxwell?"

"Sorry." She smiles. "I should've known that would be your next move."

"It's fine," he says. "We think alike, so don't worry about this case. I've got it." He leans back in his seat. "I'll also revisit the wedding venue, and catch up with the officers at the scene, since we need to locate the shell casing and bullet."

Madison sips her water. "I know we're meant to be working on different cases, but if you come up with any new theories about the Ridgeway murders, feel free to share them with me."

"You know," he says, wiping his mouth with a napkin, "I can't get that little girl out of my head. How afraid she must've been listening to her mom being attacked in the next room."

"I know," she says. "And to slip a pillow under her head *after* he'd already murdered her? That's sick. But I do think it suggests he may have known her and was remorseful. Maybe he was expecting Denise to be alone."

"Or does it suggest it was a random intruder who didn't know Denise had a kid?" Steve rubs his jaw. "I don't know. We need to speak to Ryan Simmonds again. Let's see whether he knew about Denise's affair and her other child. We shouldn't be blinded by his emotions. Let's not forget some criminals are excellent actors."

Madison sighs. She can't ignore that Ryan does make a good suspect. "What if *he* was the intended target?"

Steve's eyes light up. "That would explain why he was so devastated. I mean, I know he's lost his partner and child, but if he suspects it's because of something *he* did or someone *he* pissed off, that would make it even more unbearable, right?"

"Absolutely." She watches as the woman Nate was talking

to gets up and leaves. When she's gone, Nate approaches their table.

"Hey." He nods to Steve before leaning down to kiss Madison. Steve looks away. "Are you rushing back to work," asks Nate, "or do you have time to get married?" He smiles in that devilishly handsome way of his.

"At the courthouse?" she asks.

Vince overhears them as he clears Nate's vacated table. "What? You can't get married without any guests present. Come on, guys, don't spoil it for the rest of us. Do you know how much time and energy I've invested in your relationship? Some of us have waited years for this moment."

Nate laughs. "Fine, you can come to our second attempt." He looks down at Madison. "And I can call Owen and tell him to meet us there."

"Don't we need an appointment?" she says dubiously.

"We'll find out when we turn up. We can at least get the paperwork." His smile fades. He must see the doubt in her eyes. "You don't want to get married?"

Her phone rings. She sees the chief's name on screen. She stands. "I have to take this. Of course I want to get married, but there's no rush to do it today." He looks so disappointed that she feels compelled to add, "Don't worry, we'll do it this week! I just don't want to squeeze it in between murders."

Vince snorts as he carries more dirty dishes to the kitchen. Steve heads to the exit, giving them some privacy.

"Promise it'll be soon," says Nate.

"I promise." She kisses him as her phone falls silent. She's missed the call. "I really have to go. I'll call you later, okay?"

He nods, but Madison can tell that despite being in therapy for almost a year and a half, his self-esteem isn't quite where it needs to be yet. She has every intention of getting married this week, but if she's honest, a courthouse wedding seems too much like being at work. She'd rather do it anywhere but there.

Nate walks her out, and when they reach her car, her phone rings again. She kisses him goodbye. "I'll see you later."

He smiles before heading to his own car.

Madison accepts Mendes's second attempt to reach her. "Hi. Sorry I missed your call."

"Ryan Simmonds is at the station," says Mendes. "He wants to talk to a detective."

Madison's heart rate spikes. She wonders if he's there to confess. Steve has already set off for the lodge, and as Mendes wants them to split the workload, it's down to her to interview Ryan. "Understood. I'm on my way."

CHAPTER FOURTEEN

"The press is relentless," says Stella as Madison passes the dispatcher's cubicle. Stella has her headset around her neck and looks stressed. It's not a job for the faint-hearted, yet somehow, she's done it for decades. She keeps threatening to retire but never does. She slips a chocolate into her mouth, adding, "They're annoyed we haven't given them a statement on the wedding shooter yet, and now they've got wind of the double homicide too."

Madison passed a reporter outside who filmed her entering the station. She's also had a couple of texts from Kate Flynn, who works for the local news channel. She takes a deep breath. "Okay. Tell them to get here in an hour or so, and I'll update them in the conference room. I'm about to interview the boyfriend and father of this morning's victims. That could overrun, so make sure they're aware." The press can be demanding and easily irritated, but most of them are nice enough and just in the pursuit of the truth. "In fact, if they get a little antsy, have Adams update them. He knows as much as Steve and I do."

"Oh, he'll love that," says Stella with a grin.

Madison smiles. She likes throwing Adams in at the deep end, knowing how much he loathes holding press conferences.

"Chocolate?" Stella holds up a box.

Madison picks a heart-shaped one, hoping it has a strawberry filling. "Thanks." She pops it in her mouth and heads to her desk, the artificial strawberry flavor giving her a sugar boost.

Chief Mendes is waiting for her. "Mr. Simmonds is in interview room one," she says. "I made him coffee. He's alone, without an attorney, so I don't think he's here to confess anything. He says he wants an update."

"An update?" Madison says, exasperated. "It's only day one of the investigation! Does he expect us to have located the killer already?" She takes a deep breath, trying to put herself in his position. She'd probably be as frantic for news as he is. At least, she hopes that's why he's here. "I guess it's better that he's here voluntarily, since I was going to ask him to come anyway."

"Is he your best suspect right now?" asks Mendes.

Madison nods. "I need to find out if he knew about his girlfriend's affair, and if so, when he found out."

"His background check didn't show anything concerning," says Adams, joining them. "Just some speeding tickets."

"That may be so," says Mendes, "but we all know a clean criminal record doesn't necessarily mean someone has never committed a crime. They've just never been caught."

"True." He goes to his desk. "Want me to sit in with you, Harper?"

She considers it, as having someone else present to interpret Ryan's body language could be useful, but decides against it. "No thanks. I don't want him to feel ganged up on. I need him to feel at ease." She grabs a notebook and pen from her desk. "Wish me luck."

The door of the interview room is ajar, but Madison knocks as she enters. It makes the thirty-two-year-old jump. Ryan's bedraggled hair looks like he's run his hands through it countless times in despair. He cuts a tragic, lonely figure, and she can't help feeling sorry for him. She wonders then whether he has any family to support him through this difficult time.

"Thanks for seeing me again so soon," he says, straightening. His coffee is untouched. His eyes dart around the room, and Madison suspects he's checking whether she's switched the camera on or if there are other recording devices in here.

"Sure," she says, sitting opposite him. "How are you holding up?"

He scoffs as though he doesn't know how to answer. "I'm a mess." He shifts in his seat. "You're not recording this, are you?"

She clears her throat. "I'd like to record it, as much for your protection as mine."

He takes a second to think about it, which gives Madison a bad feeling. His body language is off. Finally, he leans back. "Fine, record it. I have nothing to hide."

Relieved, she switches the camera on. She explains he's here voluntarily and he can have a lawyer or relative present if he'd like, even though she doesn't need to because he's not under arrest. She's trying to build his trust by being transparent. When she's done, he relaxes a little.

"Colt Ridgeway showed up at the house after you told him and Bernie about the murders," he says.

Madison stiffens. "Were Denise and Lucy's bodies still there?" She hopes they didn't witness that.

"No, thank God. They'd already been removed by the medical examiner's team." He shakes his head in sorrow. "The look on Colt's face was horrendous. Losing them could kill him. His heart won't be able to take it. I feel like mine won't, and I'm a lot younger than him."

His concern for Denise's father seems genuine. "What did he say to you?" she asks.

Ryan focuses on a spot on the table. "He said it looks bad for me. That he and Bernie wanted to know straight up whether I'd killed them." A couple of tears escape his eyes. He doesn't acknowledge them. "Me and Colt always got on well, so to hear the accusation come from him is devastating. I'd expect it from his wife or mother-in-law, as they hate me. They hate most people." He finally looks her in the eye. "Listen, I *know* it looks bad for me. Especially as I wasn't there when it happened. I'm not stupid," he adds desperately. "I know it looks like I could've arranged for them to be killed and that's why I stayed away overnight, but that absolutely isn't what happened. You *have* to believe me. If I was guilty, would I really turn up like this without a lawyer? Like I said, I have nothing to hide, Detective. I want to know who did this even more than you do. Denise and Lucy were my life."

His words are delivered with passion, and she appreciates his directness. He's brave for acknowledging that it looks like he hired someone to kill his girlfriend and child. It's a risk, because if she hadn't already considered that, she would now. But coming here unprompted and without a lawyer could be a double bluff. She's seen it many times before. "It always looks bad for the immediate family," she says diplomatically, "but we're trained investigators. We know the most obvious answer isn't always the right one. We have to follow the evidence, not rumors or conjecture. So help me. Tell me why you weren't there overnight."

He wipes his face with his hand. "Denise and me, we had a kind of on-again, off-again thing going for the last ten years, mainly because of her drug problem. She'd disappear for weeks at a time, sometimes months, chasing a constant high." He raises a hand. "And before you say anything, I know it's a disease and she couldn't help it. That's why I always stuck by her. We have —*had*—a lot of history. We were so young when we met; she was nineteen and I was twenty-two." He takes a deep breath as his bottom lip trembles from the memories of their time together. "She'd been clean for the last few months, or so she said. You never really know, right? Addicts are so damn good at lying to your face and putting their high over everything and everyone else."

It's a sad, credible story that she's heard time and again. "Do you suspect now that she was using again at the time of her death?"

He shrugs. "That's just it, I don't know. Even though I loved her, and wanted to believe her, the trust was broken a long time ago. I was always afraid she'd eventually fall off the wagon again and that me and Lucy would suffer for it. So we were arguing a lot over the past few months. Just petty squabbles born out of frustration and mistrust. She knew I had my doubts about her and that probably made her feel bad, but that wasn't my intention." He rubs his face. "Maybe my doubts pushed her into secretly using again, who knows? But I wasn't at home last night because my co-worker, Neil Booth, invited me for drinks." He pulls out his phone and shows her a text he received at 5:15 p.m.

Beer? I can swing by to pick you up in an hour or two.

Ryan replied with:

Sure. 6:30.

"We got a cab back to his place when we were done drinking at the end of the night. I ended up sleeping on his couch. You can ask him. He'll tell you the same thing. He's a good guy. My closest friend, in fact."

"What's his address and phone number?" She writes it down, knowing his friend could have agreed to lie for him. And if they're *that* close, could Neil have committed murder for him too? "Which bars did you go to?"

"Only one. Joe's Saloon on Main Street. We got there

around six forty and stayed until..." He thinks about it. "Maybe midnight? I don't know. I was drunk by the time we left."

She knows the owner of the bar, and will try to verify Ryan's story, but Conrad estimated the females died perhaps as early as midafternoon, meaning Ryan could have killed them before Neil picked him up to head to the bar together. "What about the rest of your day? What did you do before Neil arrived?"

"It was Sunday, so like most people I slept all morning, while Denise took Lucy to church with her mom, Bernie. I worked all afternoon, with Neil. After that, I went home to have dinner with Denise and Lucy, but Denise was in a bad mood, so when Neil texted me, I saw no reason to stay home."

"What do you mean, she was in a bad mood? Do you know why?"

He looks like he doesn't want to say. "Don't hate me for this, but I thought it was her time of the month as she'd been cranky for a few days. Easily irritated. She was avoiding me. Giving me one-word answers and focusing on Lucy instead. I hate it when she's like that because I can't do anything right, so I gave her some space."

"You didn't visit any of your family while she was at church, or go anywhere else yesterday?"

"No." He rubs his face. "My life is pretty simple, Detective. I work six days a week, sometimes more, to keep our heads above water. Any downtime I get is split between being at home with Denise and Lucy and the occasional night out with Neil. I don't have time or money for anything else. Does anyone anymore?"

She finds herself feeling bad for him. "Who do you think did this, Ryan? Be honest with me."

He sips his coffee. "I honestly don't know. It could've been a dealer she owed money to, or a complete stranger who followed her home from somewhere."

"Do you know where she and Lucy spent the afternoon?"

"She spends a lot of her time at her parents' place, even though her mom stresses her out. She wasn't working, so she had nothing better to do. I think she and Lucy ran some errands together yesterday, after church. I know they'd been to the grocery store because the refrigerator was full. You'll probably find footage of them there. Maybe someone followed them to Denise's car. You'd be able to see that, right? And see where else they went? Everything's caught on camera these days. There could be dashcam footage, CCTV..."

Madison makes a note to ask Alex to request and watch whatever footage he can locate. "What car did Denise drive?"

"A white Ford Taurus." He frowns. "I can't remember the license plate off the top of my head, but I can call you with it later."

"That's okay, I have it already. It's the car that's still in your driveway, right?"

He nods.

"Okay," she sighs. "My team and I will look for surveillance footage to build a timeline of Denise's day." She pauses for a second, trying to assess whether Ryan is trying to misdirect her. "It's possible that they were killed by a stranger, but it's more likely that someone they knew did this, especially as the killer placed a pillow under your daughter's head and tucked her stuffed animal in beside her."

He freezes, and it becomes evident he didn't know those details. She remembers now that he'd told Shelley he couldn't bring himself to look under the blanket. His hands start to shake. He moves them under the table, onto his lap.

"I need you to think about this very carefully," she says. "Is there anyone close to you or Denise who makes a good suspect?" It's time to gauge whether he knows about Denise's affair and second child. "Could she have been seeing someone else behind your back?"

"Wait, what?" He frowns. "You think she was *cheating* on me?"

"I'm asking what *you* suspect. Apart from Denise's family, who she was obviously close to, who else was in her life?"

He leans back, and she can tell from his expression that the cogs are turning. "I told you already. She spent time with her parents or with me and Lucy. That was pretty much it."

"She didn't have any close friends?" she presses.

"She knew a lot of people, but never really invited anyone back to the house." He pauses as he thinks. "Unless you're saying she did invite someone back to the house while I was at work." He meets her gaze. "A man?" When she doesn't answer, his shoulders slump. "I guess you know about what happened with Dominic Larson."

Madison is careful with her response. "I know Dominic's a young father who's gone missing along with his two-year-old son, Charlie. And I know that Denise was Charlie's mother."

"So what?" Ryan's tone is edgy now. "I don't understand what that's got to do with my girlfriend and daughter being murdered."

"Hopefully nothing." She sits back. "When did you find out about their affair?"

"Same time as everyone else," he says wearily. "When the press wrote about it after Dominic vanished in February."

"Did you know him?"

He shakes his head. "Never even heard of him until that point."

"You must've been pissed off, right? Not just that Denise had an affair *and* another child, but that you had to find out that way."

He gives her a hard stare. "I was blindsided, sure. But that doesn't mean I killed her, Detective. If I was really that pissed about it, wouldn't I have killed her months ago, when it all came out?"

She nods, but his anger could have been building over those months. He could have been plotting her murder. But would he really kill his daughter over it too? Maybe. If Lucy had inadvertently witnessed what he'd done to her mother. "You have to admit it's strange that Dominic and Charlie would vanish, and then Denise and her other child are killed."

He falls silent for a minute. Until, "Holy crap." His eyes widen. "What if *Dominic* killed them!"

She frowns. "What?"

"What if Dominic Larson *pretended* to vanish so he wouldn't be suspected of her murder?"

Madison's rendered speechless as her mind races with a potential new angle. Until now, she hadn't even considered Dominic could be involved in the homicides. But if he is, he's managed to fool them all.

CHAPTER FIFTEEN

Article from the *Lost Creek Daily*, February 14, 2022

Appeal for Missing Father and Son

The Lost Creek Police Department has appealed for information about a father and son who have seemingly vanished from their home. Dominic Larson, 28, was last seen by a neighbor on the evening of February 13 at his home on Brooker Street. His two-year-old son, Charlie, was last seen when his father collected him from daycare at 6 p.m.

Dominic, a retail manager at a local grocery store, got on well with his co-workers, who said he was in good spirits when he left work at 5:30 that day. They reported there was nothing unusual about his demeanor or actions in the days or hours leading up to his disappearance.

Dominic's father, Henry Larson, states, "I need them to come home because I can't sleep without knowing they're safe. If anyone has any idea where they might be or why Dominic might have left town without telling anyone, call me or the police immediately. Don't worry about it being a false sighting or a possible mistake, because it could lead us to them. Please, I'm desperate to get my boys home."

Detective Steve Tanner from the LCPD declined to comment on any potential signs of foul play, but asked the community to remain vigilant, and for Dominic to contact the department if he's left town of his own volition. The careful wording of his statement suggests law enforcement isn't currently considering any third-party involvement: *It's not a crime to walk away from your life, but with a young child to consider, we just want to know that you're both safe. We're putting time, money and resources into looking for you, so if that's unnecessary, I'd appreciate a call to our office as soon as possible. Anything you tell us will remain confidential. Alternatively, if anyone has seen Dominic or Charlie since their last known sighting, I'd urge you to get in touch immediately.*

A neighbor who wishes to remain anonymous stated that Dominic is a great father who always puts Charlie's needs ahead of his own. She can't understand why he would vanish and says that everyone in the neighborhood knows and likes the pair. "He's raising that little boy all by himself for reasons unknown to the rest of us, and he was doing a great job. He'll do anything for anyone. Nothing is too much trouble. In fact, Dominic once painted my entire bedroom for me because he couldn't afford to pay me for babysitting Charlie one time. I just hope nothing bad has happened to them."

As stated, all potential sightings should be reported to the LCPD.

Article from the *Lost Creek Daily*, February 27, 2022

New Information Regarding Missing Local Father and Son

Missing father and son Dominic and Charlie Larson remain unaccounted for two weeks since they were last seen. However, the identity of two-year-old Charlie's mother has recently been revealed. Dominic's father has told investigators at the Lost Creek Police Department that he believes she is local woman Denise Ridgeway, 29. This has been verified by Charlie's birth certificate. When approached by reporters, Ms. Ridgeway declined to comment, saying she is "already going through hell." It's not known why Charlie was being raised by his father, but neighbors told us Denise also has an older child with her current partner.

Detective Steve Tanner from the LCPD issued this update: *We've spoken to Charlie's mother, and are confident she has no information on the whereabouts of Dominic or Charlie Larson. She is not a person of interest at this time. We don't know what's happened to them and any theories doing the rounds on social media are just that, theories. I'd caution against any speculation and ask that you try to imagine how Charlie's mother is feeling while he remains unaccounted for. When the police department has any updates in the case, we'll be sure to notify the press.*

It remains to be seen whether Detective Tanner's statement will reduce the speculation currently circulating online.

CHAPTER SIXTEEN

As the sun lowers in the sky, casting shadows across the neighborhood, Nate pulls over outside the home of Gail Smith, mother of missing Sharon Smith. Sharon's father died some years ago apparently, and she had only one sibling, a brother who joined the army as soon as he was old enough and who's never returned to Lost Creek.

Brody barks from the backseat. Nate swung by the house to collect him on his way here, figuring the dog had probably had enough rest by now and would be keen to get back to work. He turns and strokes Brody's head. "Ready, boy?"

The dog barks again, his tail thumping the backseat in anticipation. They exit the vehicle, where Brody gets to work sniffing Gail Smith's front yard. Nate didn't call her in preparation of his visit. He prefers she doesn't have time to prepare her answers or her reaction to a private investigator being hired to look for her daughter who has been missing for thirty years. According to Pam, Sharon's parents didn't care that she vanished, but he finds that hard to believe.

A woman dressed in yellow shorts and a white T-shirt appears from the open garage. Short, and carrying all her excess weight around her middle, she gives him a hard stare with cold, calculating eyes. She pulls back her thin white hair with one hand and ties it up. "Help you?" she says.

Brody stands alert as Nate steps forward with his hand outstretched. "Hi. My name's Nate Monroe. Are you Gail Smith?"

She ignores his hand and glances at Brody. "What's that got to do with you?"

He lowers his hand. "I'm a private investigator. I've been asked to look into your daughter's disappearance. I was hoping you'd help me with some background information about Sharon."

Gail rolls her eyes and turns her back on him. "I guess you better come in then."

Surprised to be invited in, Nate follows her. "Can my dog come, or should I make him wait outside?"

"He's more welcome than you are," she responds over her shoulder. "We can sit in the backyard and watch him play."

Nate motions for Brody to follow him to the yard. Once there, Gail points to a plastic patio chair and tells Nate to sit before approaching Brody and giving him her hand to sniff. He must catch a whiff of something interesting, as he nuzzles it for some time before she strokes his back, running her fingers through his thick brown fur. "He's a handsome devil," she says. "I've seen him with you on the TV news. Never thought I'd get to meet him." She moves to sit opposite Nate, slipping a pair of sunglasses on so he can't see her eyes. "I assume Pam's the one paying for your services?"

He nods, even though he's investigating for free. "She's not trying to upset anyone. She just wants to know what happened to Sharon. I'm sure you do too."

Gail shrugs. "I know what happened. She got herself pregnant and ran off to California."

"California?" He shakes his head, confused. Pam never

mentioned California. He realizes he needs some backstory that he didn't get from Sharon's girlfriend. "How about we start at the beginning. What was Sharon like? Did you and your late husband have a good relationship with her?"

Gail takes a deep breath, suggesting she has a lot to say. "She was a good kid until she hit puberty. Isn't that always the way?" He nods to keep her talking. "She was close with her brother until then too. After that it quickly turned to shit for all of us. She started getting fanciful ideas of her own self-importance." With a scoff, she adds, "She turned into one of those young people who crave attention."

"How so?" he asks.

"Well, see, she had this friend called Emma who one day suddenly announced she'd been molested by her uncle. The uncle was arrested, Emma was hailed a hero and told how brave she was for speaking out, even got given a therapist. Sharon watched that play out and I think she was envious of the attention her friend got, so she suddenly announced to us one day that she was attracted to women." She raises her crudely drawn-on eyebrows as though she's still shocked by the suggestion. "She's one of those people who cry wolf to get some of the spotlight on them, you know?"

Nate tries to keep his expression neutral, but he's horrified a parent would say that about any child, never mind their own. He considers whether that's because he isn't a father, and he doesn't have any experience of what it's like to raise a child. He knows that not all children are innocent angels, and some are capable of heinous crimes, but still. It seems overly harsh to him.

"She wasn't a damn lesbian," she continues. "She just wanted to be seen as different, but the truth was, she was the same as the rest of us: ordinary. I tried telling her there's nothing wrong with being ordinary, but she wouldn't have it. She accused us of hurting her feelings and being insensitive to who she really was, but that was BS. If she liked women, they why'd she move in with Justin Asher the first chance she got? He was good for her too, if you ask me." She lifts her sunglasses now the sun has disappeared behind a cloud. "She settled down with him for a year or so and talked of having babies. We thought she'd dropped the whole lesbian thing until she eventually left Justin and started talking crap about wanting to live her authentic self and all this mumbo-jumbo that could only have come from a self-help book."

At the risk of offending her, Nate can't help himself, asking, "Why could it only have come from a book? Why couldn't it have been her true feelings?"

"Because it was odd to think like that back in the late eighties, early nineties," she says. "Nowadays, everyone's trying to be different and everyone's neuro-damn-divergent or whatever they call it, but back then it wasn't a thing, or if it was, you kept your thoughts to yourself, knowing how ridiculous they sounded. She was ahead of her time, I'll give her that. Believed she was misunderstood." She inhales deeply and runs a hand over her hair. "It's hard having a child on a different wavelength to you. And I don't mean the lesbian thing. Whether that was true or not, she fought everything I ever said to her. If I looked outside and said, 'Well, Sharon, it's a lovely day out there today,' she'd come back with, 'No it isn't. I can see rain clouds in the distance.' Honest to God. Her problem was she read too much. Self-help books, fiction... Always at the library, that one. It gave her ideas above her station. I guess it was too difficult for her to accept she wasn't going to be anything other than ordinary and that's why she took off, frustrated that she couldn't prove to us that she wasn't."

It's difficult to listen to a parent talk so disparagingly about their own child. Could Sharon really have been so insufferable that Gail detached herself emotionally? Or is Gail's disregard for her daughter's best interests a sign that she was a horrible mother? "So what do you think happened to her?" Nate asks.

The woman looks over at Brody, who's lying on the deck, enjoying the warm evening breeze. "I don't think she's dead, that's for certain. I think she probably gave her baby to child services to take care of so she could make her way out to California and be famous."

"Famous?" Her theory just gets wilder.

She looks at him like he's stupid. "Yeah, *famous*! Why so shocked? You look like you haven't listened to a word I said. She had *grand designs*, Mr. Monroe. She sought *attention*. What better place than Hollywood for that? I'll tell you one thing, she had the looks for it." She gets up and disappears into the house before returning with a photograph in hand. "Look at her."

He takes the photo. There's no doubt Sharon could have made it in Hollywood on looks alone, but something about this theory doesn't ring true to him. "Don't you think you would've seen her on TV by now if that were the case?"

She waves the suggestion away. "Nah. Girls like Sharon are ten a penny in Hollywood. She would've been swallowed up and spat out by some predator pretending to make her rich." She says it with no pity or sorrow for what might have happened to her only daughter. It's bizarre.

"You don't think she would've come home with her tail between her legs?" he asks.

She looks him dead in the eye. "No. I truly don't. She would've hated for me to see I was right." Tears unexpectedly fill her eyes. "I may sound blasé, Mr. Monroe, but I loved my daughter regardless of the ideas in her head. That doesn't mean we were meant to be in each other's lives forever. I just hope that wherever she is, she's happy, and that my grandchild got the best start in life, with or without her."

He takes a deep breath, trying not to judge her. "If she was really feeling so at odds with who she was and who you wanted her to be, could she have harmed herself?"

She shrugs. "I mean, anything's possible, right?"

Anything except her daughter telling the truth when she stated she was attracted to women, apparently. "When did you last see her?"

"A few months before she supposedly vanished, which would've been February 1992, when she was twenty-three years old. She was with Pam, and pregnant. I could see her bump through her thick winter coat. They were eating ice cream of all things, even though it was cold out, and walking along Main Street giggling like a pair of schoolgirls. I remember it because I thought to myself at the time, 'I sure hope Justin doesn't catch her with Pam.'"

Nate leans in, his interest piqued. "Why would Justin have cared? I thought they'd already split up?"

For the second time she looks at him like he's an idiot. "Because it was embarrassing for him. She was flaunting her relationship with her so-called girlfriend in front of the whole town! Imagine how that made *him* look in the eyes of his friends, neighbors and co-workers. Not only was she pregnant with another man's baby, but she left him for a *woman*! Talk about humiliating."

Nate leans back in his seat as he considers Justin's position. If he felt humiliated, it's possible he could have hurt Sharon. Which means he should pay the guy a visit, see what he has to say about the situation. "Where does Justin live now?"

She scoffs. "Don't even bother asking. There's no way he'd talk to you. And I'll be calling him as soon as you leave here, just so you know. I wouldn't want him blindsided like I was. It's not fair."

Nate can't understand why she wouldn't want his help to find her. He feels like he's talking to a suspect rather than the mother of a missing woman. "That's fine. I'm not trying to trick anyone, Ms. Smith. I'm just looking for your daughter, that's all." When she doesn't respond, he asks, "Do you know who got Sharon pregnant?"

She shrugs. "All I know is that Justin told me it definitely couldn't have been his."

Interesting. "Any theories on whose it could have been?"

"Well, my husband joked that she and Pam used a turkey baster." She chuckles to herself as though it's an original or funny comment. When Nate doesn't laugh, she turns serious. "I don't know. She probably slept around with the intention of getting pregnant. If so, it could be anyone's."

He thinks she probably doesn't even know how offensive some of her comments are, let alone care. Ordinarily, he tries hard not to judge people, but he can understand why Sharon and her brother wanted out of this house. Her brother joined the army the first opportunity he had. And Pamela told him that Sharon agreed to move in with Justin even though she didn't love him. Probably because she was desperate to escape her mother. But was that reason enough to leave town too? "Would you be interested in a reunion if I find out she's alive and well?"

Gail lowers her eyes as she considers it. "My husband died five years ago, and my twin sister died within months of that. Sharon never returned for their funerals. Never even called me to offer her condolences or to apologize for the hell she put us all through when she left town. So no, actually. I'm not interested in a reunion."

He nods slowly. "Fine. What if I find out she never left town at all? What if someone hurt her, would you want to know about that?"

She swallows. "No. I'd rather imagine her living as a hippie in California." Her eyes go teary. "You probably think I'm a terrible person, but I've had to build a wall around me when it comes to my daughter."

"But *why?*" he presses.

"Because I don't want to be wrong about her." She swallows. "Because if I *am* wrong, I'd have to accept that I never even knew her." It's clear her feelings are conflicted no matter how harsh she seems. It's easier for her to believe nothing happened to her daughter. It's how she manages to carry on with her life, and who is Nate to judge her for that? He's not in her position. He doesn't have to cope with having a missing child.

Their conversation leaves him emotionally drained. Gail's not the kind of person who would listen to her children. But on the other hand, she knew Sharon. He didn't. And he's getting one story from her mother and another from her girlfriend, making it tough to figure out which version is real.

CHAPTER SEVENTEEN
APRIL 1991

"Wiggle your butt for me, would you? It's wasted under that T-shirt!"

Sharon tries to ignore the headache building behind her eyes caused by the loud music she's forced to listen to throughout her shift. She keeps her back to the bar while she pours Ron Kempton a shot of whiskey. She's aware the mirrored wall of liquors in front of her will give away her reaction if she grimaces at his lewd comment, so she keeps her expression neutral. She has to. She's lucky to have this job as it offers her the freedom not to be stuck living with her ex, Justin, so she can't risk losing it.

She does a little wiggle, although she doesn't lift her T-shirt so he can see her butt. She hates how the men who drink here constantly demean her and Ginger, her co-worker. They wouldn't dare speak to the male bartenders like this, most of whom are happy to watch it all play out because it's good for business. Only Hank would step in and tell them to watch their mouths. He's nicer than most guys, but unfortunately, he's on his break right now.

She hears Ron's cackle behind her, so she fixes a smile on

her face as she turns and hands him his drink. "Don't tell anyone else I perform party tricks."

He pulls out a ten-dollar bill from his grimy, beaten wallet. "Keep the change," he says. "I have a feeling you're worth every penny."

She takes the money, feeling shame spread through her as he licks his lips like she's an animal he hunted for dinner. By accepting his tip, is she misleading him into thinking she'll sleep with him one day? He's thirty years older than her and a hell of a lot uglier. Even his wife doesn't want to sleep with him. Everyone around here knows that.

"Well, if I knew you were this generous, I'd have poured you a little extra." She winks at him, hating herself as she plays his stupid game just to earn enough money to feed herself.

She pockets the change and approaches Ginger, who's busy fending off the attention of someone even worse than Ron. Leaning in, she whispers into her friend's ear, "Bathroom break. Won't be long."

"You better not be," says Ginger, using the distraction to extract herself from her lecherous customer.

Sharon doesn't go to the bathroom, she goes to the back office to join Hank, who's just a year older than her at twenty-three. He's smoking a joint with his feet up on the boss's desk. He smiles when she enters. She knows he carries a torch for her because he's told her, so she had to confide in him about how she left Justin because she doesn't want to be in a relationship with a man. Admitting she likes women was scary, but she trusts him. And to his credit, he immediately accepted it and backed off.

"Busy tonight, huh?" he says, offering her the joint.

She declines it but sits opposite him. "Just a regular Friday night in hell."

He studies her face. "You look sad."

She sighs. "Please tell me there's more to life than this, Hank, because I can't do this forever."

He smiles. "Of course there's more to life than this. Apparently our early twenties are *meant* to be trying. They're shaping us for who we're about to become. I guess if we had it easy now, we'd have nothing to fight for, right? We wouldn't be motivated to better ourselves." He leans back. "I've never met a single person who said being our age was easy, but they say it with a knowing smile, because they accept it had to happen in order for the rest of their lives to take shape. Imagine yourself in twenty or thirty years' time, when your kids are complaining about having to work a long shift in a shitty bar for minimum wage. What advice would you give them?"

She smiles faintly. "Wear oversized clothes and suck it up. It's a rite of passage."

"Exactly!" He laughs. "We're in our *learning* phase. Someone's teaching us how to fight for what we want. So what are *you* fighting for, Sharon?"

She inhales deeply as she tries to think. "Oh, I don't know. Life's been so crappy up to this point that I don't even know what's realistic for me." Justin threw out all her belongings when she told him she was leaving him, and now she's sharing a house with two strangers and barely a dime to her name. Her parents don't even care. They told her she'd made her bed, now she has to lie in it. They're on Justin's side, but they don't see how mean he can be. He's threatened to tell all his friends that *he* broke up with *her*, because she was frigid in bed, as if she cares about him putting something like that out into the universe. She's actually hoping it'll put other men off hitting on her.

"Don't think *realistically*," Hank says. "That'll just about kill any dream in a heartbeat. Imagine money was no object. Tell me what you actually *want*. You have to manifest the heck out of that shit, otherwise it'll never happen."

She straightens. "Okay, then I want to be the mother of three children, two girls and a boy, ideally, but I don't really mind as long as they're healthy. I want a small house to call my own that no one can take from me, with a vegetable garden out back." She hesitates, before adding, "And I want a partner who actually loves me and has my back and doesn't laugh when I talk about who I really am." She feels frustrated tears building.

He nods. "Good. And you want that partner to be a female, right? Because I can probably give you the rest if you're not bothered about gender." He smiles to show he's joking but also that he would give her whatever he could if she'd let him.

"Afraid so," she says with a sympathetic smile. "I love you, Hank, but I've never been attracted to men. I don't know why, but that's just how it is. God knows, my life would be easier if I were."

"Fine. So you want a wife, a house and three kids. Well, you remember that when the assholes out there make inappropriate comments. Use what you have to your advantage in order to earn enough money to make your dreams come true."

Her face reddens. "I just wiggled my ass for a tip from Ron Kempton."

"Hey, sex is the oldest profession in the world, so don't feel bad about that," he says sincerely. "Think assholes like him feel bad for *paying* for it? I can guarantee you they don't. And anyway, who has the last laugh? Not Ron Kempton, that's for sure. It'll be *you* when you're in the bank putting a down payment on a house with the money you earned from him. He's the idiot, Sharon, not you."

She snorts. "I never thought about it like that. You're smarter than you look."

He taps his temple. "I'm a freakin' genius."

"So why are you still working here?" she teases.

"Because unfortunately, Ron Kempton doesn't want to see

me wiggle *my* butt. But if he did, I'd be wiggling that thing like a son of a bitch."

She breaks into laughter as he grins at her.

Ginger suddenly appears at the door. "How come you two get to take an extended break?" She goes to Hank and takes his joint from him, sucking hard on it. Someone follows her in. "Oh yeah, your sister's here."

"Hey, Pam." Hank holds up a hand in greeting.

Sharon turns around to see who's entered. Pam is an attractive, petite brunette around her own age but with an aura brimming with confidence. Sharon feels butterflies in her stomach as she hesitantly introduces herself. "Hi. I'm Sharon."

Pam smiles at her. "I know. I've seen you around town many times."

"You have?" She's surprised to be noticed.

"Well, yeah. You kinda stand out."

Sharon reddens. Not used to compliments, she thinks she'd like to get to know Hank's sister a little better.

CHAPTER EIGHTEEN
PRESENT DAY

Madison's exhausted when she gets home after a long day. She has so many theories about the Ridgeway murders swirling in her head that she knew it was time to leave work, head home and let her subconscious try to piece everything together while she relaxes with a glass of wine.

The enticing smell of fresh pizza hits her as soon as she enters the house. She notices a pile of wedding gifts stacked by the couch. Nate must have fetched them from the venue. She finds him in the kitchen with Owen, who's seated at the breakfast bar wolfing down a slice of pepperoni pizza. Brody's waiting patiently at Owen's feet for the inevitable spillage.

She approaches Nate. "I don't know whether to kiss you first or eat first. I'm that hungry."

He decides for her by leaning in and kissing her. "Help yourself," he says. "I need to work late, unfortunately." He looks at the legal pad in front of him, which is full of notes.

"Interesting case?" she asks.

"Very interesting. A missing person from thirty years ago." He appears to hesitate before adding, "Your dad was one of the investigators."

A rush of dread runs through her at the mention of her father. "Oh yeah?" she says breezily. She doesn't want to ask about the case as she has enough on her plate and figures Nate will tell her more eventually if he needs to. He appears to read her expression and doesn't press the matter. She takes a seat next to Owen and picks up a slice of pizza. "How was your day?" she asks her son.

Owen shrugs. "Every day's the same during summer break. Although I did shower today."

"Wow, well done," she quips. "Did you even leave your room?"

Nate answers for him. "He had a girl over."

Madison raises her eyebrows. "A real live girl? Wow. Way to go, Owen." She and Nate laugh.

Owen shakes his head, but he knows they're just teasing him. "That's it, I'm outta here." He adds two more slices to his plate and heads upstairs, followed by Brody.

When the landline rings, Nate answers it. Madison tries to figure out who it is based on his side of the conversation. "We don't know yet," he says down the line. "We haven't made any other arrangements." Then, "Sure, you'll be the first to know."

By the time he's done, it's obvious that people are calling to ask when their second attempt at a wedding will be.

"Okay, bye." He hangs up, goes to the fridge and pours her a glass of chilled white wine. He slides it across the breakfast bar, saying, "We need to talk about the wedding."

She finishes her slice of pizza and wipes her mouth and fingers on a napkin. "I know, I know."

He sits next to her with a bottle of beer. "I'm serious. We need to get married, and soon, Madison. I don't want you to keep brushing it off, because it'll never happen if you do."

She looks at him. "You're obsessed with the wedding! Why the rush? It won't change how much I love you."

He leans in and gently touches her face. "You misunderstand me," he whispers. "It's not the *wedding* I'm looking forward to. It's the wedding *night*."

She laughs as he kisses her neck where it meets her shoulder, sending goosebumps over her entire body. "I should've known! You men are all the same." She raises his chin and kisses him on the lips. He runs his hands over her body and things quickly get heated. When he starts unbuttoning her shirt, she removes his hands and steps back. "Calm down, Monroe. You're meant to be working, remember?"

He smiles. "You're forgetting I work for myself, which means I get to choose my own hours."

"Well, even so, you'll have to wait until I've showered. I smell like trash." Warm weather mixed with crime scenes doesn't scream seduction to her. She sips the wine. It tastes amazing after the day she's had. "Is it weird that I feel like we've already had a wedding? I mean, all that fuss and expense. I don't want to go through that again."

"I agree. So let's just finalize the legal part."

She nods. "Fine. But not at the courthouse. It feels too clinical."

"Alright," he says. "Leave it with me. I'll get the documents. All you need to do is sign them."

She raises her glass to his bottle of beer. "Perfect."

"Shall we open the gifts?" He nods to the pile by the couch and heads over there.

"I feel bad that we didn't even feed our guests," she says, following him. "They bought us gifts and got nothing in return."

"I don't think they bought us gifts to get a free meal," he says with a smile.

She picks one out at random, a cardboard box with no gift wrap or card. "This might not be a wedding gift." She shows him. "It could be something Owen's ordered online."

Nate grimaces. "I don't wanna know what's in there then."

She scoffs. "Ew, don't say that! I don't want to open it now either!"

He takes it from her and breaks it open. Inside is a small gift box. He pulls the lid off and finds a typed note on white paper. His face goes pale as he reads it.

"What is it?" she says. "What's the matter?"

He slowly turns it to face her so she can read it.

Congratulations on surviving your wedding. Next time, you won't be so lucky.

A chill runs through her and the pizza she ate threatens to come back up. Because this note means she was right. She and Nate *were* the wedding shooter's real targets.

CHAPTER NINETEEN

The next morning is overcast, with a chill in the air, perfectly mirroring Madison's mood. She'd had another sleepless night, tossing and turning, unable to settle in any position because she was ruminating over who sent them the threatening note and why. All she knows it that she now has confirmation that the bullet that tragically killed Lloyd Maxwell at their wedding was meant for her or Nate, or maybe even Owen. It's no wonder she feels like death warmed up this morning. She could be living on borrowed time.

Sitting in her car, she waits for Steve and Alex to show up. She's outside the home Dominic Larson shared with his son, Charlie, because she needs to know whether he could have staged their disappearance in order to come back undetected and kill Denise and Lucy Ridgeway.

Her hands tremble from too much caffeine and a lack of food to soak it up. She couldn't stomach breakfast because she can't stop thinking about who would want her dead.

A tap at the driver's-side window makes her almost jump out of her seat. She hadn't noticed Steve approaching, despite keeping a lookout. Clutching her chest with one hand, she breathes a sigh of relief and exits her vehicle.

"Sorry," he says, with Alex watching behind him. "Didn't mean to scare you."

She looks around as she checks her bulletproof vest is secured. Although she could have a target on her back, part of her suspects that if someone really wants to hurt her, they'll target Nate or Owen, which is even more terrifying than being shot herself. "Let's go inside."

Steve's puzzled by her vest. "What's going on?"

They follow Alex up the path to the front door. He unlocks it and they step inside. Madison closes the door behind her. Before they enter any of the rooms off the small, dark hallway, she has to tell them what happened last night. She explains the threatening note in the gift box, and what it must mean, and how Nate has insisted she wears a bulletproof vest while at work until they catch the shooter.

Alex looks sympathetic. "I'm sorry. That must be very frightening. If you let me have the box and note, I'll see what I can get from them. There may be fingerprints."

"Thanks," she says, relieved. "They're in my trunk. I bagged them up as soon as we read the note, but they'll obviously have our prints on them now."

"Still worth checking," he says.

Steve looks pissed on her behalf. "We need names—anyone you think it could be—and I'll work through them one by one."

"The obvious candidate would be Angie." Her sister has always hated her, and although she's been quiet since her release from prison almost a year and a half ago, that doesn't mean she hasn't been plotting. "But Angie's not stupid enough to do it herself," she says. "And as far as I know, she's not a hunter with a near-perfect shot. So if she's behind this, she would've paid a fall guy to do it."

"Agreed," says Steve. "But it seems too obvious, and like you said, she's not stupid and wouldn't want to risk going back to prison. Can you think of anyone else who has a problem with you?"

She scoffs. "How about every damn criminal in Lost Creek? I mean, it's not a short list, right? I've helped put away a lot of people, so it could be disgruntled family members, or someone recently released from prison. But none of them have issued a direct threat." She sighs. "Nate wanted to march straight over to Angie's place and confront her to see how she reacts, but I managed to talk him out of it."

"It would be stupid to openly accuse her so early in the investigation," says Steve. "Let's build a case, find some evidence and then see where we're at."

"I agree," she says. "Did we find the shell casing or bullet?"

Alex shakes his head. "No, we haven't found either, which suggests the killer didn't eject the shell at the time, or else he took it with him. Officers Sanchez and Vickers found where they think he stood, based on some disturbance to a particular area that also has a gap in the trees providing a perfect view of where Lloyd Maxwell was standing when he was hit. I went up there and managed to get a couple of partial shoe prints, although they could belong to hikers. Also, a woody shrub was damaged as though someone had kneeled on it, perhaps while taking aim, but that could have been disturbed by an animal."

She's disappointed they don't have anything more concrete.

"Oh, and I found this not far from the spot." Alex pulls a clear evidence bag from his pocket.

Madison smiles when she sees what's in it. "Brody's bowtie from the wedding."

He smiles too. "It seems Brody tracked the shooter to the same location we did. His bowtie was hanging from a nearby branch. It must've caught on it as he raced past."

"Wow. He's such a good boy." She'll let Nate know how

close Brody came to catching their killer. That'll make him smile.

"I know Nate would never carry a weapon after what happened last time," says Steve, referring to when Nate reluctantly agreed to arm himself when the Grave Mountain Stalker was active. That situation ended with him spiraling into depression after being forced to fire his weapon. Ever since then, Madison's never suggested he arm himself again, and nor will she, even though she'd feel better if he did. "But what about Owen?" he asks. "Does he have firearm experience?"

Her stomach flips with dread at the thought of Owen being a target. "No. But maybe now's the time I take him to the shooting range, since he wants to be a police officer one day."

"It makes sense," says Steve. "I'd be making sure he was an experienced shot if he were my son."

He's right. But the thought of Owen having to defend himself makes her feel sick. Sometimes she wishes she never became a cop. Doing so has inevitably made her and her son, as well as Nate, a target. "Okay, let's focus on our other cases: the murdered Ridgeway females and the missing Larson males. To be specific, we're here because we need to figure out whether Dominic could've been involved in Denise and Lucy's murders."

They nod as she leads them into the eerily quiet living room.

CHAPTER TWENTY

Madison has never been inside Dominic Larson's home before. Steve led the investigation while she focused on other cases. With the weather being overcast and the drapes closed, the living room is in darkness, so she opens them, coughing at the dust it unsettles. The house has sat undisturbed for four months, with Dominic's father covering the bills in the hope his son and grandson will eventually return. The contents have been untouched since the place was abandoned. It looks as though the inhabitants will return any minute and continue their lives, seamlessly picking up where they left off.

She hopes they will, but experience tells her otherwise. The only sign that the home was briefly considered a crime scene is the fingerprint dust over the hard surfaces where Alex checked for prints, plus the couch and furniture are slightly askew after they were searched for clues about the father and son's disappearance.

"The only things I've taken from here," says Alex, "are personal possessions such as Dominic's cell phone and their birth certificates."

"You didn't find anything of interest on his cell, did you?" She tries to remember the specifics from the case.

"No. Dominic didn't appear to use social media very much, and the only people he regularly messaged were co-workers and his family. Everything I saw suggested he hadn't fallen out with anyone."

"Just remind me," she says, "do you have their passports?"

"Dominic's, yes. Charlie didn't have one. I also have some of Dominic's bank cards, so if he left voluntarily, it would be difficult for him to leave the country. No transactions have taken place since his disappearance."

"It would be difficult, but not impossible," she says. He could've slowly amassed a stash of cash if his disappearance was planned, and purchased a fake passport. She moves to the kitchen, which has clean dishes stacked next to the sink as though they were recently washed. With no signs of a disturbance, she heads upstairs next. The two-bedroom home is small, and Dominic's room is neat and tidy, with few possessions other than clothes and furniture. In contrast, Charlie's room looks like it's been hit by a twister. Various toys cover the floor and surfaces. His bed is messy, with stuffed animals scattered around the perimeter like they're waiting for him to come to bed and join them for a nap. It makes Madison smile, as it's similar to Owen's room when he was young. There's nothing out of the ordinary here. Toddlers' rooms are supposed to be messy like this. The fact he has so many toys suggests he was well loved.

A framed photograph on the wall near the bed shows Dominic and Charlie with Dominic's father. They're in the backyard, smiling together. Someone, presumably Charlie, has drawn a heart over both men's heads. The sweetness of it brings a lump to her throat.

Steve joins her. "Dominic was last spotted by a neighbor at around seven fifteen at night. He was putting trash in the garbage can out front. Nothing he threw out yielded any clues. Alex checked at the time."

"And Charlie wasn't spotted again once Dominic collected him from daycare, right?" she says.

"Yeah, at six o'clock that same day."

"So the neighbor who saw Dominic that evening didn't see Charlie?"

"No."

Madison chews the inside of her lip as she thinks. "Dominic could've harmed his son any time after six p.m. before then fleeing town on his own."

Steve looks alarmed. "Wait. You think he killed Charlie?"

"I don't know," she says, glancing at the family photograph. "I'm just running through all the possibilities. It's just so damn odd that there are no signs of a struggle in the house, no one saw them after that night and Dominic hasn't spent money on his cards or phoned anyone he knew. I mean, look at this place. There are no clues here at all. If someone broke in, or even if they were invited in, and then harmed the pair in some way, there would be something, wouldn't there? Blood spatter, furniture in disarray, evidence of an attempted cleanup operation?"

Steve nods thoughtfully. "It's a puzzle, that's for sure. Dominic's father was the one who reported them missing. Talking to him was gut-wrenching. The poor guy's devastated. He's called me at least twice a week since then to see where we're at with the case. He told me he'd take his own life if it ever looks like he won't get them back, because they're all he has."

Madison remembers seeing him on TV, talking to reporters in those early days. She could tell his life was ruined the moment his son and grandson disappeared. "He doesn't have any clue about what could've happened?"

"Nope. He says everyone loved them. And he's right. Everyone I've spoken to confirms Dominic got on with friends and strangers alike, and the first thing out of anyone's mouths is how good a father he was. That's why I'm not sure about your suggestion that he could've hurt Charlie."

Madison's torn. Just because Dominic appeared to be a good father doesn't mean he isn't capable of harming his son. "Maybe he killed Charlie in a bid to save him from life with a mother who was in over her head with drugs."

"But Denise wasn't interested in raising Charlie," says Steve. "He was her dirty little secret that she wanted to keep hidden from her boyfriend and family."

She takes a deep breath. "Yeah, but what if she changed her mind in the two years since he was born? If she had approached Dominic for shared custody, he could've been afraid he'd lose him and then panicked. Maybe he thought it would be better that he and Charlie died together than lived apart. For all we know, they could be lying out in the woods right now, just waiting to be found."

"I hope not," says Steve, clearly pained by the thought. "Surely he would've left a note behind to explain to his loved ones where they are and why he did it?"

"Not everyone leaves a note," she says. "And if he did leave one, it could be with his body. We've seen that before, right?" Some people pin their last words to themselves or slip a note in their pocket, knowing it will be found with their body. Others don't even consider writing a note, leaving behind many unanswered questions. It's difficult to appreciate the mysteries of suicide, and all Madison knows from her experience in this job is that most people aren't in their right mind when they take their own life, which means the decision-making process leading up to it can often make no sense to those left behind.

Steve looks away. It's clear this case has gotten under his skin, and she can see why. When young children are involved, emotions run high.

She peers out the bedroom window and is surprised to see

Dominic's father standing outside on the sidewalk, staring at the house. It looks like he's too afraid to come inside.

Steve spots what she's looking at. "Shit. I probably should've called him to warn him we were coming here." They head downstairs and past Alex, who's taking photos of the living room to add to his earlier collection.

Outside, Madison approaches the older man. Tall and thin, with thick dark hair, he's wearing a plaid shirt over an old gray T-shirt and blue jeans. She holds her hand out. "Mr. Larson? I'm Steve's partner, Detective Harper."

He shakes her hand. "Pleasure," he says wearily. "The neighbor called me to say you guys were sniffing around."

Madison notices a shadow in the downstairs window of the house next door. It disappears as the neighbor steps back, out of her view.

"Can I assume you've had a break in the case?" Mr. Larson asks, pushing his glasses up his nose. "Is that why you're here?"

"Unfortunately not," says Steve. "We're just reviewing the interior to see if we've missed anything."

Madison thinks she smells alcohol on the older man's breath. She hopes not. It's only 9 a.m. She wants to ask whether there's any chance his son could have killed Denise, but it seems too disrespectful. Something about the hopelessness in his face stops her. She doesn't want to add to his pain. "Do you want to talk inside?"

He shakes his head. "I haven't been in there since they vanished. I can't bear to see the house empty, or to look at Charlie's toys." His eyes go watery as he pulls a handkerchief from his pocket and chokes back a sob.

Madison gets a lump in her throat. "I'm so sorry." When he's composed, she says gently, "I understand it was you who told us Denise Ridgeway was Charlie's mother." He nods. "Do you have any thoughts on why she's been murdered so soon after Dominic and Charlie vanished?" She's trying to word it delicately, but there's nothing delicate about murder.

"I'm not gonna lie," he says, "her death was a shock. And that poor little girl of hers." He shakes his head sadly. "I never understood how she could give Charlie up, but I'm glad she did. That was a good thing she did. She knew she was under the spell of whatever substance she was addicted to, and she gave Charlie the best chance in life by letting him live with his father. My son loves his boy as much as I love them both. Dominic was grateful to her, and he never once told anyone she was Charlie's mother because that's how she wanted it to be."

It sounds like there was no hostility between the former lovers. "Did your son know Denise was in a relationship with Ryan Simmonds when they had their brief affair?" she asks.

"No," he says. "She lied about being single. Dominic doesn't go looking for trouble, Detective. He's a quiet man. He met Denise at the grocery store where they both worked. She never told anyone she already had a boyfriend. It seems she built her entire life around deceiving people. Maybe that's what drugs do to a person." He takes a deep breath. "But I won't judge her for that. She turned to drugs to numb her pain. I've turned to alcohol. We all need something, right? How else are we supposed to get through the long, dark days?"

Madison glances at Steve, who says, "There's help available for that, if you want to reduce your intake and get back in control."

Mr. Larson dismisses it with a wave of the hand. "Dominic was afraid when he found out she already had a boyfriend. He thought Ryan would want revenge, but nothing ever came of it. When she realized she was pregnant, she disappeared for months so that Ryan would never find out. It was during that time that she gave birth, told Dominic he was the father and said he could raise the baby without her."

"That must've come as quite a surprise to him?" says Steve.

"Sure, but he adapted immediately. He'd always wanted kids. The minute she showed him their son, he loved that boy with all his heart." He clears his throat. "We both did."

"Do you think Ryan Simmonds could've learned of their affair and taken his anger out on Dominic?" asks Madison.

The older man shrugs. "I guess it's possible. But that's your job to figure out. I just want them back. Other than that, I don't have the energy to think about anything else. My doctor recently told me I won't see out the year. My prostate is killing me. It's spread to my bones." Madison's heart sinks. He looks exhausted. "I feel like I'm expected to come to terms with never seeing my boys again, but if I could just embrace them one more time, I'd be mighty grateful to you both. Consider it a dying man's wish."

She rests a hand on his shoulder. "We can't make any promises about bringing them back from wherever they are, but we're going to try hard to find out what happened to them. Okay?" She gives it a squeeze.

He nods. "I appreciate it."

As she watches him slowly walk back to his car, she can't help feeling that Ryan must have found out about his girlfriend's affair. That could have been the catalyst for Dominic to skip town with Charlie, either because Denise now didn't have to hide the child from her boyfriend and could claim him for herself, or because Dominic was afraid Ryan would hurt him or his son out of revenge for sleeping with his girlfriend.

Either way, her gut tells her that the two cases are linked, and if she solves one of them, she'll solve them both, and potentially bring little Charlie home to his grandfather before it's too late.

CHAPTER TWENTY-ONE

Nate can't stop thinking about the note they received that was masquerading as a wedding gift. He doesn't like being threatened. And he sure as hell doesn't like Madison being threatened. He's made Owen promise to set the alarm whenever he comes and goes from the house, and to be more aware of his surroundings in case he's targeted. And he's tried to stop him from wearing headphones twenty-four-seven, but Owen's at that age where he can't live without music and social media. Ultimately, though, he knows his mom's job sometimes puts them in the firing line, so Nate has to trust he'll look after himself. What choice does he have?

The early-morning cloud has dispersed by the time he pulls up outside a single-wide trailer in a run-down mobile home park. He switches his engine off and tries to relax. His jaw is clenched, knowing he's about to enter the lion's den. He doesn't want to go in all guns blazing, but he needs to issue a warning to the person who lives here because he refuses to watch the woman he loves toss and turn every night, anxious that one of them is going to die. It's not fair that after everything she's already been through, Madison can't even enjoy her own wedding without looking over her shoulder.

He sighs as he looks at the ancient trailer ahead of him. It's dirty and basic, unlike most of them, where the residents have taken pride in their small space and kept their homes spotless. No such love has been wasted on this one, its occupant without money or inclination to claw themselves out of the situation that brought them here.

Nate's gut instinct made him come. He suspects Madison's sister is behind the wedding shooting, although he hasn't told Madison that. Her first reaction was also to question whether Angie was involved, but she's torn because she wants to believe the woman has changed since her release from prison, and that she's no longer a threat. Considering Angie was responsible for most of Madison's problems, Nate strongly disagrees. Experience has taught him that when someone shows you who they really are, you need to pay attention. But he can also understand how Madison's willing to overlook certain things because she craves family in her life, since all her other relatives have passed.

Brody leans in from the backseat and licks his ear, sensing he's worked up. He takes a deep breath. "I know, I know. I need to relax." He wants to take the dog with him, but doesn't think either of them will be welcome, so he leaves Brody in the car. "Wait here. I shouldn't be long."

Brody snorts angrily, suggesting he doesn't want to be left behind. Nate smiles. "Okay, fine. You can get out, but you're not coming in. She can't be trusted." He wouldn't put it past Angie McCoy to shoot a dog.

He slams the car door closed once Brody's out, and climbs the steps to Angie's door. He knocks once and waits, bracing himself for a barrage of vitriol.

He's met with silence, so he knocks again.

"What?" yells Angie from inside before launching into a coughing fit.

"It's Nate Monroe. I want to talk to you." He tries to keep his tone neutral.

After a few seconds of hesitation, she shouts, "It's open."

He rolls his eyes. In an act of defiance that's so typical of Angie, she won't even lower herself to answer the door to him. "Fine," he says, grabbing the handle. "I'm coming in." He hesitates, considering whether she could be standing on the other side of the door with a gun pointed at his chest.

"What are you waiting for, a written invitation?" she yells.

He steps aside and pushes the door open before peering in. Angie is lying under a thin blanket on the couch in her darkened living room.

"Leave the door open," she says. "I need some fresh air."

Nate slowly enters, and doesn't notice Brody rush in behind him until it's too late. "Shit, sorry." Brody sniffs everything before making his way to Angie. She smiles at him.

"Hey, dog." She makes no move to stroke him, probably because she looks like she's on her deathbed.

Nate wasn't prepared for this. He's shocked to see her so thin and fragile. Her eyes have sunk into her skull and the place smells horrible. With no A/C, the air is stagnant. Takeout food trays litter the floor in front of her. "What's going on, Angie?" he asks. "Are you sick?"

She scoffs. "Yeah. You can tell Madison I finally got what was coming to me."

He steps forward, guiding Brody away from her. "What do you mean?"

"Lung cancer. Terminal. She'll get her wish to see me dead."

Nate's surprised to feel pity for the woman, as well as sadness that he'll have to break the news to Madison. He lowers himself onto a worn armchair and runs a hand over his face.

"She doesn't want to see you dead. She never wanted that. All she ever wanted was a family she could rely on."

Angie's eyes narrow. "Yeah? Well, so did I."

He meets her gaze. "I'm sorry, Angie, but you of all people cannot play the victim card. Not after everything you did to her."

She breaks eye contact and bursts into another coughing fit. It's so alarming that it prompts Nate to fetch her a glass of water. As he passes it over, she takes it with both hands, and he sees how thin her wrists are now they're out from under the blanket. While she drinks, he pulls the worn drapes apart to try to get some daylight into the room.

"Hey, I closed them to keep the sun out," she says. "It gets too hot in here."

"Calm down, I'll close them again before I leave." He starts collecting the trash that Brody's sniffing on the floor. It stinks. Most of the food is barely touched.

"That's Bob's doing," she says, nodding at the trash. "An old neighbor. He works at the nearby burger joint and brings me food some days. But he moved in with his boyfriend last week, so I'll probably die of starvation before long if the cancer doesn't beat it."

Nate's animosity toward her dissipates. She shouldn't be left to die alone like this. "When did you last eat?"

"Yesterday. Some of those cold fries you just threw out." Her lips look dry.

"Want me to make coffee?"

"Screw coffee," she says. "If I'm going out, I want to go out drunk or high. Open that cabinet above the stove. I have a small bottle of vodka right at the back. Couldn't get to it myself."

"Angie," he says doubtfully. "That's not going to help."

"Says who? Are you a doctor now too, Mr. PI?"

He battles with his conscience for a second before figuring

it's her life, she can do what she wants. "Okay, but I'm making coffee as well."

He opens a window and spends some time cleaning up the mess around the place, then makes them both hot drinks, while Angie swigs on the vodka before screwing the lid back on. She winces in pain as she tries to sit up, so he pushes some cushions behind her back, but they're so flat and worn they barely make a difference.

Brody sits on the floor staring at her, probably remembering the tension he's witnessed in the past between this woman and his mom.

"What did you come here for anyway?" Angie asks as Nate sits opposite her with a cup of black coffee. The fridge was empty.

He takes a deep breath. "I don't know." He can't tell her he thought she was responsible for ruining their wedding day, as that's highly unlikely given her current condition. Although he wouldn't put it past her to have hired the shooter as one last act of vengeance before she dies. Still, he doesn't think that's the case. Not now she's so sick. "I guess I was in the area and Madison said she hadn't spotted you around for a while."

"Well, she has my address. There's no reason not to call on me once in a while. Although she better hurry if she wants one last hurrah."

"Is surgery or treatment an option?" he asks.

She snorts. "Some of us aren't rich like you." She looks away. "Chemo was an option about six months ago, but I don't have health insurance or money. And now it's spread too far."

He shakes his head in disappointment. He wishes she'd come to them. Despite everything, he would've helped her, for Madison's sake. "Do you know how long you have?"

She shrugs. "How long's a piece of string? Still, it's not all bad. I can just about get to the bathroom if I ignore the pain, so there's that." She glances at him. "I have pain meds. They're not as effective as they were, though, so if you want to get me something a little stronger, I'd be grateful."

He nods slowly. "Sure. We'll come back with food and meds. Anything you need. You have Madison's number, right?"

"Yeah. But she won't want to help. I'm sure of that. My sister hates me."

Nate shakes his head, picturing Madison seeing her like this. "She doesn't. You can trust me on that." His phone pings with a text.

How's your investigation going?

It's Pamela Smith. He should be working, so he stands. "Do you have a spare key so I can lock up on my way out? You shouldn't leave your door unlocked, you never know who might walk in."

Angie studies his face, looking like she can't understand why he'd help her. "I'm not your responsibility, Monroe. You can walk out of here and never see me again. Never even tell Madison what state I'm in. Why would you choose to come back?"

He thinks about it. He doesn't want to tell her it's because he pities her. "Because it's what Madison would want. Owen too, probably."

At Owen's name, Angie looks away. Angie's late husband, Wyatt, was Owen's father. Owen once had to live with the pair, and Angie claims she loved him like her own child, which is a bone of contention between her and Madison because she put the boy in harm's way for years, though she'll never admit it. "The spare key is in the cabinet by the door." She nods to it. "Open the other windows before you go, and close the drapes like you promised."

He does as she says. After Brody exits the trailer, Nate turns back to look at her. "Before I go, I need to know something." He pauses. "Are you done hurting her?"

"What do you mean?" she says, playing dumb.

"Madison. You're not going to try one last trick to get at her, are you? By targeting me or Owen, or even her."

She scoffs. "You're so paranoid, Monroe. I guess prison made you that way."

"No, Angie," he says, bristling. "People like *you* made me that way. Promise me. Otherwise I won't come back, and I won't tell Madison about your diagnosis. I'm serious. We've been through enough. We just want to be left alone." His voice falters. The pressure of having a target on his back and never knowing who to trust is getting to him.

Angie's smile fades. She looks him in the eye. "I'm not like that anymore. Wyatt made me that way, and he's dead. I just want to leave this earth pain-free and not completely alone. I promise you I'm not going to hurt anyone."

It's the first time she's ever spoken candidly to him, without some barbed insult or in a patronizing tone. He nods. "Fine. Then we'll see you later."

He exits the trailer and locks the door behind him, a heavy feeling of sadness weighing on his chest.

CHAPTER TWENTY-TWO

Madison enjoys the emerging sunshine on her face as she sits in her vehicle outside Ruby's Diner, watching a recording of Sergeant Adams's press conference from yesterday. He did a good job of sticking to the facts and not being drawn into speculation about the two homicide cases, which is more difficult than people realize. While listening, she regularly checks her mirrors in case she's ambushed by the wedding shooter, but that could be any of the supposed customers coming and going around her, which makes it difficult to relax.

When Adams takes questions from the assembled reporters, she recognizes Kate Flynn's voice as she asks, "Is it true that Ryan Simmonds was brought in for questioning yesterday? He was spotted entering the station."

"No," says Adams. "That's not true. He came in voluntarily for an update on the case."

"So he isn't a person of interest for the murder of his partner and daughter?" Kate presses.

"Not right now, no."

Madison sighs. Ryan's still their best suspect at this point.

Or is it Dominic? She can't shake the feeling that the young father might have panicked and done something terrible.

"And how does Detective Harper feel about the victim's family saying they have zero trust in her to arrest the killer," asks Kate, "who they very firmly believe is Ryan Simmonds?"

Madison's blindsided. "When did they say that?" she mutters at the screen, disappointed that the Ridgeways would bad-mouth her to the press.

"You'd have to ask her," Adams says diplomatically, before ending the conference.

She lowers her phone to her lap, feeling like their comment was unjustified. It's only been a day and a half since Denise and Lucy's bodies were found. How can the Ridgeways expect an arrest so soon? They might not be considering anyone else a suspect, but she can't work like that. She can't just arrest anyone. She needs evidence.

She considers whether to try to obtain a search warrant for Ryan's cell phone. Maybe there's something on there, messages between him and Denise that suggest increasing tensions or an abusive relationship. She texts Adams.

See if we can get a search warrant for Ryan's phone. It might rule him out if nothing else.

Adams quickly responds with a thumbs-up emoji. She's tempted to ask why he didn't tell her about the disparaging comment from the Ridgeways, but decides against it. He probably didn't think it was worth worrying her. But it's eating at her. She starts her engine, intending to pay them a visit. She wants to reassure them that she and the team are doing everything they can to identify Denise and Lucy's killer, and to explain that if they're correct about Ryan, she needs time to build a case against him.

. . .

Colt Ridgeway opens the door to her, but he's on his cell phone. "I've got to go, honey. The detective's here about your sister. Bye." He lowers his phone. "You couldn't have called first? I don't want Bernie unsettled by your sudden appearance."

"Sorry," she says. "I figured a visit was better than a phone call as it gives you both the chance to ask questions." He reluctantly opens the door wider so she can enter the house. "Was that Denise's older sister on the phone?" she asks.

"Yeah, Toyah," he says wearily, closing the door behind her.

"Is she okay? Because she can call me if she wants updates. She's in Denver, right?"

He nods. "Right. She's devastated, so we're planning to visit her soon. We don't want to be apart right now, and this place is full of memories." He nods to a doll sitting on a sideboard. It must be Lucy's.

"Sure, I get it," she says.

He leads her into the living room, where Bernie is seated on the couch next to an older woman with a severe expression and mean eyes that drift critically over Madison, sizing her up. Bernie takes the woman's hand in hers. "This is my mom, Ida."

"Pleasure," says Madison, even though Ida looks like one of those people who dislikes anyone in law enforcement. Perhaps she has good reason to. Madison knows better than most that a badge doesn't automatically make you a good human being. There are plenty of crooked cops out there. That's why she works extra hard to show the majority of law enforcement isn't like that. "I'm sorry to come unannounced. It's just that I understand you're concerned that Ryan Simmonds hasn't been arrested, so I wanted to reassure you and explain why that hasn't happened."

"Because you're useless," spits Ida.

Madison's taken aback, especially as neither Bernie nor Colt react. She has to remind herself that this family is grieving. Tensions are running high, so it probably isn't personal. "I'm sorry you feel that way, but the truth is there are procedures we need to follow in order to make sure that whoever we eventually arrest is the right person. If we spend too much time on a theory we have no proof of, it could derail the entire investigation, never mind the hope of eventually bringing charges."

Ida rolls her watery gray eyes. "Ryan found out about Denise's affair and that baby she had. It's obvious he killed her out of spite. Some men can't handle being emasculated. If we can see that, why can't you?"

Madison takes a deep breath. "Well, he's certainly on my radar, but I don't have any evidence to back that up right now. Homicide investigations take time, and the more thorough we are before we make an arrest, the more likely the charges will result in convictions once the case reaches court."

"So what are you doing here, then?" says the older woman. "You're wasting everyone's time. And if you're not careful, someone else will do your job for you and you'll find yourself fishing Ryan Simmonds out of the lake with half his head missing."

Bernie pats her mother's hand but remains silent.

Madison's shocked. "I hope none of you are thinking of taking matters into your own hands, because that's not going to bring Denise and Lucy back, it's just going to add to your heartache." She looks at Colt. "I'm sure I don't have to tell you that murder is murder, regardless of the rationale behind it. The law doesn't differentiate. If someone hurts Ryan, they'll spend a long time in prison for it. How is that going to help you and your family?"

"It would be worth every second if you ask me," says Ida.

Madison studies Colt's face. He looks beaten down, either from living with this woman or due to losing Denise and Lucy. But he also seems to be considering Ida's words. He might think that killing Ryan is his chance to finally gain his mother-in-law's approval. "Mr. Ridgeway, I'm counting on you to let me do my job. I don't want to arrest any of you for something you'd regret."

"*I* wouldn't regret it," says Ida. "Neither would he, I'm sure." Despite her age and frailty, it's clear that she's quite the antagonist in this household.

"Ida, stop," says Colt. His weary expression suggests there's no love lost between him and his mother-in-law.

"Don't tell me what to do in my own home," she replies, her eyes on him. "You can leave if you don't like it."

Colt glances at his wife to see if she'll stick up for him, but Bernie's eyes are firmly fixed on the floor.

Madison thinks it's best she leaves before her presence makes things worse. "Let me reassure you that the entire department is working on this case as a matter of urgency. We just need time to do our jobs." When no one answers, she turns to leave. "I'll see myself out."

She thinks she hears Ida mutter, *Good riddance*, but she can't be sure. Outside, she breathes a sigh of relief to be leaving, but she worries that if she doesn't arrest someone soon, she could have another homicide on her hands.

CHAPTER TWENTY-THREE

Once she's back at the station, Madison calls Ryan's friend and co-worker, Neil Booth. She wants to see if he'll verify Ryan's alibi for the time Denise and Lucy were murdered. He answers on the fourth ring. "Hello?"

"Hi, is that Neil Booth?" she says.

"Who wants to know?" A radio station plays so loudly in the background that she can barely hear him. He must be in the auto repair shop where he and Ryan work. Ryan won't be in any fit state to return to work anytime soon because of what happened, so she figures Neil should be able to talk freely without being overheard or influenced.

"I'm Detective Madison Harper from the Lost Creek PD," she explains. "I'm investigating the Ridgeway murders. I understand you're a close friend of Ryan Simmonds, is that correct?"

"Hold on, let me turn the music down." His tone has changed. He sounds worried now. People don't like being called by the police. When he's ready, he says, "Sorry about that."

"That's okay," she says. "I'm looking into Ryan's whereabouts on the day his girlfriend and daughter were killed so I can rule him out as a suspect. Can you help me with that?" She intentionally keeps the details of Ryan's alibi to herself, wanting to hear Neil's version instead.

He takes a deep breath. "Sure, he was with me the night before he found them. I dropped by his place around six thirty in the evening and we went to Joe's Saloon for a few beers."

That's what Ryan said. "What time did you leave the bar?"

"Probably around midnight."

"Was he with you the entire time? He didn't dip out for anything, a cigarette maybe, or to get some fresh air, make a call?" The distance from the bar to Ryan and Denise's house would take ten minutes in a car, she's checked. If Ryan was gone for thirty minutes or more, it's possible he could have killed them during that time, before returning almost unmissed.

"He had a couple of cigarette breaks. Why?"

"How long would you say he was gone during those breaks?" she presses.

Neil sighs as he thinks. "I don't know, five minutes max."

"Were you both drinking all night?"

"Sure were."

"How did you get home?"

"I dro—" He stops, realizing he's incriminating himself as he clearly drove while over the limit. "I can't remember. Probably ordered a cab."

She lets it go since she has more pressing matters to deal with, but it's frustrating that he would make the inexcusable decision to get behind the wheel of a car after drinking all night. "How did Ryan seem to you throughout the evening?"

"Fine, I guess. He was a little tired and got drunk faster than usual, but I knew he'd been arguing with—" He stops himself again, not wanting to incriminate his friend.

She needs to keep him talking. "Ryan's already told me that he and Denise weren't in the best place and had been arguing a lot, so you're not snitching on him if that's what you're worried about."

"There's nothing to snitch about," he says with an edge to his voice. "All couples argue, and he had it worse than most because Denise was an addict. He couldn't trust her. Doesn't mean he didn't love her."

"I understand that," she says. "What was their relationship like in general? Were they good together in your opinion?"

"I don't know. I never really saw them together much, so I only know what Ryan would say about her."

"Which was?"

"It was all good, mostly." He's sounding more guarded as the conversation goes on, which isn't unusual for the friends and relatives of a potential suspect.

She sips some water before asking, "Did you see Denise and Lucy when you dropped by the house to pick him up?"

He hesitates for a few seconds as he considers whether to be honest. Eventually, he says, "No. Ryan was waiting outside, smoking a cigarette."

Ryan had told her that Denise was in a bad mood that day, so although he'd gone home to have dinner with her and Lucy, he soon changed his mind. But as Neil didn't see either female, she only has Ryan's word that they were still alive at that point. He could have already killed them before his friend showed up. "Did he seem agitated or upset?"

"Nope, just tired and ready for a drink."

"Did he sleep at your place after the bar, or did you drop him at home?"

"He didn't want to wake Lucy, so he stayed at my place. Slept on the couch."

"Do you know if he stayed all night?"

"I assume so. I don't know what he did while I slept, but I didn't hear him leave until the morning. He didn't say goodbye or anything, but I heard him open and close the front door at around ten past five." She hears voices in the background. "Look, I gotta go," he says. "I have a customer waiting."

She's unsure how much she can trust this guy, but unless she finds anything to suggest that he and Ryan are lying, she has to accept his statement for now. "Sure. Well, thanks for your help. Oh, and I strongly recommend you stop driving while intoxicated. I wouldn't want to have to visit you or someone you hit in the hospital, or worse, the morgue."

He hangs up without responding just as Alex Parker approaches her desk. He hands her a flash drive, which she inserts into her computer. "CCTV footage?" she asks.

"Yes." He sits beside her with a half-full cup of tea. "We have footage of Denise and Lucy shopping at the downtown grocery store on the afternoon they died."

She hits play and watches as Alex points to a white car in the parking lot. Denise helps Lucy get out of her child seat before taking her hand and leading her into the store. They're both laughing at something. Denise doesn't act as though she's under the influence of anything. They look like any other mother and daughter running errands together. Denise is totally focused on her daughter and it's clear they were close. The video ends when they disappear into the store.

"This one shows them inside." Alex opens the next clip. "No one appeared to take any special notice of them or followed them out to their car afterward. I watched their entire shopping trip. They were served by a busy female cashier who paid them no particular attention."

On the screen, Lucy runs toward a display of toys for sale and picks up a stuffed animal that on closer inspection looks like the unicorn that was tucked up beside her lifeless body. She runs back to her mother and appears to be pleading to be allowed to have it. Madison's stomach flips with dread. Denise would have had no idea that in just a few hours, she and her daughter would be dead. She clears her throat. "Start the next one."

The third clip shows the pair returning to their vehicle, with

Denise holding two bags of groceries. Lucy's hugging the unicorn tightly to her chest. Madison scans the parking lot to see if anyone's waiting to approach them or follow their car home, but she can't see anything that gives her cause for concern. When they drive off, no one appears to follow them out, suggesting they weren't being stalked directly before their deaths.

"I also have footage from Joe's Saloon," says Alex. "It confirms what time Ryan Simmonds and his friend entered and left, matching what he told you when he came in yesterday. Want to watch it?"

She leans back in her seat. "His friend, Neil, just told me that Ryan took some brief cigarette breaks outside, but none were long enough for him to return home to commit murder. Does the footage confirm that?"

"Yes. Nothing out of the ordinary happened. I checked the camera footage from the rear of the property too, to see if he slipped out that way, but he didn't. It confirms his alibi."

She's deflated. Either Ryan killed them before he left home or he's not their guy. "Did their house yield anything of interest other than the lamp found in the bathroom?"

Alex sips his tea before responding. "Nothing at all. I've sent some fibers and hairs from their clothes to the lab along with the lamp, in case they become useful once we have suspects, but if Ryan killed them, he can explain those away by the fact he lives with them."

She nods.

Alex's cell phone rings. His face lights up when he sees who's calling, which means it's Nora from the lab. "Nora!" he says. "How are you?" They exchange pleasantries for so long that Madison starts to feel like a third wheel, so she gets up to leave, but Alex stops her by saying, "You've tested the cord from the lamp already?" He listens as Madison waits. "And the unicorn?" Silence, until: "Okay, well I'll let Detective Harper know. Thanks for prioritizing that for us. As always, I really appreciate it." He and Nora exchange even more pleasantries as they end the conversation, making Madison feel awkward again. Even so, she's hoping these two get together one day as they're clearly made for each other.

Finally, Alex lowers his phone, his face flushed. "Nora had no luck finding anything useful on the items at the scene, including the cord used to strangle Lucy. But only Lucy's DNA was on the cord, not Denise's."

Although disappointing, at least it confirms Denise didn't kill Lucy in some kind of thwarted murder-suicide. Madison's relieved she can rule that out.

"She did, however, find some rubber particles, which suggests their killer wore gloves to avoid detection."

Madison sighs. "We just can't catch a break."

"We'll find something," says Alex, reminding her they're still early in the investigation. "Killers almost always slip up somewhere. And at least now we know for sure that we have the murder weapon, which can only help us when the case eventually goes to trial."

She nods. "I guess." She knows she shouldn't be impatient, but it's difficult. She clicks play to watch the footage of Lucy in the store again. The little girl looks so happy with the brightly colored unicorn in her hand as she runs to her mom.

Madison's mood turns as she thinks about the kind of person who could drag a child out from under their bed by their ankles and strangle them to death. She has to find Lucy's killer. He can't be allowed to get away with what he's done.

CHAPTER TWENTY-FOUR

Frustrated with the lack of leads, Madison spends the next few hours trying to track down known drug dealers to see if anyone will admit to selling to Denise over the past year or so. But it's a frustrating waste of time that yields no answers, and Ryan isn't able to help her as he's not from that world. So for now she's unable to pursue the theory that Denise might have owed money to her dealer and they came to collect, resulting in a deadly altercation.

Although it would be good to know for sure that's not what happened, Madison has serious doubts given how Lucy was found, with a stuffed animal next to her and a pillow placed under her head. Her gut tells her it was someone who knew the family, and as no drug paraphernalia was found at the home, she doesn't really believe Denise was using in the months leading up to her death. But the toxicology results will prove that one way or the other.

As she's getting ready to quit work for the day, Nate calls and asks her to head home, saying he has something important to tell her. She thinks he means about getting married, but the tone of his voice suggests it's something more serious than that.

He tells her not to worry, but anxiety builds in her chest on the drive home as she considers all the worst-case scenarios.

When she finally enters the house, she finds Nate sitting with Owen in the living room. "What's going on?" she asks, dropping her keys on the sideboard. She looks at Owen, who shrugs as if he has no idea. Nate gets up, takes her by the hand and leads her to the couch before sitting next to her. Nerves immediately kick in. She feels like someone's died.

"I went to see Angie today," he says, blindsiding her.

Owen's head snaps up. "What? Why would you see *her*?" He obviously has bad memories of living with Angie and Wyatt McCoy. Wyatt was a dangerous criminal, and Angie's blind allegiance to her husband made everything worse.

Madison's chest fills with dread. She wishes Nate hadn't told her this in front of Owen. She doesn't want her son to worry. "Oh God. You're going to tell me it was her who tried to kill us at the wedding, right?" A surge of adrenaline makes her want to get up and pace the room. Just when she thought she'd found some kind of truce with her sister, she fears she's going to be proven devastatingly wrong.

"No," says Nate, holding her hand. "In fact, I'm almost certain Angie isn't involved in that."

"How can you be so sure?" she asks, studying his face.

For some reason, he's reluctant to answer.

"Just tell me," she urges. "Please, I can't bear this." When it comes to her sister, she can't control her anxiety.

"Angie's sick." He glances at Owen, before adding, "She's not going to make it. She has terminal cancer."

Madison blinks. That's the last thing she expected to hear. "You're kidding, right?"

He slowly shakes his head. "Afraid not. I went to confront her about the wedding shooter to see if she was involved, but as soon as I saw her, I knew it was unlikely. I found her wasting away in her trailer. She's so frail she can't even get up for long enough to make herself a meal." He squeezes her hand. "I don't think she's got long left. I'm sorry."

After a few seconds, Owen gets up and silently leaves the room, his expression difficult to read. He heads upstairs. Maybe he's glad Angie's dying. He can finally put the past behind him.

Madison's eyes fill with tears, surprising her. "Are you sure? How does she know it's terminal?"

"She's seen doctors. It might've been treatable last year, but she couldn't afford it, so she didn't do anything about it."

"But we could've helped her!" she says in frustration. "I would've gone with her to the hospital, paid her bills, helped her recover." Tears stream down her face. "She's so damn stupid! Why didn't she tell me?" Despite everything Angie's done to them over the years, she's devastated. She doesn't care about the past. Not in this moment. And the thought of losing her sister brings back the pain of losing her parents all over again. She's worried she'll be overwhelmed with grief when organizing the funeral. Packing up Angie's pitiful belongings... She can't face it.

Nate embraces her as she sobs. "I'm so sorry. You know what she's like. She probably wouldn't have accepted our help even if we offered it."

She doesn't know what to say, what to think. She can't deal with this right now. Every time her life feels like it's getting better, something cruelly ruins it for her when she least expects it. When she finally stops crying, she stands. "I need to see her."

Nate stands too. "Sure. I'll tell Owen we're heading out."

"He can't come," she snaps, before feeling guilty. "Sorry. It's just... I don't like the thought of Angie having access to him. Even now." It's a reflex. She's tried to protect Owen from her sister ever since Angie was arrested. But if she's frail and unable to stand for long, how much harm could she do? "Is that wrong of me?" she asks. "I mean, it's not like she can hurt him now, is it?"

He rubs her arm. "It's not wrong. You're just being a mom. Let me go speak to him. I'm sure he'll understand."

She nods, grateful that she has Nate to help her through this.

Madison's only visited Angie a couple of times since her sister's release from prison, and not in the last year or so. It just seemed easier to avoid her. But now, as she knocks on the door of the trailer, she wishes she'd come more often. She wishes they'd had a chance to get to know each other properly now that Angie's husband isn't around to pit them against each other.

"Who is it?" yells Angie from inside, before coughing her guts up.

"It's me," Madison says to the door. It's after eight. The trailer sits in the shadows of the mountains, the sun lowering behind them. When she's met with silence, she starts thinking Angie doesn't want her here.

"Your boyfriend's got the spare key."

Nate unlocks the door, letting Madison enter ahead of him. The first thing that hits her is the heat, mixed with the smell of decay. Whether that's coming from the state of the trailer or Angie, she's unsure. Nate tried to prepare her for how withered her sister is, but when Madison spots her lying under a thin blanket on the couch, she thinks it's a different person. She almost gasps.

Angie laughs at her reaction. "I look that good, huh?" She sighs, adding, "I hope you brought food. My stomach hurts I'm so hungry."

On their way over, they loaded up on healthy food, strong painkillers and drinks they can leave in the cooler bag they brought with them. It should mean Angie doesn't need to get up too much.

Madison crouches in front of her sister and hands her a

chicken salad and coffee. "Is this okay? We have a variety of stuff in here." She puts a bag of non-perishable food items next to her and passes Angie a fork.

"It's fine," says Angie. "I probably won't manage more than a few mouthfuls anyway." She looks at Madison with eyes that have sunk into her face. She looks ten years older than she should. "If you come back again, bring milkshakes. They're easier to keep down."

Madison swallows back a sob. She gets up and sits on the only other chair in the room while Nate stands. When she's composed herself, she asks, "Why didn't you tell me? We could've helped you before it got this bad."

Angie puts the salad aside. "Maybe I don't feel like I deserve help."

Maybe she doesn't, but it's the saddest thing Madison could hear right now. She bursts into tears, unable to hold them back any longer. Everything about her relationship with her sister is messed up, and has been since they were teenagers. And now she has to come to terms with knowing that will never change. They'll never be able to resolve their differences or start over. She feels like she's already mourning the sister she wishes she had, which makes her feel guilty for the woman in front of her.

"Jeez," says Angie. "Anyone would think *you* were dying, the way you're carrying on." Her attempt at a joke shows she's unable to lower her defenses, even now.

Before Madison can think about it, the words are out of her mouth. "You're moving in with us. We'll take care of you." She looks up at Nate, who, to his credit, nods without flinching.

Angie frowns, distrusting of the offer. "Nah, that's okay. I'll be fine here."

"Absolutely not," Madison replies. "I'll need to check with Owen first, but we have a spare room. I can hire a nurse to help care for you." Maybe Owen can stay with a friend if he doesn't want to be in the house with Angie. She knows he'll understand.

"No," says Angie, resolute. "I'm staying here. But you can keep bringing me food and drugs. Or maybe leave me with your service weapon." She snorts.

The thought that Angie would rather die alone in this hovel rather than accept her help infuriates Madison. "For once in your damn life let your guard down, Angie." She stands. "Give me a day or two to get everything sorted. In the meantime, we'll be back tomorrow." She takes a deep breath. "Call me if you need anything. If I can't answer because of work, call Nate."

A smile hovers on Angie's lips. She looks past Madison to Nate. "She always this bossy?"

Nate smiles. "You'll do what she says if you know what's good for you."

Angie lowers her eyes. "Fine. I guess you better give me your number then, Monroe."

Madison realizes her hands are trembling at the thought of inviting her sister to live with them. Maybe it's a terrible mistake, and maybe Angie is playing them for fools, but she has to do something. It's the only way she'll be able to live with her conscience once her sister's gone.

CHAPTER TWENTY-FIVE

The next morning, Nate pulls up outside the house of Justin Asher, Sharon Smith's ex-boyfriend. He's arranged to meet Justin to find out what he thinks happened to Sharon thirty years ago, and to try to judge whether he played any part in it. It's not like Nate's expecting him to confess to anything, but he was pleasantly surprised when the guy agreed to meet with him. Maybe he wants to know what happened to her too. Or perhaps he wants to be seen as the concerned ex-boyfriend in order to hide his involvement.

Nate rubs his temples as the morning sunshine warms his face. His head is throbbing thanks to staying up late with Madison as they tried to figure out a plan to help Angie move in. Madison tried to source a suitable bed and a caregiver, but had no luck as it was getting late, so it's on the back burner for now, just like their wedding. Surprisingly, Owen didn't balk at the idea of his aunt moving in. Like his mother, he's chosen to show compassion during Angie's final weeks, although he *is* planning to keep out of her way, which is probably for the best.

A tap on the window takes Nate by surprise, making Brody bark behind him. He looks up to find a bald man in his mid-fifties standing there, peering down at him with his morning coffee in one hand. Opening the window, Nate says, "Justin?"

"Yeah," he replies. "Can we talk out here? My wife's inside and I don't want to upset her. She hates talking about the past and I could do without the trouble it'll cause me."

Nate nods. "Sure, get in." He leaves the A/C running as the car is sitting in the direct glare of the sun.

A big guy, Justin squeezes into the passenger seat and stiffens as Brody leans in from behind to sniff him.

Sensing his fear, Nate tries to reassure him. "He's friendly."

"That's what they all say." Justin raises his arm to show a pink scar that weaves between his faded forearm tattoos. "A small dog attacked me when I was a teenager. I've hated all dogs ever since."

Nate turns to look at Brody. "Lie down, boy."

Brody does as he's told and stretches out on the backseat.

Justin tries to keep an eye on him in the rearview mirror as he says, "So tell me, man, why are you digging up the past after all these years? I mean, I know Pam's hired you, because Gail told me. She called me after you went to see her. But I'm wondering why now. Is there a new lead or something?"

Nate shakes his head. "No. If there were a new lead, the police would reopen the case. I think Pam's just at a point in her life where she feels as though if she doesn't give it one last shot, she may regret it." He eyes Justin, who's stroking his bushy beard with his spare hand. "I'm sure you have plenty of unanswered questions too. What do you think happened to Sharon?"

"Oh man, who knows, right? Her mom thinks she's in California and Pam thinks she was either abducted, murdered or both, probably by me." He chuckles, as if the thought amuses him.

Irritated, Nate asks, "Why would she think that? Was your relationship volatile? Had you threatened Sharon?"

Justin scoffs. "We weren't even together when she disappeared. Why would I threaten her?" He casually sips his coffee.

During their first meeting in the diner, Pam told Nate what Sharon had disclosed to her about the relationship she'd had with Justin. He'd often scared her, apparently, but never physically harmed her. Sharon had described how he'd beaten her down mentally, making her feel worthless. He'd say things that, to an outsider, wouldn't seem threatening, but Sharon was sensitive to their real meaning because she knew she was living with a dangerous person. Nate recognized the signs of domestic abuse in her description of the relationship, but it sounds as though Justin was clever about it, as many abusers are. He made sure his punches weren't physical, so that the signs went unseen by other people, including close family members.

Because of that, Nate has contempt for the man sitting next to him, even if it turns out he isn't the reason Sharon vanished. "You weren't upset that your ex had gotten pregnant by someone else?" he asks. "Or that she was attracted to women instead of you?"

Justin averts his gaze, looking out the windshield as his smile fades. "I was pissed she'd lied to me for over a year. I could've met someone better. Instead I wasted all that time with *her*." His tone suggests he's still mad about it, which is odd considering he's now married to someone else.

"When did you last see Sharon?"

Justin tries to be flippant. "I don't know. I can't remember, it was so long ago. It'll all be in my police statement. All I know is that the last time I saw her she had a huge baby bump, and she was with Pam. They were laughing like they didn't have a care in the world."

Sharon was eight months pregnant when she vanished, so if Justin saw her with a huge bump, it can't have been long before then. "Why does it bother you that they were carefree?" asks Nate. "Didn't Sharon deserve happiness?"

Justin meets his eyes. "Don't twist my meaning. I just meant that if I was in her position—an unmarried, heavily pregnant *lesbian*—I wouldn't be flaunting it, especially back then. I'd act a little more dignified and not rub people's noses in it. If you ask me, you should be looking for someone who hates gay people. Maybe they got sick of watching her and Pam together. Maybe they thought the pair of them needed to learn a lesson." His jaw clenches. It feels like *he's* the person who wanted to teach them a lesson. It's clear that he's homophobic, and wants Nate to know it, but he isn't dumb enough to come right out and say it, even though admitting it would clearly bring him some satisfaction.

Sensing the tension in the air, Brody sits up behind them.

Needing answers for Pam, Nate has to keep the guy talking, so the last thing he wants to do is call him out on his homophobia and risk losing his cooperation. "It's a possibility I hadn't thought of yet, to tell you the truth." He writes something down. "Do you know who got her pregnant? Because it could be that the father of the baby harmed her to avoid having to pay child support." During their first discussion of the case, Pam had told Nate that she never knew the identity of the baby's father.

Justin closely watches a teenaged girl in denim shorts and a T-shirt walk by, following her with his eyes until she's out of sight. "It wouldn't have been anyone who knew me, I can tell you that much."

"Why not?" asks Nate.

"They wouldn't dare." Justin turns to look at him. His expression challenges Nate to question whether he could trust his friends not to sleep with his ex-girlfriend.

Nate moves on. "What was your reaction when you learned the cops were looking for Sharon? Did you have any hunches back then? Any names spring to mind? Because every town has its share of weirdos, right? People who act strange around women and kids."

Justin's shoulders relax. "Especially *this* town." He runs a hand over his beard. "I don't know. No one springs to mind. As for my reaction, well, her parents didn't appear concerned. They were surprised the cops were even investigating it, which made me believe Gail's theory that Sharon probably skipped town. You have to understand something," he goes on. "Sharon was flaky, so you never knew what she'd do. I mean, her history speaks for itself. One minute she's with me, then with a woman, then she's pregnant with some unknown guy's kid. I told the investigating detective the same thing, that she was unpredictable, but he didn't want to know. He seemed to think I was involved somehow, which is ridiculous, especially as I had an alibi."

"You did?" Nate acts dumb, wanting to hear if Justin's version has changed in the thirty years since he told it to the police.

"Sure. I was home with Kelly, my now-wife. We'd only been together a few months back then, so the relationship was still fresh." He grins. "We were at it like rabbits and barely left the house that first year together. She was way more interesting in the bedroom than Sharon was, if you catch my drift."

Nate tries to keep his expression neutral.

"On the day Sharon was last seen," continues Justin, "me and Kelly were busy making babies."

"Can anyone other than your wife confirm that?"

"As I told Bill Harper back then, my mother can. She called me on the landline several times over a twenty-four-hour period. The police have my call records, even though Bill tried to lose them more than once. Luckily, I made sure I kept a copy, as I knew he'd try to pin it all on me."

It's interesting to Nate that Madison's father zoned in on Justin early on. But policing was different thirty years ago in many ways. In others, not so much. The partners of missing people, and even the ex-partners, make good suspects, which means that if they can't be ruled out entirely, the investigation will always lead back to them until some new evidence turns up. In this case, nothing did, so Nate's probably doing exactly what Bill Harper did in 1992: he's going down the logical route.

There's no denying the arrogant guy beside him could have been involved in Sharon's disappearance, but if he was, Bill probably would have arrested him back then. Pam told Nate that no one was ever arrested in this case, which suggests he probably needs to look elsewhere.

CHAPTER TWENTY-SIX
MAY 1991

Sharon has butterflies in her stomach. She's waiting outside the mall, having arranged to meet Hank's sister, Pam. This is the first time they'll be alone together, having only spent time as a threesome since they met in the bar last month. She suddenly realizes her hands are clammy, making her feel like a teenager meeting her first crush, not a twenty-two-year-old woman meeting a new friend.

Several men stare at her as they pass, one even glancing back over his shoulder. She cringes. Her naturally blonde hair has always attracted the wrong attention, even when she was still just a child. Ever since she left Justin, she's been tempted to cut it all off to avoid being an object of desire for men, but she's worried Pam would hate it or think she's weird. She probably shouldn't worry what anyone else thinks, but Pam is different. Pam has a way of making Sharon feel like she's more than just an idiot.

"Are you always on time? Because that might be a problem."

Sharon jumps. She hadn't noticed Hank's sister approaching. She smiles. "Hey. Yeah, I'm always early for everything. Sorry. My mom says it's because I'm neurotic."

"Why are you apologizing?" says her friend lightly. "I was just messing with you. I'm late for everything, so you may end up hating me."

Sharon lowers her eyes. "I can't imagine ever hating you."

An awkward silence falls over them until Pam takes her hand and leads her into the mall. "I need new jeans, so you'll have to sit and watch as I try on a million different pairs." She lets go as they enter the mall through the heavy double doors. "Hank will probably turn up later. I told him I was meeting you here and he said he felt left out."

Sharon doesn't mind Hank tagging along, but she'd like at least some alone time with Pam. As they go from store to store, they discuss him, and how he's as protective of Pam as he is of Sharon, which makes her wish her own brother were as protective. Michael enlisted in the army as soon as he was able to. Although they were close when younger, he couldn't stand to be around their parents once he hit puberty. He only barely tolerated her too. She wonders if it was because he somehow knew she was attracted to women. It's either that or he thought she was as narrow-minded and unlikable as their parents.

Pam stops outside a women's clothing store. "Let's try this one."

Sharon follows her inside. The sales assistant ignores them, continuing to read her magazine while chewing gum. As Pam selects several pairs of jeans, Sharon touches clothes she wishes she could afford to waste money on.

"You should try something on," says her friend. "In fact, you'd look great in this." She hands over a little black dress that looks suitable for a nightclub.

Sharon scoffs. "I probably couldn't even get it over my hips."

"Are you kidding? You've got a great figure. Come on, you're trying it on." Pam leads her into the empty fitting room. With no attendant on hand, they go straight into a cubicle and pull the curtain closed.

Sharon feels her face flush with self-consciousness. She hasn't changed in front of another woman since high school. She worries that if Pam knew she likes women, she might be disgusted with her. She might think she's getting off on this situation. Panicked, she clutches the dress to her chest. "I'll go in the other cubicle. This one's too small for both of us."

Pam's already stripped her jeans off, revealing slim, toned legs and black underwear. "Why? You can't be shy when you look like that, surely?"

Not knowing what to do, Sharon relents. She hangs the dress on the wall and turns her back on her friend, but she can see Pam in the mirrors around her. When the bottom of Pam's T-shirt gets in the way of buttoning the jeans, she strips that off too, revealing a matching bra and full round breasts. Sharon blushes even harder. She knows she'll relive this moment a thousand times over when she's alone in the dark.

She pulls her own T-shirt off, wishing she'd worn nicer underwear. She slips out of her shorts and quickly steps into the tight black dress, pulling it over her shoulders. It hugs her in all the right places, but she can't reach the zipper at the back.

Pam steps out of the jeans and looks at Sharon. "Wow. That's stunning. You have to buy it."

Sharon watches her in the mirror. "I can't afford new clothes. Not right now. I only recently left my boyfriend, so things are tight. I shouldn't even have tried it on." She makes to slip out of the dress, but Pam steps forward and zips it up, resting her hands on Sharon's shoulders. They make eye contact in the mirror.

"I'll buy it for you."

"No. I couldn't let you do that," Sharon says. "I don't even have anywhere to wear it, so it would be a waste of money."

Pam's hands slide down to her waist. "You can wear it for me. After all, it would be wasted on a guy, right?"

Sharon's breath catches. Hank must have told his sister that she's not interested in men. But if that's the case, why isn't she worried about sharing a changing room with her? "I'm sorry," she says. "I should've told you before we came in here. I tried to leave so you wouldn't think I was looking at you."

Pam gently turns her around to face her, her touch sending shivers down Sharon's spine. They're impossibly close now. She can smell her friend's floral body spray. "But I want you to look at me," says Pam, right before she leans in and kisses her.

Sharon's too stunned to enjoy it. She pulls away. "You like women too?"

"Shh!" laughs Pam. "Don't tell the whole store." She leans in for another kiss, before adding, "All I know is that I like *you*. Beyond that, who cares?"

Having never touched another woman before, besides hugging friends, Sharon's body flutters with a mixture of nerves and lust. She follows Pam's lead when it comes to touching each other, to how long they kiss for.

"Do you need any help?" says a sales assistant. "Other sizes or colors to try?"

They freeze, worried she'll pull back the curtain.

"No thanks," yells Pam. "We'll be out in a minute!"

When the woman leaves, they try not to laugh, quickly getting changed back into their own clothes. Sharon's heart is racing. She's never had such a sensual experience before. Is this what life is supposed to be like—not full of conflict and rejection but actually filled with joy and new experiences? She hopes so, because she's had enough of toeing the line and being a scapegoat for other people's repressed anger issues.

After Pam pays for a pair of jeans and the black dress, they leave the store giggling and flushed. Seconds later, they bump into Hank, who approaches them with a smile. He sees Pam quickly drop Sharon's hand, and looks at his sister with a puzzled expression. He notices the flush of happiness on Sharon's face and quickly puts two and two together.

Sharon braces herself for his reaction. He may be cool with *her* liking women, but that doesn't mean he'll accept it for his sister.

"Are you two..." He doesn't finish his sentence.

Pam discreetly touches Sharon's hand so no one but the three of them can see it. "Yes. As of two minutes ago. Why? You have a problem with that?"

They wait with bated breath for his response. Eventually, he smiles. "No problem at all. Although everyone else will, so don't make it too obvious. If an idiot like me can figure it out just by looking at you, others will too." His worried expression suggests he thinks they're in for a tough time.

Sharon's just relieved he doesn't mind. It means she can finally live authentically for the first time in her life. As long as no one else finds out.

CHAPTER TWENTY-SEVEN
PRESENT DAY

Madison wolfs down a couple of cookies and tries not to think about her sister's condition as she waits for the rest of the team to join her in the briefing room. She's hoping that between them they've made some progress on at least one of their three current cases: the Ridgeway murders, the wedding shooter and the missing father and son.

When she's finished eating, she checks her phone and sees a link Sergeant Adams has sent her to a video on a news site. It seems that Denise Ridgeway's grandmother, Ida Randall, was interviewed by reporters yesterday, and it's clear she had only one intention in mind: to bad-mouth Ryan Simmonds.

"I read online that several of his ex-girlfriends have admitted he liked to strangle them in bed during some kind of perverted sex game," says Ida, her heavily wrinkled face grimacing in distaste. "He used so much force he almost killed one of them. Yet when his partner and daughter die from strangulation, the dumb cops still don't think he makes a good suspect!"

"Dumb cops?" Madison shakes her head, irritated.

"One ex-girlfriend told me he was secretly gay," Ida continues, "and *that's* why he hated women so much. And one of his neighbors thinks he was the one who got Denise hooked on drugs, so that he could control her easier."

Madison lowers her phone. Ida is laser-focused on Ryan as the killer, and her interview will only stir up trouble. But it's the first time Madison's heard anyone say that Ryan partook in erotic asphyxiation. She needs to look into whether there's any truth to that.

Chief Mendes enters the room carrying a tray of freshly made coffees. She joins Madison as Steve, Adams and Alex enter behind her, helping themselves to drinks. Officers Shelley Vickers and Luis Sanchez arrive last. Shelley stands close to Steve as Sanchez drops a takeout soda cup in the trash before closing the door. Madison watches as Shelley and Steve share a smile. A thirty-four-year-old brunette who's been with the department for years, Shelley broke up with her boyfriend five or six months ago. She and Jake Rubio, a local EMT with a complicated past, had been together for a while, but Madison never thought they were that suited. Now she's wondering whether there's some chemistry between her and Steve. The age gap is eleven or twelve years, but she thinks they'd actually make a great couple, and she'd love to see Steve settle down with someone who'll treat him well, unlike his deranged ex, who no one's been able to track down since she fled town in the middle of the night almost eighteen months ago.

"Are we expecting Conrad?" asks Mendes.

"No," says Madison. "He's busy at the morgue. But I have his autopsy reports if we need them."

The chief turns to face the others and gets straight to business. "Thanks for coming. Let's start with the wedding shooter. I've seen the note he sent you, Madison, which suggests you or Nate were the intended target." She looks at Steve. "Where are you at with the case?"

Steve perches on the table behind him and undoes his top

button. The heat is becoming oppressive, as the A/C isn't working and this room gets the full glare of the sun. "Shelley and Sanchez have located the area the shooter fired from," he says, "and Alex managed to get a couple of partial shoe prints, right?"

"Yes," says Alex. "They may prove useful once we have a suspect, or they could belong to hikers for all we know."

"Have we found anything else we can use to identify the shooter?" asks Mendes.

"Nothing, I'm afraid," says Alex. "We're not even close yet."

Madison looks at Steve. "Did you go through the list of guests and employees who attended the wedding?" She believes it's worth checking whether the shooter had an accomplice at the venue, perhaps feeding them information about her and Nate's exact whereabouts at any given time.

"I'm still working my way through them," he says. "With fifty-six people present, it's slow going. To tell you the truth, I don't really know what I'm looking for. If one of them was in contact with the shooter, it's not going to be obvious."

"You never know what might spark a lead," says Madison. "It's worth finishing, just so we've exhausted all avenues."

He nods. "Sure."

"We've been collecting dashcam footage and CCTV," says Shelley, glancing at Sanchez. "But we haven't found anything useful."

"And canvassing the area hasn't helped," adds Sanchez. "No one's reported seeing someone flee the vicinity that day."

The room falls silent until Steve speaks up. "I haven't questioned your sister yet, Madison. I'll head there after this if you're okay with that."

Madison thinks about how frail Angie is. How she has no strength to keep fighting for her life, never mind to keep fighting *her*. "There's no need. Angie's not involved."

"How can you be so sure?" he asks.

She suddenly feels everyone's eyes on her. Her co-workers are fully aware of her history with her sister, and how damaging it's been to all involved. "Angie's sick. She's dying of cancer. She doesn't have the strength to organize my murder."

A shocked hush falls over them.

Shelley's the first to speak. "I'm so sorry, Madison. I know you have your differences, to put it mildly, but that still sucks. I'm here if you want to talk about it."

Madison forces a smile. "It's fine. She'll be coming to stay with me as soon as I can organize it. But at least we can rule her out." She catches Steve's eye. He looks horrified at the thought of Angie living with her, but to his credit, he remains silent.

To move things along, Chief Mendes changes the subject. "Denise and Lucy Ridgeway. Where are we at with that case?"

Madison takes a deep breath. "I think we can rule out a random intruder, as we have zero evidence to back that up. The way Lucy was covered with a blanket and had a pillow placed under her head suggests they were killed by someone who knew them."

"Agreed," says the chief. "Do you have any suspects other than Ryan Simmonds? Denise's drug dealer, perhaps?"

"I couldn't find her dealer. But there's nothing to suggest she was using in the months before her death, so I'm not seriously considering that theory right now, although that could change depending on what her toxicology results show."

"Did her phone yield anything useful?" asks Mendes.

They all look at Alex. "No," he says. "It was relatively new, and she favored phone calls over messages. I didn't find anything to suggest she had tension with anyone, but that doesn't mean they weren't arguing during calls. She was clearly close with her parents, as her mother's cell phone and landline called Denise more than anyone else, followed by her boyfriend's."

"Her phone was found in her bedroom," says Steve. "And

she appeared to be doing laundry at the time of her murder, suggesting she didn't carry it around the house with her."

"She probably hated being available twenty-four-seven, like me," says Sergeant Adams. "I wish we could go back to the old days, when smartphones didn't exist."

Shelley and Sanchez share a look of amusement. They're young, from a generation who doesn't know life without smartphones and internet access, but Madison gets where Adams is coming from. She refuses to use social media, not just because it doesn't appeal to her and she doesn't have time for it, but also because in her job she sees the harm it can cause. How many predators use it to ruin people's lives. People the criminals wouldn't otherwise have access to.

"Do Ryan Simmonds or his neighbors have door cams or dashcams?" she asks.

"Surprisingly few of them," says Sanchez. "And of those who do, nothing covers Ryan and Denise's house. The killer could easily move in and out without fear of being caught. Perhaps they knew that."

She takes a deep breath. "Ryan suggested to me that Dominic Larson could've staged his and Charlie's disappearance with the intention of secretly returning to kill Denise, maybe because he was worried she would one day want custody of her son."

"We haven't found anything to back that up yet," says Steve.

Mendes doesn't look convinced. "With all the coverage his case got, someone would've spotted him around town. I doubt he could've gone unnoticed." She checks her cell phone for the time. "But until we disprove it, I guess it's a possibility. Anything else?"

Madison's about to speak when Stella from dispatch bursts into the room. "Sorry to interrupt," she says, "but I've just taken a call from Colt Ridgeway."

"Denise's dad?" says Madison. "What does he want?"

"He just found his mother-in-law dead in her bed."

Madison's surprised, but Ida must have been in her late eighties. Maybe the stress of losing Denise and Lucy caused a heart attack or stroke. "Why did he call us? Does he want an ambulance?"

"No," says Stella. "He wants you and Steve to go to the house. He says Ida was bludgeoned to death."

Madison's mouth drops open. "*What?*"

Steve meets her gaze. "Is it possible that Colt finally got sick of living with his mother-in-law?"

"Maybe," she says. "There was definitely some tension between them. But would he really be that stupid when he makes a good suspect for her murder?" She tries to think. "Ida gave a damaging interview about Ryan Simmonds to the press yesterday. I'd be pissed at her if I were him."

Steve nods. "As of right now, Ryan makes the best suspect for the murder of all three females: Denise, Lucy and now Ida."

Madison agrees. It's time to focus on Ryan. She turns to the chief. "Can you get us a search warrant for his house, vehicle and digital items?"

Mendes nods, immediately getting on her phone as Madison and Steve race to the crime scene.

CHAPTER TWENTY-EIGHT

While Chief Mendes secures a warrant for Ryan's property, Madison arrives at Colt and Bernie Ridgeway's home. With the day continuing to heat up as it approaches noon, the bulletproof vest she's forced to wear is making her sweat. By the time Alex and Steve join her on the Ridgeways' porch, she's about to tear it off in frustration, but Colt answers the door before she can, his face ashen with shock. He silently steps aside so they can enter.

Once inside, Jake Rubio, Shelley's ex-boyfriend, passes them, heading back to his ambulance. "I'll call the ME's office and advise them they're needed," he says.

Madison nods. "Thanks." Once he's gone, she notices that the formerly spotless living room is a complete mess. Someone has smashed everything up. It looks like the couple has been burglarized. She turns to Colt. "Did the killer do this?"

An animalistic scream answers for him. Bernie enters the room, howling as she throws a glass vase against the wall. They all watch in horror, averting their faces at the last minute as it smashes into pieces, the beautiful flowers it contained landing in disarray on the carpet. "I'll kill him for this!" she yells, distraught. Her face is soaked with tears, her eyes wild.

Madison goes to her and takes her arm, trying to lead her to the couch. "Take a deep breath, Mrs. Ridgeway. You're going to be alright, but you need to sit down for a sec—"

"I'm not going to be *alright*!" Bernie screams in her face. "My mother was bludgeoned to death! I'm never going to see her again!" She shakes herself free, her face almost purple with anger.

Her husband steps forward and leads her out of the room to the stairway, soothing her as he goes.

Madison overhears Bernie as she says, "I swear to God, Colt. As soon as they're gone, I'm going to march right over there and stab him in the—"

Colt doesn't let her finish. He hushes her and suggests she keeps her voice down in case the officers think she's being serious.

Alex and Steve exchange a look, shocked by Bernie's extreme reaction. "She must've been really close to her mother," says Alex.

With a deep breath, Steve says, "She clearly blames Ryan for Ida's murder."

Madison has a bad feeling about how fast tensions are rising. "We need to protect him in case she makes good on her promise."

"Once we have a warrant," says Steve, "we can search his property, seize his phone and computers and find out where he was when Ida was killed."

She nods. They don't have enough evidence to arrest him for anything yet, but if he doesn't have a good alibi for this morning, it should be enough to move forward.

Officer Kent, who was first on the scene, appears from the hallway. Their least-experienced officer, she looks like she might vomit. "The victim is back here," she says. "You'll need protective gear."

Alex hands them gloves and shoe covers, which they slip on before Madison enters a bright room at the rear of the house. Sunlight streams through the large window, illuminating the crime scene. It's the kind of space most people would enjoy as a sunroom, filling it with houseplants and a couch so they can enjoy the sun on their face while sipping coffee and watching the birds dart around the backyard, but it's been used as a bedroom for the infirm Ida, with just a bed, a nightstand, a large oak vanity and an armchair.

Madison's eyes drift to the body on the bed. Shocked at the state of Ida Randall, she's speechless for a second. She inhales. "I wouldn't have recognized her if I didn't know who she was." Ida has been brutally beaten, her features non-existent now. Her thin gray hair is matted with blood, and the blood spray from her injuries covers the wall behind the bed, even reaching the ceiling. The killer must have struck her over and over again. The scene turns Madison's stomach, and she has a second where she thinks *she* might vomit.

She takes a slow, deep breath. "Whoever did this knew her," she says. "They must have, because it takes real rage to keep attacking someone this frail when one blow probably would've done the job." It makes her consider again whether Colt did this. Perhaps Ida pushed him too far and he snapped. Maybe she was trying to force him to take the law into his own hands with Ryan, and the only way to shut her up was to silence her for good.

"Agreed," says Alex, leaning in close to assess what clues, if any, the woman's injuries reveal. His professional interest in forensics means he doesn't experience the same level of disgust at the sight of mutilated bodies as the rest of them. He takes a more scientific approach. Eventually, he pulls out his camera and starts documenting the scene with numerous photographs.

"No sign of the murder weapon," says Steve, crouching to check under the bed and furniture.

"If this is the work of the same person who killed Denise and Lucy," says Madison, "we have a serial killer on our hands. But one who seems to be targeting only this family."

"But the murders have different MOs," says Steve. "Denise and Lucy were strangled. Ida's been bludgeoned to death."

Colt appears in the doorway. Madison notices he keeps his eyes averted from Ida's body. Is that because *he* did this to her and he can't bear to look at the damage he's caused? He doesn't step inside the room. "I've given Bernie some sleeping tablets and forced her to lie down," he says. "I'm going to send her to stay with our daughter in Denver. She needs to get out of here."

"Of course," says Madison.

"I'll stay behind to arrange the funerals." He sighs shakily, looking exhausted. "You know this was Ryan, right? There's not a single other person you could blame it on."

Madison can think of one. She exits the room, leading him to the kitchen so he doesn't have to look at his dead mother-in-law as she questions him. Motioning for him to sit at the breakfast table, she settles opposite him. "Tell me what happened."

It takes a minute for him to find the words. "She was home alone," he says. "Me and Bernie went for breakfast at the diner, followed by grocery shopping. We were away for three hours max."

Madison opens her pocket notebook to take notes. She can check with Vince that the couple ate at the diner, then obtain security footage from the store. "What time was that?

"We left home at around eight thirty and returned about a half-hour ago, when I called you guys." He runs a hand down his weather-beaten face, as though dazed. "Ryan must've been watching the house, waiting for a chance to corner Ida alone."

Madison studies his expression for clues that he's lying. "I want you to know that we're taking your concerns about Ryan

Simmonds seriously. Once we leave here, I'll be questioning him on his whereabouts this morning." She doesn't go as far as to say she's requested a search warrant, as she suspects Colt would leak it to the press in order to ensure even more attention is focused on Ryan. "But I also need to consider other possibilities, such as a home invasion. So tell me, is anything missing? Was anything out of place when you arrived home?" Although the murder appears to be personal, she has to rule out all other options. "You mentioned previously that someone broke into your outbuilding not that long ago. I'm wondering if they came back and unexpectedly found Ida here, because once she'd seen them, they would've considered her a liability."

He frowns. "I don't think so. I didn't notice anything missing, but I haven't really had a chance to check thoroughly. Bernie went straight to Ida's room when we got home, to let her know we were back. That's when she found her and all hell broke loose."

Madison's heart sinks. No one should have to find their mother bludgeoned to death, especially having just lost their daughter and granddaughter. This level of trauma will be difficult to recover from. "Have you seen anyone snooping around the house?"

He shakes his head. "This wasn't a random intruder, Detective. This was *Ryan*. How many times do I have to say it?" He glares at her. "Ida said a bunch of stupid things to some reporter yesterday. He must've seen it and got mad. I told her not to speak to the press. I *told* her he'd target her next, but she never listened to me. She always thought she knew best." Frustrated, he runs a hand through his hair. "I can't believe we're going to have to bury three people at once." His eyes fill with tears, making him pull a handkerchief from his pocket. He half coughs, half sobs into it.

Madison feels for him. If he's involved in Ida's death, he's doing a good job of faking his upset. "What if it turns out this wasn't Ryan? Who else would you have me look at?" Choosing her words carefully, she adds, "Because forgive me, but from my impressions of her, Ida wasn't exactly shy in being forthright. A woman like her must've made enemies in her time."

Colt lowers his eyes as he slowly nods. "She was an old crow. That's what my dad called her before he passed. He hated the woman. Told me that if I married Bernie, I'd end up living with the devil." He scoffs gently at the memory. "Just shows how much I love Bernie that I'd put up with her mother for so long."

Madison tilts her head. Is he admitting he's relieved she's gone? She considers whether, if his alibi checks out, he could've hired someone to kill Ida. "How long did she live with you guys?"

He meets her eyes. "Since the day after our wedding, thirty-five years ago. Her husband left her before I met Bernie, so she had no one else. She and Bernie were living here in their family home. After I moved in, I always felt like the odd one out. The third wheel."

Surprised at how long they've lived together, Madison inhales deeply. "That's a long time to spend with someone who rubbed you the wrong way."

He snorts. "Bernie always said I'll get a medal when I make it to the pearly gates." Averting his gaze, he adds, "But she wouldn't say that if she knew my real opinion of her mother all these years."

She feels like he's about to confess something, so she treads carefully. "It's not a crime to dislike your in-laws, Colt. Merging two families is difficult and rarely goes how anyone would want it to. From the sound of it, you've put up with a lot. I imagine it was exhausting to have Ida living here, watching everything you do and affecting your relationship with your wife."

His eyes remain fixed on the table. "I did it for Bernie."

She freezes. Does he mean he killed Ida for Bernie? Or just that he put up with her for Bernie?

He seems to realize what he's said and straightens in the chair. "But it wasn't all bad. The old crow had a good sense of humor if you knew how to make her laugh. Usually at other people's expense, but once she had a glass of bourbon in her hand, she'd relax a little. I don't have any regrets. Bernie enjoyed having her mom live with us and that's all that matters." He suddenly stands. "I need to call Toyah. Let her know to come and pick her mother up." He considers something. "*She* won't miss Ida, that's for sure."

Madison stands. "She won't?"

"No. Why do you think she lives in Denver and not here? Neither of the girls were keen on their grandmother. Denise used to hide from her when she was little, convinced she was a witch." He smiles faintly at the memory before tucking his chair back under the table. "You'll let me know what happens with Ryan?"

Madison cautiously nods. "We can't arrest him without proof, but I'll keep you updated." Before he goes, she adds, "Make sure you keep your windows and doors locked from now on. Take extra precautions, just in case."

Colt stares for a second before exiting the kitchen, leaving Madison worried about what will happen if they *don't* arrest Ryan.

CHAPTER TWENTY-NINE

Ryan Simmonds isn't at his house, but his neighbor helpfully discloses that he was planning to return to work this morning. Apparently feeling isolated at home, he said he was going crazy just waiting around for the police to find the killer of his girlfriend and daughter. Madison doesn't know how anyone can return to work so soon after losing their loved ones, but that's not for her to judge. She understands you do whatever it takes to get through your grief, whatever works to stop the intrusive thoughts and constant despair. Still, part of her wonders whether he was lying to his neighbor, lining up a potential alibi for the time of Ida Randall's murder. It could work for him, since his friend Neil would probably agree to cover for him.

She pulls up outside his place of work. On her way over here, Chief Mendes rang to confirm she's secured a search warrant for Ryan's home and cell phone, so Officers Vickers and Kent are on standby to enter his property. Madison's hoping he'll willingly let them in.

While she waits for Steve to join her, she checks her phone and finds a couple of unread texts from Nate.

> *I've got the paperwork for the wedding. We can self-officiate. I know it's probably the last thing on your mind with Angie being sick and how busy you are with work, but I don't think we should delay.*

Then:

> *So can I plan something?*

She leans her head back, glancing in the rearview mirror for Steve. No sign of him yet. If she's honest with herself, the wedding *is* the last thing on her mind right now. But on the other hand, if not now, when? If they get it over with, it's one less thing to stress about. She looks at her phone and replies.

> *Sure. I don't have the energy to do anything fancy, though. Just keep it simple.*

He replies immediately.

> *Understood. Leave it to me.*

She smiles, wondering what he's planning, then worries they might be targeted by the wedding shooter again. Her phone pings with another message.

> *Also, I've secured a suitable bed for when Angie moves in, and I have a list of possible nurses. We can narrow it down tonight when we go see her.*

Her smile fades. She can't imagine Angie agreeing to being nursed by a stranger, but she and Nate don't have the time or necessary skills to do it themselves. Suddenly feeling drained, she replies with a thumbs-up emoji just as Steve pulls up behind her.

As she exits her car, the sound of classic rock music reaches her from inside the workshop. Several vehicles in various states of disrepair are parked outside, the bright sunshine reflecting off metal, making her squint.

Steve joins her as they approach the entrance. "Can you tell if he's in there?"

She shakes her head. "Haven't seen him." Before they enter, she looks at him. "I thought I noticed some chemistry between you and Shelley at the station earlier. Anything going on there?"

He reddens as he smiles self-consciously. "You don't miss a beat, do you?"

She grins. "They don't call me detective for nothing. Are you two dating?"

He nods. "It's still new, so don't tell Adams." Everyone knows Adams can't keep a secret. He's like a high schooler when it comes to gossip. "I don't know how Shelley feels," he says, "but I'm enjoying spending time with her outside of work."

"Good," she says. "It's about time you had something else to do other than work, exercise and play with toy soldiers." She pauses. "Hang on, have you told her about that hobby of yours yet? Because if not, don't. You don't want to scare her off."

He snorts. "Too late, she knows. She asked me to explain the rules, but her eyes glazed over pretty fast once I got into the intricacies of wargaming. Luckily, we have a shared interest in drinking."

Madison laughs. "What cop doesn't, right?" She's joking, of course, although she is partial to a glass of wine after a long day. "Okay," she says with a sigh. "Let's see what Ryan's got to say for himself."

As they step inside the building, it takes a few seconds for her eyes to adjust to the change of light. When they do, she sees a tall, overweight guy leaning over a car engine. It smells strongly of grease and oil in here. "Neil Booth?" she says.

The guy looks up and frowns. "Yeah. Help you?"

"I'm Detective Harper and this is Detective Tanner from the LCPD. We're here to see Ryan."

Neil wipes his greasy hands on his coveralls. "You just missed him. He's gone for coffee. But he'll be back in a few minutes if you want to wait." He pulls out his phone. "Let me text him for you."

She holds her hand up to stop him, not wanting Ryan tipped off that they're here. "No, don't do that. We're fine waiting, thanks."

He slips his phone into his pocket, before turning the volume down on the radio. He looks uncomfortable at the thought of making small talk with a couple of cops.

"So Ryan's back at work already?" says Steve, casually rolling up his sleeves. The midday heat makes it as hot inside as it is outside.

Neil shrugs. "What else is there for him to do? Says he was going stir-crazy at home with nothing but grief, memories and dark thoughts to occupy his time."

Madison crosses her arms over her chest. *Dark thoughts.* That's not good.

"He doesn't have any visitors taking care of him?" asks Steve. "Family, friends?"

"I don't know, man. You'd have to ask him." Neil seems afraid of saying the wrong thing, but if Ryan has nothing to hide, his friend won't be able to say the wrong thing.

"Has he been here all morning?" asks Madison. It's just after 1 p.m. now, and they know Ida was killed sometime between 8:30 and 11:30 a.m.

Neil sighs. "I guess he arrived around—" Before he can finish his sentence, Ryan appears, carrying a cup holder with two coffees in one hand and a bag of food in the other. Grease marks stain the paper bag. Madison's stomach rumbles. They haven't had time for lunch yet.

"What's going on?" asks Ryan, handing Neil the food and drinks before looking at Madison.

"Do you have somewhere we can talk without being disturbed?" she says.

His eyes give away his trepidation that he's either about to be arrested or someone else has been. "Sure. In here." He leads them to a small, messy office with only two chairs and no window to the outside world. It overlooks the workshop instead. None of them sit down. "Have you arrested someone?" he asks.

"No," she says as Steve closes the door behind them. Neil can still see them through the glass panel, as it has no blinds. "Have you been here all morning?"

He nods. "Yeah. Since nine, I think. Why?"

"And presumably Neil can corroborate that? What about anyone else? Customers, perhaps?"

He frowns, getting agitated. "What's going on? Why do I feel like I need a lawyer?"

Madison takes a deep breath. "Denise's grandmother, Ida Randall, was brutally murdered in her bed this morning," she says, watching closely for his reaction. "You know Bernie's mom, right?"

His mouth drops open, lost for words. Until: "You're kidding, right?"

"I wish I were. We're here because we need to rule you out, what with the unfavorable interview she gave about you yesterday."

His face drains of color. He reaches for the seat behind the desk and slowly lowers himself onto it. "It wasn't me. That interview was all lies and nothing more than the ramblings of a bitter old woman, so while it pissed me off, I didn't take it too seriously." He rubs the back of his neck, stunned. "I can't believe she's dead. I thought that woman would live forever."

Madison remembers something he said to her at the station a couple of days ago. "You told me previously that Bernie and Ida hated you. Was the feeling mutual?"

He looks at her before choosing his words carefully. "I'm not gonna lie, I stayed as far away from Ida as possible. She had a sharp tongue and a mean disposition and clearly didn't like me being with her granddaughter. But no one would've been good enough for Denise or Toyah, so I tried not to take it personally. If you ask me, she and Bernie are partly responsible for Denise self-medicating with drugs."

"What do you mean?" she asks.

He shrugs. "It's obvious. Bernie's always been heavily involved in her daughters' lives, living vicariously through them, homeschooling them. Her and Ida wanted them to have as many kids as possible, to continue the family line. Some people are just like that, all about their kids to the detriment of their own lives."

Madison's reminded of the decorative plaques on Bernie's wall declaring the importance of family.

"Bernie wanted Denise and Lucy to live with them," he continues, "but Denise told me she'd feel suffocated there, even if I was allowed to join them. Her mom always put a lot of pressure on her, and when Denise couldn't live up to it, she felt like a failure." He sighs shakily. "Bernie must be devastated. She's lost her mother, a daughter and her grandchild, all in the same week."

Madison glances at Steve, who's watching Ryan closely. Her gut tells her that Ryan's reactions, to both Ida's murder and that of Denise and Lucy, are genuine, especially as he admits to disliking the older woman. But the fact is, he makes the perfect suspect. And sometimes the most obvious suspect *is* the culprit, no matter how clichéd it seems.

He looks up at her. "I feel like someone's framing me for all this. Someone wants to see me locked up."

"Okay, so who would do that?" asks Steve. "Have you upset someone? Because we considered whether Denise and Lucy weren't the intended targets at your house the day they were killed. So if you've pissed someone off and they went there looking for *you*, you need to tell us immediately so we can bring them in for questioning."

Ryan frantically tries to think, his eyes darting all over the place. "I don't know! Not that I know of." When they don't respond, he adds, "Seriously, if I've pissed anyone off, I don't know about it. And it seems pretty drastic to kill my girlfriend and child just because someone's pissed at me, doesn't it? And what about Ida? She's not related to me. It doesn't make any sense."

He's right, which is why *he* makes a more likely suspect for all three murders. Although Madison can't rule out how Colt also has a potential motive for wanting his mother-in-law dead: the fact that he spent decades living with the insufferable woman just to appease his wife.

"I can give you a list of customers who've dropped by this morning," Ryan says. "They'll confirm I was here. And Neil knows I only left once, to fetch lunch."

Madison nods. "That would be useful." She watches as he makes a list of names and hands it over to her. Five customers. He knows they'll call each one, which likely means he *was* here, and he didn't kill Ida. His alibi means they can't arrest him. But they can still search his property. "Our chief has obtained a search warrant for your home and belongings so we can try to rule you out for what happened to Denise and Lucy."

His mouth drops open. "Unbelievable." He slumps back in his chair, clearly annoyed. "Fine, whatever. You won't find anything."

Steve steps forward. "I need your phone."

Ryan shoots him a look of contempt. "How am I supposed to function without my phone?"

"I suggest you buy a new one," Steve says. "Because we can't guarantee we'll return it anytime soon, especially if we find something on it that could be used as evidence."

With a disapproving shake of his head, Ryan pulls his phone out of his pocket and hands it over. "Can I at least be present when you search my house?"

A camera flash goes off behind them, making Madison turn. Someone has noticed their arrival and tipped off the press. It will add fuel to the fire around speculation over Ryan's involvement in the murders.

Neil gets in the reporter's way and shoos him away from the property.

"You can let our officers in, then wait outside until they're done," says Madison. She feels sorry for Ryan given everything he's dealing with. They have to tread carefully, as they don't want to push him over the edge. "Sorry. I know it's inconvenient and just adding to your pain at this difficult time. But look at it this way: the sooner we rule you out, the sooner you can try to put all this behind you. It'll stop the public interest in you and the press might leave you alone."

"*Might?*" he says, dismayed.

"Let's wait and see. Do you have any family helping you through all this?"

He shakes his head. "My parents are long gone, and I don't have siblings or any extended family who keep in touch."

She can't imagine getting through the horrendous early days of grief without support. "If you need help dealing with all this pressure, don't forget there are support services available. I texted you a list after I left your house earlier this week. Don't be afraid to reach out. That's literally what they're there for."

"What, for helping suspected serial killers?" He scoffs. "I doubt it."

"No," she says. "For helping people cope with grief and depression. You could see your doctor too if you're having trouble sleeping or feeling anxious. You must reach out, Ryan. Don't suffer alone. You've experienced a terrible loss, and no one is expected to manage that all alone."

He doesn't respond, so she looks at Steve.

"Ready to go?" he says to Ryan. "You should probably let us leave first, then wait five minutes so it doesn't look to the press like we're escorting you."

Ryan reluctantly nods, resigned to his fate as public enemy number one.

CHAPTER THIRTY

After speaking with Sharon Smith's mother and ex-boyfriend, Nate's leads in the missing person case are quickly diminishing, so he's checking in with Pam to see what other information he can gather. As he pulls up outside her small, single-story home, he spots her on the porch waving off a visitor, an older guy in a pickup truck. When Pam notices him, her smile fades a little and she crosses her arms over her chest as if shielding herself from bad news. Understandably, she must be dreading what his investigation is going to uncover.

Having left Brody at home with Owen after visiting the courthouse for his and Madison's marriage documents, Nate enters her house alone. "I hope your guest didn't leave on my account," he says as Pam leads him into her kitchen.

"No, that was Hank, my brother. He checks on me every day, always has, even though he has more problems than I do. I don't know what I'll do when he goes." She takes a deep breath. "What can I get you to drink?"

"Coffee's fine, if you're having one."

She turns to the coffee machine and looks for some clean cups in the cabinet above.

"Did Hank know Sharon?" he asks.

"Of course," she says. "I met her through him, as a matter of fact. They worked together at a dive bar that's long since gone. He was actually the first person we told when we became a couple."

"And he was good with that?" Nate knows times were different back in the early nineties. Progress was being made, but not fast enough.

She turns to face him. "I was lucky with my family. My parents turned a blind eye, which was the best you could hope for back then, and Hank never had a problem with our relationship, even though I always suspected he would've liked Sharon for himself." She smiles at a memory. "He helped us to feel normal. And he was excited about becoming an uncle to our child." She pours their coffees but doesn't move to the living room, so they remain standing in the kitchen.

Nate leans against the breakfast bar, cupping his drink in his hands. "I noticed you and Sharon have the same last name, and I gather same-sex marriages weren't legal in the early nineties. So is that just a coincidence?"

"No," she says. "I changed my last name when she got pregnant. The way we saw it, we were in a committed relationship, and we would've married had we been allowed." She lowers her eyes. "Our child would have shared our last name too."

Seeing how much it pains her, Nate moves on. "I've spent a lot of time looking for information online," he says. "Including searching for babies born in and around Colorado around the same time Sharon's was due. Unfortunately, as I'm not in law enforcement, there's only so much information available to me, so that hasn't yielded any results. And as I wanted to rule out whether she could've left town of her own volition, I tried searching social media for possible profiles that could match her at the age she is now, but again, I've had no luck so far. Most people have finally learned their social media accounts should be private." In the early days, everything was available for anyone to look at, but now people are more aware of scammers. While that's a positive change that reduces their risk of being targeted by criminals, it means Nate's job is harder than ever. "With the sheer number of people online, there are just too many Sharon Smiths to narrow down a search, and we don't even know if she'd still be living under her given name."

Pam nods. "There was a time I would contact at least five women a month on social media who share Sharon's name, but Smith is probably the worst last name she could've had in that respect." She seems to hesitate, before asking, "Could your partner help us with that? I mean, surely Detective Harper would want to help uncover what happened, given it's her job to find missing people?"

Feeling awkward, Nate shifts his weight. "Unfortunately, Madison can't share information with me, again because I'm not in law enforcement. They have strict data protection and confidentiality rules. Besides, she's currently busy with several other live cases."

She nods, disappointed. "My family and I have never had much faith in law enforcement anyway. Not since Sharon vanished. I think private investigators work harder because they have a financial incentive."

It's not the first time someone's said that to him. He could remind her she's not paying for his services, but he doesn't. "Trust me, as someone who has an inside view of how hard the police work, I can tell you the majority do their absolute best in extremely difficult circumstances. No one wants a case to go cold."

She sips her drink without responding.

"I've managed to speak to both Gail Smith and Justin Asher," he says, changing the subject.

Pam scoffs. "So now you know what Sharon was up against. Two of the most hateful, ignorant individuals who ever walked the planet. What did they have to say, or is it so offensive you wouldn't want to upset me?"

Nate hesitates to tell her, but he has to. "Gail thinks her daughter ran off to Hollywood after giving birth and handing the baby to someone else to care for."

She rolls her eyes. "I've never met a mother who knew their child so little. She should be ashamed of herself."

"Where did she even get that idea from?" he asks.

"From her *ass*, Mr. Monroe. From her stupid, obnoxious ass." She shakes her head in frustration. "Sorry for being vulgar, but I've had it up to here with that woman." She takes a deep breath before looking at her drink. "I should've chosen decaf since I knew this conversation would be bad for my blood pressure."

"So Sharon never wanted to be an actress?" he says. "She didn't love being the center of attention?"

"Absolutely not. She was shy and quiet, constantly battling internal demons. Neither of us wanted attention from anyone but each other."

It's confusing to Nate that Gail would get it so wrong. Unless it was intentional. "Could her mother have said that because she knows what really happened to Sharon?"

"Absolutely!" says Pam, coming alive. "Sharon told me her mother and ex-boyfriend had a weird relationship. Gail acted inappropriately around Justin while he was with Sharon. She said it wouldn't surprise her if they were involved in some kind of sexual relationship." She shudders at the thought. "Gross."

If true, it's alarming, because it would give them both a motive to kill Sharon, and a reason to cover up her disappearance with outlandish theories. But Sharon eventually left Justin, leaving him free to go official with Gail if that was what he wanted. "Do you know if they got together after Sharon left him?"

She shrugs. "They didn't go public, so I don't know for sure because no one who knew them would tell me." She sighs. "What about Justin? What did he have to say for himself?"

"He said Sharon was promiscuous and flaky. He thinks Gail's theory could be correct, that she left to go to Hollywood."

Pam quickly turns and pours her coffee down the sink. "Don't tell me anything else, my heart can't take it."

Nate feels for her. He wishes he could find a new lead. He knows Madison's father would have exhausted all options when considering Justin Asher as a person of interest, so it's probably a waste of time to focus solely on him, and Gail too, or she would have been arrested thirty years ago. He can't shake the feeling that the answer to Sharon's disappearance lies in whoever got her pregnant. "I know you don't know who the baby's father was, but you said she was working at a bar when you met her, so presumably she interacted with a lot of male customers. Were there any particular men she was close with? Someone she may have confided in about her sexuality and who might have agreed to sleep with her so she could have a baby?"

Pam has her back to him, but he notices her shoulders tense. "Absolutely not. The only male she was ever close to was my brother. She didn't have any other male friends, and she despised the people she served in that place." She turns to face him. "The kind of men who frequented that bar would never agree to help her if they knew she was a lesbian. But they'd be more than happy to take from her. That's why she left to work elsewhere. She hated those people."

She seems pretty sure of herself, and he picks up an undercurrent of disgust in her voice. "Okay, so no one offered to do her a favor. Are you suggesting someone might have done the opposite? Forced themselves on her?"

Pam swallows back a sob as tears rise to her eyes. "I probably should've said something sooner, but I figured you'd get there by yourself. And I don't know any details, so it doesn't really make much difference..."

Nate's heart sinks. She's kept something from him. "With all due respect, let me be the judge of that."

Pam lowers her eyes, unable to say the words that pain her so much to admit. But it doesn't really matter, because Nate thinks he's figured it out for himself.

CHAPTER THIRTY-ONE
NOVEMBER 1991

Sharon crouches as she hurriedly stuffs a bunch of beautiful pink roses into a pot containing water, pricking her finger on one of the sharp thorns due to rushing. She wants to finish up and leave work before anyone else enters the flower store. Her boss has taken the day off yet again, and it's almost time to close. She hates it here and curses the day she ever agreed to the job, wrongly assuming it would be better than working at the bar. Working with a female boss and mainly female customers, it should have been perfect. But the boss is mean to her, regularly making her cry, and she's been getting some unwanted attention lately. She hasn't told Pam about that as she doesn't want her to worry. Their relationship is the only thing that keeps her going most days. But that could all be in jeopardy once she gets home later, because she needs to tell Pam about something awful that happened.

Her stomach lurches with dread at the thought of breaking the news. Their lives are about to drastically change, and she has no idea how her girlfriend will feel about it.

The bell above the door jangles, making Sharon jump. She spills the pot of roses all over the floor. The water drenches her sneakers. "Shoot!" She looks at who has entered and breathes a sigh of relief when she sees her girlfriend standing there with a bemused look.

"Did I scare you?"

Her hand goes to her fluttering heart as she stands. "No. Yes. I don't know. I was hoping it wasn't another customer." She attempts a smile. "Give me a minute to close up. I'll meet you at the car."

Pam and her brother Hank live at home with their parents despite being in their early twenties. Hank has a double room over the garage and Pam is still in her childhood bedroom. Their parents dote on them so there's no reason to move out. They both have the freedom to live their lives however they want to, and can bring friends home too. Their parents don't know Pam's dating Sharon, so she's allowed to sleep over whenever she wants, but Sharon suspects that regardless of how cool they appear, they would soon change their tune if they knew their daughter was sharing a bed with another woman because they're romantically involved.

Sharon's hoping that one day soon she can leave the crappy house she shares with strangers and she and Pam can move into their own apartment, living as partners instead of friends. Especially now.

On the journey home, she can barely sit still. Car headlights flood the darkness, blinding her as Pam drives. And despite the cold outside, her underarms are damp with sweat. Her breathing is shallow, and it doesn't take long for Pam to notice.

"What's up with you today?"

Sharon sits on her hands. "I don't know. I'm nervous." Before she realizes it's happening, she bursts into tears.

Alarmed, Pam swerves the vehicle into a drugstore parking lot and switches the engine off. She drapes an arm over Sharon's shoulders. "Honey, what's wrong? Why are you crying? Is it that damn boss of yours again? Because you can quit whenever you like. I can see if my mom will let you stay with us, so you don't have to worry about making your rent."

Sharon wipes her face with her hands. "No. You don't understand. I have to tell you something."

Pam takes her hands. "What is it? You can tell me anything." She must read the expression on Sharon's face—illuminated by a neon sign flashing in the dark—because she leans back with a gasp. "Oh my God. Are you breaking up with me? Have you met someone else? Is that it?"

Shaking her head, Sharon says, "No. Of course not. I *love* you!"

An awkward silence falls over them. That's the first time one of them has mentioned the L word. Pam's face flushes red, and just when Sharon thinks she isn't going to answer, she says, "I love you too. Have since the day we met. Is that why you're so nervous? You thought I didn't love you back?"

Her admission makes Sharon cry harder. She melts into Pam's embrace and lets the tears fall, conscious that passersby will be staring, wondering what's going on. When she eventually pulls back, she finds a couple of napkins from the glovebox and dries her eyes and nose. Her makeup is probably smeared all over her face, but she can't bring herself to care. Cold rain starts pelting the windshield.

"Feel better?" asks Pam, smiling at her with unmistakable concern in her eyes.

Sharon doesn't feel better, but she nods. Grabbing Pam's hands, she says, "What I'm about to say is going to hurt you, but you have to focus on what it means for us, not what happened to me. Okay?"

Pam's eyebrows knit together, puzzled. "What do you m—"

"Promise me," Sharon urges, squeezing her hands. "Just remember that I'm fine *now*, and that this could be the best thing that ever happens to us, depending on how you feel about it. But if it's not what you want, be honest with me. I'd rather know now than risk losing you over it."

Pam snorts. "You're not making any sense, and you're scaring me, honey. What happened to you?"

Sharon takes a deep breath, not knowing how to put her experience into words, only knowing she has to minimize it in order for Pam to see past it. "Several weeks ago, a man forced himself on me... and now I'm pregnant."

The color drains from Pam's face. She tries to swallow, but it causes her to cough. She attempts to pull her hands away in horror, but Sharon won't let go of them. "Focus on the pregnancy, *please*. I'm going to have a baby." She forces a bright smile. "We can raise it as ours. The father doesn't need to know it's his. He lost that right when he raped me."

A single tear runs down Pam's face. "Who was it?"

Sharon's heart sinks. "It doesn't matter. I'll never tell you or anyone else, so if you're about to advise me to go to the police, you can stop right there. I have no proof that it wasn't consensual. The police won't want to know. So I've chosen to concentrate on the positive instead. It's the only way I'll get through this." She forces her girlfriend to look at her. "Pam? We can have this baby together. We can be a family. If you really love me, you'll see that something good can come out of what happened."

Pam shakes her head. "But he *hurt* you!"

Sharon blinks back tears. "For all of five minutes," she says, playing down the degradation she felt during and after, and still feels now when she lets her guard down. "I can't think about that. I'm thinking about my child instead. *Our* child." She looks into her girlfriend's eyes, desperately willing her to visualize the life they could have together. "Don't you want to be a mother?"

Pam lowers her gaze. "Of course I do, but I didn't think it would be possible."

"Then view this as a gift from whoever is controlling our destinies. Let's move in together and raise our child in a house filled with love and acceptance."

Pam looks afraid. "We can't make the people outside our home accept us, Sharon. They'll talk about us. Laugh at us. Judge us for being bad parents because our child has no father."

Sharon knows this, but she also knows she can't change it. "We only get one life, Pam, and so far mine has been pretty damn awful, so I intend to make the next twenty years great. I refuse to live in fear any longer."

With doubt in her eyes, Pam says, "You're so much stronger than me."

Sharon smiles. "Then I'll protect both of us. And we have Hank too. He won't let anyone hurt us. He'll make a fantastic uncle." She moves Pam's hand to her belly, despite there being no bump yet. "So let's have this baby and live together as a family. What do you say?"

Pam finally smiles, but it doesn't reach her eyes, suggesting she wants to make Sharon happy but understandably has some doubts about it. "Well, I love you, so... I'm in."

Sharon is swamped with relief. She's aware this could have turned out very differently. She knows it won't be plain sailing, but nothing can be worse than living with a man who secretly despises her, or with parents who don't understand her. She plans to give this baby everything she never had.

With tears in her eyes, she leans forward and kisses her girlfriend, finally not caring who might see them.

CHAPTER THIRTY-TWO
PRESENT DAY

Madison works late to avoid having to think about her sister's imminent arrival at their home. Aware she's only delaying the inevitable, she has no choice as her chest is tight with anxiety and dread over what's to come. She doesn't want to watch her sister wither away in pain over the next few weeks or months. She considers whether that's because she resents Angie for putting her in this position. If only she'd told them about her condition sooner. They could have tried to get treatment, maybe slowed down the progression of the disease.

"Madison?" Adams's voice makes her jump.

She straightens in her chair. "Sorry, I didn't notice you there. I was miles away."

"Wouldn't that be nice?" he says with a scoff. Originally from Denver, Adams has always hated living in Lost Creek. For some reason he has a superiority complex and thinks he's better than the locals, although he's not as bad as he used to be when he first arrived in town. Madison thinks he's slowly becoming one of them, not that she'd ever say that to him.

"Have you got something for me?" She nods to the folder in his hands and notices Steve turn in his chair to listen in.

With a deep breath, Adams says, "Actually, no. The officers who searched Ryan's house found nothing of interest. Alex is checking his cell phone, but as he didn't find anything suspicious between him and Denise on *her* phone, it's unlikely he'll find anything interesting on Ryan's. Unless the guy was stupid enough to use it to hire someone to kill Denise and Lucy, of course, in which case, he's screwed."

She thinks that's unlikely. "Okay. Thanks."

"Also, I called the list of customers Ryan gave us. They all confirmed they dropped by the auto repair shop at various times this morning and saw him there, which means he didn't slip away to kill Ida Randall. The timeline of their visits didn't give him any opportunity to drive to her home and back again, certainly not without washing her blood off him first."

"Okay, thanks for checking."

"Sure." After glancing at his watch, he drops the folder on his desk and shuts down his computer. "I'm off. Don't stay too late, you two. People will talk." He winks at them as he leaves.

Steve turns back to face his desk, saying nothing of his new relationship with Shelley. He must not be seeing her tonight.

Madison watches Adams leave. She looks around. The chief's office is in darkness. Dina Blake is starting the night shift on dispatch. Stella left a half-hour ago. A few officers come and go as they either end or start their shifts. Daylight has faded outside the building's windows.

She glances at her bulletproof vest, resting on the desk beside her. It's been three days since the wedding shooter struck, and she hasn't caught anyone following her or paying her any special attention. Is he really waiting for her and Nate to try to marry again before he strikes? They would make easier targets during their normal day-to-day routines. But if the shooter *is* waiting for the wedding, it suggests his vendetta is personal, which means he must be known to one of them. The thought of another attack fills her with dread. She wishes she could look forward to the wedding, but it's ruined now, just like everything always gets ruined for them.

She focuses on her computer screen and tries to distract herself by examining the photos from the Ridgeway crime scene. Although the images are ingrained into her memory, it's not unheard of for a new detail to pop out at her when she least expects it. Despite her years in law enforcement, Madison will never get used to seeing people frozen in their last positions before they died, revealing just a snapshot of what happened to them. She flips to a photo of Lucy's room. It was filled with toys, just like any other child's bedroom.

Steve wheels himself over to her desk on his chair, so close she can smell his aftershave. He peers at her screen to see what she's looking at. Lucy Ridgeway's small body is positioned in a way that makes her look like she's been tucked in for the night. It contradicts the brutality of her murder. "Whoever killed her showed remorse after the fact," says Madison. "It suggests they didn't go there intending to murder a child. Does that mean they weren't there to murder Denise either? Because it would've been obvious that if Denise was there, Lucy would be with her. So if not them, it must've been Ryan they intended to find, right?"

Steve leans back. "Perhaps the perpetrator didn't know who lived there. Maybe they weren't there for Ryan *or* Denise, they were only there to rob the place and find something valuable enough to sell, or even just for the thrill of burglarizing someone. We know home invasions happen for all kinds of reasons, many of them senseless. It could've gone wrong when they were interrupted by Denise."

She nods. "I feel like searching for their killer is getting me nowhere, so I need to change my focus."

"To what?"

She considers it for a moment. "To Dominic Larson. I just have a gut feeling that if we could find Dominic and Charlie, we'll discover what happened to Denise and Lucy. Because it's too much of a coincidence that Denise's only other child is missing, right?"

Steve tilts his head as he thinks. "But by that reckoning, it would mean Denise and Lucy *were* the intended targets."

Madison's getting a headache from overthinking it. "Okay, so who would want to see Denise dead? We've focused on Ryan and that's gotten us nowhere. She was adored by her family, and even though she used to have a substance abuse problem, there's zero evidence to suggest she was using at the time of her death." Something suddenly occurs to her. "Are the toxicology results back yet?" If they show Denise had drugs in her system, she'll know to focus on finding her dealer.

"Not that I've seen," he says.

She picks up her landline and calls the medical examiner's office. Her computer tells her it's past nine o'clock, but she knows that, like them, Conrad frequently works late.

"Hi, this is Dr. Stevens."

"Conrad, hi." She smiles at the thought of him answering the main line after everyone else has left for the day. "It's Madison. I was hoping you'd still be at work."

"I was just about to leave, as I have your wonderful chief here waiting for me," he says. "She's taking me for a romantic meal at one of Lost Creek's finest eateries, but I'm a sucker for answering a ringing phone. You just never know who it'll be."

"That's usually why I try my best to ignore them," she jokes, trying to get the image of Conrad and Chief Mendes doing anything romantic out of her head. "I won't keep you, I just wanted to know whether the tox results are in for Denise Ridgeway yet."

"You must be psychic. I saw them flash up in my email just as I was locking up. Let me open my cell phone." She waits while he explains the situation to Chief Mendes. Mendes will either be rolling her eyes at the delay, or impressed Madison's working late. She hopes it's the latter. "Here they are." He takes a minute to read them. "Okay, it seems she had no alcohol or drugs in her system at the time of her death, which means she wasn't even on any prescribed medication."

Relieved that Denise hadn't relapsed, but disappointed she has no new lead to follow, Madison takes a deep breath. "Okay, thanks. Sorry for delaying you." She wants to ask if he's managed to examine Ida Randall's body yet, but doesn't want to hold him up any longer.

"You don't want to hear my thoughts on Ida Randall's murder?" he says.

She smiles. "Well, if you insist."

He laughs. "I prioritized her autopsy due to the other murders in the family. Ida was definitely killed this morning, corroborating what her son-in-law told you at the scene, and although it's obvious, it was the severe head wounds that killed her. There's no way she could have survived them. In fact, a single blow would likely have killed her, given her age, so the following blows were unnecessary. I've requested toxicology tests, but I don't expect any significant findings given how she died. The results won't be back until next week."

"Do you have any idea what type of weapon was used?" asks Madison.

"I'd need Alex's expertise to help us narrow it down."

Unfortunately, the team didn't find the murder weapon at the scene. Madison sighs. She didn't expect Conrad's assessment to tell them anything they didn't already know, but it's disappointing all the same. "Okay, thanks for that. Have a good evening."

"You too, Detective."

She shakes her head at Steve as she hangs up the phone. "No surprises with Ida's death, and Denise had no drugs or alcohol present in her system."

"At least we know we can rule out drugs as a motive for her

murder," he says before standing. He stretches his arms behind him as though he has a backache. "It's getting late. I'm going to head home. You should too."

She sighs. "I guess you're right."

Before he leaves, he adds, "Oh, while I remember, a couple of the employees from the wedding venue have criminal records, so I'm going to delve a little deeper into them tomorrow. You never know, it could be a link to whoever shot Lloyd Maxwell."

"Fingers crossed," she says.

He hesitates to leave, his eyes dwelling on the bulletproof vest. "Want me to walk you to your car?"

She waves a dismissive hand. "No thanks. I'm good." It's nice that he wants to protect her, but Madison doesn't want to go through life with a chaperone all because some crazed asshole has it in for her.

Nate's asleep on the couch when she enters the house. The TV is on low. She doesn't want to wake him, so she takes the opportunity to check on Owen. She hangs her purse on the back of a chair and quietly heads upstairs. Owen's bedroom door is ajar, but she still knocks lightly, poking her head around the corner. "Can I come in?"

He lowers his headphones to his neck. "Yeah." He's lying on the bed, his back against the headboard, a computer game playing on the big screen. Brody is sprawled across the bed, with Bandit curled up near the dog's belly. The cat is a notorious body-heat thief.

"I wish I'd brought my phone so I could take a picture," she says. "You guys look adorable." She goes to move a gaming magazine from his desk chair so she can sit, but he stops her. "Careful with that! It's full of toenail clippings."

She grimaces. "Eww, *Owen*! Why aren't they in the trash?

In fact," she looks around, "your room looks like a bomb's hit it. Can't you tidy once in a while?" Clothes are haphazardly hung over every surface. She notices a girl's pale-yellow hoody and tries not to think about why the mystery girl took it off in here.

"They're not mine!" he says. "They're *Brody's*. Nate told me to cut them after he got back from his little adventure, so I did." Brody's tail starts lazily thumping against the comforter at the mention of his name. Owen strokes his head, annoying the cat, who jumps down and disappears out of the room, probably to go curl up with Nate on the couch.

With a look of disgust, Madison says, "That was days ago! I've known serial killers who keep mementos for less time than that." She's joking, of course, but he gets her sense of humor. She carefully places the magazine on his desk before sitting.

"So what's up?" he says. "Feeling guilty that you're about to make me live with my abusive dead dad's crazy widow?"

She gives him a look. "Don't say that."

He grins. "I'm just messing with you. It's good that you're making me face my worst fears. According to the shrinks on social media, confronting your trauma head-on builds character."

"Owen!" she says, throwing some dirty socks at him. "Stop making me feel bad! I'm not *making* you do anything." Trying to think of a compromise, she says, "You don't have to stay while she's here. Why don't you stay with a friend or return to college early to get ahead on your studies?"

He scoffs. "Yeah, right. Like *that's* gonna happen." He drops the game controller on his bed, suddenly turning serious. "It's fine, really. I'll just stay out of her way." He hesitates before adding, "But have you considered whether she could be faking her illness?"

She frowns. "I don't think you can fake cancer, Owen."

"Sure you can. Plenty of people do it for all kinds of

reasons. I googled it. All she'd need to do is drastically reduce how much she eats, to make it look like she's wasting away."

"But why would she do that?"

He shrugs, trying to act flippant, but it's clear he's given it a lot of thought, which means Angie moving in here is bothering him. "To kill us all while we sleep?"

Her mouth drops open. "You're seriously worried she's going to hurt us, aren't you?"

"Wouldn't be the first time," he says, defiantly meeting her gaze.

She stands. "In that case, she's not coming. I'll find somewhere else for her instead."

"No," he says, suddenly looking regretful. "I'm just being paranoid because it's her."

"It's fine," she says. "I'll figure something out. You can stop worrying. I won't let her come here now. I'm glad you told me how you really feel about it."

"How about we get locks on our doors?" he suggests. "So she can't get to us?" His eyes suddenly tear up, something that never happens now he's older. It makes him look like a little boy. Her heart aches for him. He's clearly still afraid of Angie.

She approaches the bed and embraces him as best she can. "I won't put you through it, Owen. You mean more to me than she does, more than anyone does. You know that, right?"

He nods while sniffing back tears. "I don't want to be afraid of her. I want to be able to show compassion, so I know I'm not as bad as she and my dad were." When Madison returns to her seat, Owen composes himself as Brody rests a paw on his thigh, keeping an eye on him. "It's fine," he says. "Let her move in. I'll deal with it. Hell, I'll even help care for her. Maybe it'll make her realize she could've had us in her life if she hadn't chosen Dad over us all those years ago."

She takes a deep breath. "You don't have to do this."

"No, I want to." He's resolute now. Challenging himself.

Trying to grow as an individual, which is to be admired because it would be far easier to run away from his fears. "Honestly. I can handle it. I was just being paranoid. If I can't defend myself against a sick middle-aged woman then I deserve whatever I get, right?" He laughs, trying to make it look like he's okay.

"She doesn't have enough strength to hurt anyone, Owen. I can promise you that much. She can barely eat or drink by herself. But if it gets too much for you, we can reassess at any point, okay?"

He nods with a bright smile and picks up his controller. "Okay." He restarts his game, signaling the conversation is over. Madison reluctantly leaves his room, her heart hurting at the thought of the three of them having to survive this one final challenge before Angie's no longer a threat to any of them.

CHAPTER THIRTY-THREE

There's an unexpected chill in the air the next morning, along with thickening rainclouds. Madison heads to what Alex Parker calls "the dark side of the moon," meaning the cold side of the police station where his tiny office is located. The sun rarely touches this part of the building, making it continually cold and miserable—not that Alex cares. He's one of those people who thrives in fall and winter rather than the warmer months. It's probably why he became a forensic technician, as doom and gloom doesn't negatively affect his mental health, unlike normal people.

His door is wide open, so she enters. "Morning," she says brightly.

Alex is seated at his computer with a radio station playing what sounds to her like nineties emo music, though she could be wrong. He turns the volume down as she looks at Mrs. Pebbles. The tiny dog was asleep in her crate, but now she's side-eying Madison as she dares to get closer to Alex than the little madam would like. Alex turns in his chair. "To what do I owe the pleasure so bright and early on a Thursday morning?" he asks.

"Hold your hand out," she says. "I have something for you."

Far too trusting, he obediently holds his hand out without considering what it might be. She places a clear evidence bag on his palm and waits for his reaction.

He frowns as he peers at the contents. "Nail clippings," he says dubiously. "You're... too kind."

She laughs as she takes a seat on the only other chair that fits in the small space. "They're Brody's. Owen clipped his nails the morning after Brody raced to find the wedding shooter. Now, I have no idea whether he ever caught up with the perp, but I dreamed about those last night, so I think my subconscious was telling me to get them checked in case they have the killer's DNA on them."

Alex beams at her ingenuity. "Amazing. I can picture the headlines now. 'Wedding Shooter Caught Thanks to Lovable Shepsky's Bravery!'"

She laughs. "I know, right? He could be awarded a medal." She looks at Mrs. Pebbles with a raised eyebrow. "I bet *you'd* never do anything that brave, would you, missy?"

A low growl emanates from the chihuahua.

"I'll send them to Nora," says Alex. "If she finds anyone else's DNA besides yours, Nate's and Owen's, we may be able to use it as a comparison sample once we have a person of interest in the case. But don't get your hopes up. It's a long shot."

She stands. "I know. But cases have been solved with long shots before, right?"

He smiles. "Absolutely." Before she can leave, he says, "Oh, by the way, I didn't find any trace evidence on the threatening note you received as a wedding gift. Sorry about that." His disappointed expression suggests he feels like he's let her down.

"That's okay," she says. "I didn't expect it to provide any answers. Thanks anyway." As she leaves his office, she feels a stab of annoyance that the wedding shooter always appears to be one step ahead of them.

. . .

The earlier rainclouds have cleared and the sun has warmed her car by the time Madison leaves the station to visit Dominic Larson's father. She forgoes the bulletproof vest today, but is mindful to be extra vigilant in case the wedding shooter tries to strike, but at this point, she's starting to think it was an empty threat meant to distract her, and suspects the killer has probably fled town or changed their mind. Vests aren't much use against someone who's as good an aim as this guy anyway, since he can just target her head if he's that serious about killing her.

She takes the route that passes Colt and Bernie Ridgeway's home, as she's been wondering how Bernie's coping. She slows as she spots a red pickup truck out front. A young woman in a pink plaid shirt and pale blue denim shorts is helping Colt lift suitcases into the back. The woman has long red hair, which suggests she's their elder daughter, Toyah, as Colt's also a redhead. Denise was blonde, but there's no mistaking the pair were sisters, as the resemblance is obvious. Toyah must be here to take Bernie back to her place in Denver for a while, to help her escape Ida's crime scene and grieve in peace.

Madison pulls over behind the pickup truck. It would be good to learn Toyah's thoughts on the murders and whether she suspects anyone other than Ryan, because her parents have tunnel vision when it comes to him. Toyah might see things differently. Denise might have confided in her about someone else who makes a better suspect.

Colt spots Madison as she exits her vehicle. His eyebrows are raised expectantly. Perhaps he thinks she's about to tell him she's arrested Ryan for the murders.

"Morning," she says as she approaches them. She notices the inside of the pickup truck is disheveled, with a child's car seat covered in old takeout bags, cups and dirty napkins. Owen lets the trash build up like this in his vehicle, and she'll never understand it. She needs her car to be kept clean, although she's not as fussy about her house, perhaps because Nate happily does most of the housework. She hit the jackpot with him.

The woman stops what she's doing, so Madison extends her hand. "Detective Harper. I'm assuming you're Toyah Ridgeway?"

Toyah nods as she shakes Madison's hand. "I am. Are you here because you have an update?"

"Not yet. I was just passing and thought I'd check how your mom's doing."

Colt shakes his head in disappointment. He turns and walks back into the house, presumably to retrieve more suitcases.

Toyah shields her eyes from the glare of the sun as she says, "Don't mind him. He's frustrated, that's all. We all are. It feels like there's no progress, and we're constantly being contacted by reporters. It's annoying." She tears up, and Madison has to remember she's lost her sister, niece and grandmother all at the same time.

"I know," she says. "I'm sorry it feels like there's no progress, but it's still very early days and homicide investigations take time. We're working hard to follow any leads we get." She takes a deep breath. "I know your parents are set on Ryan Simmonds being the culprit for all three murders, but so far we've found nothing to back that up, so I want to know what you think. Do you have anyone else in mind? Did Denise ever confide in you?"

Toyah wipes her eyes with a tissue from her pocket. "About what?"

"I don't know, about an affair she might have been having, or unwanted attention from anyone in her life?"

"We weren't that close on account of her substance abuse," she says. "We used to be, but it's heartbreaking to watch your little sister ruin her life with drugs, so I pulled away a few years ago. I couldn't put up with her lies and random disappearances, and I worried Lucy would suffer."

Madison can tell she feels guilty about keeping her distance now they're dead. "How was Ryan as a father?"

Toyah shrugs. "On the outside he appeared to be a good dad, and Lucy clearly adored him, but who knows what goes on behind closed doors, right?"

Madison frowns. "Do you think he might have been faking it? Or is it only since the murders happened that you have doubts about him?" It's possible she's been influenced by her parents' opinion.

The other woman sighs. "Look, I don't know. But happy people don't have affairs, right? Denise strayed for a reason, if you ask me."

There could be something in that. "Did you know about her affair with Dominic Larson?"

She shakes her head. "Not until it all came out in the press earlier this year."

"Have you ever met Dominic or his and Denise's son, Charlie?"

"No, never. I don't live here, remember. And I hadn't seen Denise and Lucy since..." She tries to think. "Well, it's been a few years, put it that way."

"I understand she would take off for months at a time when she was using," says Madison, "and that's how her pregnancy with Charlie went undetected by Ryan and your parents."

"Right. We knew she'd always return when she ran out of money, or when she was trying to get her life back together. She was lucky, because Ryan always took her back. Most men wouldn't be that forgiving."

It certainly shows how much Ryan loved her. But that doesn't mean he didn't kill her. He might have been pushed to his limit after learning she had taken advantage of him by cheating with Dominic.

Toyah closes the back of the truck, seemingly ready to end the conversation and begin the long drive home with Bernie.

"Your father mentioned that you and Denise were a little afraid of Ida, your grandmother," says Madison.

Resting against the truck, Toyah lowers her eyes, probably thinking about Ida's brutal murder. "That doesn't mean we didn't love her, though. She was the kind of person who called a spade a spade. Some people can tolerate that better than others, and as we got older, we realized her bark was worse than her bite."

Madison bats away a persistent bee. "Can you think of anyone who might have wanted to hurt her? I imagine her strong opinions got her into a lot of arguments over the years."

Toyah snorts affectionately. "You can say that again. But not to the point where someone would want to do *that*." She gestures to the house before breaking into a sob. Her parents must have described the scene they came home to. What Ida went through in her final moments alive.

Madison rests a hand on her shoulder. "I'm sorry. I didn't mean to upset you." She removes her hand. "Thanks for answering my questions. I'm just trying to get as many opinions as possible, so I'm glad I bumped into you." She takes a deep breath. "Are you and your mom heading out soon?"

Toyah composes herself. "As soon as Mom's ready."

Madison's glad that Colt's staying behind so she can liaise with him while they're gone. "Okay, well have a safe journey." She turns and heads back to her car. She's a little frustrated, because although it was good to meet Denise's sister, it's gotten her no closer to identifying any suspects other than Ryan Simmonds. She's starting to think there's a reason for that, and that maybe it's time to accept that he *is* responsible for everything that's happened.

CHAPTER THIRTY-FOUR

When Madison pulls up outside the home of Dominic Larson's father, she's surprised to find Sergeant Adams leaning against his vehicle, waiting for her. He approaches her car as she gets out. "Hey. What's up?" she asks.

"Alex asked me to give you these." He hands her a large envelope containing a bunch of photos of the interior of Dominic Larson's house, taken soon after he and his son vanished. "He suggested showing them to Dominic's father to see if he notices anything unexpected in them. Alex figured he'd know the home better than anyone else we can ask."

"Good idea," she says. "Want to come inside with me?"

He nods. "Sure, why not? It'll be like old times." He grins, alluding to the time they were partners. They didn't get on as well back then—Madison found him irritating and a little unprofessional if she's honest, which he's well aware of. Thankfully, he decided he was better suited to the sergeant role and now they get along just fine. "Hey, have you heard about Steve and Shelley?" he says excitedly.

Madison looks at him. "Heard what?"

"They're *dating*." He looks pleased with himself for knowing the latest office gossip.

"How do you know?" she says, feigning ignorance.

"It's obvious. They can't keep their eyes off each other! You know, I always say the sign of a good detective is knowing who's screwing who. And you had no idea." He shakes his head. "Some detective you are, Harper."

She rolls her eyes. "Oh please. I've *never* heard you say that."

"That's because you don't listen to a word I say."

He has a point. They approach the front door and Madison knocks twice. "Keep it to yourself," she says. "Let's give them a fighting chance of happiness, okay?" She's also unsure how Chief Mendes will react.

He grins. "My lips are sealed."

When there's no answer at the door, she tries again.

Nothing.

Adams turns to look at the neighbor's house. "Let me ask his neighbor if they know where he is."

Madison wanders around the side of the property, and it's not long before she hears Adams talking to an older woman next door. She can't hear what they're saying, so she peers into a side window. Everything looks still inside. The kitchen shows no sign of anyone having prepared breakfast or coffee this morning. It looks like it hasn't been used yet. The thought fills her with dread. What if he's in trouble inside? What if—

Adams returns, breaking her train of thought. "Mr. Larson's not in there. His neighbor says he was taken to the hospital by ambulance yesterday. He wasn't doing too well apparently."

Her shoulders slump, but she's relieved he's not dead inside the house. "He's battling prostate cancer," she says. "I hope he's alright." She suddenly feels pressured. Time is running out to reunite him with Dominic and Charlie before he succumbs to the disease.

"The neighbor implied he stank of liquor," says Adams. "Maybe his son and grandson's disappearance is getting to him." He sighs. "Who can blame the guy for turning to drink, right?"

"Right." It's hard not to feel sorry for him. "I should go check on him." She hesitates, worried about seeing him in pain, because he's going through the same as Angie and she doesn't want her own emotions to be triggered. When Adams heads back to his car, she follows him. "Tell Alex thanks for these." She holds the envelope up.

"Will do. Let me know if you need anything."

He drives away. Madison reluctantly starts her car, bracing herself for what she'll find at the hospital.

It takes some time for her to locate Henry Larson in the bustling maze of medicinal-smelling corridors and wards, but when she does, he's surprised to see her. "Detective?" Looking pale and drained, he tries to force himself into a sitting position, which makes his gown fall off his shoulder.

"No, don't move," she says. "I just wanted to check on you." He has a private room with a large window that lets in the morning sunlight.

"Pass me my glasses, would you?"

She looks at the nightstand, which is empty apart from his glasses and a plastic cup of water. Handing him the glasses, she says, "I just went by your house and your neighbor said you were here. How are you doing, or is that a stupid question?"

He smiles briefly. "Honestly? Each day things get a little harder. I guess I took a turn for the worse and managed to raise the alarm with my neighbor. If I hadn't, I might not be alive right now. I was severely dehydrated." He nods to the bag of fluids attached to an IV. His neighbor was right, he smells of alcohol. Madison doesn't comment, but it's no wonder he's dehydrated. Hopefully his doctor will broach the subject.

"The doctors keep telling me I shouldn't be living alone anymore," he says. "But what can I do? The plan was to move in with my son when things started going downhill, but that's obviously not going to happen now." He looks away, his lower lip quivering with emotion.

"I'm so sorry," she says. "I wish I could find him and Charlie for you. We *are* trying our best."

He coughs into a tissue. "I know you are. But I've finally accepted that even if you do find them before I die, they won't be alive. They can't be. I don't feel them with me anymore. I just feel... empty."

She takes a deep breath, saddened that he's given up hope, but it's understandable given four months have passed since their disappearance and there have been zero leads or accurate sightings. "May I?" She points to the armchair next to the bed. He nods. She has the envelope of photos that Adams gave her but doesn't want to show him right away. Gently, she says, "How certain are you that Dominic didn't leave town of his own volition, taking Charlie with him? Because based on the lack of evidence suggesting otherwise, it feels like that's more likely than an abduction."

"But why would he do that?" he asks dubiously.

"Well," she says, "I think it's got something to do with his affair with Denise Ridgeway." She crosses her legs. "I can't help thinking that because Dominic loved Charlie so much, he was afraid Denise would eventually change her mind and want custody of their son at some point."

"But surely no judge in their right mind would award her custody if they knew about her struggles with substance abuse?"

He could be right, but that doesn't mean Dominic wasn't afraid of it happening. "Perhaps he was also afraid Ryan Simmonds would find out about their affair, so he wanted to skip town to avoid retaliation." When Henry doesn't say anything, she adds, "I need to be honest with you, Mr. Larson. I have to consider whether Dominic might have faked his disappearance so he wouldn't be a suspect for Denise's murder."

"*What?*" he says, glaring at her. "You think my son killed Denise and Lucy? That's preposterous!" He finally gets some color in his face, but that's not a good thing in his current state. The machine monitoring his blood pressure starts beeping a little faster.

"You might be right," she says, trying to calm him. "But I need to consider all scenarios in order to rule them out and see what that leaves me with. I'm sorry. I'm not trying to upset you. But if there's anything you can think of that would help me dismiss that scenario sooner, then tell me."

He shakes his head, struggling to find something. "Maybe Dominic *was* worried that Ryan was about to find out about the affair. Fine, I could believe he'd skip town to keep custody of his son—even though I don't believe that's what happened—but he's no *murderer*, Detective. What has he got to gain from killing his ex-girlfriend? He didn't have to go that far. Skipping town would've been enough. He could get lost off-grid somewhere, ensuring Ryan would never find him and Denise would never find Charlie. But that doesn't make any sense, because where's he going to go with no savings and none of his possessions? His credit cards are here. I'm here. His whole *life* is here." His eyes well up. It's clear this is draining for him.

He's so passionate that Madison is inclined to agree with him. "Okay. Sorry for bringing it up. Like I said, it's my job to consider all possibilities. It doesn't mean they'll lead anywhere, it's just helpful to work through each one until they've been exhausted." It's true that it makes no sense for Dominic to skip town and then secretly return to murder Denise, risking being seen by one of the many people who would have heard about his disappearance in the press and media. Not unless that's what he's banking on the police thinking, meaning he's performed an elaborate double-bluff.

Going around in circles is giving her another headache. She needs evidence, but it's clear she's not going to find it here. She stands, then remembers the photos. "Before I go, our forensic technician asked if you would take a look at these. They're photos he took inside Dominic's house. He was hoping anything that shouldn't be there would stand out to you. Is that okay?"

He leans over to take a sip of water before nodding. She lets the photos slip out of the envelope and passes them to him. He pushes his glasses up his nose and studies each one meticulously. It's not long before his hands start trembling. "I haven't been in the house since they vanished. It's upsetting to see it without them in it."

"I can only imagine," she says gently.

He suddenly frowns, looking closer at a photo of the living room. "What's this?" He points to something on the floor in the corner of the room, half hidden under the couch.

She peers closely at it. "It looks like a stain in the carpet."

His face drains of color. "Not blood?"

"No," she says. "Our forensic tech would've already tested it if it resembled anything close to blood. Are you saying that wasn't there before?"

He looks again, even removing his glasses and holding the photo farther away to see if that helps. "Maybe I just didn't notice it before. It could be mud from someone's shoes. It's pretty dark."

His reaction is enough for her to get it checked out. "We'll look into it and get back to you." He passes her the photos, which she slides back into the envelope. "I'll leave you in peace now. Do you have anyone coming to visit you?"

"Yes," he says. "My sister's on her way."

A nurse approaches, taking readings from a machine to their left. She works silently, as if she hasn't seen them.

"Okay. Well, thanks for your help," says Madison. "And

sorry again to have upset you. Just keep in mind that we're doing everything we can to find Dominic and Charlie."

He lowers his eyes and nods. "Thank you."

As she exits his room, she feels the weight of the world on her shoulders. Because she's beginning to suspect that this case might be unsolvable.

CHAPTER THIRTY-FIVE

"Comfortable?" asks Nate.

"It'll do," says his soon-to-be sister-in-law as she pulls the covers right up to her neck, despite it being a warm day.

Madison asked him to take care of moving Angie in while she's at work. She said she'd see her sister when she gets home later. The situation is clearly stressful for her, as well as for Owen, who's chosen to spend the day with a friend. When he left the house early this morning, he implied he wouldn't be back until late, which means Nate's alone with Angie. Even Brody doesn't want to enter the spare bedroom. He's sitting outside the threshold, closely watching the ailing woman formerly known as their nemesis. He must be wondering why she's been permitted to enter their home. Bandit is the only one who doesn't have a history with her, and he's currently curled up on her bed by her feet, having gratefully accepted the tuna from the sandwich Nate made. He told Angie she should be eating it herself, but she said she was feeling too nauseous to eat, so she hand-fed the cat instead, making herself a friend for the rest of her short life.

"Don't suppose you keep any liquor in the house?" she asks sheepishly.

Nate raises an eyebrow. "I'm not going to answer that question. Now, if I can't get you anything else, I need to work. The nurse I've booked doesn't start for a couple more days, but you have my number. Call me if you feel unwell or need anything, okay?"

She nods. "Open the blinds before you go. I want to see outside."

"Sure." He moves around the bed and raises them, letting the sunlight stream into the room and across Bandit, who turns on his back, exposing his fluffy white belly to the warmth.

Angie smiles at the cat. "Isn't he just precious?"

Nate's surprised she likes animals, given it's well known that psychopaths don't. He immediately feels bad for the thought. "Anything else?" She has cold drinks in a cooler by the side of her bed, along with the TV remote, her cell phone and some snacks in case she gets her appetite back. And her meds should last another few hours before they wear off.

"No, I'm good. Have fun catching bad guys."

He laughs. "I'll try. See you later, Angie." He exits her room. Brody follows him out of the house and into his car, where he pulls out his cell phone and calls Pam. He wants to meet with her brother to get his take on what he thinks happened to Sharon Smith.

Pam answers on the third ring and sounds stressed. "Hi. Sorry, but I shouldn't be on my phone. I'm at the hospital."

"Oh, okay. Nothing serious, I hope?"

"It's not for me, it's my brother. He's not well at the moment." She lowers her voice, adding, "He has prostate cancer and he's not taking care of himself properly."

"I'm sorry to hear that," Nate says, thinking of what they're going through with Angie. It must be ten times harder when you actually love the person. "I'll call you tomorrow instead."

"Thank you." Pam hangs up.

Before he can slip his phone away, it pings with a text from Madison.

Do you have time for lunch? My treat.

He smiles as he replies.

Sure. I'll head to the diner.

He looks at Brody in the rearview mirror. "Wanna go see Uncle Vince?"

Brody's tail thumps the backseat. He lets out an excited bark, knowing that when they go to the diner, he usually gets a treat.

Madison's laughing at something Vince says when Nate enters Ruby's Diner. Brody remains outside, seated on a bench as he soaks up the midday sunshine and watches people come and go. Some people are scared of him, given his size, but others stop to stroke him and offer a little something from their takeout bags. Nate does *try* to limit how much human food the dog gets, but he figures Brody burns it all off anyway.

When Madison notices him approaching the counter, she smiles. "Hey." She's not one for public displays of affection, so he's surprised when she embraces him.

He kisses her. "Hey. Everything okay?"

She pulls away. "Yeah, I've just been visiting someone at the hospital. I guess it made me grateful that you and Owen are healthy."

He nods. There's nothing like a hospital visit to make you appreciate your health. He thinks about how Pam's currently at the hospital. "Who were you visiting?"

"I'll bring your order over," says Vince.

"Thanks," says Madison. With two coffees in her hands, she leads Nate to a booth by the window where they can keep an eye on Brody. "Dominic Larson's father, Henry. You remember I told you about that case, right?"

"Sure." He remembers the missing father and son being splashed all over the news earlier this year.

"Well," she says, "he has terminal cancer and was holding out hope that we'd find his son and grandson before he dies. It doesn't look like that's going to happen, since he's taken a turn for the worse."

Nate sips his coffee as a thought occurs to him. "Does he have a sister named Pam?" he asks. Pam took Sharon's last name. He doesn't know her previous name, but he knows her brother is called Hank, which could be short for Henry.

"He has a sister, yeah, but I'm not sure of her name. Why?"

"Pamela Smith is the woman who hired me to look for Sharon Smith, her girlfriend who vanished in the early nineties. She told me she's at the hospital visiting her sick brother, Hank. He has prostate cancer, right?"

Madison nods.

"I didn't realize until just now that Pam is Dominic Larson's aunt," Nate says. "I never thought to ask her previous name as I guess it didn't seem relevant."

"*Is* it relevant, though?"

Vince sets two plates of burgers and fries in front of them before serving the customers in the booth behind them.

"I guess not." Nate takes another sip of coffee as he thinks it through. "Sharon's disappearance thirty years ago can't have anything to do with Dominic's recent disappearance, right?"

Madison thinks about it. "Sharon may have been in a relationship with Dominic's aunt, but she wasn't directly related to Dominic. Was he even born when she disappeared?"

Nate's stomach flips with dread as something comes to him. "Wait a minute..."

"What?" She leans in.

He hesitates to say what he's thinking, as it sounds outlandish, but in this town, anything's possible. "What if Dominic is the baby Sharon was pregnant with when she vanished?"

Madison lowers her burger. "But if that's the case, why would Hank raise him as his son? Pam would've raised him, surely?" She thinks for a second. "What's Dominic's date of birth?"

He pulls out his phone. "Give me a second." He wants to double-check, so he googles articles about Dominic's disappearance. Disappointed, he says, "No. I'm totally wrong. He was born two years after Sharon vanished." He suddenly feels stupid jumping to conclusions. "I should've known. The chances of Sharon and her baby still being alive after all this time are slim to none."

"I agree," she says. "If no one has seen her since the day she vanished, it's likely she was killed on or around that day and her baby never even got a chance at life." She lowers her eyes as she thinks about how sad that is.

"Sorry for ruining the mood," he says.

"It's fine. It sounds like Hank and his sister have been through a lot. I wish I could find answers for both of them." She chews a French fry. "You said my dad worked on the Sharon Smith case, right?"

"Right." With a smile, he says, "Don't suppose you want to leak me some information about his investigation so I don't waste my time on false leads?"

She gives him a stern look. "You know I can't do that. But if my dad didn't manage to solve it, it suggests all the obvious leads didn't work out. Try thinking outside the box."

He snorts. "Gee, thanks for the helpful insight."

She laughs before turning serious. "I should probably speak to Pam to see what she thinks happened to Dominic and Charlie. As far as I know, she hasn't been questioned about their disappearance."

"Likewise," he says. "I should ask Hank what he thinks happened to Sharon. Maybe we should visit them together, once Hank's out of the hospital. Would that be okay?"

She thinks about it. "If they're alright with it, I don't see why not. But that's assuming Hank is discharged. He looked pretty bad when I saw him earlier."

That reminds him of Angie. "By the way, your sister's settled in at home now. The nurse I hired starts in two days. Until then, I've told Angie to call me if she needs anything."

Madison finishes her burger and pushes her plate away. "I don't know what I would've done if you hadn't taken care of all that. For some reason, I just get overcome with anxiety at the thought of how her final weeks are going to pan out. I guess I just don't want to face it."

"That's completely understandable, Madison." He rests a hand on hers and gives it a gentle squeeze. "No one wants to watch a family member deteriorate." Sipping his coffee, he says, "Anway, she seemed happy enough with Bandit keeping her company."

"Bandit? Really? She likes the cat? I thought..."

He snorts. "Me too. Psychopaths and animals, right?"

She shakes her head, amused. "I feel bad for even thinking it, but I can't picture her petting an animal."

"I get the feeling she's going to spend all her spare time watching the soaps on TV," he says. "You know how she loves drama."

Madison scoffs. "She could teach those show writers a thing or two about drama." Sipping her coffee, she says, "Is Owen home?"

"No, he left early, and I don't think we'll see much of him

from now on. He knows he only has to say the word and we'll find somewhere else for Angie to stay."

She nods. "I know. I still feel guilty, though. I guess I'd feel guilty for letting Angie die elsewhere too, so I can't win."

He smiles sympathetically. "You have nothing to feel guilty about."

Changing the subject, she stands. "I better get back to work."

"Sure." He finishes his coffee and joins her.

Outside, they find Vince feeding Brody something. Brody wags his tail when he sees them, looking sheepish. Vince puts his finger to his lips. "Our little secret." He strokes the dog's head.

Nate laughs. "Thanks for lunch. We're heading out."

"No problem," says Vince, hiding a greasy food bag behind his back. "See you later."

"Bye, Vince," says Madison.

Nate walks her to her vehicle as Brody follows them. "I'll let you know when Pam's free to see us both," he says as she slips into the driver's seat.

"Okay. See you later." She leans in for a kiss before closing the door.

He and Brody watch her drive away before Nate gets into his own vehicle. He thinks of Dominic and Charlie Larson, and how they've been missing for four months now. Sharon Smith's been missing for thirty years. The cases can't be linked. But as he doesn't know much about the Larson case, he thinks it's worth looking into, just to be sure.

CHAPTER THIRTY-SIX
FEBRUARY 2022

Dominic Larson straps his two-year-old son safely into the back of the car and straightens his woolen hat. "Better?"

Charlie smiles. "Better."

With a laugh, Dominic closes the door, climbs into the driver's seat and starts the engine. As he pulls away from the curb, he meets Charlie's big blue eyes in the rearview mirror. "Did you enjoy daycare today, buddy?"

Charlie nods emphatically, clutching the painting he made earlier that depicts a significantly inaccurate version of Dominic eating something unrecognizable beneath a sun so large it would kill him with radiation poisoning within seconds were it real.

"Is that supposed to be *me?*" Dominic asks. "Am I really *that* big?"

Charlie giggles. "Yeah!"

"Then I guess I'd better stop ordering pizza when we eat out." He smiles, glancing at his son in the mirror every few minutes during the ride home, his heart swollen with love for the little boy.

Every day he thanks his lucky stars that Denise did what

she did. It's not just that she could have opted to terminate the pregnancy or give Charlie up for adoption without ever letting him know she was pregnant in the first place. It's the fact that she came to him and told him the truth, then asked if he would take care of their son. Denise Ridgeway has a lot of faults, like having affairs outside of her relationship and self-medicating with drugs, but he knows she wants what's best for Charlie. She knows that if her boyfriend finds out that she and Dominic were briefly seeing each other, never mind that they had a child together, it would be over for her. It sounds like Ryan has given her several chances to turn her life around for the sake of their daughter, and one more mistake would mean him walking away for good, probably taking Lucy with him.

Dominic sighs as he pulls into the driveway of the small home he shares with his son. Denise did what was best for Charlie, but she doesn't seem capable of doing what's best for herself. He has no animosity toward her, despite their relationship ending because he found out about Ryan. He wishes she could be in Charlie's life, and that Lucy and Charlie could grow up together as the half-siblings they are. But Denise has built her life on lies, and he can't help feeling that one day it's all going to implode, leaving her completely alone in this world.

He gets out of the car and opens the back door to get Charlie. "Ready?"

"Is Mommy here?" his son asks.

Dominic's heart sinks. Ever since Charlie's been at daycare and mingled with kids who have mommies, he's been asking when he'll meet his own mommy. He doesn't understand when Dominic explains that he doesn't have one, because he can't give him a solid reason. Just to confuse matters, his best friend has *two* mommies *and* a daddy.

But Denise is adamant that she doesn't want anyone to know she's his mother. Dominic suspects that one day that will change. That she might come seeking a relationship with her son. The thought fills him with dread, because it might mean they'd have to share custody, and that Charlie could be exposed to her addiction. "No, just Daddy," he says. "And we need to make you something to eat. Come on. Bring your backpack." His son's backpack is almost as big as him and only contains one slim book and a couple of plastic dinosaurs, but Charlie acts like it's heavy as he follows Dominic into the house. "Go wash your hands, okay?"

"Okay!"

Dominic starts preparing dinner: leftover pasta from the fridge, which he splits onto two plates and then adds salad leaves and some small tomatoes, cucumber, slaw and cooked chicken. He throws the empty slaw container in the trash and realizes it's full. Pulling the bag from the trash can, he opens the side door and heads out into the dark evening. He dumps the bag inside the wheelie bin on the driveway and lowers the lid, shivering from a blast of cold February air.

"Evening, Dominic!" shouts Mrs. Lucas from the other side of the road.

He happily waves to her, even though he can barely see her in the dark. "Evening." He got lucky living on this street. The neighbors are wonderful, and almost all of them dote on Charlie. Probably because they feel sorry for him not having a mother. They've asked where she is too, and Dominic tries to be even vaguer with them than he is with Charlie, just saying she doesn't live in town anymore. So far, no one is rude enough to ask any follow-up questions, but he knows that as Charlie gets older, more questions will come. Because his son will constantly be quizzed about both his parents as he grows up. Teachers will wonder why only his dad attends parent-teacher conferences. Girlfriends will want to know why he only has a dad. Doctors will ask what health conditions run in his family, and poor Charlie will only be able to answer for Dominic's side, not his mother's. It pains him that he may one day need to lie to keep the questions at bay. He may need to tell Charlie that his mother died when he was young. But that could backfire if Denise ever reveals herself to him.

He disappears back inside the house, his chest heavy with dread. That's not the only thing he worries about. He's often wondered what would happen if Ryan Simmonds found out about Charlie. He's bound to be pissed at Denise for cheating on him, and he'll probably assume Dominic went into the relationship knowing she was already with someone. Will Ryan want revenge? And if so, will he take it out on him, or on Charlie? His stomach flips at the thought.

"Daddy, I'm ready!"

Dominic pushes the unsettling thoughts away as he closes the door behind him, safe again in their little cocoon. He sets the kitchen table while Charlie struggles into a chair, coloring book in his spare hand. "I'm going to color the T-Rex pink," he says.

"*Pink?*" Charlie giggles and Dominic can't help himself. He leans down to kiss his son's soft, plump cheek. "I'm pretty sure dinosaurs weren't pink, buddy."

"Well, mine is."

"Okay, fine. Make room for dinner." He sets a plate in front of his son and passes him a fork. "One pasta shape at a time, okay? Remember what happened last time."

Charlie giggles again. "I almost *died*."

"Well, I'm glad *you* can laugh about it, but that was very traumatic for me." Traumatic is an understatement. For a brief second, he'd seen what a life without Charlie would look like and it made him realize he couldn't go on living if anything ever happened to his son. He suddenly knew with a massive wave of certainty that there would be no point.

He sits opposite him and lifts his knife and fork.

"What does tram-tic mean?" Charlie struggles with the word.

"It doesn't matter. Eat your food." He hopes Charlie never learns what that word means. He hopes he can keep him safe from anything that will traumatize him.

They eat in comfortable silence until Charlie's full. Afterward, Dominic lets him switch on the TV in the living room while he washes their dirty dishes and tidies the kitchen.

A knock at the side door makes him jump. He's not expecting anyone. Maybe Mrs. Lucas needs something fixing.

"Is that Grandpa?" yells Charlie from the living room.

"No, Grandpa's on vacation, remember?" Dominic throws the washcloth next to the sink and wipes his damp hands on his shirt. When he opens the door, he's taken aback by who he finds standing there. "Oh. Hi." His stomach flips with dread as he realizes his worst fears are about to come true. "I think I know why you're here."

CHAPTER THIRTY-SEVEN
PRESENT DAY

Back at the station, Madison is heading to her desk with coffee in hand when she passes Alex. "I showed the photos of Dominic's house to his dad," she says, stopping him.

"Did he notice anything unusual?" he asks.

"He sure did." She leads him to her desk, where she empties the envelope of photographs, selects the correct one and points to the dark stain in the carpet. "See this? Hank wasn't sure if it was a new stain as he didn't recognize it. He thought it might be blood, but I know you would've already tested it if that were the case."

Alex smiles. "Ah, yes. I did notice it, but it wasn't blood, it was more like a grease stain of some kind. I had no reason to think it was suspicious, but I can go back and take a sample since he thinks it might be new."

"That would be great, thanks."

"No problem. I'll head over there next. But first, you should know I've been checking the messages on Ryan Simmonds's phone."

She raises her eyebrows. "And?"

"I've found nothing incriminating, I'm afraid. Which is

what we expected. I think he'd have the good sense to use a burner phone if he was up to no good, but we didn't find one during the search of his house."

"Doesn't mean he didn't hire a hitman face-to-face," she says.

"True. I think most people know by now that they shouldn't use phones for anything dodgy, although I'm always pleasantly surprised when they do."

"Not the smart criminals," she says with a smile.

"Exactly. If you really think Ryan is our killer, you need to outsmart him, because he appears to have done a good job of covering himself."

She sighs. "Got it."

When Alex leaves, Steve turns from his desk to look at her. "Well, after trawling through the list of people who were at your wedding, I found no reason to think anyone present could've been involved or might've been an alternative target to you guys." He pauses. "Until now."

Her stomach flips with excitement. A new lead is exactly what they need. "Well, don't be coy, tell me!"

He smiles. "I just discovered that one of the people present is related to the Ridgeways."

She frowns. "Really? Who?"

"Chad Peters. He works for the wedding venue as a bar manager. It may be nothing, since it feels like everyone's related to each other in this town, but do you remember seeing him on the day?"

She tries to think back and remembers Chad looked as shaken as Deborah Purdue, the venue manager, when Madison broke it to them that Lloyd Maxwell had been instantly killed. But she's unsure how him being related to the Ridgeways could be relevant to the wedding shooter's actions. "Yeah, briefly. How is he related to them?"

"He's Bernie and Colt's nephew on Colt's side."

"Bernie and Colt's nephew..." she says, thinking aloud. "I only met him at the wedding, so it's unlikely he has a grudge against me and was working with the shooter if Nate or I were the target—which we have to assume we were, based on the note, right?"

Steve crosses his arms over his chest. "What if you guys *weren't* the target?"

"But the note said, 'Congratulations on surviving your wedding. Next time, you won't be so lucky.'"

"I know, but maybe that was to put you off the scent." He stands, excited now. "Think about it. Bernie and Colt's daughter and granddaughter were murdered, followed by Bernie's mother. What if someone is targeting the Ridgeways, and they were actually trying to kill Chad—the nephew—at the wedding, rather than you?"

She has to admit it makes more sense than her or Nate being the target, as that theory has led them nowhere. "That could be why there's been no other attempts on my or Nate's lives. The note made it sound like the shooter would try again at our next wedding, but they'd know the threat alone would mean we'd take extra security measures to avoid us or any of our guests being harmed. And why wait for the wedding? We're both out in public every day. They could target us anywhere, probably with more success."

"Right," he says. "Which is why I don't think you were the targets. I think it's worth considering whether Chad was."

She'd love to believe it was Chad Peters over the alternative, but it just makes this case even odder. "Was he even outdoors when the shot was fired?" As the bar manager, it's more likely he was inside, preparing drinks for when the wedding was over.

"He was," says Steve. "I remember glancing over my shoulder to watch you walk down the aisle. Chad was stationed at the outside bar." He quickly grabs a piece of paper from the printer and draws a crude mockup of the wedding. "You and

Nate were here," he makes two circles, "and Lloyd was between you but a step back, here. And Chad was here, at the bar." When he's done, he draws a line from Lloyd to where they believe the shot was fired from, then extends the line past Lloyd to where Chad was standing.

"Wow." Madison sits back. "He was in the line of fire, but Lloyd got in the way."

Relief washes over her as she realizes she's been worrying for no reason. But it's still concerning that someone is targeting the Ridgeways.

Steve's phone rings. He stands as he answers it. "Great, thanks." He hangs up. "That was the front desk. Chad's here. I called him and asked if he'd speak to me. Wanna join us?"

She picks up her cup. "Hell, yeah."

CHAPTER THIRTY-EIGHT

Chad Peters is a soft-spoken thirty-five-year-old who comes across as genuinely wanting to help them. "Oh, sure," he says in answer to Steve's question about whether he's close with his aunt and uncle. "Bernie always says I'm the son she never had. She's very big on family."

Madison wonders why Bernie had only two children if family means that much to her. Perhaps she had medical issues that stopped her from having more. She smiles. "That must be nice, to have such a close-knit family."

He gives her a sympathetic look. "Forgive me for saying, Detective, but I've heard about *your* family in the press, given everything that's happened over the years. I can't imagine how you got through those difficult times without being able to turn to them for support, since your sister in particular has been the cause of most of your problems. I'd be lost without my family, and without Jesus, of course. Do you attend church?"

She squirms in her seat, not wanting to get into a discussion about faith, not because she doesn't believe, but because this isn't about her. "It's amazing where you can draw strength from when you really need it," she says.

"Bernie and my great-aunt Ida are firm believers that blood is thicker than water," says Chad sadly. "I'm going to miss Ida. Any issue that any of us faced, she would always say, 'This will be handled by the family,' but I think anyone can become blood if you open your heart to them. We've become so inward-focused and paranoid as a society that we no longer have a sense of community. Instead, we shut everyone out in fear." He shakes his head. "It's such a shame. I think living our lives online is part of the problem. If we started talking to our neighbors again, we'd feel more involved in our communities, which would solve most of the world's problems, in my humble opinion."

Madison smiles but doesn't respond. It must be nice to have such a positive outlook. Maybe Chad has never been betrayed by someone he trusts. She feels bad for thinking it, but sometimes experience tells you that opening your heart to people leaves it vulnerable to attack.

"We're obviously investigating the murder of Lloyd Maxwell at Detective Harper's wedding," says Steve, "and we're considering whether Lloyd was shot by accident. Now, I'm assuming you don't have any enemies, given how friendly you are," he smiles to put Chad at ease, "but we need to rule you out as the intended target."

Chad sits up straight, concern washing over his face. "Oh, I can't imagine who *I* might've upset!"

"No one at all?" Steve presses. "You've never exchanged harsh words with someone, or forgotten to pay back a debt to a friend, or cut someone off in traffic so bad they threatened you?"

"Gosh, no. That's not me at all. I'd immediately apologize if I ever hurt or offended anyone. I wouldn't be able to sleep at night. You can ask my husband, Patrick. He knows I'm a big crybaby when it comes to upsetting anyone. I'd rather be upset myself. He says I'm a people-pleaser, but I just enjoy making people happy."

Madison believes him. He appears to be one of those rare beings who thrives by helping others.

Picking up on the fact that Chad is in a same-sex relationship, Steve asks, "What about any negative reactions to your relationship with your partner? I know homophobia is still rife in some places. Has anyone ever threatened you because of that?"

Pressing a hand to his chest, Chad says, "Not at all! Especially not my family." But he hesitates for a second before adding, "I mean, Patrick and I did have to put up with some gossip at our church when we first got together, but now those very same people are the ones who invite us for lunch after the service." He smiles, looking proud of himself. "We won them round eventually."

Madison smiles.

"Okay," says Steve, dropping his pen. "Well, we had to ask. Just to be sure."

Before they let the man go, Madison asks, "How are you coping with your recent bereavements? I can't imagine how hard it is to lose three family members all at once."

Chad nods, his smile fading. "It's slightly easier when you have faith, but I see everyone around me crumbling, so it does take its toll. I guess my thoughts get stuck on poor little Lucy and what she must have suffered before finally being at peace." His eyes well up. "She was such a vivacious little girl."

Images of Lucy's final moments run through Madison's mind. How she was desperate to get under her bed, thinking that would stop her mother's killer from reaching her. Madison will never get those images out of her head, like those of so many other victims. They tend to flash through her thoughts on the nights when sleep evades her. "I'm so sorry."

"Thank you. I'm helping my uncle Colt plan the funerals, which gives me something to focus on. Bernie's just not up to it, understandably. I've picked out some wonderful hymns that should bring them comfort during what will be an unbearable day."

Madison smiles sympathetically before asking, "Do you know if Colt or Bernie have any enemies or... rifts with anyone? It's just such a coincidence for one family to experience two separate homicides in the same week. We're wondering if the attacks were personal."

"Gosh, I don't know," Chad says. "I can't imagine they've upset anyone, especially Colt, who's so mild-mannered and accommodating. He has a heart of gold, except when it comes to Great-Aunt Ida, but then that's understandable." He chuckles. "I don't like to speak poorly of the dead, Detectives, but her demise, while obviously horrible, isn't such a shock. You kind of wonder how it never happened sooner. You know what I mean?"

"We've heard she was... a force to be reckoned with," she says diplomatically.

He scoffs. "Yes, that and the rumors about her killing her husband back in the day."

Madison frowns. "What do you mean?"

"Oh, don't worry," he says. "They're just rumors. You more than anyone should know what this town is like for gossip!" He leans forward. "I guess it's okay to talk about this now she's gone, but her husband, Phil, just vanished one day. Ida said he took off with a lover, leaving her and Bernie high and dry, but because she was so... *cantankerous*, shall we say, it became an urban myth that she killed him in a fit of rage and buried him in the backyard. The kids from my school even made up a song about her." He laughs. "I can't remember how it goes now, but it came in useful having a relative with a fierce reputation. Whenever I was bullied during high school for being gay, I'd tell them I'd get my great-aunt to cut them up into little pieces and feed them to some pigs."

Steve stifles a laugh.

"Why would she kill her husband?" asks Madison. "Was their relationship bad?"

"She didn't!" says Chad, smiling. "It was just a stupid rumor. But many thought Phil was henpecked during their marriage. Apparently he toed the line in fear of her wrath." He chuckles. "I guess he finally built the courage to leave her, and who can blame him, right?"

Madison doesn't find domestic abuse funny. She can see why Ida got a reputation for having killed her husband, but it's far more likely that he took off to escape a loveless marriage, given how difficult she must have been to live with. It sounds like Bernie's father was in a similar position to Colt: henpecked. "Do you know of anyone Ida might have offended recently, or anyone who held a grudge against her?"

Chad takes a deep breath. "Well, if I were Ryan Simmonds, I'd be a little mad at the things she said about him on camera. Not that I'm pointing fingers, of course. I'm simply answering your question."

Ryan again. All roads seem to lead to him. "Of course," Madison says. "Well, thanks for coming in to see us. It was a pleasure to meet you."

Steve walks him out as Madison stays behind. She can't imagine anyone wanting to harm Chad Peters, but she can't ignore the fact that he's related to the Ridgeways, which means he makes a more likely target than Lloyd Maxwell, or anyone else present at the wedding. Her gut tells her that as that's the only potential link they have between the murders, someone might be trying to destroy the entire family. But what she can't figure out is *why*.

CHAPTER THIRTY-NINE

The afternoon speeds by as Madison gets lost in a sea of background checks, witness statements and theories. When the clock hits five, she leans back in her seat and stretches, her back aching from being hunched at her desk for too long. She's considering what to make for dinner later when her phone buzzes with a text from Nate.

Come home. We're getting married. I can't wait any longer.

Her stomach flips with nerves as she leans back in her seat. "He wants to get married *now*?" she mumbles.

Adams looks up from his desk. "What's that?" Luckily his phone rings, distracting him before she has to answer. For some reason, she doesn't want anyone to know she's about to get married. Perhaps because she doesn't want to get emotional.

She takes a deep breath and looks out the window. The late-afternoon sun is starting to cast shadows across the parking lot. It's a beautiful day for a wedding, depending on where Nate wants to do it. Maybe it's at their house, which is fine with her.

It would be good to get it out of the way. She feels bad for thinking of it like a chore, but her main focus right now is on finding the person who seems hell-bent on taking out the entire Ridgeway family one by one. Maybe she should get them some protection. Station an officer outside their property.

Her phone pings again.

So?? Are you on your way?

She replies.

Where will we do it?

His response is immediate.

Don't worry about a thing. Me and Owen have it covered. Just come home.

She realizes her hands are trembling with nerves. She self-consciously switches her computer off and grabs her purse, nervous that Adams and Steve might question where she's going. They don't. They're too busy with work. She pops her head into Chief Mendes's office on her way past. "I'm going home for an early dinner. I'll probably be back later. That okay?"

Mendes looks at her with an extra-wide smile. "Of course it is. Have fun."

Madison frowns as she leaves. Is the chief in on it? Probably. Nate must've checked it would be okay for her to leave work early. She pauses before glancing back over her shoulder and realizes everyone's stopped what they're doing to watch her leave. Adams is grinning in that inane way of his. Shelley pokes her head out of the kitchen, smiling at her with tears in her eyes.

It brings tears to Madison's eyes too. They all know. They probably all want to come too, but she'd told Nate she wanted something small and quick the second time around. It means less can go wrong.

She blinks back the tears as she exits the station on her way to marry her soulmate.

Sitting in her car outside her home, Madison's reluctant to get out. She doesn't know what the plan is. All she knows is that she's about to get married while her sister is slowly dying upstairs. The two events are on opposite ends of the spectrum and both bring different emotions, making her feel like she won't be able to enjoy the wedding.

She pushes the thought away, composing herself. For once in her life, this is about *her*, not Angie. But still, she feels anxious in case something goes wrong—which, considering how their first wedding ended, isn't impossible. Glancing at the quiet neighborhood around her, she doesn't see any potential threats. She takes a deep breath. Knowing she can't live her life in fear, she slips out of the car and heads inside, where Brody greets her excitedly at the door. He has his bowtie on again, making her laugh. "You're so damn cute, Brody Monroe. Anyone ever tell you that?"

"They tell him all the time," says Owen as he approaches her. "But nobody tells me that anymore."

She laughs. Owen's wearing a suit but without a tie, and his white shirt is unbuttoned at the top and untucked. He's dressed more casually than their first wedding and it brings her some relief. It means the event will be less formal this time around. "Where's Nate?"

"In the backyard, putting the final touches together. He says you need to change out of your work clothes into whatever makes you feel like you're on vacation."

For some reason, she wants to cry. She doesn't deserve Nate. "I'll need to shower first."

"That's fine," says Owen. "He says you're worth the wait."

Madison hugs him quickly before rushing upstairs. Angie's door is closed, so she heads to the bathroom and showers before choosing a light summer dress and sandals and fixing her makeup. Before heading downstairs, she hesitates outside her sister's room, not knowing whether to see her first. Eventually, guilt gets the better of her and she knocks lightly.

"Come in," says Angie. She's sitting in bed, propped up with cushions, with the TV on low. Her face is gaunt. "You look nice. I never see you dressed up."

Madison steps closer to the bed. "We're about to get married."

"In the backyard?" Angie snorts. "I thought your man could afford something better than that."

Madison lets the dig slide. She refuses to let her sister ruin it. "How're you feeling?"

Angie scoffs. "How'd you think? I'm in constant pain and I feel sick all the time even though I'm starving."

Madison lowers her eyes. "I'm sorry. I wish there was something I could do."

"There is. Leave your service weapon here while you go marry Prince Charming. If you're worried about the mess, I can tape a bag around my head."

Madison meets her sister's gaze and knows she means it. It makes her feel sick. "Don't talk like that, Angie. You know I can't—"

Angie waves a dismissive hand. "I know, I know. You'd never break the law. You always were a Miss Goody Two-Shoes. I guess I'll just die in pain. That would probably make you happy, right? The perfect wedding gift."

Madison takes a deep breath. "I'm not doing this. Not right before I get married. I should go."

"Wait!" says her sister. "I'm sorry, alright? It's just hard to be happy for people who still have their whole lives ahead of them." She sighs. "I'll try harder." She sips some water from her nightstand. "Tell me something. Does the fact you're letting me spend my last days here mean you've finally forgiven me for everything that happened?"

"You mean for everything you did?" says Madison, needing to hold her accountable, even now.

Angie nods resentfully.

"Depends. Do you regret it? And don't lie just because we're taking care of you and you're worried I'll kick you out if you say no."

Her sister gives her a look. "Madison, I'm *dying*. Why would I lie? I literally have nothing to lose."

"So do you regret it?" Madison presses.

"Yes, I do. Do you forgive me?"

She takes a deep breath. "I forgive you for what you did to me. But only Owen can forgive you for what you did to him. How your actions affected him."

"He's already forgiven me."

"He has?" She's surprised. She didn't even know Owen had been to see his aunt.

Angie nods. A silence falls over them, until she says, "Think I'll go to hell for everything me and Wyatt did?"

Madison opens her mouth to speak, but she's at a loss for words. Angie did some terrible, unforgivable things. But her choices also negatively impacted herself. Life hasn't been easy for her, so Madison hopes that in death she finally finds some peace. "No. I think you'll just go to sleep."

Tears brim Angie's eyes. "Let's hope God's as forgiving as you are."

Madison steps forward and squeezes her sister's hand, fighting back a surge of tears that threatens to overwhelm her. Angie is the last link to her parents. Once she's gone, Madison's the last one standing. What she'd give to have her parents back. "God, I wish we'd done things differently. Everything that happened was all so pointless." She self-consciously wipes her tears away.

Angie nods thoughtfully. "That's the problem with life. You only get one chance at it, and wisdom doesn't come until it's too late. Maybe if Dad hadn't walked out on us when we were younger, things would've been different."

Madison doesn't think so. Angie was already resentful of her long before then. She thought their father favored Madison over her, when in reality they just had a shared interest in law enforcement.

Owen knocks on the door. "Are you ready?"

Angie smiles up at him, moving her hand out of Madison's grasp. "Don't you look all grown up. I can picture you as a lawyer in that suit."

"I'm not going to be a lawyer anymore," he says. "I changed my mind. I'm going to be a cop, like Mom."

Madison's eyes fill with tears again. She's so proud of him and how he's coped with everything he's been through. He could have turned out so differently.

"A cop?" says Angie, her eyes narrowing. "Just what we need, another cop in the family." She smiles, but Madison thinks she sees traces of the real woman behind the expression, and she suddenly realizes that if her sister wasn't dying and didn't need their help, she would be exactly the same bitter person she always has been. The thought fills her with sadness, as it means Angie didn't learn from any of her mistakes.

"I need to go." She turns.

"Fine," says Angie. "But open the window wide, would you? I want to listen in to your wedding. Share in your joy and all that."

Owen pushes the window open more before approaching Madison and giving her his arm. "Ready?"

Madison nods. As they head for the door, Angie says, "Congratulations, sis. Save me some cake."

Madison turns to look at her. She's a shadow of her former self. Barely recognizable now. It's painful to see her this way, no matter what's happened between them. "Sure, Angie."

She lets Owen lead her out of the room.

CHAPTER FORTY

Madison rises above the low-level anxiety in her chest that convinces her this is going to end badly. She lets Owen lead her into their peaceful, sunny backyard. The effort he and Nate have gone to is touching. A beautiful rose arch sits at the end of the makeshift aisle, smothered in white climbing roses and humming with bees. Flowers and garlands cover every outdoor surface, their sweet floral aromas filling the air. A table to the right is filled with buffet food, a simple wedding cake and bottles of champagne on ice. It's all far too much just for them, but that's when she notices their only wedding guests: Vince Rader from Ruby's Diner, and Stella Myers from dispatch. She's glad they're here together. She's noticed how they've grown close lately.

Vince is suited, wearing his shirt buttoned with a tie, regardless of how casual the wedding is supposed to be this time around. Stella's wearing a simple pale-blue summer dress with sandals and a rose in her hair. Madison spots Bandit in Vince's arms. The cat is fast asleep, enjoying the warm evening sunshine on his face. She steps forward and hugs Stella before smiling at Vince. "Thanks for coming, you guys."

"Wouldn't miss it for the world." Vince places Bandit on a cushioned chair, then embraces Madison. He kisses her cheek before pulling back. "Now, let's get this deal sealed once and for all, shall we? Some of us are ready to call in our bets."

"Vince!" says Stella, shocked.

"It's okay," says Madison. "Adams told me ages ago that people were taking bets on whether Nate and I would ever make it down the aisle." She's glad to finally prove some of them wrong.

She turns to where Nate's waiting for her beside the rose arch. He's dressed in suit pants and a crisp white shirt, minus a jacket and tie. He looks as handsome as ever and the occasion feels more relaxed than their first attempt. As a result, *she's* more relaxed.

He holds out his hand, which she takes. "Are you ready?" he asks.

She nods, and she means it. They've delayed for too long. Brody strolls over to be near them, somehow resisting the spread Vince has prepared. Owen comes and stands between them, a few steps back. Madison frowns at him. "*You're* marrying us?"

He leans in and whispers, "Technically, all you need to do is sign the papers, but Nate thought this would be a nice touch."

She laughs. "Okay, fine."

"Wave to the camera." Owen nods to his phone, which is set up on a tripod to record the nuptials.

She rolls her eyes. "Please tell me you're not livestreaming this?"

"That's a great idea!" he says. "Why didn't I think of that?"

She and Nate wave to the camera before Owen clears his throat and retrieves a piece of paper from his pocket. He looks her in the eye as he begins. "Nate said we don't need to do any formal reading or anything, I can just ask if you agree to be married. But before I do that, I wanted to let you both know how important you are to me."

Tears immediately spring to her eyes. "Oh boy," she whispers, lowering her gaze and focusing on Brody. Nate squeezes her hand.

"The way I see it, Mom," Owen goes on, speaking louder than necessary, which makes Madison realize he's intending for his aunt to hear him through her open window. She braces herself for what he's about to say. "If you hadn't gone to prison, you would never have lost me for those years we were apart. And if you'd hadn't needed to look for me when you were released, you would never have sought the help of a private investigator." He glances at Nate and smiles.

Madison sees tears building in Nate's eyes. He must be thinking the same: that their meeting could easily have never happened. She can't imagine what they'd both be doing now if they hadn't met. It doesn't bear thinking about.

"But luckily for me," Owen continues, "you found one so loaded he could pay for my college education, meaning I never need to flip burgers at some fast-food joint in return for minimum wage."

Vince chuckles to himself. "There's always a job waiting for you at Ruby's Diner, young man," he says. "Everyone should experience financial hardship at least once in their lives. Helps build character."

"With all due respect," says Owen, "I've been through so much hardship already that I'm at risk of having too much character."

Madison shakes her head as she laughs, although he's not wrong.

Owen turns serious before continuing. "Mom, you meeting Nate was the best thing that ever happened to us, and all of us, Vince included, could see that you were meant to be together. But for some reason, you couldn't see it for yourselves. At least, not right away."

Madison meets Nate's gaze. Owen's right, of course. It took

them too long to take a chance on each other, but only because they'd both been so badly burned by the cards they'd been dealt up until now.

"Nate," Owen turns to look at him, "I know you're not my dad, but you've cared more for me in the time I've known you than my real dad did my entire life." He suddenly wipes his damp eyes. "I know I can go to you with any problem, no matter how big or small, and you'll not only help me solve it because I'm Madison's son, you'll help me solve it because you feel protective toward me. That's a good feeling. Many kids my age don't have anyone to care about them, and I'll never take that for granted, so thank you."

Nate squeezes Owen's shoulder and nods, unable to speak without his emotion spilling out of him.

Madison has no choice but to let her tears run down her face, ruining her makeup. At this point, there's no keeping them in. Stella's crying now too.

"And Mom?"

She braces herself again.

"I know that those years we spent apart were unbearable for you, and then seeing me leave for college was a reminder of that time and triggered all your worst fears, but you still allow me to live my life how I want to. I'm so proud that you're a detective, and that you spend your life helping others, even though you could easily have given up years ago. You're my motivation to try to be the best I can. I may move away, get married and have kids—"

"Wait, what?" Her heart starts thumping. "Not anytime soon, right?"

He laughs. "No. Not anytime soon. But I know that when I eventually start my own family, you'll have Nate to take care of you. And there's no better feeling in the world than to know my mom's going to be safe." He clears his throat again before looking at Vince, who's brought over a tray filled with glasses of chilled pink champagne. "So I'd like to raise a glass to my mom and Nate, two people who have every reason to be bitter at the world but who instead choose to make a positive difference to other people's lives. Cheers!"

They clink glasses before sipping the champagne.

"Oh crap," says Owen. "I forgot to ask. Mom? Do you take Nate to be your lawfully wedded husband?"

She laughs. "I do."

"Nate? Do you *definitely* want Mom as your lawfully wedded wife?"

Nate's dark blue eyes meet Madison's. "I always have, and I always will."

"Phew!" says Owen. "Then I guess you need these." He pulls a ring box from his pocket and watches as they exchange simple platinum wedding bands. "I guess you two should probably kiss to seal the deal, or whatever."

Nate takes Madison's glass and gives both hers and his to Vince, while Owen grabs his phone to capture the moment with some photos. Nate embraces and kisses her while Vince, Stella and Owen cheer. Brody jumps up at them, breaking them apart.

"Time to get this party started!" says Owen, choosing a tune from his playlist that's so weird Vince and Nate exchange confused looks.

"What the hell is this?" says Vince.

Nate shrugs. "Damned if I know. Sounds like someone in pain if you ask me."

Madison laughs. "You two sound so old. I like it!" She starts dancing with Stella.

"Can we cut the cake now?" says Owen. "Brody's been very patient."

"Sure," she says. "He can have the first slice."

. . .

Later, after posing for more formal photos, signing the necessary paperwork and enjoying the food Vince prepared, Madison and Nate leave Owen and their two guests outside with the pets as they head upstairs. Madison's carefully balancing a slice of wedding cake and a glass of champagne on a tray. She knows Angie might not want either, due to her nausea and meds, but she wants her to at least feel included.

She knocks on the door, but there's no answer. Turning to Nate, she whispers, "She must be asleep. What do you think, shall we come back later?"

"Yeah, but let's close her window so we don't wake her with Owen's *music*." He makes air quotes.

She laughs quietly before opening the door and stepping inside. Nate goes to the window, pulling it closed.

Madison turns to the bed and frowns. Her heart starts pounding a little harder as she realizes Angie's expression is slack, her skin has a gray tone to it and her lips are blue. Her sister's right hand is lightly clutching an empty glass, the one that contained water. "Oh my God. Angie?" She places the tray on the nightstand and with trembling hands tries to rouse her sister by shaking her. "*Angie?* Can you hear me?"

No response. Madison doesn't want to accept what this means. "Angie! Wake up!" Her throat seizes as she tries to hold back a sob. She needs to wake her sister. This can't be the end.

Nate silently leans in and feels Angie's neck for a pulse. He tries her wrist next before gently lowering her arm back onto the bed, defeated. With sorrow in his eyes, he looks at Madison, not wanting to say what she already knows, but knowing he has to. "I'm so sorry. It's too late. She's gone."

Madison feels the walls close in on her. She wants to keep shaking her sister. "What? No. She can't be dead." She doesn't want to believe it. She feels for a pulse, but doesn't find one. Angie's eyes are fixed, staring right through her. Speechless, she doesn't know what to think or feel. It's too soon. She thought Angie had weeks, if not months left.

She spots something in her sister's mouth. "What the hell is that?" She opens her jaw and finds two unswallowed pills. In Angie's other hand is a clear bag. Blood roars in her ears as she realizes what Angie's done. "She's overdosed."

"Impossible," says Nate. "I made sure to keep her pills downstairs. She didn't have the strength to go down there. I was giving them to her every few hours."

Madison lowers herself onto the bed, not trusting her trembling legs to hold her as shock sets in. "She either kept some hidden on her when you moved her in, or she saved them up, building a stash so she could do this." She looks at her sister's lifeless body, unable to believe she's no longer with them. A sob finally breaks free, and she turns to Nate with tears streaming down her face. "Why did she do this during our wedding?" She wipes her eyes. "Is that selfish of me? Am I underestimating how bad the pain was for her?"

Nate embraces her. He looks angry. "Maybe. Or perhaps this was her final act of vengeance." He pulls back and looks her in the eye. "She couldn't bear to see you happy, Madison, so this doesn't surprise me at all. It saddens me, and it pisses me off because we had such a beautiful wedding and she's tried to ruin it, but it doesn't surprise me. I should've known she'd try something. You have everything she ever wanted: your health, a partner who loves you, a son who's thriving... She was jealous. It's as simple as that."

Madison's bitterly disappointed. Part of her wants to believe Angie's timing wasn't deliberate. But perhaps she's too naïve when it comes to her sister and that's been the problem all along. "I wish she hadn't died all alone up here."

Nate strokes her back. "She went out on her own terms. It's exactly what she wanted. You did everything you could for her, that's all you need to focus on."

She knows he's right, but somehow, it doesn't seem enough.

CHAPTER FORTY-ONE

The next morning doesn't feel as celebratory as Nate had hoped, considering he and Madison are newlyweds. Angie's body has been removed from the house. Once Conrad confirms her cause of death, she can be released to a funeral home, then Nate can help Madison plan her sister's cremation.

Madison's holding it together, but he knows she didn't get any sleep last night. And he heard her sobbing in the shower this morning. She won't want him worrying about her, though. She wants to return to work this morning so she can focus on her investigations, so he's arranged for them to meet with Pam Smith and Hank Larson first thing. They need to see if Sharon Smith's disappearance could be linked to Dominic and Charlie Larson's. Pam texted him to say Hank had been discharged from the hospital overnight, although he's still frail apparently.

"Ready to go?" he asks as Madison enters the kitchen.

She nods, offering a weak smile. Her eyes are red from crying. He doesn't want to set her off again as he knows she won't want to dwell on Angie's death, so he resists hugging her. "Sure you don't want any breakfast? We have plenty of food left over from yesterday in the refrigerator."

She grimaces. "Owen can have that. I can't stomach anything. This will do for now." She gestures to the travel mug in her hand, which Nate filled with coffee.

"Okay." He goes to the door, followed by Brody. "You can't come this time, boy. I'll pick you up later, okay?"

Brody gives a dissatisfied grunt and slides his front legs forward on the hardwood floor so that he's resting on his belly.

Madison smiles down at him. "Go wake your brother instead."

Nate had heard Owen moving around in his room until the early hours, probably also unsettled by Angie's death. They leave the house, and Nate keeps one eye on Madison as he drives. When they stop at a red light, he says, "I've told Chief Mendes about Angie, so that none of the team say the wrong thing." But also so she goes easy on Madison. The chief suggested she take some time off to deal with her grief, but also acknowledged that probably wasn't going to happen. She was right. Madison's the type of person who uses work to distract herself from pain. She'll grieve in her own time.

She nods. "Okay." Large sunglasses cover her eyes.

He squeezes her hand. "I know it sucks right now, but once we get through Angie's cremation, we can try to move on."

She nods again, offering a brief smile. "Okay."

His heart breaks for her. Grief is bad enough in normal circumstances, but when you have a complicated relationship with the person who died, it can be even harder. Partly because you can no longer fool yourself that it will be mended one day. Instead, you have to try to come to terms with the knowledge that you never had the relationship you wanted with them, and now you never will. It's so brutally final.

When they pull up outside Hank Larson's house, Madison gets out first. It's warm as they walk to the front door and knock. The birds are singing and there's not a cloud in the sky.

Pam opens the door and smiles at Nate. "Morning." She

reluctantly nods at Madison. "Detective." Nate remembers what she said about her family not having much faith in law enforcement because Bill Harper never found Sharon thirty years ago. He thinks she might have some underlying hostility for Madison, being Bill's daughter.

They enter the house. Hank is sitting on the couch in the living room with a blanket over his lap. He's pale but alert, reading a newspaper. When he spots them, he lowers it, removing his glasses.

"Hi, Mr. Larson," says Madison. "This is my partner—sorry, *husband*—Nate Monroe." She reddens. It's the first time she's been able to call him that.

Nate steps forward and shakes his hand. "Pleasure."

Pam's studying them with interest. "I thought your wedding was interrupted by a shooter? I saw it on the news."

"It was," says Nate. "So we had a small backyard wedding yesterday evening. With no interruptions this time."

"Well, congratulations." Pam looks at Madison. "So are you Detective Monroe now?"

"No," says Madison. "I'm keeping my last name since there's no one left in my family to—" She suddenly chokes up.

Nate gently rubs her back. By way of explanation, he says, "Madison lost her sister last night. It's a difficult time."

"Oh my goodness," says Pam, pressing her hand to her chest. "I'm so sorry. I shouldn't have asked. It's none of my business."

"My condolences," says Hank, his eyes full of compassion.

Madison clears her throat and attempts to laugh it off. "Thank you, but ignore me. I'll be fine." She takes a deep breath to compose herself before turning to Hank. "Sorry to bother you when you're fresh out of the hospital, Mr. Larson—"

"Please, call me Hank." He gestures to the armchairs opposite him, so they sit. Pam chooses a seat next to her brother.

"You obviously know Nate's looking into Sharon's disappearance," Madison continues, "and my team and I are investigating Dominic and Charlie's." Hank nods. "When we learned you and Pam were siblings, we realized we should probably check whether the two cases are linked, just in case that provides us with a potential new lead."

Pam frowns. "But they happened thirty years apart, and Sharon wasn't related to Dominic or Charlie."

"I know," says Madison. "But it's incredibly bad luck for both of you to have loved ones go missing. Are you okay with us visiting you together like this or would you prefer we do this separately? Nate can talk to you, Pam, and I can stay with Hank. It's completely up to you."

Pam and Hank look at each other and shrug. "It's probably better this way," says Pam. "We need all the help we can get to find Sharon as well as Dominic and Charlie."

"Okay, great," says Madison. "Now, I don't know as much as Nate does about Sharon's disappearance, so forgive me for going back to basics, but could you tell me what she was doing on the day she vanished?"

Pam takes a deep breath, readying herself to relive it yet again. "It was her day off work—she was an assistant florist. We'd spent the whole day together, going to the pictures in the early afternoon, followed by dinner with Hank." Hank nods at the memory before Pam continues. "At around six p.m., Sharon left to go home. She lived in a small house with two other women as roommates. She told me she wanted a bath and an early night. Being eight months pregnant was taking its toll on her."

"Were her roommates questioned about what happened?" asks Madison.

"Yes," says Pam. "But it was confirmed that they'd both been at work until midnight, so Sharon was home alone from six fifteen onward."

Nate had tried to track down the roommates but discovered

they'd both moved away years ago after marrying and starting families. He has to assume Bill Harper interviewed them after Sharon's disappearance and found no reason to suspect them of involvement. Their names certainly haven't come up as potential persons of interest while he's been investigating.

"The state of her room suggested she'd gotten into bed after her bath and watched some TV," says Pam. "The TV was still on when her roommates returned home together, so they assumed she was in bed, which means no one knows what time she actually vanished."

"When did someone first notice?" asks Madison.

"I called her the next morning on the landline. Her roommate answered and offered to go wake her, but I figured I should let her sleep." Pam lowers her eyes. "If I hadn't, maybe we could have acted sooner and possibly found her before it was too late."

"Not necessarily," says Nate. "It's best not to think like that or the what-ifs will drive you insane."

"Unfortunately," says Pam, "that's easier said than done." When Hank coughs, she hands him a glass of water.

"So what time did you actually discover Sharon was missing?" Madison presses.

With one eye on her brother, Pam explains, "I went to her house at midday and let myself in using my spare key. One of her roommates was eating lunch and said she hadn't seen Sharon all morning but the TV was still on in her room. Sharon regularly fell asleep in front of the TV, so that wasn't unusual. I decided to wake her. I knocked on her door and entered, but she wasn't there. Her bedsheets were thrown back, making it look as though she'd gotten out of bed. Her pajamas were lying on top. A pair of her sneakers was missing, along with some clothes, suggesting she'd changed her mind about an early night and gone out again."

"But you don't know where?" asks Madison.

"Right."

"When did you notify the police?" she asks.

"I called them right away and was told she'd probably turn up in a couple of hours, so I shouldn't worry. It was infuriating, but there was nothing to suggest she'd been taken or hurt. No blood, or signs of a struggle. In a way, I felt a little better, because if the police weren't concerned, then I assumed I shouldn't be. That was before cell phones, you see, so we weren't used to being in touch with each other twenty-four-seven. But by the end of the afternoon, I was filled with dread, so I called the police again and they sent a detective out." She looks at Madison. "Your father."

Madison shifts position as Nate takes over. "And Bill didn't find anything concerning, right?"

"He told me he'd found no signs of foul play," says Pam. "But I felt that his eyes betrayed his concern. Especially as Sharon was heavily pregnant."

Hank's shaking his head. "It was a terrible thing."

Nate looks at him. "Pam mentioned it was you who introduced her to Sharon. Is that right?"

He nods. "Sharon was a beautiful person, inside and out. She made my sister very happy, and she would've made a wonderful mother to their child."

Madison frowns. "Just remind me, who was the baby's father?"

Pam sniffs but remains silent. Hank doesn't speak either, so Nate says, "Sharon's pregnancy was the result of a sexual assault."

"I'm sorry," says Madison. "That's terrible. Did she reveal who assaulted her?"

"No," says Pam. "But remarkably, she was able to put it behind her. She said the baby would be a blessing because we might never have become parents otherwise." She lowers her eyes. "Not that we ever did."

Nate can tell Madison's brain is in overdrive as she tries to connect the dots. "Could she have been covering for the baby's father, protecting his identity for a reason?" she asks.

Pam's head snaps up. "What do you mean?"

"Please don't take offense at this," says Madison. "But is there any possibility that she wanted to get pregnant and asked someone to help her with that?"

Pam looks away. "I don't know. I can't imagine she would have. Besides, who would she even ask? Our circle was pretty tight. It was just me, Sharon and Hank."

Madison looks at Hank, and Nate realizes this is where she meant to go. He suddenly feels stupid for not even considering Hank could be the baby's father. "Hank?" she says. "Did Sharon ask for *your* help to get pregnant?"

Pam looks at her brother, alarmed, but he doesn't respond.

"Is that what happened?" says Madison gently. "You knew your sister and her girlfriend wanted children, so you offered to help them?"

Eventually, he shakes his head. "I absolutely would've done so if they'd asked, but they didn't. They didn't need me because someone else got Sharon pregnant."

Nate knows they can't prove that without Sharon's or the baby's body.

Pam backs her brother up. "Trust me, that's *not* what happened. Sharon would have sought my permission if she was thinking of asking Hank to do something like that. You have to understand, we'd never even discussed having children before she got pregnant. It wasn't planned at all."

Madison nods. "Okay. Well, at least I can rule that out now." She takes a deep breath. "I assume you tried asking who assaulted her?"

"Of course," Pam says with tears in her eyes. "But she told me to leave it, to see her pregnancy as a positive thing for us. I respected that. What choice did I have? It was already done.

Besides, it didn't matter who the father was. Not to us. The child was going to be *ours*. With no male involvement except for his uncle."

Nate believes them. He thinks Hank would have admitted being the baby's father by now if he was, because he would've known that ruling out the father as the main suspect in Sharon's disappearance would have left the police free to focus on other individuals.

Madison moves on. "Okay. Thanks for being so open with us. I don't enjoy asking probing questions, but unfortunately, it's my job."

"I understand," says Pam, but she does look a little offended. It's understandable, as it must be difficult to consider that the person you loved so dearly could have been lying to you.

"We're just happy you're still looking for her," says Hank. "Hopefully you'll find my boys soon too, before it's too late for me to see them again." He breaks into another coughing fit.

Madison stands, offering a reassuring smile. "We're certainly trying. You take care of yourself, Hank."

Pam leads her and Nate to the front door, where they say their goodbyes before exiting.

Once outside, Madison turns to Nate. "I think they're telling the truth, that Sharon was raped by an unknown attacker, which means the baby's father makes the best suspect for her disappearance. Maybe he was a married man who didn't want to lose his wife and reputation or pay child support." She sighs. "I don't have time to reopen a cold case, and Chief Mendes wouldn't let me anyway, not without new evidence. You know how she is."

Nate nods. "The more I think about it, the more I suspect Sharon's mother and ex-boyfriend were involved in her disappearance. Justin could've harmed her as payback for supposedly humiliating him." He takes a deep breath. "Now you've spoken to Pam and Hank about it, does that mean you can at least check your dad's case notes and see if there's anything that could help me moving forward?"

She slips her sunglasses back on. "Maybe. I'll run it past Mendes and see what she says. She wants you on the team one day anyway."

He raises his eyebrows. "She does?"

Madison smiles properly for the first time today. "It probably has something to do with the generous donations you keep making to the department."

Nate had put in a proposal for his donations to build a crime lab at the station, as it's desperately needed. He also suggested that he could join the department as a cold-case investigator. But with no formal law-enforcement training, he thought it had been a long shot. He just wanted to be able to work closer with Madison, and Owen too, when he eventually joins the team as a rookie officer. "Think you could stand seeing even more of me every day?" he asks, smiling.

She snorts. "Are you kidding? If you worked at the station, I'd have someone to bring me coffee and snacks all day long."

Nate kisses her forehead before embracing her, relieved to see his wife smiling again.

CHAPTER FORTY-TWO

After going their separate ways, Madison decides to check on Colt Ridgeway. He may be able to shed some light on why the wedding shooter might have been targeting his nephew, Chad. That's not the only reason she wants to see him, though. Now his mother-in-law is dead, and his wife is staying with their remaining daughter in Denver, she's worried he may have too much time on his hands. He could be dwelling on his hatred of Ryan Simmonds. He and Bernie have been hell-bent on blaming Ryan for everything that's happened, but Ryan has an alibi for Ida's murder and Colt currently makes a better suspect for that.

She parks outside his house and exits her vehicle, stepping into the midmorning sunshine. Before she can approach the house, her phone buzzes in her pocket. It's a text from Kate Flynn, her reporter friend.

I'm hearing rumors your sister has passed away. It's not true, is it?

Madison's stomach sinks. Word spreads quickly in this town. She types a response.

It is. Happened last night. She was battling cancer.

She doesn't mention the suspected drug overdose but knows the press will find out once Conrad confirms her cause of death. Kate's quick to reply.

I'm so sorry. Brace yourself for the headlines.

Dread threatens to overwhelm Madison as she realizes the media will dredge up the past when reporting on Angie's death. They'll rehash all her crimes, and the damage done. She should let Owen know. She sends Kate a thumbs-up emoji and quickly texts her son.

Avoid the news. They've heard Angie's dead, so it's a matter of time before they cover it. Please don't watch it.

He replies instantly.

Sure. I guess it was inevitable. RU OK?

She smiles.

Fine. Keeping busy. Make sure you do too.

Before she can slip her phone away, Kate texts again.

Call me if you need me, or if you ever just want to let off steam and get drunk.

Madison would love to get drunk, but knows she can't. She has killers to catch.

Will do. Thanks.

She hasn't seen enough of her friend lately, and Kate will probably be mad when she finds out she wasn't invited to yesterday's nuptials, but Madison didn't want a fuss. The evening was perfect with just the five of them present. Or it was until Angie passed. She still can't believe her sister's gone. It doesn't feel real yet.

Pushing the thought aside, she slips her phone away and approaches Colt's house. She knocks loudly on the door, then turns her face to the sun to try to soak up some vitamin D while she waits for him to appear. When she realizes no one is going to answer, she tries again. Colt's car is in the driveway, so there's no reason to believe he's out running errands or visiting friends. She spots a rolled-up newspaper on the front lawn. Maybe he's still sleeping. She checks her phone for the time. It's almost 10:30 a.m.

She walks along the porch and peers into the living room window. The blind is drawn but there's a gap at the bottom where it doesn't meet the windowsill. She uses her hands to shield the sunlight so she can see inside. The vase Bernie smashed is still on the floor. Colt's made no attempt to remove the broken glass. She notices the large oak sideboard by the door has two of its drawers pulled open. The surface is almost empty, meaning the family photos are gone.

She straightens, wondering what's going on. Did Bernie take the photos with her, even though she was visiting Toyah for only a few days? That doesn't seem logical.

Her gut tells her something's wrong. What if Colt's been killed and the house ransacked? With three members of the family already murdered, and the added break-in attempt at this location recently, she can't ignore the disarray inside the property. She pulls out her phone and calls the couple's landline as she walks around the building to the rear of the house. The phone rings inside, but no one answers. She tries Colt's cell next, but it's disconnected. "What the hell?"

The closest neighbor is some distance away, their property obscured by trees, blocking their view of this place, but Madison runs over there to see if they know where Colt is. An elderly woman answers the door, leaning on a walking stick and pulling her glasses down from the top of her head. She can barely hear Madison, so it's unlikely she heard anything untoward from next door. "Sorry, I don't have a clue," she says when asked. "I don't mind telling you I steer clear of that family. That Ida woman wasn't my cup of tea. She used to let her dog run amok in my yard until it got run over on the road. Tried to blame me, but I was on vacation when it happened."

Not wanting to waste time, Madison thanks her and runs back to the Ridgeways' property. She needs to get inside to see what she's dealing with. She calls dispatch and asks Stella for backup before transferring to Chief Mendes to explain the situation. Mendes tells her to try calling Bernie before she enters the property, but agrees that if Bernie can't be reached, she should go ahead and force entry based on the possibility that Colt could be lying injured or dead inside. Stella finds Bernie's cell number for her, but the phone is switched off, so Madison leaves a message asking for a callback, then waits for backup to arrive before her next move.

It doesn't take long for Officer Sanchez to arrive, closely followed by Steve. They approach her on the porch. "What's going on?" asks Steve.

"I think something's wrong," she says. "There's no answer when I knock, Colt's cell phone is disconnected, Bernie's is switched off and their house is still a mess. I'm worried they may have been burglarized, or targeted by the killer. Bernie should be with Toyah in Denver, but as far as I know, Colt was staying here. What if whoever killed Denise and Lucy came for him, knowing he was an easy target in there on his own?"

Steve glances at the car in the driveway. "Is that Colt's?"

She nods.

"Want me to force entry?" asks Sanchez.

"Do it."

It takes seconds for him to get the front door open. He enters first, weapon raised. "This is the Lost Creek Police Department!" he yells as he cautiously enters the living room. "Make yourself known."

They're greeted with silence. Madison sniffs the air. It smells fragrant. She's relieved. But if Colt was killed within the last few hours, it wouldn't smell bad yet. Sanchez quickly sweeps each room on both levels, yelling, "All clear!" from upstairs when he's done.

Madison turns to Steve. "So where's Colt?"

He shrugs. "Maybe he's gone out in Bernie's car."

If that's the case, he won't be happy when he returns home to find they've broken in. She looks around. The two open drawers in the sideboard are almost empty, but she doesn't know what was meant to be inside. Several books and photo frames lie on the floor in front of the bookcase as though someone was searching for something.

Steve returns from the kitchen. "Everything looks fine in there. No signs of an altercation."

They move to the hallway, where Sanchez is descending the stairs, pocketing his weapon. "Several drawers in the bedroom vanities have been almost emptied. The gun safe is wide open, and empty too."

"They had guns?" says Steve. He looks at Madison. "I wonder if Colt's a hunter. If he is, could he be the wedding shooter?" He frowns as he thinks about it. "But if Chad was the target, that would mean Colt tried to kill his own nephew. Why would he do that?"

"I don't think he would," she says. "Chad told us he was helping Colt plan the funerals. It sounded like they were close." She pauses. Unless Colt's having some kind of breakdown that's causing him to take out every single member of his own family one by one. She shudders at the thought. "Call Chad. See if he and his family are safe, and whether he's heard from his aunt or uncle today."

Steve pulls his phone out. It doesn't take long for Chad to answer, and it appears he's safe and well. Madison's relieved. She heads upstairs while Steve questions him, and wanders around the three bedrooms, but other than the open vanity drawers in the main bedroom, and the empty gun safe, she doesn't spot anything suspicious. The safe wasn't forced open. Whoever retrieved the weapons used a key. And it's as clean and tidy up here as downstairs was on her first visit to the house. Several vases filled with wilting flowers are dotted around, probably sent to the couple with condolences after Denise and Lucy's deaths. Madison wonders if anyone sent their condolences when Ida was killed, but doubts it. Perhaps she's being too harsh. The old woman must have had *some* redeeming qualities.

She returns downstairs as Steve ends his call. "Chad hasn't heard from Colt today, but he's due to meet him at a funeral home tomorrow to confirm arrangements. I've told him not to alert Bernie or Toyah that we're worried about him yet. We don't want to cause them any more upset if this is all just a misunderstanding. He could be fine for all we know."

She nods, but she doesn't think this is a misunderstanding. "Maybe he's on his way to stay with them."

"It's possible," says Steve. "He could have realized he was a sitting duck here. But why's his car here? Why are some of their belongings missing? And why is his phone disconnected?"

"I don't know, but it doesn't look good." Usually when someone's phone is disconnected it means either the owner doesn't want to be located or something bad has happened to them. Her heart skips a beat as she suddenly wonders where Ryan Simmonds is. What if it *was* him who murdered Denise and Lucy, and now he's killed Colt with a view to taking out the rest of the family?

Trying to remain calm, she looks at Steve. "Call Chad back and tell him to get out of his house immediately. He and his family need to go somewhere safe in case Ryan's snapped and is on the rampage. Then call Adams and ask him to locate Toyah Ridgeway's address and phone number. If Toyah can't be warned over the phone, tell him to contact the local police department to request a welfare check on the occupants of the address."

Steve pulls his phone out, but looks confused. "You think someone's going to kill the rest of the family?"

"Yes." She pauses, her heart hammering in her chest now. "And I think we need to locate Ryan Simmonds asap."

CHAPTER FORTY-THREE

Patrol has been instructed to locate Ryan at home or at work and take him directly to the station for questioning. Before Madison leaves the Ridgeways' house to head there, she wants to check their outbuilding to figure out why someone wanted to break into it. Perhaps it holds clues as to what's been happening to this family. "Come with me."

Steve follows her out the back door while Officer Sanchez remains stationed at the front of the property in case Colt returns.

The outbuilding is padlocked with a chain, so Steve retrieves a pair of bolt cutters from Sanchez's cruiser before breaking it open. Inside the wooden structure the air is cool and stagnant. Madison doesn't detect any foul odors. A large space, it houses a bunch of junk from the looks of things: lawnmowers, tools, spare car parts and old tires. She walks around, peering in drawers full of nothing but mismatched screws and tools. It looks like no one uses any of this stuff anymore. Turning to Steve, she says, "Why would someone want to break in here?"

He opens a couple of toolboxes to check their contents. "Could've been kids messing around, or an addict looking for something to sell in order to score their next high. There's no evidence the break-in was linked to the murders."

He's right. She sighs. "I'll get Adams to check whether any other break-ins have been reported in the area." As she moves, a huge rat appears from behind a damp box and scurries over her foot, making her jump back. "Oh dear God!"

Steve tries to stifle a laugh.

"I'm not scared of them," she says defensively. "It just took me by surprise, that's all."

He wisely turns around and pretends to look at something else.

"I guess we can go." As she walks to the open door, trying not to run, her foot kicks a floorboard that's sticking up at an angle. It looks like it's been forced from its position. She stops as she notices the whole floor is covered in them. It makes her wonder what's underneath. "Remember what Chad told us about his great-aunt Ida?" She looks at Steve. "The rumors about her killing her husband, Phil Randall."

"Yeah, but we both know this town thrives on rumors."

She considers it. It's true that people who are considered a little strange or mean get unfair reputations, mainly started by kids, but she can't shake the feeling that someone broke into this outbuilding for a reason. And since it happened so close to the time of Denise and Lucy's murders, she wants to put her mind at rest. "Dig it up."

Steve frowns. "What?"

"Let's dig it up." She nods at the floor. "All of it. Let's see if the rumors are true. Because then we'll know whether Ida Randall was capable of murder. I'm sure Sanchez won't mind helping."

He rests his hands on his hips. "Madison, Chief Mendes would never let us dig this up based on a rumor."

"It's more than that, though, isn't it?" she says. "This family is being targeted by someone, and we need to find out who. If there's a body under here, that gives the victim's family motive for wanting Ida dead, and maybe the rest of her family too. If Mendes can't see that then she shouldn't—"

He holds his hand up, stopping her. "Alright, alright. Let me call her."

Madison smiles. He's used to her wild hunches by now. "I'll go tell Sanchez he won't need to go to the gym tonight."

Steve laughs as he dials the chief's number.

When she walks back through the house, Madison hears raised voices. Sanchez is arguing with someone out front. "Get on the ground *now*! I won't ask you again."

She reaches for her weapon and rushes to the front door. Outside, Sanchez is aiming his service weapon at Ryan Simmonds. She gets a knot in her stomach. She'd hoped patrol would have picked him up by now. She cautiously steps out of the house. "Ryan? What's going on?"

Keeping his eyes on Ryan, Sanchez says, "He tried to get inside and now he's refusing to drop to the ground."

"Let me see them!" shouts Ryan. His eyes are wild, darting all over the place, but his hands are empty. "I just need to talk to Colt and Bernie, that's all." His words are slurred.

Madison takes a few steps forward. She can hear Steve talking on the phone in the living room. He must've come to see what's causing the commotion. "What's the matter, Ryan?" she says. "Talk to me."

When he doesn't answer, Sanchez tells her, "He said he's carrying a firearm in the back of his pants."

She tenses, wondering if it's the weapon taken from the safe upstairs.

"Of course I'm armed!" says Ryan. His body language is aggressive, his arms wildly gesticulating as though he's drunk. "Someone entered my home and killed the two loves of my life. What if I'm next? It's for my *protection*. I'm not gonna hurt anyone!"

She doesn't know what to believe, but they need to get him under control. "If you lie face-down on the ground, we can remove your weapon and then we'll talk. Okay?"

"I don't want to talk to you," he says. "I want to talk to *them*." He motions to the house behind her.

"They're not here," she says. "We think they've left town."

"I don't believe you."

"Well, if you let us disarm you, I'll let you go in and take a look for yourself." She's trying to figure out whether he's doing this as some kind of stunt to make it look like he's not involved.

"Fine." He gets on all fours before dropping his chest and head to the ground with his arms behind his back. But his hands are too close to his concealed weapon for her liking.

"Put your arms above your ahead like Superman, hands flat on the ground." Sanchez pulls out handcuffs while they wait for Ryan to do what Madison says. "I've got my weapon trained on you," she adds. "Stay still while Officer Sanchez cuffs you, okay?"

Ryan nods, his face in the grass.

Sanchez speedily rushes over to him, removing the weapon from Ryan's pants before pulling his arms back and cuffing them behind him. Madison pockets her own weapon as Sanchez helps him to stand. "Want me to arrest him?" he asks.

"No," she says. Because technically, he hasn't committed a crime, assuming the weapon is his and he has a license for it. "Take him to the station."

"What?" says Ryan. "You said I could look inside!"

"Sorry, but I can't let you contaminate a potential crime scene. You'll just have to take my word for it. None of the Ridgeways are in there." She suspects he already knows that.

Indignant, Ryan shakes his head in disgust as Sanchez leads him to the cruiser.

Steve steps out of the house. "What was he thinking, turning up here *armed*?"

"Maybe he was planning to kill Colt," Madison says with a sigh, suddenly feeling tired after her sleepless night. "How'd it go with Mendes?"

"She said you'll probably make her life hell if she doesn't agree to the search, so she's getting a warrant authorized."

Madison nods. Part of her is pleased to be able to dig up the floor of the outbuilding, but another part dreads what they might find.

CHAPTER FORTY-FOUR

Chief Mendes has secured a search warrant for the Ridgeways' property, so while she arranges for a digger to be delivered so work can start on revealing what lies beneath the outbuilding, Madison and Steve have returned to the station to question Ryan. As they missed lunch and are waiting for Ryan to sober up before questioning him, they grab a quick break to eat whatever they find in the kitchen. Madison's chosen a couple of slices of toast, as that's all she can stomach thanks to the nausea that began with Angie's death. Steve's working his way through a tuna and potato salad he made himself, along with a protein bar.

"I didn't want to mention it before," he says, "but I'm sorry to hear about Angie. For all her faults, she was still your sister, so I imagine it was tough to find her... gone. And the timing couldn't have been worse."

She leans against the wall with a sigh. "Yeah, she found a way to upstage me at my own wedding. That would've given her a lot of satisfaction." She smiles faintly before taking a bite of toast.

He studies her face. "How does it feel to know she can't

hurt you or Owen anymore? Part of you must be relieved, since she was always your greatest threat."

He's right, of course. She swallows her mouthful. "You know, I haven't even thought of that yet. I imagine I'll be relieved once the cremation is over. At the moment, I just feel numb. And so damn tearful." Just saying the word makes her well up.

He steps forward like he wants to hug her, but thinks better of it now she's a married woman. Madison knows he's always had a soft spot for her, because he once told her. She was surprised by it, and suspected that if Nate hadn't been in her life, she and Steve might have dated.

He finishes his protein bar. "Look on the bright side," he says, smiling. "At least her passing means we have one less suspect for anything that happens to you in the future."

She snorts. "That's true."

Adams enters, carrying an empty cup. "I see you've brought Ryan Simmonds in. Have you arrested him yet?"

"We're figuring it out," says Madison, finishing her second slice. "About to question him after this."

"Well," says Adams, "Sanchez says the guy has a headache, so I've come to get him a second cup of coffee."

Steve retrieves a bottle of water from the refrigerator. "Did you manage to get in touch with Toyah Ridgeway?"

"No." Adams pours coffee. "She didn't pick up, so I've arranged for my old police department to perform a welfare check. They'll let me know what they find. I've told them it's urgent."

Madison's stomach flips. "I really hope she and Bernie haven't been hurt."

"Oh, and Chad Peters called," says Adams. "He wanted to know how long he has to hide and whether you'd located Colt yet."

She rinses her plate before taking the cup of coffee from

him. "Hopefully we can answer that once we've spoken to Ryan." She looks at Steve. "Ready?"

Steve throws his wrapper in the trash. "Yep."

They leave Adams in the kitchen. The door to the interview room is ajar. Inside, Officer Sanchez is keeping a close eye on Ryan, who's no longer cuffed. They're giving him the benefit of the doubt because of what he's been through, but if Madison senses he's behind any of the murders, she won't hesitate to arrest him.

She looks at Sanchez. "Thanks, Luis."

He nods before leaving them to it. Steve switches the camera on and explains to Ryan that he's not currently under arrest but is being recorded. "You can have an attorney present before we ask any questions if you would prefer that. Understand?"

Ryan's holding his head in his hands, so Madison places the cup of coffee in front of him. "Here. This might delay the hangover." He sips it gratefully. "So do you want an attorney present?" she asks.

He shakes his head. "No. I haven't done anything wrong."

She's always surprised when people assume an attorney is just for people who have something to hide. If she was ever arrested for anything again in the future, she wouldn't speak to anyone without an attorney by her side. "You haven't? So how did you get to the Ridgeways' house?" She takes a seat opposite him, next to Steve. "Did you drive while intoxicated?"

Shame burns Ryan's face as he realizes he's been stupid.

"We could arrest you for that alone," she warns. But as she wants him to be honest with them, she doesn't. His face shows the pressure he's under. He looks like he's on the verge of a breakdown. "Ryan, what's going on?" she says gently. "Why did you go to their house carrying a weapon?"

"It's my right to carry a firearm."

"You have a license for it?" asks Steve, even though they already know he does. They checked.

"Yeah." Ryan sighs. "I wanted answers, okay? And none of them are picking up their damn phones."

"But what do you think they can tell you? They don't know who killed Denise and Lucy."

He looks her in the eye. "Don't they? Are you sure about that?"

She frowns. "What do you mean? You think her *parents* killed her?"

He looks away.

"Why would they kill their own daughter, never mind their granddaughter? From what we've heard, they were very big on family, and you said yourself that Denise spent all her spare time with them." When he doesn't answer, she asks, "Was there a rift we're unaware of? Some family dispute no one's told us about?" If there is, she's going to be pissed that it's been kept from her.

He shakes his head but remains silent, so she tries a different approach. "Ida Randall told the interviewer she spoke to that there were rumors you enjoyed strangling previous girlfriends during sex. Is that true?"

Clearly offended, he says, "What are you *talking* about? Of course it's not true. I'm not a weirdo, Detective. I don't get off on hurting women."

"Can we call some of them?" asks Steve. "To confirm you're telling the truth?"

Ryan looks annoyed. "That would be difficult, seeing as I've never slept with anyone but Denise."

Madison's surprised. "You're saying you have no ex-girlfriends?" If so, that leaves them with no one alive to confirm his sexual preferences. But he could be lying.

"I already told you we met when we were young," he says.

"Denise was my first and only girlfriend. My best friend too. That's why I took her back every time she screwed up. I loved the damn woman. I wanted more kids with her if she stayed clean. So I was devastated when I found out she'd had a baby with that other guy."

She looks at Steve and can tell he's wondering the same thing: was he devastated enough to kill Dominic over it? "You previously told us you'd never met Dominic or Charlie," she says. "Are you sure about that? Because if you did, now's the time to tell us."

A knock at the door makes Ryan jump. Madison gets up to see who it is, as she knows they wouldn't be interrupted if it weren't important. Alex is waiting for her, so she steps out and closes the door behind her to ensure Ryan doesn't overhear their conversation.

"Sorry to interrupt," he says, keeping his voice low. "But I heard you were interviewing Ryan Simmonds, so I thought it might be useful to know the stain Henry Larson pointed out on his son's carpet was actually oil."

"Oil?" she says. "Engine oil or cooking oil?"

"Engine oil. And as Mr. Simmonds works as a car mechanic..." He doesn't need to finish. She knows where he's going with it.

"Damn," she says, her heart fluttering with equal parts dread and excitement. "Ryan had no reason to ever go inside Dominic's house. He said he never met the guy."

Alex raises an eyebrow. "We'll need to have it tested to figure out the type so we can compare it to the oil Ryan works with, so don't get too excited, but it's something to bear in mind as you question him. There's always a chance it got there from Dominic's shoe. Maybe he was working on his vehicle before he vanished."

She nods, knowing it isn't enough to be able to hold Ryan.

Not until the test results come back. "Thanks, Alex. I'm going to need those results asap."

He smiles. "Of course." He turns to leave, then stops. "Oh, by the way, Nora got back to me about Brody's toenail clippings. She found traces of DNA underneath. After using elimination samples from you, Nate and Owen, she confirmed they belong to someone else, but the database didn't return a match, so it's someone without a criminal record."

"Brody gets around a lot," Madison says, "so presumably it could be anyone's DNA, right?"

"Yes," he admits. "But when we have a suspect in custody for the wedding shooting, we can compare samples. If they match, and the suspect is someone who's never previously been around Brody, it could suggest they met on the mountain that day. It may not be enough to secure a conviction, but it's another tool in our arsenal, along with the partial shoe prints I took from the location where we believe the shot was fired from."

She nods. "It's a long shot alright, but I agree that every little piece helps." If she didn't already know Ryan was at work during the wedding shooting, she'd consider him for that, but he can be ruled out.

She re-enters the interview room and closes the door. Once seated, she says, "Do you want to answer my previous question?"

Ryan looks at her. "I never met Dominic Larson or his kid. I only found out about the affair after he vanished, when it all came out in the press."

"So you've never been inside Dominic's house?"

He frowns. "No. Like I said, I never met him. How many times do I have to repeat myself?"

She holds her hands up. "Fine. I just wanted to make sure I've got that straight." It's good to have it on record for when

Alex's test results come back. "How long have you worked at the auto repair shop?"

Ryan drops his head in his hands and goes quiet. He looks like he's close to breaking point. She doesn't know whether it's his grief for Denise and Lucy or guilt, but this is clearly not a well man in front of her. "Are you okay? Do you need something to eat?"

He shakes his head and sighs loudly. "I don't want to be here anymore." The way he says it suggests he's not just talking about the station.

Alarmed, she glances at Steve. He seems concerned too. "Why, Ryan?" he says. "What's going on?"

"What do you mean, what's going on?" Ryan snaps. "My life ended the day Denise and Lucy died, and now everyone thinks it was me. I won't do time for this, Detectives. You hear me? I can't. I wouldn't survive in prison." Tears run down his face. It's not the first time Madison has seen this kind of emotional display from a suspect, an attempt to gain sympathy in order to blind the police to their true personality. She can't tell if that's what he's doing.

"Do you want to talk to a doctor?" she asks. "We can get you some help."

He shakes his head, wiping his eyes with his sleeve. "I'm not seeing a shrink."

She takes a deep breath. She doesn't know what's best to do, but it's clear he's in no state to be questioned further right now. "Okay, well, I don't feel comfortable interviewing you while you feel this way. I want you to speak to someone who can help you. Would you do that if I arrange it?"

He rubs his eyes. "I'll be fine, I'm not going to do anything stupid. I just need some sleep, that's all. I haven't slept in days."

She studies his face and thinks he's right. He needs to sleep this off. "Fine. I'm going to call your friend Neil and see if he'll drive you home and stay with you for the rest of the day." She can explain that Ryan needs watching closely. He can also keep Ryan's gun away from him. "We can pick this up tomorrow morning, okay?"

He nods, relieved to be able to go home. It could be exhaustion and grief making him act erratically. Or it could be guilt. Either way, she intends to make sure patrol keeps a very close eye on his house, just in case this is all an act and he intends to skip town the minute he gets out of here.

CHAPTER FORTY-FIVE

Having drawn a blank in the Sharon Smith case so far, Nate has more questions for Justin Asher, Sharon's ex-boyfriend. Wanting to take him unaware this time, he's turned up unannounced at his house. A scrawny black cat flees the porch as Nate climbs the steps and knocks on the door. A thin, tired-looking woman around fifty years old answers—presumably Justin's wife. She takes one look at him before saying, "No salesmen."

She's about to shut the door in his face, so he holds up a hand. "Wait! I'm not a salesman. I'm a private investigator looking into the disappearance of your husband's ex-girlfriend." He talks fast. "He's already spoken to me about what happened, but I have some more questions. You've heard of Sharon Smith, right?"

She eyes him suspiciously. "Justin's at work."

Figuring that might work in his favor, he says, "Then do *you* have a minute to talk?" When she seems dubious, he extends his hand. "My name's Nate Monroe. I'm sorry, I don't know yours."

She's surprised into shaking it. "Kelly Asher. I guess you'd better come in." She turns and heads inside.

Bookcases line every wall of the living room, filled with physical media—DVDs, CDs and computer games. "Wow. You guys must really like watching movies, huh?" he says.

She scoffs. "They're Justin's. He's too cheap to pay for streaming services, so if we can't find it at the thrift store, we can't watch it."

Nate suddenly feels nostalgic as he reads the titles of some of the DVDs, including old films and TV shows dating back to the eighties that he remembers from his childhood. "I bet you never get bored with all this at your fingertips?"

She sits on the couch, so he takes a seat opposite, on a worn-out armchair, and places his notebook on his lap. Owen teases him for still using a pen and paper to take notes, but Nate likes to point out that a notebook can't be hacked and no thief would want to steal it, unlike a cell phone or a laptop. "How long have you and Justin been married?"

She lights a cigarette. "Almost three decades. I was the first woman he started seeing after Sharon vanished. Well, unless you count her mother."

He raises his eyebrows, surprised by her comment. "You mean Gail Smith?"

She nods as she blows smoke. "You didn't know about them already? Some investigator you are. I thought the whole town knew."

"Well," he says, shifting position, "I've heard rumors, but you're the first to confirm it." He has many questions, but decides to start at the beginning. "When did he and Gail first start seeing each other?"

She snorts. "It's just sex, Mr. Monroe. They were never *seeing* each other. They started screwing while he was living with Sharon." She shakes her head in disgust. "What kind of mother does that to her own daughter, right?"

What kind of mother indeed. "Did Sharon know about it?"

"I don't know. I doubt it. She probably would've left him

sooner if she did. It makes me sick just thinking about those two together."

"Did you know Sharon?" he asks.

"Kind of. I knew *of* her. We'd smile and say hi if we passed each other in the street, but that's about it. You couldn't really miss a woman like Sharon. She was beautiful."

He nods. "What did you think when you heard she'd disappeared?"

She takes another puff of her cigarette, her eyes not meeting his now. "Women don't just vanish on a whim, right? It's obvious she and her poor baby were murdered. From what I heard, she and her girlfriend were looking forward to the birth. She had no reason to leave town without telling anyone."

For Nate, it's refreshing to talk to someone who isn't playing mind games or trying to hide something. "Did you ever hear rumors about who might have been responsible for hurting her?"

She quickly shakes her head.

"How soon after she vanished did you and Justin get together?"

"We started dating while she was still alive, but she'd already moved out of his place. I can't remember exactly. It was all so long ago."

The thirty-year gap means it's been difficult to find witnesses able to recall facts correctly. Time has a way of skewing things, but on the other hand, it also has a way of changing people's alliances. Those who once didn't want to speak out because they were close to the suspect may now be more willing. "Did he ever talk about Sharon to you? Or show any interest in what she got up to after they broke up?"

She appears to think carefully before she speaks. "He was surprised when he learned she was pregnant. Pissed too. He wanted kids with her, but she never got pregnant for some reason. I guess she wasn't as stupid as me. She probably lied about stopping birth control. Sometimes I wish I had." She reddens, quickly adding, "Not that I don't love my kids."

He senses she's bitterly disappointed with how her life has turned out. "How many kids do you guys have?"

"Three. I would've stopped at one if I'd have known what an asshole he was." She suddenly looks afraid. "Don't tell him I said that. I'm just kidding. In fact, I probably shouldn't be speaking to you at all. It's just, well, no one ever talks to me. My opinion doesn't count for anything. And while I'm home alone watching the kids every evening, he's out screwing Gail, probably others too."

Nate's mouth drops open. "They're still in a sexual relationship *now*?"

She nods. "They think I don't know, but I do. I'd leave if I had any money." She looks at the bookcases. "If I had any sense, I'd pack mine and the kids' things, take a bunch of his prized possessions—some of them are worth a pretty penny—and sell them to fund a new life somewhere far from here." She finishes her cigarette. "But he's sucked my will to live out of me, and besides, I don't know how he'd react. It's not like I could go far. He'd track me down soon enough. So I don't do anything. I just stay here, wash his clothes, feed him his favorite meals and bitch about him behind his back. It seems the safer option, for now at least."

Nate feels for her. She seems far too exhausted for her age. Life with Justin obviously hasn't been kind to her. "Is he violent? Because I can help you to—"

She shakes her head. "No, it's more indifference than anything else. He doesn't care enough to hit me. Maybe if he did, I'd finally do something about it. He doesn't get physical. Well, not..."

He leans forward. "Go on."

She looks him in the eye. "He's weird in bed, but all you men are, right? You're all sex freaks." She laughs it off.

"No," says Nate. "We're not. If he's forcing you do something that makes you uncomfortable, that's not okay, Kelly." He doesn't know how far to push this, as it's none of his business, and as a male he's aware he shouldn't be probing her about her sex life, but he also can't sit back and let her believe any kind of violence is acceptable, especially as Justin's ex-girlfriend vanished after breaking up with him thirty years ago.

"He has this stupid fetish, I guess you'd call it," she says. "It was back in the early days. He doesn't do it much anymore. Not with me, anyway." She blushes, lowering her voice. "He squeezes my neck during the deed sometimes." She tries to laugh it off again, before suddenly standing.

Nate's no prude, but he thinks there's something seriously wrong with getting a kick out of combining sex with violence. He's alarmed. Especially as he knows Denise and Lucy Ridgeway were murdered by strangulation. But Madison told him neither female was sexually assaulted, thankfully. It makes him wonder whether Justin could have strangled Sharon all those years ago. He remains seated. "If you don't like something he does during sex—"

She quickly changes the subject. "I hope you find out what happened to Sharon, Mr. Monroe. But I have things I need to do, so if you wouldn't mind..."

It's clear she doesn't want to talk about her relationship. He stands. "Sure. Just one more question." Meeting her gaze, he asks, "Do you think your husband is capable of killing someone?"

She takes a deep breath. "Honestly? I think everyone is capable of killing someone if they're in the right emotional state." She's deliberately being evasive.

"Okay, so let me ask you this," he says. "Do you think Justin killed Sharon?"

She lowers herself back onto the couch. "I've thought about it a lot over the years."

"And?" he presses.

She shrugs. "I think he makes a good suspect. But so does the man who got her pregnant."

"Could that have been Justin?"

She bites her lip before answering. "Who knows, right? He swears it wasn't him, but he's a proven liar."

"What does your gut tell you?" he presses, since she's being so open with him. It feels like she's been itching to talk to someone about this for years.

She sighs heavily. "Put it this way, Mr. Monroe." She looks up at him. "If you came to me tomorrow and told me my husband had been arrested for her abduction and murder, I wouldn't be surprised."

He keeps his expression neutral, but he *is* surprised. He's surprised she'd live with a man who she believes is capable of such a thing.

"But that doesn't mean he did it," she adds. "I'm a paranoid person by nature, so maybe my dissatisfaction with our relationship is clouding my judgement. I'm certainly not accusing him of anything, and I would never stand up in court to repeat what I've just said to you. Not unless you had concrete evidence that he did harm that poor girl. In which case, I'd do my best to help her rest in peace. It would free me too. So if you do find anything, you come back and visit me, okay?"

He nods. "Of course." She's right to protect herself, since she doesn't know for sure. "Thanks for your honesty. I appreciate it."

"So what now?" she asks wearily. "Are you going to arrest him or something?"

He smiles. "No. I'm not a cop. And I have zero evidence about what happened to Sharon. But maybe now I know where to focus my investigation." He hesitates, before adding, "Where does that leave you? Do you want help getting out of your relationship? Because there *is* support available."

She nods thoughtfully. "I've been thinking about it for a while. This might be the push that I need. I've joined some groups online that talk about places me and the kids could go while I get some money together, but I have to make sure the timing's right."

"Good," he says. "Just a word of warning. Keep your plans to yourself. It's probably best that Justin doesn't find out until you're out of harm's way." He's relieved she's looked into it, but also concerned. Because if Justin did hurt Sharon all those years ago, Kelly's risk of being harmed will increase dramatically when she tries to leave him.

CHAPTER FORTY-SIX

At the station, Madison's taking a minute to read her father's account of what he did thirty years ago to try to locate Sharon Smith. Several photos have been uploaded to their database, so she opens them one at a time and realizes they were the photos used on the missing person poster. Sharon's smiling face looks familiar. An attractive blonde who appears shy when being photographed, she was an obvious target for a sexual predator. But on the other hand, she was eight months pregnant, so Madison would like to think that would put a rapist off, but experience tells her that they don't care as long as they get what they want, which is control as well as sex.

She sighs. Seeing her father's handwritten notes on screen tugs at her heartstrings, especially now. She's overcome with a strong sense of homesickness. What she'd give to go back to being a teenager, right before her father left them to go hunt serial killers in Alaska. She could change everything that happened afterward, and try to keep her family together. Maybe she and Angie would have had a chance to become close. She swallows the lump in her throat and pushes the thought away. She shouldn't dwell on the past, but grief is making her nostalgic.

When she overhears Adams taking a call, she listens in. It sounds like he's talking to someone from his old police department. They'd agreed to perform a welfare check on Toyah Ridgeway for him. She leans back in her chair to peer over her computer screen.

"Okay, got it," says Adams down the line. "Hold off until we know what we're dealing with. I need to run it past the team here." After hanging up the phone, he looks at her. "There was no answer at Toyah's address, but they managed to contact the landlord. He met them at the apartment and let them inside to look around."

"And?" she says, noticing Steve is listening in now too, until his phone suddenly rings and he turns back to his desk to answer it.

"It was empty," says Adams.

She nods. "They must've gone out. Are the police going to return later and try again?"

"No, you don't understand," he says. "It was empty of personal belongings. Clothes and valuables. The landlord thinks Toyah's skipped out on him. Only the furniture that came with the apartment was left behind."

Madison feels a tightness in her chest as her gut tells her something is very seriously wrong. "What the hell is going on with that family?"

"Sounds to me like none of them are missing," he says. "Including Colt. His place wasn't ransacked, Madison, he's fled, along with Bernie and Toyah. Maybe they're terrified that they'll be next. I mean, you can't blame them given three of their family members were murdered and there was also an attempt on their nephew's life."

"Maybe," she says, her heart rate quickening. "Or maybe *they* killed Denise and Lucy. Perhaps Ida too."

He raises his eyebrows. "But why would they do that? Had they fallen out with Denise? Did she have something they wanted? Because we know greed is one of the best motivators for murder, right? That or rage, jealousy..."

Before she can answer, Steve ends his call and turns to them. "You're never gonna believe this."

"What?" she says.

He takes a deep breath. "That was Sanchez. They've found what looks like human remains under the Ridgeways' outbuilding."

"*What?*" Madison stands. "You're kidding?" She glances at Adams, who looks as surprised as she is. "So the rumors about Ida killing her husband and burying him in the backyard are true." She grabs her keys off her desk. "Adams, tell Conrad we need him out there asap."

He picks up his desk phone. "On it."

She glances at Mendes's office but the chief is out. She turns to Steve. "Coming?"

He nods before following her out of the station.

Officer Sanchez meets them at the front of the Ridgeways' property to give them a heads-up that Chief Mendes is already here. Apparently she was having lunch nearby with Conrad when he got the call from Adams. Madison and Steve follow Sanchez to the rear of the property, where the medical examiner is crouched over an open grave. The outbuilding's floorboards are almost all lifted, along with a large amount of soil. A small digger sits empty outside, waiting to finish the job. Now that remains have been discovered, it's going to be a more delicate job to search the rest of the area. They don't want to inadvertently destroy evidence.

Madison nods to the chief before peering over Conrad's shoulder. Someone has already set up scene lighting, helping them to see what's hidden in the earth. Peeking out of the dirt is some black plastic, a large bag or cover. Within that, at Conrad's feet, Madison can see a beige dome-shaped object covered in creepy-crawlies. Goosebumps prickle her flesh. It looks like the top of a skull, with clumps of hair still attached to it in several places. The rest of the remains are covered in fabric that has turned brown with decomposition. Her eyes skim the contents of the plastic. A metal belt buckle sticks out of the dirt, where it catches the glare of the bright light above it.

She and Steve share a look. Chief Mendes waits patiently beside them while Conrad inspects the remains, using a brush to remove some lose dirt from around the skull. When he moves, Madison catches a whiff of something foul coming from the grave and has to cover her nose briefly. She's surprised it still smells, considering how long Ida's husband must have been down there. Perhaps being entombed under this building and away from the elements has helped to preserve him, hopefully along with any evidence, since it would be nice to catch a break for once.

She folds her arms over her chest. "The occupant's nephew told us about rumors that Ida Randall, the elderly matriarch of the family, killed her husband and buried him on the property years ago."

"Really?" says Conrad, glancing up at her.

She nods. "But he didn't seem to give the rumors much credence. I guess he was wrong."

Conrad sits back on his heels. "How long ago was that supposed to have happened?"

"Oh, decades," she says.

He stands, brushing dirt off his knees. "Well, this is an adult's skull, and likely a male based on what I can see of the clothes. But if Ida did kill her husband all those years ago, this isn't him."

Madison freezes. How can it not be Phil Randall? She and Steve exchange a horrified look. "It isn't?" says Steve.

Alex Parker suddenly appears, carrying his forensic kit. He nods in greeting before peering at the remains.

"No," says Conrad. "This body is much fresher than that."

Madison gets a horrible sinking feeling. "How fresh?"

"Well," he says, "I'd obviously need to examine it thoroughly before giving an accurate estimate, but I don't think it's been down there more than six months. Maybe less, based on the stage of decomposition and the bugs present."

Steve kneels next to the remains, careful not to touch anything. He studies the belt buckle with interest before looking up at Alex. "I'd like to know what color this belt is under all that dirt." The dirt is likely a combination of bodily fluids and skin cells mixed together with the soil. He looks visibly shaken and Madison thinks she knows why.

Alex crouches next to him, removing a brush with soft bristles from his kit. He skillfully brushes away the dirt that's stuck to the belt without causing any damage. It reveals lightly tanned leather.

Steve stands and clasps his hands behind his neck. "Shit." He looks at Madison. "If the rest of the clothes also match," he says, "it's possible this could be Dominic Larson."

Madison lowers her eyes as her heart sinks. She thinks of Dominic's son, two-year-old Charlie. If his father's dead, it's reasonable to assume he's buried down there too, given that there have been no credible sightings of the toddler in the four months he's been missing. "Damn." She has to swallow the lump in her throat. Hank Larson will be devastated, his sister too. And she and Steve are the ones who will have to break it to them and watch Hank's reaction as he realizes he won't get to hug his son or kiss his grandson again before he dies. "This will kill Hank."

Steve exhales as he drops his hands. "I was holding on to the hope that Dominic had fled town with Charlie."

They stand in silence as everyone takes a minute to grieve for the young father buried at their feet.

Once the shock wears off, Madison starts thinking logically. "Why would he be buried in the Ridgeways' backyard? They told us they didn't know Dominic or Charlie. They said they didn't find out about Denise's affair until *after* the Larsons vanished, when it all came out in the press."

Steve shakes his head. "They lied to us. Dominic couldn't be buried here without their knowledge, right?" He turns to look at the house through the open doors of the outbuilding. "Look how close their home is. They would've seen or heard it."

Madison tries to think. "Maybe he was buried here while they were visiting Toyah or away on vacation."

As Conrad and Alex get to work delicately unearthing the remains, Chief Mendes says, "There's always the possibility that only one of them knows about this."

Madison slowly nods. "Maybe."

Mendes looks at Officer Sanchez. "We need to dig up the rest of the area to see if Charlie's down there. Follow Alex's lead. We need to be extremely careful with whatever we unearth." She turns to Steve and Madison. "When do you want to notify Dominic's father that we've found remains?"

Madison inhales deeply. "Not until we know the clothes definitely match. Maybe by then we'll know whether Charlie is here too. I don't want to deliver two death notifications separately. I don't think he can take it." She'd rather break the news of both losses in one visit to try to minimize the impact, if that's even possible.

"Fine," says the chief.

"I'll issue a BOLO for the Ridgeways," says Madison. "We need to bring them in for questioning." She hopes they can be located before they flee the state. As she looks at the skull poking out from the ground, she considers what it means. She doesn't want to believe that Bernie and Colt could have murdered Denise and Lucy, but with Dominic buried on their property and Charlie likely to be dead too, it's clear they had no qualms about killing their own family members, despite how they claimed to put family first. Charlie was their *grandchild*, just like Lucy. And Ida was Bernie's *mother*.

Madison suddenly wonders whether Bernie is the innocent victim in all this. That perhaps Colt isn't as henpecked as he likes to make out. Maybe *he's* the one who's destroyed their family, and Bernie had no choice but to go along with it in order to survive. Perhaps he's holding her and Toyah hostage.

Adrenaline shoots through her veins. They need to find Colt before he does any more damage.

CHAPTER FORTY-SEVEN

The mood at the station is somber as the entire team tries to focus on work while anticipating what feels like the inevitable discovery of Charlie Larson's body at the crime scene. The afternoon is transitioning into early evening, and the sky outside has darkened, with cloud build-up threatening rain. From the other side of the office, Madison hears Stella fielding calls from reporters who've noticed something's going down at the Ridgeways' property. She's been given the all-clear to confirm the department has issued a BOLO for Colt, Bernie and Toyah Ridgeway, but no more than that. She's hoping patrol locates them before any more damage is done.

Steve has taken the discovery of what appears to be Dominic Larson's body particularly hard. He and Madison have spent the last few hours considering various scenarios that paint the Ridgeways as the killers now that they suspect the family hasn't fled in fear of their lives. It's far more likely they've fled because they fear being captured by law enforcement and brought to justice. But Madison's at a loss as to Colt and Bernie's motive for killing Dominic and Charlie, especially as they're Charlie's grandparents.

Officer Vickers approaches her and Steve. "Hey." She sips her bottled water before resting her hands on her hips. "I've come from talking with Chad Peters. He isn't hiding his aunt and uncle. He voluntarily let me and Officer Kent check his property. I obviously had to tell him why we suspect they're running from law enforcement. He was stunned about the remains we've found. He got really emotional. I felt for the poor guy."

As much as Madison liked Chad when he came in to speak to them, part of her wonders whether his likability was all an act and actually he knows exactly what's going on. He could be in on it with them. Or maybe she's just being paranoid. "What about extended family? Chad's father is Colt's brother, right?"

"Yeah, but he's in a residential care home. He has dementia, and Chad's mom has passed. I asked him about other family or friends who might offer his aunt and uncle a hiding place, but he said there's no one else who was close to them on account of Ida. As we know, she didn't exactly endear herself to people, and most of Chad's side of the family feels Bernie was just as bad as her mother, so relations were frosty to say the least."

That's disappointing. "Okay, thanks for checking."

"Sure."

On her way past Steve, Shelley shoots him a sympathetic smile before discreetly asking, "Are we still on for tonight?"

Steve takes a deep breath. "I hope so, but let's see how this pans out. It could be a late one."

Shelley nods. "Sure."

When she leaves, Steve's cell phone rings. He snaps it up quickly. "Hello?"

Madison watches as he reacts to something. "Oh God." He looks at her with disappointment in his eyes as he listens to the caller. Her heart sinks because she knows what's coming. They all know it's inevitable that Charlie's buried with his father. When he's done with the call, he sets his phone on the table and sighs. "That was Chief Mendes. She says they've found more remains."

Madison groans. "It must be Charlie."

He nods. "Conrad thinks there could be more than two people down there. He's found various different bone fragments."

Madison's heart drops. "So they may have killed Dominic, Charlie *and* Ida's husband. This is insane. That family is insane."

"They're not insane," he says. "They're *evil*."

She knows they need to keep an open mind, but it's difficult given what they're discovering. "I guess Ryan Simmonds is off the hook for Dominic, Charlie and Ida's murders."

"What about Denise and Lucy?" says Steve. "Would Bernie and Colt really kill their own daughter and grandchild?"

"Charlie was their grandchild too," she reminds him. She can't help feeling that everything that's happened is linked to Dominic and Denise's affair. So if Colt and Bernie killed Dominic and Charlie, was it for Denise? Did they think they were doing her a favor somehow? If so, maybe it backfired and somehow resulted in Denise's death.

"Like the chief said, maybe only one of them was in on it," he says. "Colt could've killed them all without Bernie's knowledge."

She has to admit that it would explain why Lucy was given a pillow, toy and blanket after being killed. Colt was her grandfather. He could have been remorseful for what he'd done. "But if Colt killed them, wouldn't Denise and Lucy have been buried under the outbuilding too? Not left at home to be discovered?"

"Maybe he ran out of time," says Steve, looking exhausted. "I don't know. The only motive I can think of is that Colt found out about Charlie being Denise's child and he was mad she'd kept that from them. Maybe he thought it made their family look bad. They strike me as the kind of people who don't want to be associated with scandals like adultery and love triangles."

Madison isn't convinced. "They kept a newspaper clipping of Charlie in a frame on their sideboard. They seemed sad that they never got to meet him, and proud that he was one of them. They were supposedly big on family." She thinks back to her conversations with them. "When we informed them about Denise and Lucy's deaths, Bernie was so upset she vomited. She was emotionally distraught." She pauses as she realizes something. "But she had a different reaction to Ida's murder. After she discovered her mother dead, she was angry, like really pissed. Enough to smash a vase against the wall. That seems odd, don't you think?"

"You mean it seemed like she was angry because someone had gotten the better of her?" says Steve. "Perhaps taken her by surprise?"

"Right. I don't think she'd kill her own mother, especially not in the brutal way it happened, so that must've been Colt. He obviously reached his breaking point with Ida."

Adams appears. Hearing what they're discussing, he stops beside Madison's desk. "What if Toyah's behind all this. You haven't considered that angle yet, right?"

He's right, they haven't. Mainly because she doesn't live here, so it's unlikely she's involved. Unless... Madison's heart drops as something comes to her. "Oh no."

"What?" Steve looks at her with interest.

"I should have realized." She tries to think back to the only time she's met the woman. It was when Toyah and Colt were packing Bernie's luggage into the pickup truck so she could stay with her daughter in Denver. "I met Toyah briefly outside their house. I noticed a child seat secured in the back of her truck. I assumed she had children." She looks at Steve. "Does she have kids?"

He reaches for his phone and immediately makes a call.

"Chad, it's Detective Tanner. I need to ask you something about Toyah Ridgeway. Does she have any kids?" After a second, Steve looks at Madison and shakes his head. "Does she have a partner who has kids?" he presses. After hearing Chad's answer, he again shakes his head.

Madison gets goosebumps as she considers the implications. Why would Toyah need a child seat in her vehicle if she doesn't have kids? She was Lucy's aunt, so it's plausible that she might have bought one to drive her niece around. But she doesn't live locally, so would she ever have needed to drive Lucy anywhere? "Ask him when she moved to Denver."

Steve nods. "When did Toyah move to Denver?" He listens, before repeating Chad's answer. "Mid to late February? You're sure about that?" He pauses. "Okay, thanks for your help." He lowers his phone.

Madison thinks she knows what happened. Toyah could have moved to Denver right after Dominic and Charlie vanished in order to keep Charlie hidden. Having killed Dominic, Colt, Bernie and Toyah could have abducted the two-year-old. Maybe the plan was always for Colt and Bernie to join Toyah and Charlie later, but they didn't want to leave town too soon in case it was obvious why they were moving. But that was delayed further when Denise and Lucy were murdered, because then at least one of them had to stick around to plan the funerals and answer questions from law enforcement.

As Steve lowers his phone, she says, "I have a feeling Toyah has Charlie. That he's not buried with his dad under the outbuilding."

Adams shakes his head in disgust. "If you're right, that family is evil."

Steve looks hopeful. "I can't tell you how much I want you to be right about this, Madison. Bad as it is, at least it's better than the alternative, because it would mean Charlie is still alive."

She thinks it makes sense. "That's why they've fled together. They lied to us. They *did* know about Denise's affair with Dominic. Somehow, they found out, despite Denise trying to keep it a secret. They knew Charlie was half Ridgeway, and they wanted him all for themselves. It's probably why Denise tried to hide his existence from them. She knew they'd want him in their lives, and she didn't want that. She knew what Ida was like. She wanted her son to grow up in a happy, loving house with his father."

"Which is exactly what he was doing until they snatched him," says Steve angrily.

He's right. Dominic Larson loved his son, that much was evident. But unfortunately, he couldn't protect him from Denise's family. Madison stands, looking at Adams. "Update the Amber alert and notify every police department in Colorado that we're looking for the Ridgeways. Then update the press asap. The more eyes we have looking for that family, the more likely we can bring Charlie home before the Ridgeways do something stupid."

CHAPTER FORTY-EIGHT

Chief Mendes returns just as Madison and Steve are about to leave the station. She calls them into her office to provide an update on the crime scene. "Conrad's team has been busy retrieving the first set of remains," she says, slipping out of her wet rain jacket and hanging it on the wall behind her desk. Outside, the thickening cloud has caused a serious of short, sharp showers. "They found a wallet in the pants pocket, confirming Dominic's identity, so we'll need to notify his father as soon as possible."

Steve lowers his eyes. Even though they suspected the remains belonged to Dominic, it's another thing to have it confirmed.

"Understood," says Madison. She takes a deep breath before updating Mendes on what they think happened to Dominic and Charlie and how the Ridgeways are involved. The chief seems taken aback at the suggestion the little boy could still be alive. "We need to find him before the Ridgeways panic," says Madison. "Because if they suspect we're on to them, they might try to... destroy the evidence."

Stella appears at the door. She lowers her headset. "Patrol

has located Colt Ridgeway at a gas station on the edge of town in an unregistered vehicle. He's alone and he didn't put up a fight. They're bringing him in. ETA is ten to fifteen minutes."

Madison glances at Steve. "Holy crap. We could get answers sooner than we thought."

"That's good," he says. "But where are Bernie and Toyah? Do they still have Charlie with them? Or, God forbid, has Colt murdered them all in his bid for freedom?"

Her hands clammy from adrenaline, she shivers. "I don't know. Maybe Colt's acting as a decoy to give them time to escape with Charlie. That would be better than the alternative."

They return to their desks to await Colt's arrival. Madison prepares interview questions as rain pelts the windows on and off. She realizes she needs to let Nate know she'll be working late, so she messages him.

Won't be home anytime soon. Had a breakthrough in the Ridgeway case.

He quickly replies.

Sure. Don't worry about us.

Officer Kent appears at the other end of the office and leads Colt Ridgeway to interview room one. His eyes are lowered and his hands are cuffed behind his back. He looks drained but defiant, as if he's ready to do battle.

Madison slips her phone away and stands. "He's here."

Steve looks up, then grabs his notebook and stands. "Let's go."

They follow Officer Kent into the small interview room. "Want me to uncuff him?" asks Kent. "He's been read his rights."

Madison nods. "You're not going to cause us any problems, are you, Colt?"

He gives her a hard stare but remains silent as Kent removes the cuffs and leaves them to it.

Madison doesn't want to reveal yet that they've discovered remains under his outbuilding, as she wants to hear what excuse he has for trying to flee with his wife and daughter. When Steve switches the camera on, she reminds Colt of his rights. He says he doesn't want a lawyer yet but may reconsider. She's relieved she can get straight down to business. "Where were you headed when our officers caught up with you?"

"I was getting gas," he says wearily. "Is that a crime now?"

"Only if you're using it to flee law enforcement," she says. When he doesn't reply, she asks, "Did you know Bernie and Toyah are missing?"

He looks away.

"Aren't you worried about them? The person who killed Denise and Lucy could have harmed them for all we know."

He surprises her by sitting forward and looking her in the eye. "I don't want to spend another second with my wife, so if you find her, don't bring her to me. She can rot in hell for all I care."

Madison glances at Steve in surprise. It seems the Ridgeway family isn't as harmonious as they like to portray.

Steve says, "Why, Colt? What's going on?"

Colt leans back in his seat. "Let's just say that Ida's death has given me the incentive I need to finally leave that family. I should never have married Bernie. If I hadn't, my life would've been a hell of a lot better than it is now."

"Why though?" says Madison. "You're talking in riddles, and we don't have much time. Don't you want to help us find Denise and Lucy's killer?"

He falls silent again.

Knowing they need to find Charlie as fast as possible,

Madison decides to speed things up a little. "We've found a body under your outbuilding. Maybe more than one."

His head snaps up. She can see the cogs turning behind his eyes as he tries to decide whether it's better to deny everything, confess or lawyer up. Eventually his demeanor visibly changes from defensive to despairing. He takes a deep breath and his shoulders sag. "Bernie's capable of anything right now. She's devastated after losing Ida, Denise and Lucy. She's not thinking straight. And she's armed. She needs to be stopped before she fully transitions into her mother. But don't go in all guns blazing in case you hurt the boy."

Madison doesn't dare breathe. Not while he's confessing. "What boy?" she asks, playing dumb. She wants to hear it from him.

He lowers his eyes to the table. "They have Charlie."

Her stomach drops. She's so relieved to confirm the toddler is still alive that she can feel tears burning her eyes. She forces them back. "You're saying Charlie Larson is alive and well, and your wife and daughter have him?"

He nods. "He's our grandson, so Ida felt he should be living with us, not Dominic, and unfortunately, Bernie agreed."

"So Toyah's been taking care of Charlie this whole time?" asks Steve.

He nods again.

"Did Denise know about this?" asks Madison.

"No. She never found out we knew about the affair she had with Dominic, never mind the baby it produced."

Madison's confused. "If she didn't tell you about the affair, then who did? Dominic?"

"No." Colt shifts in his seat. "Toyah told us. Denise stupidly confided in her sister. And Toyah's always trying to win her mother's approval because she thinks Bernie favored Denise over her, so she told Bernie and Ida everything." He sighs. "I know she regrets it. She's not a bad kid. She's just trapped in this awful family, same as me."

Madison doesn't know how he can claim Toyah isn't bad after she betrayed her sister and helped abduct her nephew. "Tell us what happened to Dominic, Colt. Who killed him?"

He won't look at her. He must still be considering his options. Eventually, he asks, "Will it help my case if I cooperate, or does that only happen in the movies?"

She's annoyed that he only appears concerned for himself, but that's to be expected considering everything he's done. Ultimately, it doesn't matter why he tells them as long as they can bring Charlie home alive. "I'm sure it'll help you."

He studies her face to see if she's telling the truth. Eventually, he squeezes his eyes closed as he prepares to tell them the whole sorry story.

CHAPTER FORTY-NINE
FEBRUARY 2022

A knock at the side door makes Dominic jump. He's not expecting anyone. Maybe Mrs. Lucas from across the street needs help with something.

"Is that Grandpa?" yells Charlie from the living room.

"No, Grandpa's on vacation, remember?" He throws the washcloth next to the sink and wipes his damp hands on his shirt. When he opens the door, he's taken aback by who he finds standing there. "Oh. Hi." His stomach flips with dread as he realizes his worst fears are about to come true. "I think I know why you're here."

Toyah and Colt Ridgeway wait in the dark. "Can we come in?" asks Denise's older sister. "We have a few questions."

Dominic involuntarily gulps, feeling like he's in trouble, which is ridiculous. Sure, he unwittingly had an affair with Denise while she was in a relationship with Ryan Simmonds, but that's not *his* fault, it's Denise's. So if they're planning to start something—

"Who are they, Daddy?" Charlie appears behind him. He's staring up at their visitors. When no one answers, he holds a green plastic T-Rex out for them to see. "I'm going to paint this pink."

Dominic gets the sudden urge to slam the door in their face, scoop Charlie up and run.

"It'll only take a minute," says Colt from behind his daughter. "Then we'll be out of your hair."

Dominic realizes he can't exactly turn them away. He just has to hope his fears are unwarranted and that he's being paranoid. "Sure, come on in. This is my son, Charlie."

Toyah enters first, going straight to Charlie and crouching next to him. "*Pink?* So it's a girl then?" Her expression is strained, as though she doesn't want to be here.

Dominic forces a smile, but he can't help feeling he's being ambushed. He thinks about calling Denise and asking her to come over. She'll be able to provide her family with more answers than he can. This is the first time he's ever spoken to any of them. He knows of them, of course, and has seen them around town, but they've never been introduced, and why would they? They shouldn't even know that he and Charlie exist. The whole situation feels awkward.

He suddenly worries that it was Denise who sent them here. Maybe she finally wants custody of Charlie and doesn't feel able to ask him herself. Blood roars in his ears as his worst-case scenario gains traction. "Can I get you a drink?" he asks, hoping they'll say no.

"Sure," says Colt. "I'll have water."

"I'm good," says Toyah, taking Charlie's hand. "Charlie's going to show me his bedroom. That okay with you?"

Feeling it would be rude to say no, Dominic nods, but he feels sick doing so. He wishes a neighbor would interrupt them so he can get them out of here. Maybe he should call the police. His hands shake as Toyah leaves him alone with her father. Charlie runs upstairs ahead of her, jabbering on about his toys.

Dominic goes to the refrigerator. Against his better judgment, he turns his back on Colt. The air is thick with unspoken menace. He reaches for a bottle of water, desperately trying to think of a way to get these people out of his home without causing offense, but his hand doesn't make it. Instead, he winces in pain as he's struck with something from behind. The blow is so hard he sees stars.

He quickly goes dizzy, his entire body folding forward in shock. As he sinks to the floor, clutching the back of his head, he thinks of Charlie, and how he needs to do everything he can to stay conscious in order to protect his son.

But it's no good. Everything goes black.

When Dominic wakes, his head is pounding so hard he feels it in his teeth. And he can't see anything. Someone has placed a blindfold over his eyes and tied his hands behind his back. He struggles to break free, but he doesn't have a spare inch of space around his wrists. His mouth is bone dry and he almost gags with fear. He knows he's not at home because he feels a cold wind on his face. He's outside somewhere, but probably not in his own backyard as a neighbor would have spotted him by now. They would have called the police.

He feels disoriented. "Charlie?" he shouts. "Charlie, where are you?"

"You can stop that," says an older woman's harsh voice. He doesn't recognize it.

"Who are you?" he says, looking in the direction of the voice. "Where am I? What have you done with my son?"

She doesn't respond.

"Are you Denise's mom? *Denise!*" he yells. "Denise, they've got Charlie!"

The woman chuckles as though she finds this amusing. "Come on, let's get this over with."

A second voice pipes up. "Are you sure we should do this, Mom?"

Dominic frowns. He doesn't recognize the second voice either, but he knows it's not Denise. "Please," he says. "What's going on? Can't we talk about this? I just want to know my son is okay."

"He's *our* son now," says the first woman. "He'll be raised a Ridgeway, not a Larson."

Her words send chills down his spine. He can't believe what he's hearing. This must be Denise's mother and grandmother. Goosebumps cover his entire body. He's heard rumors about Ida Randall. He knows Denise is afraid of the pair of them.

"You and Denise had no right keeping him from us," says Ida. "We should've been in his life from the day he was born."

Stunned by her logic, he yells, "What are you talking about? He's my *son*! You're not taking him from me! Denise didn't want you to know about him and now I know why. You people are crazy!" He tries to break free of his restraints, but it's hopeless. "You can't just take my son from me," he pants with exertion. "I'll go to the police. I'll tell everyone what you've done."

He suddenly realizes he's playing this all wrong. He's made himself a threat to them and their terrible plan to keep Charlie for themselves. He needs to reason with them instead. Appeal to their better nature. Tell them they can see Charlie whenever they want.

But his realization comes too late, because something suddenly explodes inside his chest, silencing him forever.

CHAPTER FIFTY
PRESENT DAY

Madison glances at Steve, who looks like he'd happily wring Colt's neck for his part in Dominic's demise if it wouldn't see him arrested himself. She turns to Colt. "Who shot him?" she asks. "Was it Bernie or Ida?"

"Bernie," he says with a sigh. "She wanted to prove to her mother that she was as tough as her."

"What do you mean?" asks Steve, confused.

Colt looks at him. "Ida killed her husband—Bernie's father—years ago, back when Bernie was just a teenager. Then she forced Bernie to help bury the body. You'll find Phil's remains somewhere near Dominic's."

Madison can't believe what she's hearing. It goes some way to explaining why Bernie let her mother get away with being so domineering all her life. She was probably terrified of putting a foot wrong in case Ida killed *her*. She steers the conversation back to Dominic's death for now. "You saw Bernie fire the shot?"

He nods. "I refused to do it for them. All I did was overpower him and bring him to our backyard."

"And what was Toyah doing at the time?" she asks. "Taking care of Charlie?"

Steve shifts in his seat beside her. "Please tell me Charlie didn't witness his father's murder."

A flash of anger passes over Colt's face. "Of course not," he snaps. "She took Charlie from Dominic's place straight to her home in Denver."

That explains why there were never any local sightings of the boy. "Does Charlie know his dad's dead?" asks Madison.

He shrugs. "I don't know what Toyah told him."

Thinking of the oil stain in Dominic's house, she says, "You tried to frame Ryan Simmonds for his murder, right? With the oil stain. His father didn't recognize it, which means it must've been added after Dominic and Charlie vanished."

Colt nods grudgingly. "Ida thought Ryan made a good suspect since it could look like he found out about Denise's affair with Dominic."

Madison bristles. "That man's going through hell right now, and you framing him for murder could've tipped him over the edge. I hope you realize that."

Colt straightens. "Can I get some water? And a lawyer?"

Her heart sinks. She still has so many questions, especially about what could have happened to Denise and Lucy, and whether Colt killed Ida and Lloyd Maxwell. She regrets pushing him. He might not have asked for a lawyer otherwise. "I can get you both, but first would you consider telling us where Bernie and Toyah are now? We need to make sure Charlie's safe, and I'm sure you'd agree that while he's with those two, he's in a lot of danger, especially as patrol is looking for them."

Colt appears to consider it for a long time before sighing heavily. "God help me," he mumbles. He looks her in the eye. "They're hiding at the campsite over near Fantasy World amusement park, waiting for me to return with a fake passport for Charlie. We were going to try to leave the country, but I couldn't do it. I sat at the gas station knowing it was just a matter of time before I was apprehended. I guess I gave up when I realized spending the rest of my life in prison would be easier than living with them and watching them ruin that poor little boy." He looks ashamed of himself as he adds, "He would've been so much better off with his dad."

"Yeah," says Steve. "And he would've still been with him if it weren't for you."

Madison jumps out of her seat and motions for Steve to follow her. Outside the interview room, with the door ajar, she says, "Get Adams in here to watch him. I'll tell dispatch to send officers to the campsite immediately." She has more questions for Colt but no time to ask them. They'll have to wait. Charlie's life is in danger.

Steve nods. "Got it."

Colt stops them. Approaching the door, he says, "Wait! Remember, Bernie's armed. Toyah shouldn't give you any trouble, though. Don't shoot my girl, okay?" He looks desperate as he adds, "She's literally all I have left."

Madison can't bring herself to feel sorry for him. He's brought this on himself. She abruptly turns and leaves.

The sun has set. The campsite is shrouded in darkness. Madison and Steve raise their weapons as they cautiously approach a red and white campervan that Officers Sanchez, Vickers and Kent believe is where Bernie and Toyah are located. The officers got here first and scoped the place out after having spoken to the campsite's owner and prepared them for what's coming. This particular camper is parked in an isolated location away from the others, obviously in a bid to hide the occupants from view. Sanchez reported hearing kids' cartoons coming from inside.

Knowing Bernie's armed, the whole team is wearing bulletproof vests. They move as silently as possible, hoping the element of surprise works in their favor. Madison approaches the door while Steve stays back to keep an eye on the windows. They haven't seen any movement inside, which makes Madison nervous. Bernie and Toyah may already know they're here.

She puts her ear to the door and listens carefully. The only sound coming from inside is the TV. It should be past Charlie's bedtime, so hopefully he'll be safe in a back room while they go in and—

"Get down!" yells Steve, breaking her chain of thought.

She doesn't have time to drop to the ground before a blast rings out. She collapses painfully onto all fours when she feels shards of glass raining down on her. In her peripheral vision she sees Steve fall to the ground as if hit, just as Officer Kent opens fire. "Shots fired from the window!" yells Kent. She fires a second shot herself.

They hear a surprised yelp from inside. Someone's been hit.

Madison glances at Steve, who's currently being dragged out of the line of fire by Sanchez. She can only pray his vest protected him from the impact. Facing the campervan, she knows she has to move fast. She motions for Shelley to approach. Despite being worried for Steve, Shelley instantly moves behind her, staying focused. With a deep breath to steady her nerves, Madison pulls the door toward her. It's unlocked. She steps back as it swings wide open. She waits for another loud blast to rip through the air. When it doesn't, she raises her weapon and steps inside.

Bernie Ridgeway is lying on her back on the floor, blood spilling out of her arm. She's still conscious. Her weapon is discarded next to her but within reach. Madison lunges at it, pulling it out of the way just as Bernie tries to kick her in the face.

"Don't move or I'll shoot!" yells Shelley. She trains her

weapon on the woman as Madison spins around to look in the seating area. Toyah Ridgeway is seated with her hands under her thighs, rocking back and forth like she's self-soothing. She has tears streaming down her face.

"Hands in the air!" yells Madison.

Outside, she hears Sanchez on his radio. "Shots fired! Officer down! We need two ambulances immediately at this location."

Madison doesn't allow herself to think about Steve. She needs to focus on the boy. "Where's Charlie?" she barks at Toyah, who has raised her hands.

"In the back bedroom." She points past her mother.

"Get on the floor with your hands behind your head," barks Madison. "Are you armed?"

"No. My mom had the only weapon." Toyah slowly lowers herself onto the floor.

"Don't say a word, Toyah," spits Bernie, who's now cuffed face-down and writhing in pain.

Madison steps over her to approach two closed doors. She considers whether anyone is hiding back here with Charlie. Perhaps Bernie's nephew Chad. "This is the police!" she says forcefully. "If anyone is in there, make yourself known immediately!"

Silence.

She keeps her weapon raised as she pushes the first door open and steps back. When nothing happens, she switches the light on and peers inside. It's an empty bathroom. She hurries to the next and opens it, moving out of the way in case more shots are fired. Nothing happens, but she hears weeping coming from inside. She switches the light on and looks at the bed. Little Charlie Larson is sitting in bed dressed in Spider-Man pajamas, sucking his thumb as tears stream down his face. He's terrified.

Madison has to push back her own tears of relief at finding him alive. She slips her weapon away and goes to the boy.

Forcing a smile, she sits on the bed and takes his free hand in hers. "Hey, Charlie. My name's Madison. I'm going to take you to see your grandpa, okay?"

Charlie's eye light up. "Grandpa?" It comes out as a hiccup, due to his tears.

She wipes some sweaty hair away from his eyes. "That's right. Grandpa can't wait to see you."

Charlie jumps out from under the cover and holds his arms up to her. Madison gladly picks him up and clutches him close, tears building behind her eyes. She only wishes his dad were waiting for him too.

CHAPTER FIFTY-ONE

Madison brings Charlie to the station. He's been evaluated by an EMT and found to be physically fine, thankfully. His earlier tears from hearing the exchange of gunfire have passed, but he may need emotional support over the coming days and weeks, when it's carefully explained to him that he'll never see his father again. But for now, while they figure out the next steps in the investigation, Stella has offered to care for him now that Dina's arrived to take over from her on dispatch.

Stella's face lights up when Madison brings him over to her in the conference room. Charlie's dressed now, clutching a plastic dinosaur in one hand and holding on to Madison for dear life with the other. He doesn't appear to be a shy child, but he's timid now, and clearly unsettled by finding himself at the police station. Stella's put some toys in the middle of the room so he can play while she watches him, along with a drink and some snacks.

"Hello, Charlie," she says, leaning in. "My name's Stella and I'm going to play with you for an hour or so. Is that okay with you?"

"Is Daddy here?" he asks hopefully.

Madison's heart breaks for him. She takes a deep breath as she exchanges a look with Stella. "No, Daddy's not here but you'll see your grandpa soon, okay?"

Charlie glances around the room like he knows something's off. Eventually, he looks at Stella. "Do you like dinosaurs?"

Madison smiles as Stella emphatically declares her love of dinosaurs, despite probably not knowing half as much about them as he does.

Before Madison leaves, Stella asks her if there's any update on Steve's condition "He was still conscious when I left the campsite," she says, "but he was hit in the thigh, so they've rushed him to the hospital. I'm not gonna lie, he looked terrible." The color had completely drained from him, and it was clear he was in a lot of pain. "Officer Kent exchanged fire and hit Bernie Ridgeway in the arm. Bernie will be fine, but she's also on her way to the hospital."

Over Stella's shoulder, Madison spots Shelley leading a man in a suit, presumably Toyah Ridgeway's lawyer, toward the interview room. Toyah immediately requested an attorney once she was arrested. "I should go," she says. "The lawyer's here."

"Sure." Stella takes Charlie by the hand and leads him to the toys. The poor boy seems okay, despite everything that's happened. But Madison can't help wondering how he'll cope as he grows up and discovers that his mom and dad were both murdered. With a heavy heart, she turns to head to the interview room, but someone calls her name, stopping her.

"I just heard what happened," says Nate rushing over, looking frantic. He pulls her in for a hug. "Are you okay?"

Brody follows him.

"I'm fine," she says after she lets go. "Toyah Ridgeway is here. I'm about to interview her."

"So it was the Ridgeways who killed Dominic?" he asks.

"Right. Hank doesn't know yet, but Charlie's safe. He's here."

Nate takes a deep breath. "Thank God. Hank's going to be ecstatic to see him again. Can I come with you when you tell him? I can make sure Pam's there too, for moral support."

"Sure," she says. "I don't see why not." She glances at the clock on the wall. "I know it's getting late, but if you stick around while I interview Toyah, we can take Charlie to see them as soon as I'm done here."

Chief Mendes approaches, pulling her jacket on, about to head to the hospital. "Who's helping you with the interview, Madison?" She looks around the office. With Steve out of action, the next best person to sit in is Sergeant Adams but he's busy on the phone. "Maybe you should wait until the morning."

Madison doesn't want to wait. She wants answers for when she visits Hank. "What if Nate joins me?" she says. "He knows Charlie's grandfather, Hank, and he's been investigating a cold case for Hank's sister."

"I won't say a word," says Nate. "I'll just be another pair of ears and eyes."

Chief Mendes wouldn't normally let him, but with resources stretched and so much still to be done, plus the fact he's proven himself trustworthy over the years, she relents. "I guess if it's okay with Toyah's lawyer, then fine." She looks at Nate. "But everything you see and hear is strictly confidential, understood?"

"Of course," he says.

Madison quickly turns and heads to the interview room before Mendes can change her mind. Nate follows her. She knocks on the door. "Ready for us?" she asks the lawyer.

He nods and stands, offering them both his hand. She hasn't met this one before. He's tall and slim with thick dark hair. "Dean Miles," he says. "Pleasure."

Madison introduces Nate as a private investigator who sometimes works with the department. Dean doesn't have a problem with him being present, and once they're all seated and the camera is switched on, he says, "My client is fully prepared to cooperate with your investigation, as she's keen to help you."

Madison glances at Toyah, surprised. This isn't usually how it goes. "She is?"

Toyah lowers her eyes. She's nervously rubbing her hands together. Her long red hair hangs limp around her shoulders, needing a wash. It looks as though the events of the past week have taken their toll on her. Madison sees signs of her sister in her face. They have the same high cheekbones and long eyelashes.

"Yes," says the lawyer. "She feels she's also a victim of everything that's happened."

Madison tries not to scoff. She can't wait to hear what makes Toyah think she's a victim. But looking at the woman, she does appear remorseful. Distraught even. She's clearly ashamed of her part in all this. Madison almost feels sorry for her but then remembers that Steve is lying injured in the hospital and Charlie has lost both his parents because of her actions. "Your father, Colt, has been helpful in filling in some gaps already," she says. "He's the one who told us where to find you and your mom."

Toyah nods as though that's what she was expecting. "Dad and I aren't like Mom and Grandma. Never were. Neither was Denise."

Madison isn't sure that's strictly accurate given how Toyah and Colt have both played a part in everything that's happened. "I understand your sister confided in you about her affair with Dominic and how they'd had a baby together. Colt told me you took that information straight to your mom. Why did you do that, Toyah? Weren't you and Denise close? Didn't you realize they'd want Charlie for themselves?"

"No, I didn't." Toyah glances at her lawyer. He nods to indicate that she should answer. "You don't understand," she says quietly. "In this family, you do what you're told, because you know that if you go against Mom or Grandma, you're effectively no longer one of them. When you're in, you're in, and that comes with protection. But when you don't toe the line, you're no more their blood than anyone else is."

"And blood was important to them, right?"

Toyah scoffs. "Apparently. Although they didn't mind..." She tails off, not finishing her thought.

"What, Toyah?" says Madison gently. "Tell me what's bothering you."

"It's just... my mom..." She falls silent. Her lawyer has his pen poised to record whatever she says, despite knowing he'll have access to the recording and any statements taken here today.

Madison leans in. "Your dad told us it was Bernie who shot and killed Dominic Larson. They wanted to keep Charlie for themselves. Is that right?"

Toyah nods.

Madison still can't understand their logic. He was their grandson; they could have just asked to be a part of his life. Dominic was the kind of person who would have let them. "Did your mom always want a son? Is that why she abducted Charlie?"

Toyah shifts uncomfortably, suggesting she could be right.

"Was she extra hard on you and Denise because you weren't boys?" she presses. "I know some parents feel like they need a son in order to keep the family name going, but I'm wondering why she didn't just try for another baby. That's what most people do. Or did she have a medical issue that stopped her having a third child?"

Toyah meets her gaze with scorn. "My so-called mother never gave birth to a baby in her life," she says bitterly. "She had fertility issues."

Madison frowns. That's not what she was expecting. "Oh.

So if she didn't give birth to you and Denise, were you adopted?"

"No."

"She used a surrogate?" asks Nate, unable to help himself. He seems as frustrated by Toyah's infuriatingly short answers as Madison is.

"No." Toyah sighs heavily. "Dad told me recently that the date of birth I've been using my entire life was fabricated. So was Denise's."

"Fabricated?" Madison's confused. "Why on earth would they give you fake birthdays?" She tries to figure out where this is going, but only knows it can't be good. Perhaps that's why the sisters were homeschooled, because they had no official identifying documents, or maybe they did have ID but Bernie didn't want them to know their real dates of birth for some reason.

"I always felt like an outsider when it came to my mom and grandmother," says Toyah wearily. "And it finally made sense when Dad explained everything. Turns out I'm not related to Bernie and Ida at all. They may have raised me, but we aren't blood relations."

Nate leans back in his seat beside Madison. She senses he's figured something out, but she's still a step behind him. "What do you mean?" she asks. "Why did they fake your birthdays? Aren't you related to any of the Ridgeways?"

Toyah shifts in her seat. "I'm Colt's daughter, and I'm Denise's sister, but we weren't born two years apart. We're actually twins."

Madison takes a second to try to figure out why the Ridgeways would keep that from the girls.

"I thought I was thirty-one, and that Denise was twenty-nine when she died. But according to Dad, I was only born nine minutes before my sister."

She tries to piece everything together. "So how old are you really?"

"Thirty. We're fraternal twins. I look like my father, but Denise looked much more like our mother. Our *birth* mother."

Madison's mouth goes dry as it dawns on her where this is going. She hopes she's wrong, but the fact that Denise and Toyah were born thirty years ago suggests she's not. "Tell me, Toyah," she says, needing it confirmed. "Who's your birth mother?"

Toyah looks her in the eye. "Her name was Sharon Smith."

Nate shakily exhales beside her, stunned. He's been looking for Sharon and her baby, but he could never have predicted this outcome. Did he ever consider the Ridgeways as suspects for her disappearance? She doesn't know, but *she* can't understand the link between them and Sharon. All she knows is that she and Nate wrongly suspected that too much time had passed for Sharon or her baby to still be alive. Yet one of Sharon's children is sitting before them, alive and well but currently under investigation for the abduction of Charlie Larson, who Madison suddenly realizes is Sharon's grandson by way of her daughter Denise. And Lucy Ridgeway was her granddaughter.

Stunned by the implications, it explains why the photos of Sharon from her missing person poster reminded her of someone. She looks like her children, especially Denise, who had the same blonde hair.

Breaking the stunned silence, Madison reluctantly asks, "What happened to Sharon thirty years ago? Did your father tell you that much?"

A tear rolls down Toyah's face as she nods. "What they did to my mother was despicable."

Madison feels Nate brace himself beside her as a shiver runs through her own body. "Tell us, Toyah," she says. "We need to know."

CHAPTER FIFTY-TWO

MAY 1992

Sharon's back is killing her. Her bump is so big now that some customers have joked she might be having twins. She hopes not, but admits there is a small possibility given the fact her mom is a twin. Of course, she would already know one way or the other if she had actually attended any doctor's visits, but she and Pam can't afford to get into debt, and she worries she'll be judged for not being married to the baby's father. If the doctor's office knew she was in a relationship with another woman, they might even contact child services. Sharon's heard stories about that happening to other same-sex couples who have children, so she's steering clear of medical professionals and letting nature take its course. She trusts that she'll learn everything about her baby when the time comes.

If she's honest with herself, those aren't the only reasons she's avoided doctors. The idea of being probed by a male gynecologist triggers her, given how she had gotten pregnant in the first place. Letting a strange man examine her down there will feel too much like what Colt Ridgeway did to her that night he stopped by the store to supposedly help her close up. She had insisted she could do it alone, but he stayed anyway. Colt had always viewed her with hungry eyes, but never really said much to her, which made his behavior even more creepy. Since he was her boss's son-in-law, Sharon had no one to complain to about him, so she just had to deal with him staring at her.

She realizes now that she should have left her job. But new jobs are hard to come by. She's only hanging on financially by a thread and she really doesn't want to return to bartending, as men like Colt are everywhere in that line of work, except they're more overt about their sleaziness. Colt hadn't forced himself on her, not really. He'd cornered her in the storeroom after locking the store and switching the lights out. He'd implied Ida was on the verge of firing her, which she probably was, but he said he could persuade her not to. All Sharon had to do was stay quiet and it would be over with in a matter of minutes. He was right. The physical act took less than five minutes. The shame has lasted longer and will probably never go away.

He left shortly after and never tried it again, thankfully. She's seen him a handful of times since and he knows she's pregnant but has probably convinced himself someone else is the father. So because of Colt Ridgeway, she's given in to her fear and steered clear of all doctors during her pregnancy in case she's triggered and breaks down in front of them. That would be awful. They might assume her panic attacks mean she's not fit to raise her child. When the time comes, at some point within the next four weeks by her estimation, she's planning to have a home birth, with just Pam and Hank present. The pair of them have researched what to do during labor by reading books from the library. They're the only people she trusts, so she's content with her decision. If anything goes wrong, well, then they'll call an ambulance, but she doesn't think it will come to that.

She's almost finished her last chore, filling all the vases with water so the flowers don't wilt overnight. It's meant to be her day off, but Ida called asking her to top up the vases as she'd forgotten to do it herself. Despite the fact she'd already been in bed, Sharon agreed, because she's scared of her boss. Ida was mad as hell when she first noticed Sharon's bump, claiming it would cost her time and money to hire a replacement. To appease her, Sharon agreed to continue to work as close to her due date as humanly possible, and over the last few weeks things have seemed better between them. Ida's anger and disgust suddenly subsided out of nowhere. Sharon's even been allowed longer breaks now and she doesn't have to lift heavy items anymore. It's like the older woman has finally discovered a maternal side.

Sharon yawns, feeling like she could fall asleep on her feet. Being pregnant has been no fun this last two months. The bell above the door jingles, so she turns, ready to tell the customer the store's closed, but it's Bernie Ridgeway who steps in. Bernie's taken more of an active role in the business lately, and seems a lot friendlier toward Sharon than previously. Sharon's noticed pregnancy can do that—make other women more interested in her, more likely to start conversations. It's been nice in most cases, but she's been uncomfortable around Bernie ever since Colt took advantage of her.

"Locking up?" asks Bernie, her eyes hovering on Sharon's huge bump.

"Yeah. I'm done now." Sharon pulls her apron off and switches the lights out before a sharp stabbing pain in her lower stomach stops her in her tracks, making her groan.

"You okay?" asks Bernie, stepping forward.

Sharon feels an urge to use the bathroom, but it quickly passes. A second stabbing pain shoots through her lower back. She winces. "I'm fine. I probably spent too long on my feet today."

"Is Pam picking you up?"

"No, she thinks I'm at home in bed. It's meant to be my day off." She approaches the exit and steps out into the cool evening.

Bernie follows her and locks the door. "I can't let you ride the bus in your condition. I'll take you home."

"Oh no, really, it's fine," she protests. "It only takes fifteen minutes from here."

Bernie smiles at her. "Don't be silly. What if your waters break on the bus, or you fall over when it pulls away? I'd feel terrible. And I'm going that way anyway. Let's go." She walks to her vehicle.

Sharon really doesn't want to get in her car, but she can't think of a polite way of saying it without sounding ungrateful. Besides, the shooting pains are getting more pronounced, making it feel like someone's shoving knitting needles up her ass. She waddles to the car and slips inside, slowly pulling her swollen feet in after her.

Bernie drives out of the strip mall's parking lot. It's quiet on the roads. The warmth from the car and the hum of the engine make Sharon sleepy. She's always sleepy lately, and falls asleep at the drop of a hat. Pam says it's because she's busy growing a baby. She leans her head against the rest as the car stereo plays soft music.

Sharon jolts awake. She's confused at first, not remembering where she is. Then she becomes aware of being lifted. Someone has hold of her underarms, and someone else is holding her ankles, their grip painfully tight. She tries to open her eyes and realizes they're covered with something. She's so confused she assumes she's dreaming, until she hears a voice say, "Put her on the mattress."

Her blood runs cold. "What's going on?" she says. "Argh! That hurts. What are you doing?"

The shooting pains in her back and stomach are getting

worse. She worries they could be contractions, but it's too soon, isn't it? She wonders if she passed out in Bernie's car and has been brought to the hospital for monitoring. But when she tries to move her hands, it becomes clear they're bound together. Fear envelops her. She stops breathing as she's placed on what feels like a mattress on the floor—it has no bounce and she can feel the hard ground beneath it. "What the hell is happening?"

Someone tears the blindfold off her. She desperately looks around and sees she's in some kind of outbuilding or shed that's dark except for a few small lights dotted around. Bernie and Ida are hovering over her, eyeing her like she's an experiment. Colt's here too, but he's exiting the building so she can only see his back. Presumably he helped carry her here from the car. The walls close in on her as she tries to figure out what's happening.

"You were contracting," says Ida. "We're taking care of you. Bernie and I will deliver your baby."

Sharon stares at them in horror. "I don't want to give birth here. Take me home. Or to the hospital. Call Pam. I need her!"

Ida scoffs. "There's no time for that. You're in labor."

Sharon doesn't understand. She doesn't know why they'd bring her here instead of to the hospital. But she doesn't get long to think about it, because an almighty pain tears through her insides, making her scream out in agony. Ida gets on her knees and pulls Sharon's dress up. She roughly removes her underwear, causing embarrassment to wash over her. "No, please," she begs. "Not you guys. I want Pam. I want the hospital!"

Ida looks up at her daughter. "It won't be long. Get everything we need, including the pain meds."

Bernie nods before leaving them alone together. Sharon's embarrassment at having Ida see her naked below the waist reduces the more the contractions tear through her. She needs this baby out of her, and she doesn't care who does it.

. . .

Hours pass. Sharon's unsure how many, as she's been in so much pain and she's feeling delirious from whatever pills Ida forced down her throat. She remembers bursts of consciousness. Being yelled at to push through the pain of contractions. Someone pressing on her belly, making her want to vomit. And the feel of her insides being pulled out as she used what little strength she had to scream while praying she didn't burst a blood vessel.

She rouses to the sound of a crying baby. She forces her head off the mattress and realizes her hands are no longer bound. "Did I do it?" She notices a hell of a lot of blood covering the mattress below her waist. She feels like she's wet herself. Surely that's too much blood? She probably needs to get to the hospital as fast as possible, but she can't imagine ever standing again. She just doesn't have the energy. Her legs feel like jelly and her whole body is trembling, making her teeth rattle together. She sees Colt hovering in the doorway, too afraid or embarrassed by her nakedness to step inside.

Bernie's proudly holding a baby in her arms. "You sure did. This is Toyah."

"A girl!" Sharon sobs at seeing her beautiful baby for the first time. She has fine red hair and her face is scrunched up like she's unhappy about something.

She frowns as she realizes Bernie has named her daughter. That's not for her to do.

Ida steps forward holding a different baby. "And this is Denise."

Sharon blinks. "I had *twins*?" She thinks of her mom. Perhaps having twin granddaughters will bring her and her mother back together since her mother is a twin. Her heart flutters with hope. They might be able to repair their broken relationship.

Baby Denise has fine blonde hair and is silently peering around the room.

"Give them to me." Sharon holds her arms out, yearning to feel her babies on her chest. It's such a powerful need that she can't imagine ever having empty arms again. But the strength goes from her, making her arms drop back onto the mattress. Something isn't right. She needs some glucose, or food. Something sugary to boost her strength.

"Afraid not," says Ida, looking down at her. "They're our babies now."

An overwhelming surge of dread creeps through Sharon's chest, so strong she can't breathe. "What do you mean?" She goes lightheaded and is desperate for some water.

"We know Colt is their father," says Ida. "We know you seduced him in order to get pregnant. Which means these babies are Ridgeways, not Smiths. Don't you worry, though, we'll take good care of them."

Sharon scoffs, thinking they're playing a terrible prank on her. "You're not serious? Why would you joke at a time like this? Give me my babies! I want my babies *now*."

But Bernie and Ida turn away and leave, taking Colt and her daughters with them.

The door closes behind them, leaving her with just the soft glow of a single light. Her head falls back on the mattress. Void of all strength, she can do nothing but sob. Her arms are empty, her body is empty, and she's not allowed to kiss her beautiful babies.

Minutes turn into an hour, maybe longer. She lies still, tears streaming from her eyes in disbelief. Someone will save her. Or Bernie will realize this joke has gone too far. She'll show some compassion and return with her daughters.

She fades in and out of consciousness again. The pain meds begin to wear off, making her aware of an intense burning sensation down below. "Please don't hurt my babies!" she sobs every few minutes.

After a while, the pain becomes more bearable as she goes lightheaded. She gets a sensation of passing out, before coming round and remembering what happened. "Wait until Pam finds out," she mutters. "She'll kill you for this."

Her eyes close as she fades away.

CHAPTER FIFTY-THREE
PRESENT DAY

Toyah is sobbing by the time she's finished relaying what Colt told her. "He said he buried my mom in the backyard, but I don't know where. I was too traumatized to ask questions."

Madison closes her eyes. Sharon must be in the same grave Dominic was found in, where Ida's husband was presumably buried too.

"Dad said he almost called the police on them because he felt so terrible watching it all play out without intervening," says Toyah, trying to regain her composure. "But he couldn't do that without admitting he was the father of Sharon's children, so he left her to die alone in that awful place, having never had the opportunity to hold me and Denise."

Silence fills the room. Madison is on the verge of breaking down herself. She knows what it's like to have a child taken from her, but she and Owen were eventually able to reunite. Sharon never got to spend a single second with her daughters. The Ridgeways may not have killed her with a weapon, but all three of them are responsible for letting her die. And Colt may be remorseful now, but he's the one who set this terrible series of events in motion. He's the one who raped Sharon Smith.

Getting her pregnant caused a butterfly effect that has ruined so many lives.

Anger makes Madison clench her jaw. It's too late to bring Ida to justice, but she's determined to make sure Colt and Bernie pay for what they did.

Toyah's lawyer drops his pen on his pad. "I think it best that we end the questioning for today. My client is clearly emotional and it's getting late."

"I agree," says Madison. "But I just have one more question." She looks at Toyah, who's wiping her eyes with tissues. "Why help them abduct Charlie knowing what they'd done to your mother?"

"I didn't know any of that in February," she says. "My dad only told me everything when we got to the campsite yesterday. He waited until we were alone. After he told me, he said he was leaving to secure fake passports for us. Before I could do anything, Bernie was back from her walk with Charlie and I was stuck in the campervan with her, desperately trying to hatch a plan to escape."

"You could've called the police," says Nate.

Toyah looks at him. "I was seriously considering it, but I was afraid. I knew I was in too deep." She wipes her nose. "I promise you both that I didn't hurt anyone, but I *was* an accessory to what they did because I'd taken Charlie from his home to mine. I hid him for months. So I was afraid that if I called the police, I'd go to prison for that, even though I took care of him as best I could. I loved having him with me." A tear runs down her cheek. "He's such a special little boy, and he wouldn't stop asking about his dad."

Madison doesn't say it, but it's likely Toyah *will* go to prison for her part in all this. She stands. "Okay, we're done here. I'll have an officer escort you to the cells once you two have had a chance to talk."

The lawyer nods. "Thanks."

She and Nate leave. Outside the room, Madison turns to him. "I know it's late, but we need to tell Pam and Hank everything."

He rubs the back of his neck, clearly dreading it. "This is going to be painful."

She touches his arm. "I know. But at least they'll have Charlie back with them. Hopefully that will help soften the blow." She pauses. "Did you know Sharon worked for Ida Randall?"

"No. I knew she worked at a place that no longer exists called Phil's Flowers. The owner was on my list of people to contact, but I hadn't gotten around to it yet. I guess Ida bought the place from this Phil guy?"

"No, Phil was her husband," Madison says. "He supposedly left her for another woman back when Bernie was a teenager, but rumors suggest she killed him. We're expecting his remains to be with Dominic's, and I guess Sharon's too."

"Jeez." Nate takes a deep breath. "I had no idea the place was owned by anyone linked to the Ridgeways. I wish I'd focused my attention there sooner now."

"Doesn't matter," she says. "The outcome would've been the same either way. Sharon was murdered thirty years ago. Nothing you could've done would have helped her."

He nods. "I guess. Do you still think Ryan Simmonds killed Denise and Lucy? And what about Ida's death, was that Colt?"

She sighs. "I have no idea. It's possible. I intend to interview Colt and Toyah again in the morning. Maybe Colt will admit to killing all three of them. If not, that leaves us with Ryan." She's exhausted just thinking about it, especially as she can't understand where Lloyd Maxwell's death fits into all this, especially if she and Steve are right and Chad was the real target of the wedding shooter. She hopes things will become clearer once she's had some rest.

Nate pulls his phone out. "I'll call Pam, let her know we're heading over to Hank's place with news. Hopefully she can meet us there."

Madison returns to the conference room to get Charlie. He's being carried around the room on Adams's back. Adams is on all fours, sweating from exertion and making weird noises, presumably pretending to be some kind of dinosaur. She smiles. You can say what you want about the guy, but at least he's good with kids. Stella notices her at the door and stands as she enters.

"Hi, Charlie," says Madison as he slips off Adams's back. "Are you ready to see your aunt Pam and your grandpa?"

His eyes light up. "Yeah!" He swings around in a circle, clearly excited by the prospect.

She holds her hand out. "Come on then. Let's go."

Before they can leave, Adams approaches her. "I had an update from Chief Mendes about Steve. He's scheduled for surgery in the morning as they need to remove the bullet, but the docs think it'll be straightforward. He's bright and alert, already joking about what to do with his time off. Mendes doesn't think we need to worry about him. Shelley's going to stay with him overnight." He grins. "Told you they had a thing going."

Madison's relieved the injury isn't life-threatening. "Okay. Thanks for letting me know, and for taking care of this little one."

She turns to leave. It's time to reunite Charlie with his grandfather.

CHAPTER FIFTY-FOUR

Madison pulls up outside Hank Larson's home in the dark, with Charlie falling asleep in the back of her vehicle. It's approaching 11 p.m., and although she's exhausted, she suspects the evening's events will keep her awake well into the early hours of the morning.

As she switches the engine off, she sees that Nate and Brody have beat her here, as did Pam Smith, who's standing on the porch, listening with growing horror as Nate relays everything they learned tonight about what happened to her nephew, Dominic. They agreed it was best she knew before Hank, so she can help break the news to him as delicately as possible.

"Aunt Pam!" Charlie points to her through the back window.

"That's right," says Madison, smiling. She's so glad he has some family to take care of him. She exits the vehicle, opens the back door and undoes the clasp on the child seat. Hoisting him out, she balances him on her hip as she approaches Pam and Nate. Holding a child this way reminds her of when Owen was little. She used to love walking around with him like this. He'd usually suck his thumb and rest his head in the crook of her neck. But those days are long gone.

Pam looks completely overwhelmed when she sees her young nephew for the first time in months. She holds her arms out to Charlie, who wriggles into her embrace. "Charlie!" she says, her voice thick with emotion. "We missed you so much!" She kisses him all over his face, with tears streaming down her cheeks. Eventually, she looks at Madison. "Is he okay? He wasn't harmed?"

"He's fine. He was well cared for." Madison clears her throat, feeling terrible that she has to deliver more bad news before they go inside. "I gather Nate's told you about Dominic, but unfortunately, we also have an upsetting update about Sharon."

Pam glances at Nate, her eyes widening. "You do?"

Nate nods.

She lowers Charlie to the ground but keeps hold of his hand. She studies their faces. "It's bad, isn't it?"

"I'm afraid so," says Nate, exhaling heavily with sadness. "Before coming here, we learned that Sharon died the same night she vanished."

Pam's hand flies to her mouth. "Oh God, no!" She lets go of Charlie's hand and covers her face, prompting Nate to squeeze her shoulder briefly.

"I'm so sorry," he says. "She died due to blood loss during childbirth."

Pam sobs. A few minutes pass before she manages to compose herself. She wipes her eyes, completely overwhelmed. It's then that she frowns. "Wait, I don't understand. She was in labor? At the *hospital*? But I called them. They said she wasn't there. And Bill Harper checked all the nearby hospitals for any sign she'd been there." A second passes before she realizes there's an even more important question she hasn't considered.

Slowly, with a hand pressed to her heart, she asks, "Did the baby survive?"

Charlie lowers himself onto the porch steps to stroke Brody. Madison keeps an eye on him.

"She didn't go into labor at the hospital," says Nate. "Unfortunately, she was abducted by the Ridgeways. It was Colt who sexually assaulted her. Ida and Bernie found out he was the one who got her pregnant, and since Bernie was unable to have children of her own, they took Sharon to steal her child."

Tears stream down Pam's face. She looks like she might pass out. "I can't believe what I'm hearing."

"I know," says Nate. "It's terrible. But we learned tonight that Sharon gave birth to twins. And they were both born healthy."

Pam swallows, looking back and forth between them incredulously. "We had *twins*?"

Madison could cry for Pam right now. The babies' biological parents were Colt Ridgeway and Sharon Smith, but Pam had been preparing to welcome Sharon's child into her life. She was preparing to become a mother. Losing Sharon *and* the baby must have been a terrible double blow for her.

"That's right," confirms Nate.

"Where are they now?" says Pam eagerly. "Can I see them?" She looks desperate to get a glimpse of the closest link she has to her girlfriend.

"The Ridgeways raised the girls as their own," says Nate. "They named them Denise and Toyah."

A look of terrible sadness spreads across Pam's face as realization hits her. "But Denise and her little girl were murdered recently, right? I read about it in the news."

Nate nods. "I'm afraid so. Denise is gone, but Toyah's still alive."

Pam blinks as she absorbs the news. Nate fills her in on Toyah and Colt's involvement in Dominic's murder and Charlie's abduction. Her joy at learning one of Sharon's daughters is still alive is quickly replaced with growing horror at everything that Toyah and her family have done. She reaches for the porch railing to hold herself up. "My God. This is too much."

They give her a couple of minutes to let it all sink it.

"You need to try to focus on Charlie now," says Madison. "He needs a guardian. With your brother's ill health, that might fall to you."

Pam nods slowly. "So Charlie is Sharon's grandson, isn't he?" She chokes back a sob. Wiping her eyes with her hands, she says, "I couldn't raise our daughters, but I can raise our grandchild. I think that's what Sharon would've wanted, right?"

Nate nods, but doesn't speak. Madison can tell he's getting choked up. Like her, he becomes emotionally invested in the cases he investigates. It takes its toll.

"I'm sure she would've loved that," says Madison. With a deep breath, she adds, "But right now, we need to tell Hank about Dominic. Do you think he can take it? We don't want to risk his health deteriorating."

Pam thinks about it, then looks at Charlie, who's nodding off on the porch. "He's gone downhill fast over the last week. But seeing Charlie will help him with his grief." She scoops the little boy into her arms and plants a gentle kiss on his cheek, keeping hold of him as Nate takes her keys to enter the house. She lets Madison and Nate enter ahead of her then follows them inside, leaving the door ajar for Brody to come and go.

They find Hank dozing on the couch. The living room is lit with the soft glow from the TV. Nate switches it off as Madison turns on some lights.

Pam sits beside her brother on the couch, with Charlie still in her arms. "Hank? Look who's come to see you."

Hank rouses. As his eyes adjust to the light, he squints at Madison and Nate, confused. "What's going on?" he sputters.

"Look who it is," says Pam.

Hank looks at Charlie and blinks. Charlie rouses, suddenly noticing who he's sitting next to. "Grandpa!"

Hank gasps as Charlie leaps into his arms. He squeezes his grandson tight and tears roll down his face. "Charlie? You're back! Oh, Charlie. I missed you so much! Am I dreaming? Have I died?"

Madison becomes overwhelmed. She feels Nate's arm around her shoulders. It's a touching moment to see them reunited, but it's spoiled when Hank looks past them toward the open door, clearly expecting his son to be there. "Where's Dominic?"

She tries to compose herself. "I'm so sorry." Not wanting to say too much in front of Charlie, she shakes her head to signal Dominic won't be coming home.

Pam gently touches her brother's arm. "We won't get to see Dominic again, but we have Charlie back. We need to focus on that."

He looks crestfallen. Charlie is a wonderful consolation prize, but at some point, Hank will have to come to terms with his son's murder.

Pam's been trying to hold it together, but she suddenly crumples under the pressure of her own grief. Her voice thick with emotion, she says, "I need to go to Dominic's house to pick up some spare clothes and toys for Charlie." She gets up and hurries out of the open front door just as Brody enters.

Brody sniffs the room, and when he gets close to Hank, his demeanor visibly changes. His stance becomes stiff, and he starts barking forcefully at the older man.

Madison glances at Nate questioningly.

Nate tries to pull the dog away, but he doesn't want to come. His aggression scares Charlie, who tightly embraces his grandpa. "He can probably smell your meds," says Nate, knowing Hank must be taking pain relief for his cancer. "Sorry, he's a former K9, trained to alert us to all kinds of things. Let me get him out of here." With some effort, he tugs Brody away and out of the house, slamming the front door behind him.

Madison's embarrassed. "Sorry about that. Don't worry, Charlie, he won't hurt you."

"Never did like dogs," says Hank. Still holding Charlie, he gets out of his seat and goes to the front door to lock it so Brody can't return.

Madison doesn't take it personally. Not everyone is an animal lover.

Hank approaches a sideboard and opens a drawer, his back to her. Madison can hear Brody going wild outside. It sounds like Nate's struggling to control him. He's going to start attracting attention from the neighbors if he carries on like this. It's odd, because he never usually causes this kind of scene unless someone's in danger. But why would any of them be in danger?

Her mouth suddenly goes dry. A shudder runs through her as it slowly dawns on her what Brody's trying to tell them. *Shit.* She tries to swallow. "Hank," she says cautiously. "Have you ever met Brody before?"

He turns to look at her, which is when she sees what he retrieved from the drawer. A gun. He nods. "I have. The day of your fancy wedding, in fact."

Madison's blood runs cold as she realizes just seconds too late that Hank Larson is the wedding shooter.

CHAPTER FIFTY-FIVE

Madison swallows back her fear. She's torn between drawing her service weapon and racing to grab Charlie from Hank's arms. She wishes Nate were still here. They should have known to trust Brody's response. He's rarely wrong. But they came here to deliver bad news, not to arrest a killer.

She dares to glance over Hank's shoulder to the window overlooking the driveway. If Nate looks in, she could try to signal to him that she and Charlie are in danger, but she watches with growing dread as he concentrates on getting Brody into the back of his car. Pam slides into the passenger seat. He must be giving her a ride to Dominic's place. Madison wills him to look over at the house one last time before getting into the vehicle himself.

He doesn't, which means she has no backup. Somehow she'll need to get herself and Charlie out of here without either of them being injured.

Hank closes the drapes, blocking her view of the outside. "Sit down," he says, moving back to the couch and seating Charlie on his lap. The little boy has fallen asleep. He's dead to the world after his eventful day.

Madison reluctantly lowers herself onto the armchair opposite them, facing the window.

"They can't get in," he says, "even with Pam's keys. I've bolted the door from the inside." He coughs. "I'm not going to hurt you. I just want the opportunity to tell you my side of the story."

She's not worried for herself, she's worried for Charlie. Hank has nothing to lose at this point. He's already dying. And now that he knows his son is dead and he's about to be exposed as a killer, it might push him over the edge.

"I didn't know it was *your* wedding," he says, gun by his side. "Not until it was in the news."

"But you sent me a note," she says. "Why pretend I was the target if I wasn't?"

"It was an attempt at misdirection. I had to hide who my real target was." He takes a deep, weary breath before explaining. "I was out there hunting that day, letting off some steam, but I spotted Bernie and Colt's precious nephew working the event. I could see it was a wedding, but I didn't know whose. All I know is that I saw Chad working the outside bar and I took my opportunity for revenge." He runs a hand down his face. "I'm sorry for hitting the wedding officiant instead. I regret that terribly."

Madison's confused. "Revenge for what? Are you telling me you already knew Dominic was killed by the Ridgeways at that point?"

"I didn't know anything for sure, but Ida gave me enough clues to figure it out."

She shakes her head. "I'm sorry, but I don't understand." It's true, she doesn't. But she's also buying time for Nate to return and realize he's locked out. Maybe then he'll figure out why Brody was barking at Hank.

Hank sighs. "When my son and Charlie vanished, I was bereft. I didn't sleep. I was a wreck of my former self. I started drinking heavily just to get through the miserable hours. The day before your wedding, I bumped into Ida Randall outside the grocery store. She was in her wheelchair, smoking a cigarette as she waited for Bernie and Denise to finish shopping. I've known Ida for years, just in passing. She was a horrible woman, but I was lonely, so I sat beside her on the bench. She told me I reeked of liquor. I said I didn't care. That my boys were missing so I had a reason to drink in the daytime. She said maybe it was karma." He shakes his head in disgust. "I said karma for what?" He pauses. "Do you know what she replied?"

"No," says Madison, "but knowing Ida, it won't have been good."

He nods. "You're right. She said they could've vanished as karma for keeping Charlie from his real family for so long. It was then that I realized she knew Denise was Charlie's mom. My stomach was in knots, as Dominic had made it clear to me from the outset that Denise didn't want her family knowing she'd had another child. I figured it was because she was embarrassed about having an affair, but now I know it's because they would've wanted to keep Charlie close, make him as bitter and twisted as they are. She didn't want that for her little boy. She wanted to give him a fighting chance of a life filled with love. That's why she let Dominic raise him. And it would've worked out great if they hadn't found out about his existence."

Madison keeps her eyes on his weapon. "Denise confided in her sister, Toyah," she says. "And unfortunately, Toyah told Bernie and Ida about the affair and Charlie's existence."

Hank nods, everything making sense now. "Once I realized Ida knew about Charlie, it wasn't difficult to figure out what had happened to my son. I knew about her reputation. I'd heard rumors she'd killed her husband back in the day. My gut told me she was behind Dominic's abduction. And the only reason she would do that was to get to Charlie."

"So what did you do?" asks Madison.

"I wanted to kill her with my bare hands right there and then. Instead, I went home and stewed over it. The next day I got my gun and went hunting. That was when I saw Chad at the lodge. Maybe subconsciously I'd gone nearby to hunt because I knew he worked there. It makes no difference now. The bottom line is, I had a clear aim, so after making a split-second decision, I took it. Like I said, I'm sorry for hitting Lloyd Maxwell instead, but by then the wheels were set in motion for everything that followed."

Her hands are slick with sweat. She's trying to assess whether she could pull her weapon faster than he could raise his. But Charlie's sleeping against his chest. There's no way she can fire shots while he's in the way. "Chad is innocent too," she says. "Why target him when your beef is with Colt, Bernie and Ida? Why not come to the police with your suspicion?"

He scoffs. "Oh please. You guys never found Sharon, so Pam and I never had any faith in law enforcement." His stare turns cold. "Besides, I wanted to hurt them by taking out someone they loved, just like they did to me. If they were dead, they wouldn't feel an ounce of what I'm feeling."

Madison's stomach flips with dread. She thinks she knows what's coming. "It was you who tried to break into their outbuilding, wasn't it?"

He nods. "I wanted to find proof of what they'd done. I thought they'd killed Dominic and possibly Charlie too, given how evil they are, so it would make sense for them to dispose of the bodies on their land, but I didn't find anything."

Madison swallows. "We found Dominic's body under the outbuilding earlier today."

He squeezes his eyes closed with grief. Madison considers lunging for his weapon, but he quickly opens them again. "In that case, I don't feel so bad about killing their daughter."

Her mouth falls open in shock. "It was *you* who killed Denise and Lucy?"

He nods. "But it's not what you think. I didn't go there with the intention of hurting anyone." He swallows. "I went to see what Denise knew. I wanted to find out where my boys were. She said she didn't know anything, but I didn't believe her. Rage and alcohol got the better of me because she was the reason my boy was taken. If she had been honest about not being single, Dominic would never have started a relationship with her! I strangled her out of frustration. I didn't mean for her to die! I wanted to scare her into being honest." A sob breaks out. Eventually, he adds, "Her little girl saw me. She was a witness. I knew I had to kill her too. I didn't want to. But if I was locked up, I'd never be able to find my boys and get the proof I needed."

Madison's horrified. Denise and Lucy died because her family abducted Charlie. This was all a battle between two families, neither of whom came to the police for help. Equally guilty of something, they wanted to settle it themselves, but that just made everything so much worse. She watches with disgust as Hank wipes his face dry with his sleeve.

"I couldn't use my hands on the little girl," he says. "I used a cord instead. It felt less like murder."

It's difficult to listen to his story. Madison hides her contempt as she asks, "Why did you cover her afterward, and put a pillow under her head? You put a stuffed animal beside her like you were tucking her in to sleep. Why?"

He won't look at her. "Why do you think? I was remorseful. I wanted her to know I was sorry."

Unable to help herself, she shakes her head in disgust. "She was already dead, Hank. So all that did was make *you* feel better." When he doesn't respond, she says, "Bernie Ridgeway wasn't Denise and Toyah's real mother."

His head snaps up. "What?"

"Charlie wasn't the only child they abducted. Thirty years ago, they made your friend Sharon give birth in that very same outbuilding your son is buried under. They took her babies from her as she bled out. Those babies that Sharon and Pam were so looking forward to raising together were instead raised as Denise and Toyah Ridgeway."

The blood drains from his face as he realizes he's killed one of Sharon's children. "No. Please don't tell me that. I loved Sharon like a sister. Pam would never forgive me if she found out. Please tell me that's not true."

So Pam doesn't know what her brother has done. She isn't involved. That's something at least. Madison shakes her head. "I'm afraid I can't, because it *is* true."

He looks winded as despair washes over him. "Then I can never again look my sister in the eye. Not now." His grip tightens on his weapon as he raises it. "I have nothing left to live for."

Madison freezes in fear as she anticipates the gunshot blast.

CHAPTER FIFTY-SIX

Nate drops Pam at Dominic and Charlie's house so she can pick up some of Charlie's clothes and toys. She's already starting to come to terms with what's happened, probably because she has the little boy to focus on. He thinks it would be different if Charlie had also been killed.

Brody still hasn't quit barking by the time Pam exits the vehicle. It's giving Nate a headache. "I better get him home," he says. "Will you be able to make your way back to Hank's when you're done?"

"Sure, I'll get a cab." Before she closes the door, she says, "I need to thank you for investigating Sharon's disappearance. I was convinced her mom or Justin had something to do with it. Now I know it was that awful Ridgeway family, and where she's buried, I can organize a funeral for her. I'm hopeful that will give me some closure." She tears up.

Nate feels for her. "I'm just sorry it wasn't better news." He hesitates. "Do you think you might want to speak to her remaining daughter one day? Because Toyah was remorseful over her part in Charlie's abduction. She only learned yesterday that Bernie wasn't her real mother. She was devastated when she found out what happened to Sharon."

Pam considers it. "I think Sharon would want me to show her forgiveness, so maybe I'll send her a letter while she's in jail. Perhaps we can build some kind of relationship out of all this devastation."

Nate nods. "I'm sure she'd love that. She'll need family around her over the next few months, and as you were supposed to raise her with Sharon, I'd say that includes you."

A tear runs down Pam's face. "Thank you for saying that. I know Sharon and I weren't married, but I did feel motherly toward the unborn baby." She pauses. "Of course, we had no idea she was expecting twins." She quietly closes the door and walks to the house.

Nate starts the engine and pulls away from the curb. When Brody squeezes through the gap into the front passenger seat, barking directly in Nate's ear, he knows he needs to listen to him. "What's the matter, boy? Is it Hank's place?"

More barking. It's times like this he wishes Brody could talk. He had intended to drop him at home before returning to pick Madison up, but his gut tells him he needs to turn the car around instead and head back to Hank's place immediately.

As he drives, he runs through the possible triggers for Brody. It could be the cancer meds Hank is taking, or maybe cannabis he bought to help with the pain. Or perhaps Brody smelled blood at his place. But again, that could be due to Hank's illness causing nosebleeds or something.

Waiting at a red light, he strokes Brody to soothe him. "It's okay. Everyone's safe. You can settle. We'll be going home soon enough." Maybe he's hungry. Nate shakes his head. That can't be it, as he's already been fed. The lights change as he considers another possibility. "Is it *Hank*?"

More barking.

Nate's chest tightens. But how could Brody know Hank? They've never met before.

He suddenly remembers Brody's overnight vanishing act. He'd run after the wedding shooter when Lloyd Maxwell was killed. His heart hammers in his chest. Ignoring the green light, he looks at the dog. "You met him in the woods on our wedding day, didn't you?"

Brody barks even louder, standing now, his tail thrashing the passenger window as he fills the entire space.

Nate's stomach flips with dread. "*Shit.*" If he's right, that would mean Madison and Charlie have been left alone with a killer.

He steps on the gas and floors it, needing to reach Madison before it's too late.

CHAPTER FIFTY-SEVEN

"Wait!" says Madison, her heart hammering so hard she can barely breathe. Hank's weapon is dangerously close to Charlie, and she can't tell where he intends to point it. "Think about how Pam will feel if you hurt yourself or Charlie. Let me take him from you. You're not thinking straight right now."

"You're not taking him anywhere." The old man's eyes are watery with anguish as he considers whether to take the easy way out instead of having to face his sister after she learns what he's done.

"Fine." She tries to relax her posture to disguise how she desperately wants to lunge at him. Shifting his attention, she says, "I have one more question. Was it you who bludgeoned Ida to death?" He had been admitted to the hospital later that same day from exhaustion and dehydration. She assumed it had been caused by his illness, but it was more likely the result of overexertion. Ida's death had been brutal.

Hank lacks remorse as he nods. "If anyone ever deserved a painful death it was that woman. She started all this by abducting Sharon all those years ago. If she hadn't, everyone else would still be alive."

He's not wrong, but he's acting like he didn't have a choice in killing Denise and Lucy. He could've notified the police about his suspicions. Instead, he wanted revenge. He wanted the Ridgeways to suffer like he was suffering. Denise and Lucy didn't deserve that, no matter what happened to Dominic. They were innocent, and Denise knew nothing about what her family had done. Poor little Lucy had tried to scramble to safety under her bed. Hank dragged her out by her *ankles*.

"I think the Ridgeways knew it was me," says Hank. "But they couldn't go to you guys because they knew that if I was arrested, I'd tell you why I did it. I'd tell you how I suspected they took Dominic and Charlie, which would mean you'd search their property and find all those bodies."

That would explain why they kept trying to blame Ryan instead. He made a good suspect, and his arrest would have given them time to get away with what they'd done. That would also explain why Bernie was so angry after finding her mother dead. She had realized Hank was coming after all of them. When she'd declared, *I'll kill him for this*, she wasn't referring to Ryan, she was referring to Hank. That's why Colt quickly led her upstairs and away from them, to avoid her letting something slip.

Charlie stirs in his grandfather's arms, slowly waking.

"Let me take him so he doesn't get hurt," says Madison, leaning forward.

"He's already hurt!" shouts Hank, the weapon shaking in his hand. "His dad's dead. His grandpa's a murderer. He'll be raised in foster homes until they spew him out at sixteen with nowhere to go. He has no chance at a happy life, not now. It would be kinder to take him with me."

Madison's hands sweat from an adrenaline rush. "Don't be stupid, Hank. Pam can raise him. He has everything still to live for. He's just a *child*."

Charlie reaches for the barrel of the gun as Hank weeps. He sticks a finger inside, intrigued by it.

Madison stands, unable to sit and watch any longer. "Come on, Hank, give him to me."

He looks up at her. Tears run down his face. "No. I won't let you take him, Detective. I'm warning you." He raises his weapon to aim at her chest.

Terrified, Madison braces herself. Before she can even think of reacting, a pane of glass shatters in the kitchen behind Hank. The loud noise startles Charlie, who jerks, knocking the gun out of Hank's hand. Madison braces as it hits the floor, convinced the impact will make it go off.

It doesn't. Instead, Brody suddenly appears, making a beeline straight for Hank. He holds himself back when he notices the child in Hank's lap, but it doesn't stop him from barking menacingly.

Madison takes the opportunity to grab Charlie from his startled grandfather, but Hank resists at the last second. He pulls Charlie closer to him, his arms wrapped around the child's torso. "No!" he yells. "I don't want him to suffer!"

"But you're already making him suffer!" Madison yells back.

Charlie screams in fear as big fat tears roll down his face.

"Let go, Hank! This isn't good for him."

Brody lunges at Hank's right arm, making him give up his grip. He howls in pain, doubling over as he tries to pull away.

Nate sweeps in, taking Charlie from Madison, who is laser-focused on removing the gun from Hank's reach. Brody doesn't let go of Hank's right arm, but Hank's left hand reaches for the weapon and manages to grip it before Madison can stop him.

Within seconds, a shot rings out, stunning her. Time slows as she steps backward, waiting to be hit. The bullet missed her, so she looks at Nate.

Nate has stopped in his tracks, clutching Charlie to his chest.

Frozen in place, Madison doesn't dare breathe. She and Nate exchange a look before realizing they're both okay. Charlie is okay. The shot went into the ceiling.

In the confusion, Hank has time to raise the weapon to his own head. "Tell Pam I'm sorry."

Nate immediately turns Charlie away from witnessing what's about to happen. He runs for the kitchen as Madison steps forward, attempting to stop Hank from firing. "No!"

She's too late. Blood splatters the wall behind him. He instantly slumps forward. Gone.

Madison falls to her knees, her entire body trembling. She didn't want it to end this way.

CHAPTER FIFTY-EIGHT

Madison watches from the back of an ambulance, with Charlie on her lap, as Nate breaks the news of Hank's suicide to his poor sister. Pam listens, horrified, as she learns how her brother killed Denise, Lucy, Ida and Lloyd Maxwell, all because Ida and Bernie killed his son and tried to claim Charlie as their own. Eventually, she collapses into Nate's arms, prompting an EMT to go check on her. She's led away to another ambulance, her face white with shock and despair.

Nate comes to check on Madison and Charlie. The little boy is sucking his thumb and resting his sleepy little head in the crook of her neck. He's a comforting weight, and she finds herself wishing he were Owen. That she could go back in time and do everything differently in order to experience the whole of his childhood this time around. Not just part of it.

Nate enters the ambulance and sits beside them. He looks exhausted. When he takes her hand and asks if she's okay, she bursts into tears. "No. How can I be after all this?" She motions to Hank's house.

Jake Rubio appears at the doors. "Sorry to bother you. Can I take Charlie for an assessment?"

She nods, reluctantly handing the little boy over. He groans for a second but soon melts into Jake's strong arms. She and Nate watch as Jake takes him to the same ambulance Pam's in. "He reminds me of Owen at that age," she says.

"Owen called me when he couldn't reach you," says Nate. "I've told him we're both fine and that we'll be home soon." He pulls her close, kissing her forehead. "I love you."

She swallows back tears. Sometimes this job is too much. Being in law enforcement means witnessing the worst things imaginable before returning home to your family for dinner as though nothing has happened. Her only saving grace is that she goes home to people who understand what the job takes from her.

Chief Mendes appears at the ambulance doors. She looks at Madison. "Tough night?"

Madison snorts as she nods, wiping tears from her eyes. "You could say that. How's Steve?"

"He's fine. His surgeon says the operation is nothing to worry about, although he may be out of action for a while as he recovers."

Madison groans. "Does that mean I'll have to partner with Adams again in the meantime?"

The chief laughs. "Afraid so." She looks around and they follow her gaze to where Hank's body is being removed from the house on a covered gurney. With a deep breath, she says, "I'll expect a full report in the morning."

Nate bristles. He's about to give Mendes a piece of his mind, but the chief notices and holds her hand up to stop him. "*Then* you can consider yourself on vacation. You two need a honeymoon. I don't want to see or hear from you for at least a week, and before you return to work you need a mandatory session with our therapist. Understood?"

Madison nods, then looks at Nate. "Does a honeymoon sound okay to you?"

He squeezes her close. "What do you think?"

"Good work, you two," says Mendes. "You make a pretty good team." Brody appears beside her, so she pats him on the head. "You too, Officer Brody." She smiles at them, then disappears.

Brody jumps into the ambulance and lies at their feet, also exhausted. He's been checked over by an EMT too. Nate was worried he could've been hurt when breaking through the glass-paneled door in his bid to save Madison. But he's fine. His thick fur protected him. Madison thinks of his nail clippings, the ones she gave Alex. It's highly likely they'll find Hank's DNA on them, which will help confirm he'd met Brody before.

She strokes Brody's beautiful face as she imagines going on honeymoon. "I guess we're gonna have to find a resort that's dog-friendly, huh?"

Nate snorts. "Of course. We can't leave Brody behind."

"What about Owen?" she says, half joking.

"Well, we may as well take him with us." Nate smiles at her. "He can keep Brody occupied while I keep *you* occupied."

"Oh really?" she says. "In that case, what about Bandit? Is he coming on our honeymoon too?"

Nate pretends to think about it. "Nah, Bandit can go stay with Uncle Vince."

She laughs, knowing the cat would probably prefer that anyway. "Okay, then I guess we're going on vacation." She rests her head in the crook of his neck. She may be physically exhausted, but she feels blessed to have such a wonderful family, albeit a very small one these days.

A LETTER FROM WENDY

Thank you for reading *As They Lay Sleeping*. I hope you enjoyed book nine in the Detective Madison Harper series.

You can receive updates about my books by signing up for my newsletter.

www.bookouture.com/wendy-dranfield

You didn't think Madison and Nate's wedding would go smoothly, did you?! I had no idea what was going to happen as I sat, like you, watching the happy couple hold hands in front of the officiant, eager to exchange vows on that beautiful summer's day at the beginning of the book. But I did have a bad feeling about how well things were going, so I wasn't too surprised when a shot was fired!

Now that Madison and Nate are married, they've overcome their traumatic pasts and their adversaries are no longer around, I feel like the series is coming to a natural close. At the time of writing this, I'm planning only one more book. I never expected the series to last this long, and I don't know what the future holds, but for now at least, I feel it's time to move on and wanted to give you advance notice. I know some of you will be disappointed that it's ending, but I hope you've enjoyed the time you've spent with the characters. I know I have. I'm so grateful for your support over the years and have always written with you in mind. I'm sure I'll soon miss the characters, and I never say never, but once book ten is finished, it's time for a break.

If you enjoyed this book, please leave a rating or review (no matter how brief) on Amazon. This helps it to stand out among the thousands of books published each week.

As always, thanks so much for reading.

Wendy

www.wendydranfield.co.uk

ACKNOWLEDGMENTS

Thank you to all the readers who have given one of my books a try, and I'm very grateful to the loyal readers who have followed me from the beginning of my career and cheer me on with each new book. Thanks also to the advance readers and bloggers who review my books with so much enthusiasm.

As always, thank you to everyone at Bookouture who worked on my latest book.

And a special thanks always goes to my wonderful husband, the reader of all my first drafts.

PUBLISHING TEAM

Turning a manuscript into a book requires the efforts of many people. The publishing team at Bookouture would like to acknowledge everyone who contributed to this publication.

Audio
Alba Proko
Melissa Tran
Sinead O'Connor

Commercial
Lauren Morrissette
Hannah Richmond
Imogen Allport

Cover design
The Brewster Project

Data and analysis
Mark Alder
Mohamed Bussuri

Editorial
Harriet Wade
Sinead O'Connor

Copyeditor
Jane Selley

Proofreader
Ian Hodder

Marketing
Alex Crow
Melanie Price
Occy Carr
Cíara Rosney
Martyna Młynarska

Operations and distribution
Marina Valles
Stephanie Straub
Joe Morris

Production
Hannah Snetsinger
Mandy Kullar
Nadia Michael
Charlotte Hegley

Publicity
Kim Nash
Noelle Holten
Jess Readett
Sarah Hardy

Rights and contracts
Peta Nightingale
Richard King
Saidah Graham

RAISING READERS
Books Build Bright Futures

Dear Reader,

We'd love your attention for one more page to tell you about the crisis in children's reading, and what we can all do.

Studies have shown that reading for fun is the **single biggest predictor of a child's future life chances** – more than family circumstance, parents' educational background or income. It improves academic results, mental health, wealth, communication skills, ambition and happiness.

The number of children reading for fun is in rapid decline. Young people have a lot of competition for their time, and a worryingly high number do not have a single book at home.

Hachette works extensively with schools, libraries and literacy charities, but here are some ways we can all raise more readers:

- Reading to children for just 10 minutes a day makes a difference
- Don't give up if children aren't regular readers – there will be books for them!

- Visit bookshops and libraries to get recommendations
- Encourage them to listen to audiobooks
- Support school libraries
- Give books as gifts

There's a lot more information about how to encourage children to read on our websites: **www.RaisingReaders.co.uk** and **www.JoinRaisingReaders.com**.

Thank you for reading.

Made in United States
Orlando, FL
07 November 2025